DINOTOPIA
»LOST«

DINOTOPIA
»» LOST ««

ALAN DEAN FOSTER

ACE BOOKS, NEW YORK

This Ace Book contains the complete text of the original hardcover edition. It has been completely reset in a typeface designed for easy reading, and was printed from new film.

DINOTOPIA LOST

An Ace Book / published by arrangement with Turner Publishing, Inc.

PRINTING HISTORY
Turner Publishing, Inc. hardcover edition / 1996
Ace trade edition / September 1997

The Putnam Berkley World Wide Web site address is
http://www.berkley.com

Make sure to check out PB Plug,
the science fiction/fantasy newsletter, at
http://www.pbplug.com

ISBN: 0-441-00462-8

ACE®
Ace Books are published by The Berkley Publishing Group,
200 Madison Avenue, New York, NY 10016,
a member of Penguin Putnam Inc.
ACE and the "A" design are trademarks
belonging to Charter Communications, Inc.

PRINTED IN THE UNITED STATES OF AMERICA

10 9 8 7 6 5 4 3 2 1

For Jim Gurney, of course.
Fellow traveler.

I have wrought my simple plan
If I give one hour of joy
To the boy who's half a man
Or the man who's half a boy.

—INTRODUCTION TO
SIR ARTHUR CONAN DOYLE'S
THE LOST WORLD

≫ I ≪

PUNDU SINGUANG AND CHALK WERE WATCHING THE ocean, similar thoughts running through their minds though they were very different in appearance. The *Centrosaurus* was nearly fourteen feet from beak to tail, with a stocky, muscular body that weighed somewhere between four and five tons, depending on when he had last eaten. His huge skull swept back into an armored, bony frill lined with short spikes while a single massive horn thrust upward from just behind the horny beak. His personal name derived from his unusually pale appearance.

His human companion was shorter, slighter, darker of skin, and completely unarmored, though he did have a rather prominent nose. Together with a family of torosaurs they worked the farm, sharing proportionately in its bounty of rice and tropical fruit.

Presently they were standing atop a small hill, a tree-covered blip on an otherwise typically flat corner of the Northern Plains. Arms crossed over his sweat-streaked, bare chest, Pundu leaned back against the supportive sweep of Chalk's frill. The farm spread out behind them. Nearby rose a cluster of neat thatch-roofed structures designed to accommodate humans, dinosaurs, farm equipment, and the twice-yearly harvest.

Before them stretched a brackish quilt of untamed reeds, palms, and finally mangrove swamp. Beyond lay a narrow beach of pure white sand, a wide lagoon, and at last the extensive reef that encircled all of Dinotopia. Leaping from a cobalt sea, deformed by powerful, unnavigable currents, ivory breakers shattered themselves against the unyielding coral shoulder.

The sky was a paler hue, its homogeneous blue marred only by a few patches of sooty cloud escaped from some unseen northern squall. Except along the line of breakers, where the sea warred with the accumulated skeletons of long-dead corals, all was tranquil and calm.

"It looks peaceful enough," Pundu remarked to their visitor. At the sound of his voice Chalk also turned to regard the runner. "Are the weathercasters certain?"

The swift *Gallimimus* had come from the south only that morning. Twin saddlebag-satchels decorated with official seals and trailing bright blue and yellow streamers were strapped across the rose-tinted skin of her back. An ornamental hood topped by a flowering of shorter yellow streamers protected her face from wind and dust and covered most of her head while simultaneously signifying her status to any who saw or encountered her.

Though no translator was present, she was still able to recognize the uncertainty in the farmer's voice. By way of reply she held out the official document, pinching it firmly between two of her claws. The warning was written both in human and dinosaur. Having already read it, Chalk continued to stare out to sea. Only humans felt the need to peruse the same words over and over, as if to assure themselves of their validity. Dinosaurs were far more accepting of reality.

There was no equivocation in the warning, which was clear and forthright. It stated that Dinotopia's six-year weather cycle was coming to fruition, and that all the signs indicated that the culmination of this particular cycle should be particularly robust.

Like anyone whose family had long farmed the damp, hot lands of the Northern Plains, Pundu Singuang knew what that meant. So did Chalk. Raising one hand facing forward, Pundu touched his palm to that of the runner and nodded once. The *Gallimimus* returned the gesture, turned, and trotted down the gentle slope. With each stride, she covered twice as much ground as the best human sprinter could manage.

She paused only long enough to bid farewell to Pundu's wife, Lahat, who was hanging out laundry in front of the bamboo-framed farmhouse. Their two children followed the runner as far as the dirt road, one of them riding atop Singlewhack's back. Singlewhack was Chalk's daughter. She was still young enough for her nose horn to be little more than a stub above her beak.

As they concluded their hopeless pursuit of the runner, the children's laughter drifted up the hill. Pundu watched the now tiny bipedal form of the *Gallimimus* turn left on the road and accelerate, dust rising from beneath her flying, three-toed feet, her silken streamers stretched out behind her.

Pundu knew that the children, human and centrosaur alike, ought to be helping with the chores, but at that moment neither he nor Chalk was inclined to discipline them. Let them have their fun while they could. There would be hard work for all soon enough—harder work than they had yet known.

Again he turned to stare out to sea. The last several six-year cycles had been relatively benign. It had been some time since he had been forced to think of the ocean as a threat.

It took many days with everyone working together to empty the house and barn. Everything that could be moved, from kitchen utensils to the big iron plow, was packed, piled, or stuffed onto the six-wheeled farm wagon. Lahat's treasured set of shadow puppets, handed down in her family from generation to generation, was wrapped in rice paper and stowed carefully beneath the seat with the other fragile household goods.

Chalk grunted patiently at the youngsters, chivying them along, while the two huge torosaurs, ceratopsians like Chalk only bigger and with eye horns like a *Triceratops*, tried to make themselves comfortable in the wagon harness. Chalk and his mate would follow behind, pulling a second, smaller wagon piled high with farming implements.

They were good companions and good farmers, Pundu reflected as he watched his ceratopsian compatriots at work. He was lucky they had chosen to mingle their lives with his own. Human and dinosaur families alike benefited from the mutual cooperation. They worked together, lived together, often played and ate together.

And now, he reflected grimly, they would flee together.

In his desire to be on their way, Chalk was displaying an almost human impatience. Pundu's mood lightened as he watched his old friend. Just like a *Centrosaurus*: always anxious to check out the fodder over the next hill. Chalk and his relatives liked the Northern Plains, where there was thick forage and good farmland in abundance.

That was why so many of the plains farmers had chosen to form working alliances with ceratopsians or stegosaurids. With a torosaur or *Triceratops* supplying willing muscle, plowing a field or raising a dam became feasible for a single family. For their part, the ceratopsians and stegosaurids were very fond of rice and bamboo, which humans raised with skill and in abundance.

He wondered how his neighbors, the Manuhiris and Tandraputras, were progressing with their preparations to evacuate. It was a scene that was being repeated several hundred times all across the Northern Plains: families piling everything they owned, from the implements of everyday living to family heirlooms, onto wagons, swamp carts, and broad dinosaurian backs in preparation for flight.

Most would head for Bent Root, Pundu knew, it being the nearest town of sufficient size to provide the necessary accommodations and assistance for an exodus of such size. Others would travel farther in search of less crowded quarters, to Treetown and even Cornucopia. The smaller towns in the foothills of the Backbone Mountains would take their share. All across the region, people and dinosaurs would pitch in to help the temporarily displaced. It was the Dinotopian way.

The most fortunate among the uprooted had relatives or close friends in the towns, but it wasn't necessary. Any stranger would help another. You might need his help tomorrow.

The voice of his son interrupted his thoughts. "Father, come and help with this!" Selat and his sister Brukup were struggling to load the headboard from the front bedroom. The bed was one of Lahat's delights because it had been carved and decorated by Pundu himself and two of his friends in the months before their wedding. It hurt to see it traveling in pieces, like so much lumber.

For the moment we are all displaced, he mused as he started forward. *People and furniture alike.*

Together they eased the heavy piece of wood onto the wagon. Chalk helped with the last shove, careful to use the side of his mouth so that his nose horn wouldn't damage the carving. Wiping sweat from his forehead, Pundu turned to gaze out across the paddies. Most of the rice and taro had already been harvested and sold. This was fortunate, because he knew that if the weathercasters were right, they would miss at least one planting, maybe two. There were mangoes and rambutan still to be gathered, but the runner from Sauropolis had been insistent about the departure window. The ripening fruit would have to ride out, unpicked, whatever the six-year cycle had in store for the farm.

Pundu shrugged. It could be worse. Without the work of the weathercasters there would be no warning, and then a man could lose more than a little fruit.

They could lose it all, he knew. Or they could return to find everything, even to the fruit hanging ripe on the trees, intact and unharmed. There had not been a truly bad six-year storm in his lifetime. But he knew the stories and the histories. Every six years precautions had to be taken. It was the law . . . not to mention common sense.

The evacuation, at least, held no surprises. He had been through it half a dozen times before. In the outside world, it was said, people tried to resist the forces of nature instead of bending with them. It was difficult to imagine. How could one do otherwise but than to bend with what might be coming at the end of the six-year cycle? The thought of attempting to resist such a thing flew in the face of all reason.

Turning from the fields, he let his gaze linger lovingly on his children and the supple form of Lahat. Noticing his stare, she smiled back as she drew her arm across her high forehead. Though they were acclimated to the heat and humidity of the Northern Plains, the hard work still made them sweat.

As he moved to help her with the pots and pans from the kitchen, he glanced again to his right, toward the sea. It was hidden from him now, concealed by trees and distance. That was why the weathercasters' warning was so important. If the outcome was a bad one, there would be no time to see it coming. In that case, the conclusion of the cycle would bring death instead of renewal.

Out there the wind and the water were starting to stir. Pundu fully intended to have his family and friends well upland in the event that the elements' mood turned sour. *Best not to nap next to the sea-god*, he remembered his mother telling him, *when he decides to walk in his sleep.*

Bigfoot, the male torosaur, turned in his harness to snort at Pundu. "Yes, yes, I know we need to be going," the farmer called back. The strapping ceratopsian was eager to be on his way. The sooner they arrived in Bent Root, the sooner he could slip out of the tack.

Pundu turned to take a last look at his house. If the sea-god only walked in his sleep, all would be unchanged when they returned from Bent Root. If he had a nightmare . . . well, the thatch was thinning and some of the bamboo was old and starting to splinter. A new house would not be such a bad thing.

Placing his palms together in front of his chest, Pundu faced the sea and bowed. The religion and culture of his family was a gentle, accepting one, ideal for a farmer. For a while his lips moved.

Then there was nothing more to be done. Straightening, he mounted the wagon, reaching down to give Lahat a hand up. The children would ride gleefully behind, on the broad backs of Chalk and his mate. For his part, Pundu had grown old enough to desire a softer seat.

Gathering up the reins, he stood on the footrest and shouted, "Hai! Bigfoot, Browneyes! Time to go!" The torosaurs did not understand the words, but Pundu's tone coupled with a gentle chuck of the reins was eloquent enough. Stout legs started forward, and the heavily laden wagon, creaking and groaning with its load, began to roll out of the farmyard on its six strong wooden wheels.

Behind him, Pundu heard his children echo his words. They were excited and unafraid. To them the displacement was an adventure.

Reaching the farm road, the torosaurs turned right, toward

the shadowed line of the Backbone Mountains. No one looked back. Pundu and Lahat could not see over or around the heavily laden wagon, and no ceratopsian could see behind itself without turning its body.

Now that they were on their way, he relaxed. There was no need to guide the torosaurs. They knew the way to Bent Root better than any human, being able to follow olfactory as well as visual signs. Flooded rice paddies and taro fields lined both sides of the road.

By midday they were part of a growing line of vehicles, humans, and dinosaurs, all creaking and groaning as they made their way toward the green foothills. They traveled on an elevated road fashioned of packed earth paved with cut stone, built centuries ago to allow access to the rich loam of the Northern Plains. Maintained by crews of humans and dinosaurs, it permitted year-round travel across a flat countryside that was frequently deluged by torrential rains. At such times, ordinary ground-level roads were reduced to impassable rivers of thick, gluey mud.

The gathering stream of humans, dinosaurs, wagons, and carts wound its way steadily southwestward. Though it represented a coming-together of all the inhabitants of the Northern Plains, the roadway was not overwhelmed. The transitory nature of life on the plains reduced its appeal. Despite the fertility of the soil, farming there did not promise an easy life, nor were there many families willing to gather up everything they owned and shuttle it back and forth every six years. Families also had to endure isolation from the excitement of cultural centers like Sauropolis and Waterfall City.

But there were rewards, Pundu reflected as he and his family jounced along in the steadily moving line. Beauty, tranquillity, the joy of watching things grow. He would not have traded it for any other life.

Turning in his seat, he offered a friendly wave to a farmer he recognized. Otera and his family lived farther down the coast, closer to Crackshell Point. There they fished the bountiful lagoon as well as farmed the land. They knew each other, as did all the residents of the Northern Plains, from periodic encounters at festivals and markets.

"Ho, friend Otera! How goes it?"

"It goes well enough," the stout fisher-farmer replied. Otera was of Maori ancestry. His son was already heavier than Pundu, who came from far more diminutive physical stock. Oblivious to all the activity, four-year-old twins slept soundly in a hammock suspended between the great eye horns of Quickpush, Otera's mature female *Triceratops*. A male *Stegosaurus* led the way, his back plates strung with cord. Household goods were piled high between the triangular plates.

"What do you think of the weathercasters' predictions?" Otera asked him. As the humans conversed, triceratops, stegosaurs, and torosaurs spoke in low rumbles, like a polite earthquake.

Pundu glanced north, toward the ocean. The convoy had climbed high enough now for the sea to appear as a distant dark blue stripe between earth and sky.

"Too early to tell, I think."

"Perhaps the weathercasters are wrong. Perhaps this will be another moderate six-year storm." Otera rubbed his forehead, which was decorated with intricate blue-black whorls and dots. The tattooing had been done by his uncle over a period of several years.

"Perhaps. One can only hope. It has happened so before."

Otera's wife, Teita, who was also a good deal bigger than Pundu, sniffed skeptically. "You men are deluding yourselves. The weathercasters are almost always right. Hoping a thing will not happen will not change that."

"Hoping is not deluding, my love," her husband reminded her. "Would you rather live in Sauropolis?"

"What," she blurted back, "with all that noise and bustle? No, thank you! I would rather live by the sea. It is like any child. Most of the time it giggles and coos and is a blessing to you. You have to expect the occasional tantrum. That's all I'm saying."

"I feel the same." Pundu relaxed against the back of the wagon seat. "The city is too busy for me. Where are you going?"

"To Cornucopia," Otera replied. "It's farther, but we have cousins there."

Pundu nodded. Bigfoot and his mate edged toward the shoulder of the road. Since Otera's group had farther to go, others courteously offered them the right-of-way on the narrow thoroughfare.

It wasn't all ceratopsians and stegosaurids on the road. There were ankylosaurs and a fair number of duckbills as well. Ankylosaurs were excellent excavators while duckbills were particularly good at working both paddies and orchards. No sauropods, though. The true giants of Dinotopia were a bit too massive for farmwork. A *Diplodocus* might be fun to gambol on the beach with, but you wouldn't want one mucking about in your taro patch.

City folk didn't have to evacuate their homes every six years, Pundu knew, but they had other problems. That was the wonderful thing about Dinotopia: there was a region and lifestyle to suit everyone, human and dinosaur alike.

A larger, darker cloud had appeared in the sky. A harbinger of more to come? Pundu wondered. He nodded sagely to himself. It was always best to follow the advice of specialists outside one's own area of expertise. He was glad their departure from the farm had gone so smoothly.

As the long line of humans, dinosaurs, and their goods climbed slowly and steadily out of the Northern Plains and into the foothills of the Backbones, Pundu Singuang found himself remembering the jovial Teita's likening of the sea to an infant. Giggles and coos, laughter and tears, he told himself. Yes, that was as good a description of the ocean's moods as any. It was only natural that in return for its bounty those who lived by its side should expect to have to put up with an occasional fit.

The only question now was, in its coming distress and upset, how loudly would it scream, and how hard would it kick?

➤➤ II ◄◄

WILL DENISON WHISTLED PIERCINGLY. THE GI-
gantic, columnar leg paused in midstride and settled to the earth with a muffled thud. The brachiosaur's neck
dipped down and to one side as it searched for the source of
the whistle.

Will had been partly concealed by a bush and the big
sauropod had nearly overlooked him. Like all its kind, it had
excellent hearing. According to the librarian Nallab it was
an ancient development originally intended to allow them to
detect the approach of marauding carnivores.

By way of apology, the brachiosaur sniffed gently through
the nostrils located atop its head. Will tapped the greenish
snout and smiled to show that he was unharmed. Then he
turned away quickly as the head shuddered and convulsed.
The sneeze stripped half the leaves from the bush Will had
been standing alongside. Once more the brachiosaur offered
his apologies.

Sauropods were among the most polite of dinosaurs, a
consequence of their enormous size. Unable to eschew an
innate clumsiness, they compensated by moving with extreme care and precision when in the presence of those
smaller than themselves ... which meant nearly everyone
else. Will had been amazed the first time he'd seen one pacing prissily down a street in Waterfall City. It was something
to see a thirty-ton *Apatosaurus* prance.

"No harm done," Will told the giant. Raising his voice,
he called to his fellow instructor. "Geina, you ready?"

She waved back enthusiastically, buoyed by shouts from her covey of half a dozen teenagers. Will moved away from the bush to eye his own group.

"Everybody ready? We're going to beat them, this time!" Cheers came from the six young men and women gathered nearby.

The elegiac little forest stream that separated the two groups could be cleared by a good leaper, the watery barrier being more metaphorical than real. Taking up a stance close to the creek edge, Will picked up the two-inch-thick rope in both hands and snugged it close to his left side.

"All set?" Half a dozen young voices responded eagerly. He raised his voice and directed it across the stream. "On three, Geina? One, two . . . three!"

Immediately, Will's team dug their heels into the ground and pulled . . . and just as immediately found themselves being dragged toward the creek by the other group.

Each end of the rope was gripped in the mouth of a dinosaur. Shortfoot, a juvenile male brachiosaur, fortified Will's team, while Gaptooth, a young *Camarasaurus*, pulled for Geina's. Gaptooth was older and larger than Shortfoot, but it was an equal contest because brachiosaurs are especially good at tug-of-war since their front legs are longer than those behind.

As he was dragged toward the water, Will wondered if he'd judged the slope correctly. If it was much steeper than the one on Geina's side, his team wouldn't have a chance. Then his descent was arrested as Shortfoot's resolve stiffened and the immense legs dug resolutely into the soil. Cheers rose from the youngsters hanging on to the rope behind him, while the two dinosaurs huffed and chuffed like idling locomotives.

To a cry of triumph from the other side, Will's feet slid into the water. Shortfoot strained determinedly and pulled Will clear. The partial dunking didn't bother him. The morning was hot and humid, unusually so for Treetown, and he was glad of the rinse.

He'd come to Treetown not only to further his education, for his father had insisted on it, but to give back in service some of the help and assistance that the citizenry of Dinotopia had shown to them both. He found that he enjoyed working with others. As a qualified apprentice skybax rider, he'd given some consideration to becoming a flying instructor under the master Oolu. That meant acquiring some practical teaching experience.

As wise Nallab had told him, "If you would become a teacher, you must be always a student. I have lived over a hundred years and read many thousands of books, yet each piece of knowledge I acquire only reminds me of my ignorance, because it invariably teases me with hints of a dozen new things I have no knowledge of." When the opportunity to work at one of Treetown's youth camps had been offered, Will had jumped at it.

It gave him great satisfaction to be able to help. In addition to his minding his own group, all the youngsters as well as their instructors and leaders found his tales of the contemporary outside world fascinating, if a bit unnerving. The concept of money was one they found particularly amusing.

Six years he and his father had dwelled in their new home, learning and prospering. Now Will found himself participating in a tug-of-war with a dozen youths slightly younger than himself, and two creatures believed long extinct who in size and strength would have given pause to Hercules.

The participation of the twelve young humans was very much incidental to the game itself. Though well-intentioned, their exertions fooled no one, least of all themselves. Their combined body weight was a fraction of that of either the brachiosaur or *Camarasaurus*, and their most strenuous efforts could not affect the outcome. Which wasn't the point. It was the participation that was important, the sharing and the learning that was taking place between human and human, human and dinosaur.

For their part, the two juvenile sauropods enjoyed the play as much as their human counterparts. The only difference was that they calculated their weight, as opposed to their maturity, in tons instead of pounds. Socially and intellectually, they were the equal of the dozen bipeds.

No adult supervisors were present. By the age of fifteen, one was supposed to act like a grown-up. Freedom and play were encouraged; irresponsibility was not.

Despite the steeper slope, Shortfoot succeeded in using her longer forelegs to back onto level ground. Once that had been achieved, Will's team was able to pull Geina's, laughing and squealing, into the creek. This accomplished, Will and his charges joined them in splashing and throwing water. So did the two sauropods, using their forefeet and long necks to send water flying in all directions. Gaptooth caught Will with a mouthful that, squirted between peglike teeth, sent him sprawling. A sheepish expression on his face, he came up thrashing energetically, much to the amusement of the others.

He wasn't worried about catching cold. All of Treetown and the surrounding mountains seemed slightly wilted in the exceptional heat. Those not working lay in the sleeping baskets that dangled like wicker-wrapped fruit from branches fifty feet and more off the ground. There they did their best to catch the occasional breeze. It was much cooler up in the branches of the firs and redwoods, gingkoes and sequoias, than it was down on the ground.

Even the winds that normally flowed down the slopes of the Backbone Mountains had been affected. Uncharacteristic warm, moist breezes rose from the hot Northern Plains, making sleeping difficult and the inhabitants uncomfortable. This didn't surprise those who had heard the official predictions of the weathercasters. The weather in Dinotopia was nearing the end of one of its regular six-year cycles, at which time strange things happened. Clouds dispersed over the Rainy Basin, and isolated thunderstorms raked the Great Desert. The prevailing winds shifted from the west to the north, and climatologically speaking, everything turned a little backward.

Those who lived in the mountains dealt with this temporary onslaught of tropical weather as best they could, changing from temperate attire to clothing more suited to the plains or the Hadro Swamp. Everyone knew it would pass. In any case, they suffered far less than the farmers of the Northern Plains, who temporarily had to change much more than just their clothing.

Though most had made Bent Root, Cornucopia, and the other lower towns their destination, Treetown, too, had received its share of evacuees. Will had studied these arrivals with interest, adding the details of their situation to his store of knowledge without becoming personally involved. After all, he called Waterfall City home, and it lay far away to the south, safe from any drastic changes or dangers.

Noticing that Shortfoot and Gaptooth were panting heavily, he and Geina guided the group downstream to deeper water so that the young sauropods could cool more than their feet. Exchanging their light clothing for swimming trunks, the youngsters plunged into the deep pool with abandon, improvising games of tag and hide-and-seek around the legs and under the bellies of their two gigantic companions. On request, dinosaurian tails became living springboards, sending competitive would-be divers flying through the air in intricate flips and curls.

Farther downstream they came to a waterfall perhaps twenty feet in height. The falling water had cut a deep plunge pool out of the surrounding granite. Shelves of polished gray and beige stone lined the pool, forming perfect places on which to sit or lie while soaking up the sunshine. Redwoods and firs grew all around while smaller growths clung to the exposed rock walls and the rim of the falls, giving them a landscaped look.

Circling around through the forest, Shortfoot waded into the pool and contentedly placed the side of his head against the top of the falls, occasionally ducking it under the foaming white cascade. Those swimming in the gently churning water could climb onto the nearly submerged back and shinny up his neck all the way to the top of the falls. Cheered on by those below, the most accomplished among them would execute intricate dives into the pool, while others volunteered whoops and yells as they took running leaps off the precipice.

Those for whom formalized aerial acrobatics held no interest gathered around Gaptooth on the far side of the basin. The *Camarasaurus* obligingly lifted one swimmer after another out of the water, scooping them up on her head before flicking them skyward with a violent muscular contraction of her long neck. Screaming and squealing, the individual thus camarapulted would fly halfway across the pool before

landing, sometimes in an incongruous position, with a sat-
isfyingly loud splash.

Attracted by the noise, a party of strolling hypacrosaurs
and corythosaurs stopped by to chat. Though they preferred
the country around the Hadro Swamp far to the southwest,
they were as comfortable elsewhere in Dinotopia as any of
their cousins. Settling themselves in the shallow end of the
lake, they entertained the gamboling youngsters and sauropods with their sonorous, reverberant singing.

As evening crept timorously into the hills, the youth
groups unpacked their personal gear. Having attended first to
their own needs, they then proceeded to assemble long-
handled, stiff-bristled brushes and devices that resembled
garden rakes more than hygienic accoutrements.

With these they commenced to scrub and groom the two
sauropods, who lolled luxuriously in the shallows as the
young humans attended them. Rather than a reward for services rendered, the grooming was a sign of mutual affection
and respect. It was not regarded as work by the youngsters,
but a joint activity to be enjoyed.

As for the sauropods, a brachiosaur can do many things,
but there are plenty of places it can't scratch. The Backbone
Mountains were notoriously deficient in rolling hollows, and
it was forbidden to scratch against a tree because such activity, if done repeatedly, would wear away the bark and kill
the growth.

It was this comfort gap that a dozen energetic young humans filled admirably.

Necks and backs were scrubbed clean, tails raked, parasites located and removed. Using a compact, specially designed two-handed saw, a pair of sixteen-year-olds neatly
trimmed toenails the size of half dinner plates. Peglike teeth
were polished until they shone.

A person hasn't heard contentment, Will decided, until
they've heard a brachiosaur purr.

Once the youngsters had dried and dressed themselves, the
entire party bid the recently arrived duckbills farewell and
started back toward Treetown. Some chose to walk, examining and trying to identify the many plants they encountered. Others rode communal backsaddles secured to broad

sauropodian spines while Will and Geina occupied the observer's seats located just back of each head, in Will's case some thirty feet above the ground. The saddle shifted back and forth with the gentle, swaying movement of Shortfoot's muscular neck.

Treetown was a unique community, even for Dinotopia. It was one of the few places where the human inhabitants could peer out their windows and always be sure of looking *down* on dinosaurs. This was because every human structure in Treetown was literally up a tree, the buildings resting on broad branches and connected to one another by an intricate system of ladders, bridges, ropes, and cables. Even the marketplace sat nearly eighty feet aboveground, each stall occupying its own niche or branch.

The dinosaurian portion of the citizenry spent the nights in huge barns that had been constructed in special clearings. Sturdy sequoias were used to buttress the walls. Though much higher, Treetown was close to the Rainy Basin, and it was not unknown for an occasional ambitious or addled carnosaur to make the climb in search of fresh food.

Besides, sauropods enjoyed being indoors. It was a novelty supplied by human ingenuity, and allowed the great creatures to survive chillier climes than they would otherwise have been inclined to tolerate.

Bidding good day to his young charges and to Geina (who was nice, but not as nice, he thought, as his Sylvia), Will made his way toward the tree in which the guesthouse where he was staying was located. Ascending a huge Douglas fir by means of a spiral stairway that encircled the trunk, he crossed via a rope suspension bridge to a redwood, climbed a series of ladders, and paused on a viewing platform.

Most of the buildings in Treetown had open sides that could be covered with canvas flies in the event of bad weather or to provide privacy. These were open now, their flaps furled to reveal the activity inside as well as to allow cooling breezes to pass through. A pair of oropendula flashed by beneath Will's platform, warbling like drunken flutes.

Except for such avian visitors, the human population of Treetown had the treetops largely to themselves. Only some of the smaller dinosaurs, like the ornithopod and dromaeosaurs, felt comfortable more than a few feet above the ground. The lack of an opposable thumb with which to grip branches and bark was responsible for some of this reticence, an inherent psychological disinclination to climb for much of the rest.

Sauropods quite liked Treetown. The weather was usually comfortable, there was ample space between trees for them to walk, and they enjoyed browsing the lower branches of those growths that had not yet evolved out of their reach. In turn, humans could sit in baskets or on the lower branches and look eye-to-eye with the tallest dinosaur. This had the added benefit of keeping them out of the sauropods' way, which meant that a wandering *Saltasaurus* could be less concerned with where it was stepping.

Geina had retired to her parents' home and the various youngsters to their respective dormitories. It was early supper-time, but despite the day's activities Will wasn't hungry yet. He preferred to linger on the platform and await the sunset.

Had he done well today? He always felt that he could set a better example. At least he'd taken the lead in the tug-of-war. Already he'd learned that being a good teacher required patience even more than knowledge. He'd also learned that he couldn't be first at everything. His father had warned him about that.

Still, being such a recent immigrant to Dinotopia, he felt compelled to excel, if only to prove that he belonged. His ambition was to be certified the youngest master skybax rider ever.

As he left the platform and entered the guesthouse, a sudden sharp wind, chill and unpleasant, rocked the branch and forced him to grab a hammock to steady himself. Slicing through the mugginess like a sword, it was unexpected and disturbing.

Reaching his own sleeping hammock, he turned to watch Lyra Aurelius. Across the open room, the laundress was making up a fresh, unoccupied hammock in anticipation of guests yet to arrive. Not far away her four-year-old, flaxen-haired Tlinka, played on the edge of a sheer sixty-foot drop. The children of Treetown quickly learned to tolerate open spaces. Even so, a padded babyline was snugged tight around the little girl's waist. If she stumbled off, she'd fall no more than ten or fifteen feet before the line brought her up short, bobbing like a tadpole on a string. A few such tumbles were sufficient to teach local children to mind their step.

Since his arrival Will had marveled at the skill displayed by local youngsters in swinging from branch to branch and tree to tree. The boldest among them made such leaps without the aid of ropes, or walked fearlessly two hundred and more feet above the ground along branches no more than an arm's width across. They were startled and admiring when Will joined them. As a skybax rider, he had absolutely no fear of heights.

He didn't worry about the hundred-foot plunge he'd sustain if the boards beneath him gave way. Like every structure in Dinotopia, the buildings of Treetown were designed to last. ("The Roman influence," Nallab had told him. "Very demanding, those Romans.")

Slipping into his hammock, he rolled onto his left side and found himself gazing in the direction of the weather station. Located atop the tallest trunk in Treetown, on the crown of an ancient redwood, it looked out over the surrounding temperate forest and the mountaintops beyond.

Sited among the uppermost branches were devices designed to measure rainfall, wind, even changes in atmospheric pressure. To reach the station, an instrument reader would have to ascend a series of ladders and ropes that put the mainmast rigging on the largest clipper to shame. Normally such readings were taken every few days, but with a six-year storm threatening to break, careful measurements were being taken every morning and evening.

"Monsoonlike," Arthur Denison had declared when explaining the condition to Will, "only at once more extreme and unique to Dinotopia. I think it might have something to do with temperature changes in the sea."

Dinotopia was probably located somewhere in the southern Indian Ocean, Will knew. A watery expanse where nothing was supposed to exist, home to great mysteries. Perhaps even to a contra-monsoon, if his father's suppositions were correct. Arthur Denison had told his son of how the Indian monsoon periodically devastated the southern shores of many countries. It was hard to imagine any such catastrophe striking peaceful Dinotopia.

Yet the commerce of Dinotopia was turned inland, away from the sea, and the Northern Plains in particular were devoid of large coastal communities. This was not the consequence of someone's whim.

Will had watched along with everyone else as refugees from that fecund coast had begun to flood into town, filling the guesthouses and spare bedrooms of friends and relatives. These travelers had been told to leave their homes and farms. Only temporarily, to be sure, but such periodic mass exoduses suggested a potential for devastation on a scale hitherto unknown to Will. What was going to happen, if anything? He hadn't taken the time to look into it very deeply, and those involved seemed too busy to pause and talk.

Well, he would find out soon enough. Presently it was the meteorological station and its readings that intrigued him. A really serious storm might interrupt his training, though as Nallab had once told him, "Sometimes the inimical is more instructive than the benign. In between screams, try to pay attention."

Reaching a decision, he swung out of the hammock and left the guesthouse. A flying fox was utilized to cross long distances between trees, and it was this device he settled into in order to travel directly to the weather tree. A woven wicker chair was suspended from an overhead cable fashioned of fine strands of strong rope. Settling into the seat, he proceeded to pull himself along hand over hand, his legs dangling in open space. The hard ground lay seventy feet below.

Climbing out of the suspended chair, he walked along a branch lined with handrails until he was standing near the trunk. Tilting back his head, he was able to make out an ascending series of ladders and rope tunnels. These vanished into a smear of rust-colored bark and green needles. The weather platform was firmly secured to the tree's crown, more than four hundred feet above the ground.

Two older men were working nearby, repairing rigging. A third sat in an open-sided shed, recording information in a thick book. Sensing the eyes of the first two on him, Will walked over to the side of the shed. Looking up, the inscriber noticed the emblem sewn into the shoulder of his visitor's shirt and smiled politely.

"Something I can do for you, apprentice?"

Will returned the smile and gestured upward. "Is weather-caster Linyati taking the evening's readings?"

The recorder nodded. "Yar, he's up there, like a bird in its nest. He'll be down soon, if you want to talk to him."

"No." Will tilted his head as far back as it would go in a futile attempt to penetrate the grandfather redwood's upper recesses. "I want to go up."

"D'you, now, lad?" The wizened scribe scrutinized his young visitor closely. "Have you done it before, then?"

"This'll be my first time."

"I see. If you don't mind my asking, what d'you want to go to the top of a mere tree for, you bein' a skybax rider already and all?"

Will smiled at him. "Because I *haven't* done it before."

"Obviously not afraid of heights," the oldster murmured. "Climbing's not the same as lying athwart a soft saddle, though. If you fall, the tree won't dive down to catch you."

"I know. That's another reason why I want to do it."

The recorder grinned. "Have at it, then, apprentice, and good luck to you."

Will reached for the first rung of the bottom ladder and paused. "Linyati won't mind, will he?"

"Mind?" The recorder swirled his pen in its shallow jar of ammonite ink. "He never gets any company up there."

"Some people don't like company."

Mildly irritated, the old man gestured with his free hand. "D'you want to talk or climb? Get along up with you, apprentice! What d'you think, that Tswana's a rogue from the Rainy Basin? He'll be glad of the visit." With that the scribe returned his attention to the work at hand.

Will nodded, took a deep breath, and resumed his ascent, careful always to keep at least one hand or foot on the guide ropes at all times.

In places he climbed through a tunnel of cables that swayed with his weight. As he moved higher the wind strengthened, until the oppressive humidity of the past few days was reduced to a discomfiting memory. This was fortunate, because he was sweating heavily. Peering down, he discovered he could no longer see the ground, or even the recorder's perch: only a confusing tangle of leaves and branches. Someone afraid of heights could never have done it. Accustomed to executing complex maneuvers on the back of a giant *Quetzalcoatlus*, Will was in his element.

Six years ago almost to the day, he'd astounded the crew of a transoceanic sailing craft by scampering boyishly to the top of the mainmast at the height of the howling storm that had eventually cast him and his father adrift on these dinosaurian shores. The weatherwood was taller than that mast, but much steadier.

At last he could see the observation platform, constructed itself of sturdy redwood planks, and climbed the last few woven rungs to the top. Few needles brushed his cheeks now, and branches were sparse. Emerging onto the rough-hewn surface, he straightened as he hailed the weathercaster.

Linyati turned to greet his visitor, a broad grin creasing his dark face. "Will Denison, isn't it?" He extended a hand palm out, which Will grasped in his own. "I'm Linyati, six mothers Tswana," he said in the traditional Dinotopia greeting. "I've heard of you."

"And I of you." The weathercaster wasn't much older than himself, Will decided. Mid- to late-twenties, perhaps.

Linyati chuckled. "I'd heard you were a quick study. Pick up names as well as information, do you?"

Will shrugged, at once embarrassed and flattered. "When your father is a scientist you learn to remember everything." Gratefully he turned his face to the cooling breeze. It was much more comfortable up here atop the canopy than down on the ground.

In the distance the high peaks of the Backbone Mountains were clearly visible. Beyond, thanks to Dinotopia's pristine, unpolluted air, he could just make out the snowcapped crags of the higher Forbidden Mountains, hovering like pale dreams at the edge of perception.

A speck of wind-borne dust landed in his left eye and he turned away, blinking. "What do the readings say?"

Linyati glanced down at his writing tablet. Shipwrecked Chinese had introduced the art of papermaking to Dinotopia hundreds of years before it reached Europe. Their descendants had raised it to an art form. Papermaking parties were an important social event among many notable families. Nor was anyone who wanted to participate left out. Dinosaurs shared enthusiastically in the pulping process.

"There's a storm coming. No question about that." Linyati flipped pages. "A *big* storm. What we're trying to decide is just how big."

Will looked to the north. Even from the weather platform you couldn't see the ocean from mountain-locked Treetown, though it was possible to do so from Bent Root.

"Obviously the master weathercasters think it's big enough to warrant a mass evacuation of the Northern Plains. Is the danger really that great?"

"It's a traditional precaution," Linyati explained. "Why do you think there are no large towns in the Northern Plains, no permanent settlements?" He shrugged. "It may be nothing will happen. There will certainly be heavy rain and localized flooding, and probably some wind damage. Anything more extensive is hard to predict, which is why the guild wants the information on local conditions continuously updated." He tapped his tablet with a stylus. "That's my job, and the job of other observers."

"What happens if it turns out to be a *really* big storm?"

Linyati lost his smile. "If it's a once-in-a-generation Norther, then you'll surely see something."

"What?"

"Hard to say."

Will made a face. "For a follower of a supposedly scientific discipline, you're not very specific."

"It's hard to be specific where the weather is concerned, and I'd rather not commit myself. Not for a week or so, anyway. Come back then and ask me again."

"The last six-year storm was what shipwrecked my father and I on the northwest coast near the Hatchery. It's hard to imagine a storm bigger than that one."

Linyati's smile returned. "You may think you've seen a major storm. A six-year tempest is something, to be sure. A once-in-a-generation storm is, well, something *else*."

"Have you been through one of those?"

"No, but I've read about them. Let us pray it will not be so." His attention dropped to his tablet. "The signs are not good."

Will would have pressed the observer further, but Linyati had asked him to wait a week. It would have been impolite to continue.

"You're a skybax rider, I see." Linyati put his tablet aside.

Will leaned back against the railing, indifferent to the four-hundred-foot drop on the other side. "That's right. Fully qualified apprentice."

"I thought as much." Moving to a strange instrument situated in the center of the platform, Linyati began to check the fluid levels in multiple glass vials. The device allowed weathercasters to monitor changes in atmospheric pressure, making sure to allow for Treetown's altitude in their calculations.

"Your avocation explains how you were able to make the climb up here." Linyati jotted numbers on his tablet. "The height is too much for most people."

"It's something that's never bothered me," Will replied. "I've always been lucky that way. Back in Boston I used to climb out on top of the highest church steeples." He chuckled at the memory, part of an earlier life already half forgotten. "The deacons would call the police, and I'd run away over the rooftops before they could catch me."

"Everyone has his own fears," Linyati added. "In my family, there are old stories of giant crocodiles overturning dugouts and eating fishermen. Can you imagine what my ancestors must have thought when they fetched up here and saw their first dinosaurs?" He laughed gently at the memory.

"My father and I were afraid, too, when we had our first encounter. That was before we came to know dinosaurs. Funny how intelligence changes your perception of someone, even if that someone has spikes and claws and weighs as much as a fishing schooner." Will thought of his genial, patient skybax, the great-winged Cirrus. "Or looks at first like a gargoyle set free from the top of some cathedral."

"Dinotopia teaches everyone to look beneath the surface."
Linyati shifted to the other side of the barometric device.
"It's what's inside that makes a person, even if that person
weighs fifty tons.

"Fortunately, my ancestors encountered civilized dinosaurs right away. Can you imagine their reaction if they'd
come first upon the carnosaurs of the Rainy Basin? An allosaur would munch crocodiles for breakfast."

Will nodded agreement as he looked back out over the
treetops. "However big it's going to be, when do you think
the storm is going to hit?"

"Can't say. Despite what you may think, weathercasting
isn't an exact science yet, though we hope that someday it
will be." He raised his eyes to the clear blue sky. "If only
we could look down from higher up than the mountaintops.
Attach a telescope to a balloon, perhaps, and somehow relay
what it sees back to the ground." He lowered his gaze. "An
unworkable notion, of course."

"Oh, I don't know." Crossing his forearms on the railing,
Will rested his chin on the support they formed. "My father
thinks that through science a great many things are possible.
Maybe even a flying telescope." A glimmer of excitement
sparked his suggestion. "What if I were to take one up on
a skybax?"

Linyati considered. "You know, you may have something
there, young Denison. As you are aware, the winds that circle
Dinotopia are treacherous, but who knows? In my family
there is a saying: 'It is better to have the wit of a mongoose
than the heart of a lion.' I will pass your idea along to my
superiors."

Will wasn't sure whether to be flattered or not. Didn't he
also have the heart of a lion? Putting the question aside, he
and Linyati fell to discussing how a covey of specially
trained skybax riders equipped with proper instruments might
add to the body of Dinotopian meteorological knowledge.

"Sky galleys are not as agile as the skybax," Will noted,
"but they can stay up longer. What if you could send one up
really high?"

"What about the winds higher up?" Linyati argued.

"How would you control such a craft, and what would happen when the air grew too thin to breathe?"

"My father has devised machinery that allows you to breathe underwater. Surely such equipment would work just as well at altitude?"

Deep in conversation, they paid no attention to a fleeting gust of wind that whipped through the top of the redwood, rustling needles and jolting the mercury in the main thermometer. The gust was a harbinger, a scout, a forerunner of winds to come.

Far out to sea, well to the northeast of Dinotopia, the storm was gathering strength in its headlong rush southward. It was dark and intense, and it pushed heavy seas before it like the hand of an angry god. Already it was stronger than a six-year storm, stronger even than a once-in-a-twenty-year storm.

It was a once-in-a-lifetime storm, and its like had not struck Dinotopia in over a hundred years.

"I'M WORRIED ABOUT THE BOY, NALLAB."

Hands resting on the smooth sill, Arthur Denison stood staring out the high window of the library. The ever-present rumble of falling water echoed through his head. A set of the colorful ear dampers that were part of the apparel of every resident of Waterfall City reposed untouched in his pants pocket. They came in many designs, colors, and thicknesses and were worn as much for ornamentation as for practicality. He chose not to insert them. If he wanted peace and quiet, he could always shut the window.

"What, what's that?" The aged third assistant librarian wandered over, removing his own dampers and automatically raising his voice as he did so. Living surrounded by waterfalls, longtime residents of the city were able to adjust their voices to varying conditions as skillfully as opera singers. Within the thick walls of the library, it was rarely necessary to shout.

"I said that I'm concerned about Will."

"*Tch*, I wouldn't worry about him." The librarian possessed the ability to concentrate on two entirely unrelated subjects at the same time; Arthur could see him mentally filing and sorting even as he participated fully in the conversation. "He's an unusual boy, your Will."

Arthur turned back to the view through the window. "He's up at Treetown, and that's awfully close to where the storm's supposed to come onshore."

"*If* it comes onshore." Nallab wagged an admonitory finger at his friend. "The center could miss Dinotopia entirely and then all we'll get is some wind and a lot of rain, which we can always use." He frowned slightly and began searching a nearby table piled high with ancient scrolls. "Now, where did I lay that *Finale* by Homer? You'd think that after all these centuries we'd finally have that overflow from the library at Alexandria sorted out."

Arthur sighed and waited for Nallab to find what he was looking for. The shelves that lined the great domed room were filled to the ceiling. Many of the works he was looking at had been lost to the outside world. Others were utterly unknown, being the product not of human but of Dinosaurian origin. There was history, fiction, poetry, music: a wealth of inspiration and scholarship that would take many lifetimes just to casually peruse.

Everything was safe here, too. Unlike the ignorant and barbaric elsewhere, the citizens of Dinotopia did not burn or censor their libraries, even when they disagreed with their contents.

"I know he's been out on his own for a while." Arthur absently fiddled with the ends of his mustache, which in the past six years had become flecked with white. "But we've never been so far apart in a situation like this."

Outside, the sky over Waterfall City was clear, with only upwellings of the omnipresent mist to occasionally mute the sunlight.

Nallab glanced up from his scroll searching and spoke in his distinctively direct manner. In the outside world it might have been taken for rudeness, but here it was understood for the honesty it represented.

"Well, then, Arthur, it's about time he dealt with a crisis or two on his own, without your advice. How old is he now—seventeen?"

"Eighteen."

"You don't say, you don't say? Excellent! One more strong back to help with the evacuation. There's much to be done up there, you know. Just in case."

Again Arthur turned from the window. "I understand it's already under way."

"Oh, yes! A necessary precaution. It's traditional, you know."

"Why not wait until the weathercasters know for certain?"

Nallab's perpetually elfin grin softened slightly. "Why, because by then it might be too late. These things happen quickly, Arthur. Very quickly indeed."

"What sort of 'things'?"

"Well, for example there is the . . ." Nallab broke off, trading words for gestures. "Come with me and I'll show you some pictures. There are excellent drawings and some fine watercolors." He put a hand on the other man's shoulder.

"Maybe I should go up to Treetown and see for myself?"

Nallab urged his friend toward the door. "Now, Arthur, leave the boy be. He can take care of himself, and if you're constantly looking over his shoulder, you'll only embarrass him. Young men must learn by mistake as much as by success. You can't understand the latter without having first experienced the former."

Arthur Denison looked down at the man he knew to be far wiser than himself. "Nallab, he's all I have. Through him I still feel connected to his mother."

"I understand," said Nallab gently. "Not to disabuse you of compassionate memories, but weren't you and that flute player on the path to becoming more than just good friends?"

"Oriana?" Arthur smiled. "She's a fine woman. We see each other."

Nallab's index finger wagged again. "I think she'd be a fine match for you. High-spirited, as I recall."

"Very high-spirited." Arthur's smile widened.

At that moment Enit came bounding in. The head librarian was tapping his fingers together. As they happened to terminate in long claws, this action generated a regular, almost musical clicking sound. It was a habit remaining from the days when the *Deinonychus's* ancestors used to grasp prey instead of ideas. The long, sickle-shaped claw on his second toe tap-tapped impatiently against the floor.

"Well, what is it?" Even as he spoke to his superior, Nallab was winking at Arthur. Enit's fussiness was a source of much good-natured humor among the library staff.

The *Deinonychus* growled softly in his own tongue. With his human palate Nallab was unable to reply, but as long as communication was kept simple, he was able to understand much of what Enit said.

"No, no. I'm sure that we had the delegation from Chandara scheduled in at four o'clock, not two." Taking up pad and stylus, Nallab wrote out his reply in the familiar dinosaurian calligraphics.

Enit glanced at the response and rumbled a comment. Alone among the carnivorous dinosaurs it was the human-sized dromaeosaurs who had managed to moderate their natural appetites sufficiently to allow them to participate in Dinotopian civilization. Subsisting largely on a diet of fish and invertebrates, they had successfully subdued their baser natures. Their considerable intelligence was a great asset to the advance of Dinotopian science and research, and far more spiritually and intellectually rewarding than making a meal of their neighbors.

The two librarians, one human and the other dinosaur, conversed energetically by means of gestures and scribblings while Arthur stood quietly nearby, temporarily forgotten. With a resigned sigh, he turned away.

Nallab was right, of course. He usually was, even when he turned the subject under discussion into a gentle joke. After Arthur had found time to ponder what the old librarian had said, the wisdom that underlay each humorous anecdote or jest inevitably shone through.

Will had to grow up on his own. Much as a loving father might want to, Arthur knew he couldn't coddle, couldn't watch over his son every minute of every day. There would come a time, he knew, when he wouldn't be there at all, to answer questions or give advice or even offer simple comfort.

Why, Will already had a fiancée, the splendid Sylvia, and a career as an accomplished skybax rider. He'd also retained and developed his interests in scholarship and the sciences. Whether he would become a master skybax rider or take up a life of advanced academia remained to be seen. Either way, these were decisions he must necessarily make by himself.

Just as he would have to handle his part in the forthcoming crisis on his own, without his father's assistance.

Arthur Denison blinked. It struck him then that what was troubling him was not that he would be unable to offer Will help or advice. It was the realization that his rapidly maturing son might no longer need it.

≫ III ≪

GULLS AND TERNS RODE THE STORM FRONT, THEIR wild cries rising above the wind as piercingly as any trumpet call. Effortlessly they surfed the sky currents, rising and dipping to tease the waves that clutched futilely at their supple white-winged forms. More than anything they resembled fragments of foam cast free from the crests of breaking rollers.

Whole tree trunks sent down rivers or torn free from squall-scoured shores tumbled and snapped in the waves. Teak from Siam and mahogany from Java, mangrove from Sumatra and bamboo from Borneo, marked the leading edge of the tempest, riding the breakers like jackstraws. There were clusters of branches still clinging futilely to their remaining leaves, dead fish stunned to the surface by the fury of the churning debris, a forlorn handmade fishing net ripped from its moorings, and whole rafts of coconuts bobbing in the swell like so many abandoned punctuation marks in search of a paragraph.

Riding high above this roiling confusion of flotsam, her foremast snapped, unreefed sails tattered and shredded, and taking on water, was the three-masted barkentine *Condor*. Designed not for speed like a tea clipper but for hauling cargo, she was proving her seaworthiness now. Her heavy keel and reinforced hull were all that had kept her anxious crew from being cast upon the mercy of the waves many days and leagues earlier. A more handsome but lesser vessel would have broken up at the mere sight of such a storm as raged about her rigging now. Not that there was a man-jack aboard who didn't believe that to be her ultimate fate anyway. Not given the furies that thundered and raged all about them.

A few men gazed longingly at the immense seas surrounding them, whose crests frequently overtopped the sodden deck, and silently wondered whether a quick end by drowning might not be preferable to the unending battering they were being forced to endure. Even if they somehow managed to survive and outrun the storm front, the inevitable exhaustion of their meager supplies promised a slow death from starvation. A step to the nearest railing, a quick jump, and the sea would welcome them with her eternal impartiality.

Raging for weeks, the storm had carried the *Condor* and her crew hundreds of leagues off course, driving them steadily south and west into the empty vastness of the Indian Ocean. According to the best contemporary charts, in all that great expanse of water there was not a single friendly isle or welcoming shore on which they could hope to be cast up.

Only the energy and ravings of their indomitable captain kept them going. Cursing and beating them from one task to the next, he refused to let them concede their ship, much less their lives, to the relentless gale. Any man who chose to leap overboard knew he'd best sink quickly lest the *Condor*'s captain have him gaffed and brought back aboard, to face a wrath no less terrifying than that of the tempest.

Brognar Blackstrap's anger was as capacious as his stomach, and few dared tempt it. Though his expansive gut heaved and rolled like one of the green swells beneath the bow, rash and foolish was the man who dared to challenge the face above. Of indeterminate age, he was strong as an ox and just as stubborn.

His personal history was as difficult to navigate as a London fog, in which very city he was rumored to have done some trading. Subsequently moving (or chased) to the Americas, he'd dabbled in various enterprises while keeping always one step or, if fortune happened to be smiling on him, two ahead of the authorities. Eventually his luck had run out and, betrayed by a comrade whom he had importunately cheated in a matter of business, he had been captured, tried, and sentenced to the prison at Hobart, Tasmania, from which no ordinary man had ever escaped.

But then, Brognar Blackstrap was no ordinary man.

In bright sunlight the impressive dome of his skull shone with a pinkish radiance, as if inlaid with rose quartz. From the sides and back, long black hair flecked with gray cascaded in rippling waves, as if mocking those long-forgotten follicles that had once thrived upon that now vacant globular terrain. Heavy brows served to introduce the enormous downward-pointing mustache, which burgeoned from beneath his bulbous nose like an ebony octopus emerging from its coral hideaway. The deep-set eyes were black as night, though not entirely without humor. Teeth showed scattered and broken in his jaws, as irregular as neolithic monuments. One was fashioned entirely of gold cast from a watch Blackstrap had appropriated in the course of an argument with a forgotten but now wiser gentleman planter of Jamaica.

Woe betide the seaman caught shirking his work. Not that Blackstrap was a cruel captain—no. He was too crafty a leader to employ such blatant methods on his own crew. Instead, he preferred to employ the subtlety that had characterized his shady business dealings across half the globe.

Not that he was averse, mind, to cracking heads when the occasion demanded.

Preister Smiggens was another matter entirely. Self-taught as a seaman, possessing more brains than the heads of any three jack-tars slapped together, the only man aboard the *Condor* who had suffered any advanced formal education, the tall first mate was as lanky and weathered as a length of driftwood. Encountering Blackstrap in the course of their mutual sojourn in quaint Hobart, Smiggens had recognized in the captain qualities of survival that he himself did not possess. To his credit, Blackstrap saw many complementary traits in Smiggens. While engaging in the not so very restful prison pastime of breaking up large rocks with small hammers, the two men shaped an informal partnership, which had, to date, endured for several years.

A partnership that the relentless storm seemed about, any day now, to dissolve.

Presently both men were standing aft, behind the wheel and the wizened Nantucketer who held it. Determination rode the helmsman's face like a harpooner in the bow of a whaleboat, but hope had long since taken flight from his eyes. Scrambling about the rigging and clinging to the wave-swept deck, the rest of the crew did their best to keep the *Condor* from capsizing.

As it had for weeks, the wind blew steadily from astern. The obdurate current that had caught them in its grip carried them ever farther from land, ever deeper into uncharted waters.

A small, tattered flag fluttered from a mizzen stay. Currently it was Dutch, a memory of their recent visit to Batavia. Previously, while they had been conducting business in Hong Kong, the crew had flown the Union Jack. Packed neatly below in a small sail locker were the flags of some thirty nations, each to be brought out and run up as the occasion required.

In point of fact, while the crew of the *Condor* hailed from many of those countries, they recognized and honored none, professing loyalty to their comrades rather than to larger and more restrictive societies. The one flag they did salute was run up only in the course of serious enterprise. That flag consisted of a skull and bones rampant on a black field.

Wind buffeted the barkentine and she heeled sharply to starboard. Standing six-foot-four and weighing well over three hundred pounds, Blackstrap slid not an inch sideways. He was as much at home in the sea as any fish, and about as compassionate.

"Keep a weather eye there, Mr. Ruskin."

"Aye, Cap'n." Ignoring the sting, the helmsman wiped saltwater from his eyes. He was old and small, but if you gagged and blindfolded him he could smell out a course between two close-lying islands by comparing the odor of land with that of coral. What he could not do was fight clear of the damnably insistent current and storm.

Preister Smiggens interceded on his behalf. "Do your best, Ruskin. There's little we can do in weather like this save try to stay afloat."

"Aye," growled Blackstrap. "Curse this current! She

makes the Gulf Stream feel like a bloody creek!'' Enormous hands contracted, forming hairy, gnarled masses.

Smiggens clutched at a line to steady himself. ''If the wind would change, we might have a chance to break free.''

''The wind, the wind,'' Ruskin groused. ''I've never seen the like, current and wind acting in such concert. Off Cape Horn 'tis something like this, but never so steady or for so long. Never!'' A wave crashed over the bow and the spray reached even those in the stern. ''If the sea wants us, she'll have us.''

''Belay that kind of talk, Ruskin!'' Blackstrap rumbled. ''I'll not stand for any nonsense of that sort on any ship of mine.''

''Sorry, Cap'n.'' The aged helmsman subsided.

''How be that caulking forward, Mr. Smiggens?''

''Still holding, Captain.'' The first mate's voice was growing hoarse from the need to constantly shout above the wind. ''I've made up some glue which I think will be stronger than mere tar and—''

''Spare me your learned dissertations, Mr. Smiggens! Will the caulking hold or not?''

''For a time, sir.'' Though it was not always apparent to outsiders, the two men, so different in background and upbringing, had the greatest respect for one another. The first mate squinted forward into the rain and spray. The faint outlines of numerous seamen, exhausted from being driven before the storm and their equally relentless captain, struggled with the rigging.

''It would aid our efforts tremendously if we could ground on even the tiniest spit of sand and make more permanent repairs to the damaged planks.''

''Don't you think I know that?'' Blackstrap muttered. ''There be no dry land hereabouts, Smiggens, unless one counts a turtle back. Be that not so, Mr. Ruskin?''

''On this course, not till we fetch up on the shores of Africa, Cap'n. Or so the maps insist.''

''Africa!'' Blackstrap unclenched his fists and promptly slammed his hands together behind his back. ''Fate seems determined to make us cross an entire ocean simply to reprovision and repair.''

"I dunno, Cap'n." Ruskin strove to inject a note of optimism in what was becoming yet another fatalistic conversation. "The distance we've covered already and the speed we're making would put the *Flying Cloud* herself to shame. The sea may claim us yet, but she seems bound and determined to show us as much of herself as possible before she does so!"

"Just like a woman," the captain growled. "I wouldn't have thought this old crate would hold together as long as she has."

As if to underline his evaluation there was a violent groan from amidships. Rushing to the rail, Blackstrap bellowed into the rain.

"Avast there, you shipworms! Get that cannon secured! D'you want to meet Davy Jones with crushed bones?"

Sailors hurried to tighten the lashings restraining one of the *Condor*'s twelve-pounders. A loose cannon banging about on deck in the midst of a storm could do as much damage to ship and crew as an angry whale.

Blackstrap watched until he was convinced the crewmen were doing a proper job of it, then returned to Smiggens's side.

"So Africa be the nearest land, be it? By Triton's scaly backside, then, we'll run to Africa if we must!"

The first mate eyed the captain admiringly. Blackstrap might be a liar and a cheat, a thief and a cutthroat, and as treacherous a captain as ever fondled a gold sovereign or unread contract, but he was afraid of nothing, not even the sea itself. There was something inside him that insisted that if one couldn't laugh at death, one could, if given enough time, at least try to outwit it.

"You might say that we're in desperate straits, sir."

Blackstrap glared at him. "I'll thank you to keep your witticisms to yourself, Smiggens." He'd always been suspicious of his first mate's book learning, quick as he was to recognize its value. But if he ever caught the other man openly laughing at him, no one aboard doubted that the *Condor* would find itself in immediate need of a new first mate.

For his part, Smiggens suspected that the captain was simply too mean to die. When the storm finally abated (as surely

it must, he told himself), when the tropical sun emerged from
behind the clouds and began to bake ship and crew, when
the last of the food and water had run out, Brognar Blackstrap would still be standing, back to the mainmast and fist
upraised, cursing the elements themselves.

The crew was nearly done. They'd had no rest for weeks
and no opportunity to rotate the watch. Every hand was
needed at all times to keep the ship afloat.

If only, Smiggens thought, they hadn't tried to make off
with that chest of ingots from the treasury at Batavia. A well-
thought-out and prepared plan had been spoiled by a cabin
boy who'd fallen asleep where he oughtn't to have been.
He'd escaped to another room and sounded the alarm.

Alerted to the true nature of the outlaw barkentine in their
midst, two Dutch warships in the harbor had hauled anchor
and given chase, only to be joined outside the Sunda Strait
by Her Majesty's frigate *Apollonia*, on watch for the *Condor*
ever since her notorious escapade at Hong Kong. Portuguese
warships, too, were on the lookout for Blackstrap's vessel,
thanks to her boarding and sinking of a well-connected man-
darin's junk near Macau.

Previously the crew of the pirate vessel had always managed to stay one step ahead of the Southeast Asian colonial
authorities. Now it seemed that every warship in the South
China Sea was in on the hunt. Smiggens felt unnecessarily
persecuted. They were no more than small-time brigands at
best. Piracy in the region was no longer a growth industry.

None of which would have mattered had the *Condor* been
able to slip out of Batavia to the east, where it could have
lost itself in the thousands of islands that constituted the East
Indies. But the *Apollonia* had forced her to turn west and
south, through the strait and into the teeth of the brewing,
boiling squall from which there seemed no escape.

At least they had shaken the pursuit, Smiggens believed.
Probably their pursuers thought them dead. He wondered if
their British and Dutch tormentors had been sunk or had
managed to escape the grasp of the storm. Somehow he could
not find it in himself to be grateful. Leg irons, hardtack, and
a nice dry hold would be preferable to what they were presently being forced to endure, and certainly an improvement

over the starvation to come should they somehow manage to ride out the storm.

He thought of the purloined goods banging about in the hold below: the fine bales of tea, the now shattered porcelain, the rolls of silk and crates of spices. Not quite the equal of gold ingots, but valuable nonetheless. All worthless unless the crew could make port.

Give old Ruskin his due, he thought admiringly. Many times during the storm the helmsman had tried to turn them north, toward Ceylon and India, but without success. The combination of current and wind was simply too strong. The *Condor* could do nothing but ride before the storm.

They were now somewhere near the Tropic of Capricorn, where the southeast trade winds acted in a manner most contrary and the threat of entering the horse latitudes loomed over their most strenuous efforts to escape. A hopeless situation. If they held to their present course the weather would eventually turn cold, and they would freeze before they had a chance to starve.

Africa, he mused. Unless they could fly like an albatross they hadn't a chance of making it all that way. Slave unceasingly and battle the storm as they might, the crew of the *Condor* were condemned men.

There on the storm-tossed deck he recalled his early life. He'd been a tutor, and a respected one, much in demand by the aristocratic families of London. It was a taste for strong drink (and other things) that had brought about his eventual downfall. There was one particular pupil, the attractive young daughter of a certain duke, whose tutoring he had perhaps accelerated beyond reasonable bounds. Certainly her father had believed so. It was only by the grace of God and good fortune that Smiggens had been able to obtain passage on a ship leaving for the West Indies just before the outraged nobleman had set upon him with pistol, sword, and police in hand.

He'd thought his escape a clean one . . . until his ship was intercepted at the mouth of the Thames and boarded by the authorities. There was no chance for him, of course, in a court dominated by the good duke, his innumerable solicitors (countless as the sands on a beach, Smiggens remembered), and a magistrate bought and paid for by friends of the suitably outraged.

So it was that he'd found himself shipped off in gaol to the most remote and barren prison on earth, that of Hobart in Tasmania, there to live out the rest of his natural life immersed in misery and hard labor. It was there that he'd made the acquaintance of the scum of the earth, of whom Brognar Blackstrap was among the most notorious. As well as the most clever, the first mate reminded himself. The friendship they had struck up was most certainly an odd one.

Smiggens's intelligence and Blackstrap's boldness had organized the theft of a small fishing boat. Escaping Hobart, they had made their way north along the Tasmanian coast. In this they were helped by the poor Aborginals, who recognized, in the escapees, individuals as persecuted by the authorities as they were themselves.

From there they had somehow managed to cross the unforgiving Bass Strait and slip into the booming port town of Sydney, hiding out until their identity was discovered. In the company of a band of equally desperate men, they had stolen a larger ship and sailed north. One of those who had placed himself under Blackstrap's protection was the helmsman and navigator Ruskin, without whose skills they surely would have foundered on the terrible barrier reef that guarded Australia's eastern shore, reefs that had given even the immortal Cook pause.

Against all odds they'd done it, turning west north of Cape York and making their way into the riches of the Indies. Along the way they acquired sailors of every nationality, desperate men with no hope. From such human flotsam was a willing crew forged.

There were Filipinos and renegade Chinese, failed farmers from Java and American whalers who'd jumped ship, free Africans and escaped Melanesians, small-time thieves from Europe and the Orient. Given a chance at booty and freedom, they served Blackstrap willingly. Every pursuit they'd managed to outrun, every battle they'd succeeding in winning. Until now.

You could not defeat the sea, Smiggens reflected. As old Ruskin had declared, if the sea wanted you, she'd have you, and there was nothing a mere man could do about it.

It was at that moment that the lookout, strapped into the crow's nest lest he be carried away by the unrelenting gale, sang out.

"Land ho!"

Land, land? What manner of nonsense was this? Smiggens wondered. The lookout would not be the first member of the crew to go mad.

Shielding his eyes as best he could from the driving rain, he staggered forward and directed his shout at the top of the mainmast.

"Ahoy in the nest! You've been too long off the deck, Mr. Suarez! Come down and we'll send up your relief!" Wind ripped his words into syllables.

Disdaining a possible fall, the excited lookout leaned over and made his reply as clear as possible. "No, sir! She is land, for sure! Due south she lies!" Extending an arm, he pointed vigorously for emphasis.

"What's all this, Mr. Smiggens?" Blackstrap had come up behind the first mate.

"It's Suarez, sir. He says there's land to the south. But that's impossible."

"How know you what's possible in these latitudes, Smiggens? There's naught but a great blank space on the charts." He looked around sharply. "Where's me glass? No, never mind that." Cupping his hands to his mouth, he roared up at the lookout.

"What manner of land, Mr. Suarez?"

Clinging to the top of the mainmast, the Cuban somehow managed to raise a spyglass to his eyes. "Flat, sir, with mountains farther in!"

"An island?" Smiggens chewed his lower lip, tasting the salt. "There can't be an island here. We're still at least a thousand miles east of Madagascar."

"And who has been here before us, Preister Smiggens? Cook himself never sailed these seas." Moving to the rail, Blackstrap bellowed at the deck, "Stir yourselves, you lazy lot of limp lungfish! Did you not hear the lookout? Put on sail!" Raging about the deck below, he lashed out with fist and boot. Most of his slaps and kicks missed, for the crew was already bustling with renewed energy, an energy born of desperation. Unlikely as it might be, if there *was* any land thereabouts, they would not, could not afford to miss it.

Then a cloud broke, and there it was for all to see. A line of dark green backed by high mountains, just as the lookout had claimed. Mountains meant snow, and snow meant clean, fresh water. A ragged cheer arose from the men.

Just when it seemed they had been rescued from certain death by a kindly Providence, another shout sounded from the mainmast.

"Reefs, sir! Reefs dead ahead!"

"Blast and damn!" Blackstrap tore his way back up to the wheel and took half of it from the grip of his helmsman. "Hard aport, Mr. Ruskin, afore 'tis too late!"

Despite their combined efforts, the rudder refused to respond.

"She won't come around, Cap'n! The current's too strong!" There was fresh panic in the helmsman's voice.

His face turning red with effort, Blackstrap bawled at his first mate, "Mr. Smiggens, lend a hand here!"

Smiggens did so, but it was no use. Propelled by irresistible winds and unrelenting current, the *Condor* continued on a course bound for disaster.

Soon they could see as well as hear the great breakers as they crashed on the wide reef, feel the threatening swell beneath the keel. As they drew nearer, there hove into view a sight to chill the bones of any seaman.

Skeletons. Not of men or beasts but of ships. Broken and gaping on the reef were the remains of Chinese junks and Arab dhows, Ceylonese fishing boats and old Spanish galleons. There were ruined merchantmen and men-o'-war, and even what looked like a New England fishing schooner.

"Every man look to his Maker and brace yourselves!" Blackstrap roared, clutching the wheel like a talisman as the *Condor* rose on the crest of a wave most monstrous. There was at that moment on board ship more prayer than had been heard in those quarters in all the previous year.

High, higher still they rose, floating in the air for what seemed an impossible time. The ship's timbers groaned under the strain and her remaining masts threatened to splinter.

Then the wave came crashing down.

Men screamed as water inundated the deck . . . and flowed off through the scuppers. The *Condor* heeled dangerously to starboard, swung back on her oversized keel, and stabilized.

All that broken porcelain in the hold, Smiggens thought numbly. *Priceless pieces so strenuously acquired now surely reduced to ballast.*

"Look out!" came a shout as the main topgallant came crashing down. Sailors scattered and the only casualty was a bruised thigh.

The wave swept on, slamming into a line of mangroves, but not before leaving the *Condor* behind. Miraculously, the ocean had had enough of her, and she floated, battered but intact, in the calm waters of the lagoon behind a reef that seemed no longer an assassin but a friend.

"Mr. Johanssen!" Blackstrap yelled. "Take a man below and check the damage!"

"Aye, sir!" The strapping ex-whaler vanished like a badger down a hatch.

Gathering their strength along with their wits, other members of the crew set about repairing what damage they could. Unsalvageable debris was thrown over the side and the carpenter's tools brought out and passed around. The man whose leg had caught the glancing blow from the falling spar was treated by the ship's barber.

Johanssen reappeared, almost smiling. "A few new leaks, sir, but they're all small. The hull's held. Nothing that can't be fixed, I think."

"Yes, fixed." Turning, Smiggens studied the reef. Beyond, the storm was finally waning. It was an impossible landing, but they'd done it, thanks to the thrust of a freak wave. "We're safely in, but can we get out again?"

A huge hand clapped him on the back. "We be alive and aground, Mr. Smiggens—two things which were badly wanted. 'Tis best not to tempt fate with too many requests at once. We don't want her to think us greedy."

"What, me?" Smiggens grunted.

"Interesting landfall, don't you think?" Blackstrap guided his first mate to the railing. They could see mangroves lining the shore and, farther in, dense high reeds.

"Might be cannibals," the ever-pessimistic Smiggens avowed, "or worse."

"I'll match any cannibal mouthful for mouthful, for unlike some men, I've no aversion to long pig." Blackstrap's energy had been renewed by their escape from the storm. "I see no signs of men; no canoes, no fish traps. Only growing things and the promise of fresh water. We've found this land, Mr. Smiggens, and by all the gods of the sea, she's ours! I, Brognar Blackstrap, claim her. Let any who dare, dispute me."

He glanced aft. "How I wish now those Dutch and British ships still pursued us, for surely the miracle which cast us safely into this lagoon would not be repeated twice. It would please me greatly me to see them splintered and ground to dust on this reef, to hear their screams and wails as they were thrown into the sea, pleading for our aid."

"They probably turned back long ago to escape the grip of the storm," Smiggens reminded him.

"Aye, I know, I know." There was a murderous gleam in Blackstrap's eye. Smiggens recognized it, having encountered it numerous times before. "But I can see it in my mind's eye, Mr. Smiggens, and delight in it there."

He straightened. "We'll make repairs and reprovision here. Perhaps there'll be natives to help with the heavy work."

"D'you think they'll be friendly, Cap'n?" the helmsman inquired.

"It matters not, Mr. Ruskin. We've eight cannon aboard and if the powder's stayed dry, any locals will see soon enough that it's in their best interests to obey our orders. 'Tis well known that a few shots of grape and chain will tame the most reluctant village. If there be any individuals worth taking, we can use them for ballast and sell those who survive in the market at Durban."

"You mean to continue on to Africa?" the helmsman asked him.

"I do, Mr. Ruskin. I've had enough of the pestilential Indies to last me some time."

It was then that something caught Smiggens's eye.

Caught up on an inner shelf of coral were the hulks of

three ships. Reduced to keel, beams, and wood skeletons that refused to rot, they were barely identifiable.

"Have a look at that, won't you!"

A preoccupied Blackstrap frowned as he glanced at his first mate. "A look at what, Smiggens? Why are you wasting your time staring at dead ships that can be home only to dead men? They can't help us. Unless," he added, brightening, "you see something useful aboard one of them. Guns would be welcome, a powder barrel or two more so."

"Such items are not to be found on any of those ships, Captain."

Noting the first mate's stare, several other seamen turned their attention to the trio of wrecks. "What manner of ships be those, Mr. Smiggens?" one finally inquired.

"I can scarce believe it myself." Smiggens shaded his eyes as he examined the hulks. "See those holes along the side of each? They're oar ports. Those craft were meant to be rowed as often as sailed. Roman triremes, is my guess. Nothing less than a trireme would survive in these waters from such ancient times."

"Roman?" Now Blackstrap was interested. "What d'you mean, Roman, Mr. Smiggens? Do they use such strange vessels in the south of Europe these days?"

"Not these days, sir. These are the ships of the Caesars, which once made of the Mediterranean a Roman lake. But how did they get here?"

"The Caesars, you say?" Blackstrap smiled thoughtfully. It was an uncharacteristic expression for him and his face had difficulty with it. "Now, Julius I know. There was a man after me own heart. What of the third vessel, then?"

"I'm not sure. Older still, from the look of it. Egyptian, perhaps, or Phoenician. See the outline of an eye painted on the bow? Their presence here is a mystery I can't explain."

"Why don't you ask their helmsmen?" Ruskin let out a wheezing cackle.

"I fear to query any seaman who's been dead a thousand years or more. His ghost might answer." Smiggens spoke solemnly, and Ruskin's smile vanished instantly.

"Bah!" Blackstrap wasn't impressed. "This be a veritable

graveyard of ships, thanks to those infernal currents. But we have survived. A fine omen.''

"I don't know, Captain." Smiggens turned away from the wrecks to face the land. "Something doesn't feel right about this place."

"To perdition with your 'feelings,' Mr. Smiggens. If 'tis dry and has fresh water, 'tis good enough land for me." The first mate didn't respond, preferring to keep his concerns to himself. Blackstrap would be unresponsive anyway.

⇒ IV ⇐

As THE CREW SECURED THE SHIP, CRIES AND strange calls occasionally resounded inland. These served only to increase Smiggens's unease, but they had an entirely different effect on the less imaginative crew.

"Wild cattle." Johanssen rubbed his hands together expectantly. "Fresh meat!"

"Buffalo, if we lucky." Tough little Anbaya hailed from the Moluccas and was as peppery as the spices that grew there. "Hunting party, Captain?"

"Soon enough, you hungry heathen," Blackstrap replied with good humor. His gaze roved the deck. "Where's that accursed African? Tell him to get up from belowdecks. We're not going to sink." Two men disappeared through a hatch in search of the Zulu warrior.

Wind continued to buffet the ship, ruffling Smiggens's ponytail, but it was much reduced in intensity. However, the sky to the northeast remained resolutely dark and foreboding. Inland, mist began to rise from the land, obscuring the distant mountains.

"What think you now, Preister?" Blackstrap nodded at the beach. "She looks harmless enough."

"So do the Fijis," Smiggens replied, "and they're home to the most notorious cannibals in the Pacific. Except perhaps for the wild men of New Guinea, whom they say—"

"That's enough. Will you never learn when to shut up? We'll go ashore, I think, and raise what food, water, and hell, we can." He raised his voice. "O'Connor, Treggang—put a boat over the side!"

Smiggens did not object. He was as anxious as any of them to stand once more on a surface that did not roll underfoot.

Two dozen men were shuttled to the narrow beach, leaving an equal number aboard to maintain watch and continue making repairs. Each time the boat crossed the calm waters of the lagoon, the men aboard commented on the abundance and strange look of the fish life below. The warm shallows were home to other peculiar creatures as well, which none could identify. Smiggens would have lingered to study them, but Blackstrap would brook no delays. If it couldn't be eaten or converted into gold, it didn't interest him.

Finding a small opening in the wall of mangroves, they left half their number to explore the beach. The rest pushed through the dense vegetation and soon found themselves rowing up a narrow, meandering stream. To everyone's delight and relief, the water soon turned from brackish to sweet.

Mangroves gave way to sedges, reeds, and other water-loving plants. Smiggens was certain he saw papyrus sharing the shoreline with cattails and wild rice. Another food source to add to the fish they'd already seen. This land would feed as well as water them.

Soon the current grew swifter and the men had to row harder. At least now they had no shortage of water to quench their thirst. They pulled with renewed vigor.

When the stream grew too shallow for the whaleboat to negotiate, they beached it on a crescent of white sand. Grass as high as a man's knee offered a sweet-smelling and not impassable obstacle through which they advanced enthusiastically, rifles and swords close at hand.

Despite the seeming calm, Smiggens remained uneasy. "Keep a sharp eye out, mates. No telling what sort of wildlife might roam a country as foreign as this."

"Yes, yes," concurred Anbaya. "Watch you feet."

"My feet?" The man who spoke wore a patch over a vacant eye socket and was missing the middle two fingers

of his left hand, a consequence of an involuntary close encounter with a passing cannonball.

The little Moluccan smiled. "Snakes like high grass."

Several of the men started visibly and began taking more
care where they set their boots. Anbaya chuckled, but no one
shared his sense of humor in this matter. A French merchantman armed to the teeth would not have given a man among
them pause, but not a one of them was overly fond of creatures that had not even the decency to have feet.

They saw no snakes, poisonous or otherwise, as they left
the grassland behind and advanced into a region of low hills.
Like old friends, trees of many lands presented themselves
for observation, from scrub oaks to palms. Some hung heavy
with fruit. Smiggens looked for monkeys, who would invariably consume such fruit, thereby showing a man what was
safe to eat and what was not. But there were no monkeys
nor any signs of them. He remarked on their absence to
Blackstrap.

"So there be no monkeys—so what?" Blackstrap used his
sword to casually hack at an inoffensive philodendron.

"In country like this you almost always find monkeys."

"Ever been to Tahiti, Mr. Smiggens?"

"No, sir."

"Big islands, lots of fruit. Looks not unlike this. No monkeys." That settled the matter as far as Blackstrap was concerned.

Chirping sweetly, several birds appeared. They flew
straight toward the landing party, utterly unafraid. One of the
men raised his rifle and took aim at what looked like a fat
pigeon with a crimson topknot. His companion slapped the
barrel aside. The would-be shooter glared at him.

"What's the matter, Mkuse? Don't your people eat fowl?"

"We'll eat just about anything we can catch." The Zulu
warrior's English was oddly stilted. "But if we're going to
open fire on the countryside and warn whatever's living here,
I'd like to catch something more substantial first." Coming
to rest on a nearby branch, the birds eyed the intruders curiously.

The shooter mulled this a moment, then nodded grudging
approval. Save for Smiggens, the seamen were not an edu-

cated bunch. Neither were they stupid. Stupid pirates didn't live very long. The party moved on.

Anbaya found not snakes, but a grove of papayas. The men lingered there, eating their fill, until the Malay Treggang came running back into the grove, his face frozen not in fear, but in amazement.

"Come quick, Captain, Mr. Smiggens, you all come quick now!"

"Settle down, man." Blackstrap wiped juice and seeds from his mouth. They lingered in his mustache. "What's the trouble?"

The Malay was fairly hopping back the way he'd come, beckoning frantically. "You come see, Captain sir, come see now!"

"What the devil is he on about?" Irritated, Blackstrap drew his cutlass. "Speak up, man, or I'll cut out your tongue!"

"We not only ones gathering fruit!"

"Natives?" Rising from where they'd been sitting or leaning, the other men were instantly alert.

"No natives, no natives. You come see quick!" With that the Malay whirled and vanished back into the brush that filled the gaps between the trees.

"Can't be all that bad if Treggang's going back for another look." Johanssen brushed papaya pulp from his trousers. "Might as well see if he's found something or just gone mad."

When they caught up with the excited crewman, he was crouching low within the brush and pointing. As soon as they discerned the nature of the other fruit gatherers, their eyes grew no less wide than the Malay's, quite irrespective of individual ancestry.

Not only were the creatures methodically gathering fallen papaya not natives, they were not even human. Nor were they the monkeys Smiggens had hoped to encounter.

"What in the name of all that's sanctified be *those*?" Blackstrap strained for a better view.

Alone among the landing party, only Chin-lee, an escaped thief from Canton, was confident he knew.

"There dragons here, Captain!"

Blackstrap turned a dubious gaze on the smaller man. "Dragons?"

Chin-lee nodded energetically. "Yessee, sir! Dragons."

Smiggens was as stunned by the sight as any of them, but of one thing he was certain: there were no such things as dragons. They were medieval superstitions, though the source of such legends was now plain to see. These creatures weren't even especially impressive. Dragons were monstrous beasts armed with fang and claw, who breathed fire and left devastation in their wake.

These beasts, for all their self-evident uniqueness, had not a fang among them and ate fruit, and all they left in their wake were papaya seeds.

But if not dragons, then what were they?

Altogether they were five: two adults (or at least two larger specimens) and three smaller ones. Their undersides varied from beige to a pale yellow in color, while intricate rose-colored mottling decorated their necks, backs, and tail. They had long, slim necks held erect in a flexible S curve; narrow, birdlike snouts; slim tails that extended stiffly out behind them like rudders; and wide, active eyes. The mature specimens stood six and seven feet tall, while the smaller trio varied in height between five and six. Lissome of build, even the adults did not appear to weigh more than a couple of hundred pounds.

"See there, see!" Mkuse gestured at the browsing wonders.

"Keep your voice down, man!" Blackstrap growled, even as he saw what the Zulu was pointing at. A leather pouch of some kind was slung over the shoulder of the tallest specimen.

Blackstrap turned to his first mate. "See the pouch. But how did this beast get hold of it?"

Smiggens considered. "Probably it was hanging on a tree where it had come to rest and these creatures came running past. Or it floated in from a wreck. That big one caught it on its neck and it's hung there ever since. They're probably used to it, since it doesn't seem to be bothering them. See how they use their front paws to pull down the branches."

"The Chinaman thinks they be dragons. What about you, Preister? Have you ever seen the like?"

"No, Captain." Smiggens's brow furrowed. "They have the aspect of lizards, but they walk on two legs. It seems to me I should know what they are, but the identification escapes me."

"I have seen like them." The Zulu had moved up alongside Blackstrap. "In my homeland, but with feathers." Both men turned to the warrior. "The Dutch have a word for them, too, but the English say 'ostrich.' "

"Ostrich," Smiggens murmured. Indeed, the wondrous creatures looked very much like that famous flightless bird. To be more exact, like one whose feathers had been blown off in a storm. Perhaps these were near relatives who molted completely at certain times of the year. But looking at them, that explanation didn't seem to fit, either. For one thing, no ostrich or any other bird had long, dexterous, clawed forearms. Those aside, the similarities were astonishing.

"Dragons." Chin-lee was insistent. "But little ones."

"They're not much bigger than we are," pointed out Samuel, the black American. "Tall, but not heavy."

As the men watched from cover, the creatures continued their foraging, seeking out the ripest papayas and varying this diet with large, fat white grubs dug from the trunk of a fallen tree. Occasional thorns slid harmlessly off their tough hides. The colorful patterns visible on several of the sensitive faces seemed almost to have been painted on. Occasionally they chirped and whistled at one another. The smaller individuals were especially vocal.

The pirates had no way of knowing, and would not have believed in any case, that these intricate whistlings constituted complex communication, that they were in fact a highly evolved language. It never occurred to them that the family of *Struthiomimuses* they were so avidly spying upon was anything other than a clutch of dumb animals. As far as they were concerned, the leather pouch worn by the adult male was present as the result of blind accident, nothing more.

Relaxing near the end of their extended camping and foraging trip, the struthie family was assured of their solitude. Certainly they felt in no danger. It was impossible for the carnosaurs of the Rainy Basin to reach the Northern Plains; therefore there wasn't anything to threaten them except the occasional poisonous snake. Even the children knew enough to keep a wary eye out for those. So their attention was focused on the trees and the ground and little in between.

When not picking fruit or eating, the three siblings chased each other around trees and through bushes, playing an elaborate game of tag in which tails were off limits. Mother and father lingered nearby, letting the children romp. They would be back at studies soon enough. All three were fleet of foot, agile and graceful in their leaps and sudden changes of direction. The fruit-gathering expedition was in the nature of a reward for their eldest, Keelk, who had performed exceptionally well in the most recent Junior Olympics at Pooktook.

Unlike humans on a campout, the *Struthiomimuses* needed little in the way of gear, being quite able and even eager to live off the land. The Northern Plains were a bountiful place and there'd been no trouble finding adequate food. Normally they would have stayed with different farm families along the way, but the humans and dinosaurs who usually worked the land had recently been compelled to move to higher, drier ground.

So they had slept out in the open, beneath the canopy of stars. Humans did the same, when the climate was sufficiently salubrious. But this was a family outing, and they had come alone.

Shremaza looked over at her mate, half a papaya held loosely in one limber, clawed hand. "We should be starting back toward Bent Root," she whistled eloquently, not seeing the men crouched low in the dense brush.

Hisaulk's body did not move, but with his long, flexible neck he had no difficulty looking directly back over his body. "I know. Probably we shouldn't even have come here. It's depressing to see all the abandoned farms. But the children would have been *so* disappointed. They've been looking forward to this for a long time. Just the family, alone in the countryside, away from civilization, living off the land in the manner of the ancient ones."

Her head bobbed with precision. All the ornithomimosaurs had evolved an intricate language of neck and body gestures to emphasize their whistling speech. It was mirrored, to a lesser extent, by the equally long-necked but much less flexible sauropods. Privately the ornithomimosaurs thought their much larger relatives clumsy body speakers, though they did not make a point of saying so. It would have been discourteous.

Besides, it was impolitic to laugh at someone several hundred times your weight.

Together they turned to watch the children. Content, they entwined their necks, looking for all the world like a pair of oversized naked swans.

"Interesting behavior." Smiggens kept low. "I've never heard of ostriches doing that."

"And what do you know of ostrich behavior, Smiggens?" Blackstrap turned to the attentive Zulu. "What say you, Mkuse?"

"Ostrich are not common where I come from, Captain."

"It doesn't matter," Smiggens insisted. "These aren't ostriches. I don't think they're even close relatives. They just look alike."

"Then what the blazes are they?" snapped another member of the crew from behind.

"I don't know." The first mate strained to remember something from long ago, but without success. "It strikes me that I've seen something very different and yet like them once before, many years ago."

"Many years ago, indeed." Blackstrap eyed his mate. "I wasn't aware that you'd been to Africa, Mr. Smiggens."

"Haven't, Captain. No, the things I saw that were like these I saw . . . in London."

"London!" Blackstrap nearly burst out laughing but remembered to keep his voice down. They didn't want to send the creatures fleeing in panic. "I thought John Bull rode horses for his amusement, not naked birds." A couple of the men chuckled softly, the wind camouflaging their amusement.

"What I saw wasn't alive," the first mate replied, undeterred.

"What you saw was the bottom of a grog tankard, most likely." Blackstrap's eyes glittered as they tracked the deli-

cately prancing creatures. "Has it occurred to you, Mr. Smiggens, what such marvelous beasts might be worth to a circus
or zoological society?"

"Worth?" Smiggens blinked. "No, Captain, I hadn't
thought on it."

"Then do so." Blackstrap clutched the first mate's shoulder. "What would you say, then? How much am I bid for
the world's only bird-dragon?"

"There's no way to say. I'm sure no one's ever seen anything like them anywhere before. They're absolutely
unprecedented. If I could only remember . . ." His voice
trailed off in frustration.

Blackstrap looked back at Chin-lee. "How much one of
the Hongs pay for a live dragon, eh?"

"Anything, Captain. Gold, slaves, silks, whatever you ask
for, they pay."

"I thought as much. A thousand gold sovereigns?"

"Anything! You ask, they pay."

The big man turned back to the struthies. "We'll have the
bloody Hongs bidding against each other, and the English
against the Americans. We'll sell one beast per country and
up the price as our stock diminishes. And we won't have to
kill anyone. Think of it, man!" He shook Smiggens. " 'Tis
a prize greater than any bloated merchantman!"

"Yes," Smiggens murmured, sounding oddly detached,
"a great prize."

"Come on, then." Blackstrap directed a silent retreat back
through the brush, leaving only Anbaya and Mkuse to keep
watch on their intended victims.

"You two!" He gave the order to O'Connor and Chumash
as soon as it was safe to talk. "Get yourselves back to the
ship. Bring back all the ropes and nets you can carry, and
another dozen men."

"But the repairs, Captain—" someone started to argue.

"Hang the repairs! They can wait. We don't know how
many of these things there be, and if we hesitate we may
lose our chance."

"The boarding nets," Smiggens suggested.

"Aye, to be sure, the boarding nets!" Blackstrap agreed
enthusiastically. "Sound thinking, Mr. Smiggens." There

were several of these, large fishing nets acquired in Manila. Stronger than was needed for simple fishing, weighted on the outside, they were dropped when boarding a prize vessel from that ship's own rigging, to entangle and confuse her defenders. Properly employed, they would make an ideal and inescapable trap.

If the crew could take the creatures by surprise, Smiggens decided, they could indeed make them captives. The creatures had powerful hind legs, but the forearms seemed weaker. And they had no teeth, only sharp but in no way formidable beaks. The thing was doable.

"Like as not we'll only have one chance." He was now fully caught up in the spirit of the enterprise. "You've all seen their hind legs. I'll wager they can outrun any man, and without strain."

"Let's see them outrun a net." Blackstrap waved at his designated runners. "Be off with you, then, and there's an extra gold piece for the man what reaches the ship first." At that the two seamen whirled and vanished into the brush, the sound of their departure quickly fading behind them.

It wasn't an easy thing to keep an eye on the *Struthiomimuses* without alarming them, but among the crew of the *Condor* were men who had spent much of their lives evading pursuit. In addition, individuals like Anbaya and Mkuse knew the ways of many animals and were themselves experienced trackers. Though their quarry gradually began to wander southward, the tense pirates managed to keep them in sight. It helped that the creatures paused frequently to eat or to gather around unremarkable rocks and logs to chitter and whistle mysteriously at one another.

Throughout it all the creatures remained quite unaware that while they were studying the land, others were studying them.

≫ V ≪

HISAULK ROSE WITH THE SUN. OPENING HIS JAWS A full hundred and eighty degrees, he yawned prodigiously before clapping them shut with a snap. Remaining in his sleeping position, his legs folded neatly beneath him, he reached out with a hand to caress the back of his slumbering mate. Shremaza was still asleep, her neck coiled to allow her to rest her head on her back.

At his touch her neck straightened. She whistled softly at him and they touched beaks, opening and closing them in a series of rapid jawing movements, clicking affectionately against one another in an intricate and meaningful duet. Then she rose, her legs straightening beneath her, the long narrow tail thrust out stiffly behind. The children slept soundly nearby, three rose-hued lumps in a pile of moss and soft green leaves.

Hisaulk turned to the sunrise, which was enhanced rather than muted by the storm clouds that seemed to hover just offshore.

"A beautiful morning, though if those clouds come onshore we'll get wet." A quiver ran down his spine as he stretched. "I'll wake the children."

Striding over to the makeshift mattress of leaves and moss, he gently drew the back of two fingers along each slender neck in turn. The youngsters woke slowly, rising and expanding like flowers under his caress.

"Must we go, Father?" The youngest of the three, Tryll, rose and stretched, kicking out first one leg and then the other as she shook off the clinging vestiges of sleep.

"It is time. We are due back in Bent Root, and there's no telling when the storm will finally strike." He gestured seaward. "The signs are not good. If it's as bad as they have been saying, we don't want to be caught out here on the plains. Not after everyone else has already left. By this evening I want us to be on higher ground."

She nodded as her brother and sister performed their morning exercises around her. *Struthiomimuses* as well as their close cousins the dromaeosaurs, oviraptorosaurs, and others were very fond of an introduced human exercise called tai chi, and had made it a part of their morning ritual. Their intricate and precise execution was not noticed by the group of pirates nearby, most of whom were resting at a distance. The pair on watch listened only for rustling in the bushes and looked only for flashes of color, and in so doing missed a demonstration that might well have changed their opinion of the intelligence of their intended quarry.

After a breakfast of fruit and bugs, and a last look at the comfortable temporary bower in which they'd spent the night, they departed on a course intended to take them up into the higher foothills. A day's walk would bring them to the trail that ran into a major road linking the mountain towns with the farms of the Northern Plains.

The youngsters darted in and out of bushes, exercising their growing legs. Energetic, excited whistles and clicks filled the air, counterpoint to the bird song that drifted down from the trees. The two adults maintained an easy, measured pace, keeping their strides short. This was, after all, their final day of vacation and they saw no reason not to make it last.

There was no need to keep a lookout. Save for the threatening storm, the Northern Plains were devoid of danger. A nice place to live, Hisaulk mused, if one didn't mind picking up and leaving every six years. Completely at ease, he let the children set the pace.

The botanical blend through which they walked was unusual even for Dinotopia. Tree ferns and cecropias grew side by side with pines, small firs, and palm trees. Mango, papaya, starfruit, and rambutan shared fruiting space with the ancestors of modern berries.

There being no farms or other habitations in this section of the foothills, the path they followed was thickly overgrown from long disuse. As the vegetation closed in around them, the youngsters fell in behind their parents, who with their larger bodies could more easily make a path through the verdure. Shremaza would be glad when they finally picked up the farm path. From there it would be a short walk to the Galinga road.

She smiled as she remembered how Arimat had argued for remaining still another day or two. "I'm not afraid of any storm!" the youth had declared. Patiently she and Hisaulk had explained that a six-year storm was no ordinary northeaster, and that the absolute worst place for a sensible dinosaur to be caught out in one happened to be the Northern Plains. He was mildly rebellious, Arimat was, and needed strong schooling.

She watched while her offspring took turns trying to clear a huge fallen tree. Though no more than six feet high, it still took each of them several tries to make the jump. Arimat did it first, and Tryll next. Keelk, with great dignity, lowered her head and walked under the barrier.

Clever, my Keelk, Shremaza thought. *Someday you will go far*. Fine youths all, they were maturing well. A little headstrong, but that was normal for their age.

It was so peaceful in the forest, so beautiful, that when the first scream was heard, she didn't react.

"That's Tryll!" her mate chirped. Simultaneously they broke into a run to catch up with the children, who had playfully raced on ahead.

In an instant they had caught up with their offspring, but the sight that greeted them was so unexpected and made so little sense that both adults simply stood and stared, unable to believe what they were seeing.

Hisaulk's first thought had been that the children might have encountered a rogue carnosaur. It was rare for one to make its way across the Backbone Mountains, but not unprecedented. Juvenile meat-eaters especially were prone to wander, before maturity and satiation reduced such desires to infantile afterthoughts. Still, the masters of the Rainy Basin were nothing if not unpredictable. Perhaps the unusual weather had set some to roaming.

Yet it was not some ambling allosaur that threatened their offspring. At first glance it appeared to be a wholly natural phenomenon. Peering carefully over the edge of the steep-sided pit, Hisaulk saw Tryll and Arimat standing in the bottom and looking up. They appeared dazed but unhurt. He turned to Keelk.

"What happened?"

"I don't know, Father. We were running and playing, and then suddenly the ground seemed to give way beneath Arimat and Tryll. I barely escaped falling in myself."

"The ground gave way?" Dipping her snout to the earth, a baffled Shremaza began to sniff of the palm fronds and reeds that covered the approach to the pit. Mixed in with these strong plant odors was another smell. The ocean . . . and something else.

Hisaulk considered the problem. The hole was too deep for the youngsters to escape from by jumping. Without a running start, even he would have had trouble making the leap to safety. *Struthiomimuses* had strong forearms and, though they did not possess an opposable thumb like humans, they could still grip large objects like branches. He began to make plans. They would have to find some strong vines. . . .

A startled Shremaza whistled loudly, interrupting his thoughts. "Someone has dug this! See how even and straight the sides are." She scuffed the edge of the pit. "This is not the work of some grubbing ankylosaur."

"There would be no reason for one of them to dig so deep anyway. One of the horned ones?"

"A ceratopsian?" she responded. "For what purpose? And right in the middle of the old trail." She kicked aside a small pile of palm fronds. "These have not fallen; they have been cut. I thought I smelled human on them. The odor's very strong, but strange."

Hisaulk leaned over the gap. "It's not lined, so it can't be a storage pit. There's no reason to put a latrine way out here. I don't understand." Humans were capable of many odd things and were full of interesting surprises, but they were as conservative of energy as any dinosaur. They wouldn't waste time excavating such a hole without a good reason.

"I know," volunteered Keelk. "It's a grave. You know how some humans still choose to waste their dead by burying them."

"A good guess, daughter." Shremaza bent again to sniff the disturbed fronds and reeds. "Except that I have never heard of a human grave so large. You could bury a dozen of them in it."

"Or one *Struthiomimus* family." A chill raced down His-aulk's spine.

Much later he saw that it was wrong to blame himself, as he did for some time, for what happened next. Neither he nor Shremaza had ever seen or heard of a live trap. Together with Keelk they were standing at the edge of the pit when a human shout sounded sharply from overhead. Then the forest seemed to collapse on top of them.

Heavy vines entangled arms and legs, weighed down neck and tail. Only they weren't vines, Hisaulk soon saw. They were ropes fashioned of some tough plant fiber that had been woven into strong nets. They stank of brine and salt.

Humans came rushing from all directions: from behind and from the other side of the pit. Several dropped from the trees like coconuts. Their combined weight on the sides of the nets kept Hisaulk pinned down.

The three struthies flailed and struggled, but while their hind legs were powerful enough to disembowel with a single kick, they were too entangled in netting to strike out. Besides, the family was too shocked by what was happening to offer any kind of coherent resistance. Had these humans suddenly sprouted wings and carried their captives off into the sky, the family could not have been more stunned.

Hisaulk tried to kick, but he was down on his side and unable to get any purchase. The tough cord proved impervious to his beak. For the first time in his life he lamented his lack of teeth. Down in the pit, Tryll and Arimat were wailing their distress.

That would do no good, Hisaulk knew. They had come to this part of the Northern Plains for its peace and isolation and there was no one around to hear their cries. He never expected to be sorry for having chosen so well.

Unable to turn his head, he called to his mate.

"I'm all right!" Shremaza replied from behind him. "What is this? What's happening to us?"

"I don't know." He tried to rise but found himself completely entangled. Human hands were on his pinioned legs, and he felt thick ropes being wrapped around his ankles.

A sunburned human face was staring down at him, eyes wide, mouth turned up in a broad grin. "What is this?" he chirped desperately at the man. "Why are you doing this to my family?" He didn't expect the human to understand. Only a professional translator could turn Struthine into Human. But he had to try *something*.

"What's going on here? What's the matter with you people? If this is some sort of a game, I don't find it amusing. I intend to protest to the first adjudicator we see!"

Blackstrap ambled out from between two young gingkoes to gaze down at the prize. "Listen to them chatter. What a racket! Like giant parrots they sound, or macaws."

"I expect they'll quiet down soon enough." Breathing heavily, an excited Smiggens was helping to roll up the edges of the nets, further imprisoning the captives. "I know seamen who favor the presence of a parrot on their shoulder. Why not try one of these, Captain?"

"Aye, now, wouldn't that turn heads in every tavern from Singapore to Liverpool?" Blackstrap roared with laughter. Elated at the success of their enterprise, a number of the men joined in.

This reaction only increased the struthies' confusion and puzzlement. "Why are they laughing?" wondered Shremaza. "Surely they can't find our situation amusing!"

"I don't know. Look at their clothing, Shremaza. Listen to their speech. I believe it is that component of Human called English. They can't be from here."

"Dolphinbacks?" An entrapped Keelk peered out from beneath another portion of the net.

"They don't act as if they've shipwrecked," Hisaulk replied. "See, their clothing is intact, and they don't look exhausted and hungry like the usual dolphinback. Something odd is going on here."

"Why don't they respond?" There was deep anxiety in Shremaza's voice, and Hisaulk wished for a way to comfort her. She was worried, he knew, not for herself but for the children. "I wouldn't expect any human to understand Struthine, but even a dolphinback should be able to recognize an intelligent gesture." Hisaulk felt her shudder next to him. "See how they look at us. I've seen humans look at birds in that manner."

That's when the second stunning realization struck Hisaulk with all its awful, impossible force.

"They don't know dinosaurs. From the way they act, I believe they consider us to be nothing more than low animals, as unintelligent as fish!"

"What are they going to do with us?" The first hint of fear had crept into Shremaza's voice. "Surely they can't mean us physical harm?"

"I don't know and can't imagine." Hisaulk tried one more time to kick and found that his ankles had been bound to a length of log that stretched between them, greatly reducing their range of motion. Thus hobbled, he would still be able to stand and walk, but only in halting, short steps. Kicking was out of the question. The log was too heavy.

"These humans are ignorant and uneducated. They are from outside. Who knows what they are capable of? We must be prepared for anything."

"Stop that!" Shremaza was calling to the humans who had surrounded the pit. They ignored her utterly as they flung smaller nets to entrap and haul up Tryll and Arimat. The youngsters were squealing and protesting mightily, to no avail.

"Calm yourselves!" Hisaulk tried to make himself heard. "Panic will not help. These strange humans understand nothing. Keelk, can you see what's happening?"

From somewhere behind him, his daughter replied, "They have Arimat and Tryll out. Now they are hobbling their arms and legs as they have hobbled ours. I think . . . it looks like the humans are being careful not to hurt them."

Shremaza exhaled a long whistle of relief. "Perhaps they are not completely uncivilized. Perhaps they are only uneducated."

She would have been less confident had she known that Blackstrap's crew was taking care not to harm their captives lest injuries reduce their market value. Damaged goods would bring less gold.

"There, that's fine work, men." Smiggens stood next to Blackstrap and they watched as the nets were carefully removed.

With difficulty the five captive creatures struggled to their feet. Their arms were roped together at elbows and wrists, and log hobbles were secured between each pair of powerful ankles and thighs. They could walk, but little else. Mkuse had suggested roping their jaws shut, for while they had no teeth, they were undoubtedly capable of visiting a nasty peck on the unwary.

Smiggens vetoed this notion, pointing out that they knew nothing of their captives' breathing requirements. Better to risk an occasional peck than to chance suffocating that which they had so laboriously and successfully worked to acquire. Blackstrap concurred.

"Mind those feet, Mr. Watford," Smiggens admonished a seaman who was checking the hobble on one of the smaller captives. "They may be bound, but they can still kick out."

"Yes, be careful." Mkuse stepped back from the larger creature he had been working with. "These two are as big and strong as any ostrich." The sailor thus warned nodded while retreating warily.

Even if their restraints had been more flexible, neither the adult nor adolescent *Struthiomimuses* were inclined to offer resistance. They had not yet recovered from the shock of the circumstances in which they found themselves. The thought of actually fighting humans, any humans, was alien to them.

"What do you imagine their purpose is in binding us like this?" Shremaza shuffled her legs experimentally. She did not fall, but neither could she run.

"Yes," added Arimat dazedly. "What do they want from us?"

"I can't imagine." Hisaulk studied their captors uncertainly. "These are not dolphinbacks, but humans who have come to Dinotopia by another means. As for what has been done to us, the old human histories of the outside world speak of such things. It seems we have been made prisoners."

"Prisoners?" Tryll chirped querulously. "You mean, they are playing the escape game?"

"Something like that, only this is much more serious. I don't believe that these humans are playing. I think they consider what they've done a part of real life, however immature it seems to us. Nor are they finished. I don't think they mean to let us go anytime soon."

"But they must!" Arimat protested. "I will miss school, and training."

Shremaza explained gently, "From the look of them, dear, I don't think that would matter to them, even if they could understand us." She shifted her attention to her eldest. "Keelk, you've said very little. Are you all right?"

Her daughter's head bobbed from side to side by way of reply. "I'm unharmed. I was just trying to puzzle out their speech. It's easier when humans only speak one language."

"They are not the words used by the humans who live among us." Hisaulk's attention was fixed on the two who appeared to be in charge. They reacted to his imploring gaze with infuriating indifference.

"I know." Keelk strained to make sense of the convoluted babble. "I think I can understand maybe a word or two."

"Keep trying," her father urged her. "If we could get some idea of what they intend, it would be very useful."

"I'll try," she replied dubiously.

Astonishingly, the humans seemed pleased with what they had done. They were in evident good spirits and moved about with every indication of contentment and assurance. To look at them one would have thought they'd just been declared the winners of the grand marathon at Sauropolis.

For a wild moment Hisaulk wondered if they were mad, then decided they were too well organized to qualify as insane.

"What shall we do, Father?" Tryll asked plaintively. Hisaulk saw that his family was looking to him for guidance.

"Nothing . . . for now. Listen and observe, but do nothing to excite them. Humans who are capable of such outrageous behavior cannot be counted upon to act rationally. We must do our best not to upset them, lest they react in an even more unpredictable manner. Meanwhile, conserve your strength . . . and wait.''

He kept whistling and chirping at the largest human, the one with the distinctive facial hair. This individual was clearly in charge. The man ignored every one of Hisaulk's entreaties, and eventually the male *Struthiomimus* gave up trying. The dinosaurs would have to find another way of making contact.

''See?'' Smiggens observed. ''I told you they'd calm down.''

Blackstrap belched. ''Maybe they're smart enough to be trained. Never saw a beast yet that couldn't be made docile by the withholding of food. I don't think we'll be having any difficulty with this lot.''

Ropes were passed around the necks of the now quiescent creatures. Their captives appeared to accept this latest imposition with resigned indifference. With a man holding fast to each makeshift rein, it was hoped that the beasts could be led instead of driven, a process that would be easier on all concerned.

Something was making Smiggens uneasy. Turning, he saw that the smallest of the creatures was staring unblinkingly in his direction. Its eyes were wide and limpid, almost like those of a child. Irritated at himself, he looked away.

They are only beasts, he reminded himself. *Nothing more*.

''How smart do you think these featherless bird-things be, Mr. Smiggens?''

''Can't say, Captain. More so than the ostriches the African speaks of, surely. See how they follow us with their eyes? Perhaps one or two may prove as intelligent as a dog.''

''Dog, eh? We'll have time enough on board to tease a trick or two out of them. Maybe we won't sell 'em all. Keep the smallest for a pet, eh?'' He nudged his first mate in the ribs, put a finger to the side of his nose, and blew prodigiously to one side. Smiggens turned delicately away.

The second largest of the captives emitted a long series of intricate whistles, chirps, clucks, and clickings. Smiggens applauded this concert. Yet, still feeling uncomfortable without knowing why, he again turned away.

"They seem docile enough already. One would almost think someone else had seen to the taming of them."

"So long as they give no trouble." Blackstrap snorted. "If they prove difficult, we'll shoot one as an example to the others. *That'll* quiet them down!" Hailing several of the men, he lumbered off to hurry them into bundling the nets. He wanted them ready in case the opportunity arose to capture a few more of the remarkable creatures.

Smiggens was left to wonder why the quasi-avian stares were unnerving him so much. It made him angry and he deliberately moved off in search of other things to do.

Shremaza silently observed the inexplicable doings of their captors.

"This isn't a game, is it, Mother?" Arimat looked up at her out of anxious eyes.

"No, dear, it isn't. I fear it's very serious business."

"These ropes chafe," Tryll protested.

"Try to ignore them, darling. They will loosen when we start walking. I'm sure these humans mean to take us somewhere, or they would not have allowed us to walk about at all."

"What's going to happen to us?"

"Perhaps they will let us go after a while." She didn't believe her own words, but she had to tell the children something, and it was better to be positive.

Tryll considered. "You don't think these humans mean to eat us, do you?"

"What are you saying?" Arimat gawked at his sister. "Humans aren't carnosaurs!"

"I wouldn't put it past this lot." They both turned to Keelk, who was studying the activities of their captors closely. "Humans will eat almost anything."

Arimat made a face. "So will struthies, but that doesn't mean I'd want to eat a human."

"Why not?" Keelk challenged him. "Meat is meat."

"But these are *humans*. Humans are friends."

"Not these humans," Hisaulk murmured.

With her arms bound, Tryll had to use her head and neck to gesture. "That one," she said, nodding in Blackstrap's direction, "has something of the manner of a carnosaur."

"Keep your wits about you, as you have been taught." Hisaulk considered his restraints. "It seems that for now, at least, they mean only to keep us tied. We must be ready for any chance to flee. The Treetown Council must be notified."

"What if we run into an evacuating farm family?" Shremaza wondered aloud. "Do you think these crazy humans will try to make captives of them also?"

Arimat sniffed. "I'd like to see them try to tie up a *Styracosaurus*."

"Yeah." Tryll badly wanted to scratch behind her right leg. "Or an *Anchiceratops*."

"I wouldn't put anything past these humans," her mother remarked. "The important thing, as your father says, is to wait for opportunity to present itself."

"I'd rather be gathering fruit," Arimat grumbled.

"Hush, now," Shremaza told him. "So would we all."

"Pay attention," Hisaulk advised his family, "and perhaps we can make some sense of what they are about. Watch and learn . . . and wait."

⇒ VI ⇐

Their captive animals offering no resistance and proving easily led, the pirates made excellent progress out of the lowlands and into the foothills in search of further wonders. Before long the slopes they were traversing became not only steep, but sheer and unclimbable. Discouraged but far from defeated, they followed the line of cliffs, traveling steadily eastward in hopes of finding a way up.

Vast mounds of brownish yellow scree had accumulated at the base of the cliffs. Smiggens paused to scoop up a handful. The rock crumbled beneath his fingers.

"See here. For true granite to have decomposed so badly is an indication of great age." He rubbed his hands together, flicking dust from his palms as he studied the perpendicular wall of stone on their immediate right. It was as unscalable and forbidding as the wall of any fortress. "This land has been here a very long time."

Blackstrap loomed close. "If you're going to waste time looking at rocks, Mr. Smiggens, at least keep a weather eye out for signs of silver or gold."

"Aye," put in a hardened sailor from Baltimore named Geary, "or diamonds and rubies."

"Why not wish for sapphires and emeralds as well?" Smiggens groused.

"We'll do that, Mr. Smiggens," said Johanssen. He and Samuel exchanged a grin. "You tell us where to start digging."

Philistines, the first mate thought sharply. *Your skulls are as dense as stone. Why not try searching for nuggets within?*

Fresh water was present in abundance, for innumerable springs gushed forth from the base of the cliffs. Men who not long ago had despaired of ever again drinking their fill now did not even bother to top off their casks, so plentiful was the supply. The water was sweet and pure. In combination with the fruit they found hanging from numerous trees, they were rejuvenated. Soon they were not merely walking but swaggering as they canvassed the cliffs for a suitable route upward.

And if they found no gold or diamonds, no town to loot, they still had their captives, whom the captain and first mate had assured them were worth thousands.

They pushed on, keeping the unscalable escarpment on their right, seeking a trail or at least suitable handholds, until they quite accidentally stumbled across something even better. The entrance to the narrow canyon lay concealed behind a dense cluster of ferns growing from a pile of rock and would have gone unnoticed by most casual passersby. But a life at sea sharpens the senses, and the unusual is quick to be noticed.

"Fortune smiles on us once more, boys." A gratified Blackstrap stood like a swollen dead tree amid the ferns. "We took all the bad luck she could throw at us and spit in her eye, and now we be repaid for our endurance and courage."

"Oi, and all along I thought all we were doin' was tryin' to stay afloat," O'Connor whispered to Watford.

"So long as she repay us quickly, Captain." Mkuse was facing seaward, his expression grim.

From their position among the ferns they could just make out a thin line of blue ocean, with the *Condor* floating quietly within. But beyond, farther out to sea, was a line of cloud as black and threatening as any they'd ever encountered. It made the squall line they'd ridden out look like a summer breeze. Too distant for its screams to be heard, lightning crackled all along the storm front.

"If that comes ashore," Samuel commented, "the boys on board will have the devil's own time keeping the ship afloat."

"You worry too much, Mr. Samuel," Blackstrap admonished the man. "The ship'll be fine in the lagoon. You all saw how wide that reef be. Mr. Leveque will see to things. He'll set the sea anchors, turn her bow-on into the wind, and ride out whatever the sea throws at him." Reassured, the men turned away from the plains.

"I no like this." Chin-lee shoved ferns aside as they started into the slot canyon. "Things going too well."

"Relax, ya heathen." Johanssen gestured ahead. "Why, it don't look like we're even going to have to climb. What more could you want?" The big, blustery American lengthened his stride, leaving the pessimistic Cantonese behind.

Chin-lee nervously eyed the towering, sheer-sided walls of granite and sandstone that rapidly closed in around them. His gaze flicked uneasily from their seemingly indifferent captives to the winding route ahead. The canyon bent and twisted like a live thing, and a man couldn't see more than a dozen yards in front of him at any one time.

"Dragons." He kept his voice to a whisper. He was tired of the others making fun of him.

As soon as she realized what the humans intended, Shremaza tried to dig in her heels. Insistent pressure on the rope looped around her neck forced her to move on or risk being choked.

"No!" she whistled. "They can't mean to!"

Hisaulk forced himself to stay calm. "Don't you see, incubator of my eggs? They are ignorant of the land and have no idea what they are doing." He examined the water-scoured, banded canyon walls. "I hope this does not go all the way through."

"If it does, it should have been marked with a warning," his mate replied.

"You saw how the vegetation obscured the opening. Not all of Dinotopia has been walked, and there are many places here in the north that have not even been properly mapped."

Tryll edged close, resisting the tugging on her guide ropes as best she could. "Father, I'm scared."

He wished he could put a reassuring hand on her shoulders, but his own arms were tightly bound. "It will be all right, child. These humans are ignorant, but they are not stupid.''

''That won't help them, or us,'' Shremaza noted, ''if they continue on this way and this canyon goes all the way through the Backbones.''

The slot canyon was an extraordinary place. Cut by millennia of running water, its colorful walls polished by innumerable flash floods, it pierced the solid rock like a hot wire dropped on a block of butter. At its widest it was no more than ten feet across. In some places it was so narrow that only one man at a time could fit through, and Shremaza and Hisaulk could advance only with much pulling and shoving.

The sky was a thin ribbon of blue hundreds of feet overhead. Lost in perpetual shade, the canyon was cooler than the plains they had left behind, and nearly devoid of vegetation. The floor was of fine sand alternating with pockets of smooth river stones. In low places water had collected, flat and clear as mirrors dropped from the sky. Fresh water trickled from cracks in the rock walls, feeding would-be streams whose ambition exceeded their volume. Each soon vanished into the thirsty sand.

Occasionally boulders that had tumbled from the canyon's rim blocked the way, but these were easily surmounted by men used to traversing sodden spars and rigging. Though not used to climbing, the struthie family managed each successive modest ascent. They had no choice, for it was clear that if they failed to attempt the climb, their captors would pull them bodily over the rough rock.

''This is madness.'' With hands and feet bound, Shremaza was forced to use her beak to pick gravel from between her toes. ''We can't go on this way. Not in the direction they are heading. We must try to talk to them.''

''What good would it do? They do not understand our tongue, and none of us can write human.''

''But father of my children, if this canyon runs all the way through the Backbone Mountains—''

''They might not go all the way. They may reach the end and decide to turn back. It's too soon to panic.''

The canyon did indeed run completely through the mountains. It took several days to complete the transition, but there was no mistaking it when they finally reached the end.

The towering narrows abruptly widened, giving way to crumbling side walls and water-swept talus. Another several hundred yards of receding cliff and they soon found themselves walking through a wonderland of greenery and color.

The strange humans were appropriately astonished. In place of the mangroves and reeds, grassland and lush riverine plains that had greeted them on arrival, there now spread out before them a rain forest as pristine and untouched as any in the world. It was a jungle worthy of deepest Africa or Peru.

The crowns of enormous tropical hardwoods vanished in swirling mist. Smiggens recognized seraya and kempas, teak and amboyna, sepetir and balau. There was dark red, light red, and even yellow meranti. And these were only the Southeast Asian timbers he knew. There were species wholly foreign to him, including several that resembled nothing he'd ever seen or heard of.

Filling in the gaps between the forest giants were a plethora of smaller trees and bushes, exotic flowers and lingering vines. There was a rampage of fungi, and vertical carpets of moss. Within the verdure unseen things cheeped and mewed, sang and chittered. Concealed insects asserted their dominance. Bird shadows flitted in muted green distances that were vital with unseen life.

Blackstrap summed it up in his usual terse manner. "Don't see no gold." He spat disgustedly to one side as a small cloud of blue-and-gold macaws emerged from one cloud of mist only to be swallowed up by another. Somewhere a bird of paradise warbled its unique song. Water trickling out of the slot canyon vanished into the greenery, which sucked it up like a sponge.

"We must make them understand, somehow." Shremaza crowded close to her mate, as did the children.

Eyes wide, Tryll looked up at her parents. "Mother, *this is the Rainy Basin*!"

"I know, darling, I know." Shremaza did her best to comfort them all.

O'Connor gestured at the family. "See how they huddle together? Ain't that cute."

"Cute!" Blackstrap barked. "Maybe this be their home." From beneath glowering brows, dark eyes surveyed the overgrown terrain. "If so, we ought to find a few more of 'em wandering about. Keep those nets handy."

As they entered the edge of the forest, Smiggens cast a curious eye at their captives. "I don't know, Captain. They don't act much like this is their home. Fact is, they seem downright skittish."

"Naw, they're just interested in the place. What with all the new sights and sounds and smells, I'm more than a bit inquisitive meself, I am." He kicked at something shiny, but it was only an innocent tree snail. "Still don't see no gold." He raised his voice. "Any of you lot see any signs of gold?"

"All I see is green, Captain." The seaman Thomas called the isle of Jamaica home, and their present surroundings were not unfamiliar to him.

"We won't lack for fruit," added another, eyeing the bounty that dangled ripe for the picking from many of the boughs they were passing beneath.

"I've had about enough of fruit." Andreas and Copperhead were both eyeing their captives with other than academic interest. The larger of the pair was fingering the haft of his sword. "Me, I say we chop the head off one of these strange fowl and see what a haunch tastes like after an evening's turn over a slow fire."

"Belay that!" Blackstrap whirled to confront the source of the unwanted culinary suggestion. "Have you forgotten what each one of these creatures be worth?"

Andreas was a big man, but he cowered beneath the captain's glare. "Just one of the small ones, Captain. You can't expect an honest seaman to live only on fruit, like an ape."

"Why not?" Blackstrap declared. "You bloody well look enough like one." As he turned away, the rest of the men enjoyed a chuckle at their companion's expense.

"Go on, laugh." Andreas straightened. "But if there's a man among you who doesn't hunger to sink his teeth into something that has to be chewed, let him confess it to my face!"

No one took him up on the challenge, a fact Smiggens made note of.

"We may have to post a night watch over our prizes, Captain."

"Fools!" Blackstrap straight-armed a branch aside, snapping it in half. "Who'd boil a chicken worth a thousand pounds? It not be like any of them is starving." He yelled back over his shoulder. "First man lays a hand on any of our pretties, by heaven I'll serve him up for supper!" The lingering laughter quickly died down.

"Aw, look at 'em. Even if you cooked 'em all day they'd probably still be tough and stringy," Samuel pointed out.

It was just as well that Hisaulk, Shremaza, and their uneasy brood could not understand English, because they would not have found the conversation to their liking. In any event, there was no more talk among the pirates (at least not openly) of retiring any of their precious captives to the broiler.

A cluster of small, gnarled trees grew from a low spot in the canyon. Anbaya winked at Andreas. "Want something to chew? Here." Using his knife on a low, curving trunk, he dug a couple of large, fat grubs from beneath the heavily scored bark. Popping one into his mouth, he offered the other to Andreas.

His fellow seaman made a face as he shied away. "Eagh! How can you eat caterpillars?"

"Not cat'pillar," the Moluccan corrected him. "Plenty good. Taste like nut-flavored butter. Very greasy, very good for you." Shrugging, he tossed down the second.

"Good for him, maybe," muttered Guimaraes. The Portuguese, too, hungered for a slab of real meat.

"One among them at least knows how to eat properly." Shremaza turned from the insect-imbibing sailor to her mate. "If we continue on like this, our luck will soon enough run out. Listen to the noise they make as they walk! We must do something." Their captors had plunged into the rain forest, though they were careful always to keep the cliff wall in sight to avoid becoming completely lost.

"I know." Hisaulk's head was twitching from side to side as he fought to interpret every sound, every movement within the trees. His wide eyes cataloged every bird and bug as he maintained an anxious watch for . . . something bigger. He and his family knew how fortunate they had been thus far in not encountering anything larger than themselves.

But such creatures were out there. This was the Rainy Basin, and those who dominated its environs did not sleep *all* the time.

Coping as best they were able with the heat and humidity, the pirates eventually settled themselves for lunch, making a meal of whatever they could harvest from the surrounding trees and combining it with the limited victuals they had brought with them. Among the latter, salt and pepper were most in demand.

They leaned back against suitable ant-free trees or spoke softly among themselves. A single guard had been set on their captives, and his attention was principally devoted to his food.

It was then that Keelk whispered urgently, "Father, Mother—I think I can free myself."

Hisaulk turned slowly to her and spoke softly so as not to alarm their captors. "Are you sure? How can this be?"

Keelk nodded at her siblings. "My bonds were never as tight as yours, and Arimat and Tryll have been picking at them when these humans were not watching." Her brother and sister confirmed this with terse head nods.

"It's true, Father," whispered Arimat. "I think she's almost loose." He punctuated his comment with a sharp, descending whistle. It was a perfectly natural thing to do, but it caused their guard to glance back. The family froze before remembering that this human understood nothing of their language. Indeed, he turned indifferently back to his food and resumed eating, exhibiting the same appalling etiquette as his companions.

"You must take great care, daughter." Restrained by her ropes, Shremaza tried to lean close. "It's obvious these ignorant humans do not know how they tempt fate."

"It would be better to try at night." Hisaulk spotted a fat beetle crawling on a nearby branch and promptly snapped it up in his beak, continuing as he swallowed. "We see better in the dark than humans."

"True," his mate admitted, "but last night they checked our bindings carefully before they began their evening meal.

If they do so again and discover that Keelk's are loose, they will tie her more securely and be doubly watchful of us.''

Hisaulk considered somberly. "That is so. My daughter, you must combine urgency with caution. Try to keep close to the cliffs until you can find a way out of the basin. That way you will have protection on one side. Do not try to return the way we came. That's the first place these humans will look for you.''

"What difference does that make, Father? I can outrun any human.''

"Yes, but they carry a number of strange devices, and they may have other capabilities we know nothing about. Also, if you were to trip or hurt yourself, they might still overtake you. Better to seek another way over the Backbones, one they do not already know.

"Bent Root is the nearest town of size. Try to make your way there. You may pass where the masters of the Rainy Basin cannot. They are not climbers, not as agile as we.''

"I will remember, Father.'' She blinked.

"Drink deep, seek peace, and go swiftly, sister.'' Arimat was able to stretch sufficiently to twine his neck around Keelk's. Tryll could only warble a soft farewell. It was not as polished as she would have wished, but even the youngest member of the family understood the need not to attract the attention of their captors.

"Go straight to any dinosaur or human in authority,'' her mother urged her. "Tell them of our plight, and what is happening here.''

"I will.'' Keelk hesitated. "I know these humans are ignorant and uncivilized, but surely they won't punish you if I manage to escape?''

Hisaulk forced confidence into his voice. "Why should they think we had anything to do with your flight? We are tightly bound; they will assume you succeeded in freeing yourself on your own. They don't know our language and so they can't question us. I don't think they believe that we talk to each other.''

He turned back to their guard. The human was digging at something on the ground between his legs. Shiny rocks, Hisaulk saw. All during the long walk through the canyon, these humans had paused to pick at shiny rocks. He wondered at the reason. Perhaps their captors had a craving for mica.

"Are you certain you can get free?" Hisaulk murmured.

She nodded. "All I have to do is twist my feet a little and this horrible log they have fastened between my ankles will fall away. The other ropes I will throw off before I run."

"Then go, daughter. Run like the wind. Run as if you are competing for the grand prize at Sauropolis Stadium. Run like you've never run before. And whatever happens, whatever you may hear, don't look back."

She would have clacked her beak in response, but chose to nod instead, wishing to make no more noise than was absolutely necessary. A glance showed that the position and attitude of their captors had not changed. Having finished their meal, a few more leaned back against supportive trees or logs, their eyes closed and hats or bandannas pulled down over their faces. But the large human, the leader of the pack, was finishing also, and she suspected that when he was done they would leave this spot.

None were looking in her direction, including their guard. She might not get a better chance.

Lifting her left foot and twisting it slightly, she gave her leg a quick shake. The liberated ropes slid down to her ankle and then off. She repeated the movement with her other leg, and the log hobble dropped silently to the leaf litter that covered the ground. Lowering her arms, she shook until the bindings dropped free. Then she was able to use her hands to remove the restraints that secured her thighs. Lastly, she loosened and removed the two guide ropes that lay draped about her neck.

She was free.

Maybe it was the action of removing the guide ropes, or perhaps the guard simply became sensitized to all the movement, however subtle, behind him. In any event, he turned and started.

"Hey. *Hey*!" Rising from his seat, he turned and yelled to his companions. "One of the beasts is loose!"

Before he'd concluded his warning, before the startled shouts of his fellows filled the air, Keelk had cleared a fallen log in a single bound and struck out into the forest, her long slim legs pumping furiously.

Human yells now resounded behind her, full of anger and dismay. Mindful of her father's admonition, she didn't look back, concentrating instead on the unknown route ahead. She kept her gaze resolutely forward even when a couple of echoing booms like miniature thunderclaps assailed her ears. She recognized their source, of course, though why the humans would suddenly decide to set off fireworks she couldn't imagine. She suspected that unlike the skyrockets and pinwheels she was familiar with from annual festivals, these had a purpose other than celebration.

Fireworks could be dangerous. She'd heard of operators who'd been burned by them, and even worse. Those who manufactured them were willing to risk such dangers in order to bring beauty to Dinotopia. She didn't know what these odd humans intended, but she doubted it was beauty.

No glittering lights excited her vision, no fiery flowers bloomed in the sky. Something like an angry wasp *did* whizz past her head, unseen and unscented. *A strange sort of fireworks*, she thought as she ran.

Clearing another fallen timber by a good two feet, she found she could no longer run in ignorance. Looking back, she saw half a dozen of the humans pursuing. As she watched, one of them stopped to point a long metal tube in her direction.

So they *were* shooting fireworks at her. Trying to burn her or dazzle her with light. Only there were no lights. Thinking them the oddest fireworks she'd ever heard, she nevertheless lowered her head, using her body for protection.

Two more booming sounds were heard and another of the invisible wasp-things sent splinters flying from a tree just ahead of her. She swerved to her right and tried to lengthen her stride. Though not as fast as an adult, she was agile and in good condition.

There is no beauty in their fireworks, she thought as she ran, *just as there is no beauty in them.*

She could hear their fading cries, sense the anger in their voices. The beautyless booming echoed distantly now, and no more of the wasp-things passed her. Maybe their supply was running low. Weaving and winding through the forest, she knew she must make a difficult target.

Though she no longer heard them behind her, she didn't slow down for what seemed like hours. Trees, flowers, tempting fruit, and obstructing branches flew past. Once, some large thorns caught her left side and there was pain. Wincing, she reached back and saw blood on her clawtips. Still she didn't slow down. Holding her arms in front of her chest in the manner of a praying mantis, she raced on.

Whatever happens, whatever you hear, don't look back, she'd been told. Though curiosity tugged at her, she did her best to comply. She knew she was running not only for her own life, but for those of her family as well.

Ahead lay the unknown and more of the Rainy Basin, which she hoped fervently would continue to remain unknown.

Having assumed the lead in the pursuit, Mkuse and Anbaya had come closest to overtaking the escapee. Seeing that it was hopeless, they finally stopped to wait for the others to catch up. Breathing hard in the heat, the bare-chested Zulu removed a bandanna from a trouser pocket and mopped at the perspiration flowing down his cheeks.

"Did you see the thing go? Very like an ostrich it runs."

"So quick!" The Moluccan sat down heavily on the moist, soft earth and rested his forearms on his knees. "Even a little one. As a boy I was the fastest in my village, but at my best I do not think I could have overtaken it."

"Not in these woods." Uncomfortably aware of their temporary isolation, Mkuse found himself staring nervously into the trees. There was no reason for his unease, he told himself. Except for their captives, they'd seen nothing larger than a bird since making landfall. Even so, something made his spine crawl. Something sensed but unseen. Had he been home he would have asked the village *sangoma* about his feelings, but knowing there wasn't a witch doctor within a thousand miles, he kept his anxiety to himself.

Besides, there couldn't be anything out there worse than Blackstrap's wrath, which they were all going to have to face shortly.

"We must double-check the ropes on the others," Anbaya was saying. "The captain, he be furious."

"Let him be." Mkuse nodded at the solid wall of green that had swallowed their quarry. "We're not going to find it in that." High in the treetops birds disturbed by the report of the pirates' guns continued to squawk their displeasure.

"What happened? . . . Did we get it? . . . Where'd it go?" The rest of the pursuers soon caught up to the two who had taken the lead.

"Gone," Anbaya told them. "Too, too fast."

A confusion of mutterings rose from the exhausted men. "Well, it's one less to keep watch over, says I," muttered Samuel.

"Yes," declared Watford. "We've still four of the beasts left, and we'll see to it that not another gets away."

Copperhead nodded. "The captain'll have to be content with that. Maybe we can trap him another."

Treggang looked less sanguine. "What we tell him?"

The big Zulu shrugged. "We tell him the truth. It was too fast for us and it got away. Ran like the devil was after it." He laughed. "Maybe it thinks we're devils." A couple of uncertain chuckles greeted this weak attempt at humor.

Informed that one of his precious pets had made good its escape, Blackstrap exploded like one of the *Condor*'s twelve-pounders. As always, it was Smiggens who finally succeeded in calming him, pointing out in concert with Mkuse that they did, after all, still retain four captives, and that if fortune favored them, they might encounter more. As for those remaining prisoners, they reacted to the escape of one of their own by staring stolidly at their captors like the dumb animals they so obviously were.

Smiggens and his companions would have been startled indeed had they been able to share the emotions that were presently churning within their captives.

Growling under his breath like a bear disturbed at its feed, Blackstrap contented himself with fetching the unhappy guard such a blow to the side of the head that the poor man's ear instantly swelled up like a cauliflower. The sailor didn't complain, counting himself fortunate that the captain hadn't been holding a sword or knife at the time.

Smiggens did his best to cheer his friend and master. "Don't take it hard, Brognar. Who knows what wonders may lurk around the next rock, the next tree? If we're lucky we may encounter beasts even more remarkable."

"Aye, I suppose you be right, Mr. Smiggens. You often are." He waved a suddenly indifferent hand in the direction the escapee had taken. "Let it go. We'll take it as a lesson." His gaze narrowed as he scrutinized his crew. "Always learn from your mistakes. I bloody well have. That's why I'm still alive." A few relieved cheers rose from the men. Compared to the reaction they'd expected, the captain's manner was proving positively genial.

How right the first mate's supposition was about encountering more beasts, none of them could imagine, but if they'd had an inkling as to the true nature of the sort of creatures that called the Rainy Basin home, their enthusiasm would surely have been considerably muted.

≫ VII ≪

KEELK RAN UNTIL SHE WAS COMPLETELY WINDED. Chest heaving, legs aching, she slowed to a halt alongside a towering cecropia. Striving to breathe silently, her head flicked from side to side as she listened for the slightest sound. Despite their size, the masters of the Rainy Basin could slip through the forest with unparalleled stealth and cunning. They also had the ability to stand completely motionless, seemingly asleep or unconscious, until the unwary wandered within reach.

Of course, most of them were so well fed by the civilized Dinotopians traveling through their territory, they didn't need to hunt. But driven as they were by ancient imperatives that eschewed logic and reason, they always had to be regarded as dangerous. This fact was made known to all inhabitants of Dinotopia at an early age.

So when a bird chirped nearby or an insect hopped suddenly from branch to leaf, she analyzed the sound and motion as much for what it might suggest as for what it actually represented. Every grove, every tree, potentially concealed unknown dangers. This was the Rainy Basin and she was alone, so alone! How far it was from the familiar, civilized surroundings of Cornucopia.

Unable to avoid the risk, she tiptoed to the edge of a running stream and dipped to drink, scooping up water with graceful arching sweeps of her head and neck. Tumbling fresh and cold from the slopes of the Backbones, the cool liquid soothed her throat. Had she truly escaped the horrible humans? There'd been neither sight nor sound of them for a long time. If so, it did not mean she was safe; only that she was safe from them. She had exchanged one threat for another.

Straightening to her full six feet, she headed toward the cliffs that were visible through gaps in the trees. The rock rampart she finally reached was too steep and too crumbly to allow climbing.

Avoid the canyon they'd used, her parents had instructed her. That meant traveling west instead of east. She wasn't entirely displeased. The mountain communities of the Backbones lay in that direction anyway.

Aware that alongside the naked stone she was utterly exposed, she reentered the forest and began making her way eastward, using available vegetation for cover. By this time she was convinced she had lost her former captors and no longer worried about them and their inscrutably aggressive fireworks.

She halted only when the night had grown too deep to make further movement impractical. A twisted ankle or broken leg would slow her far more than any amount of sleep. Besides, she badly needed to rest.

Finding a slight hollow beneath a flamboyant cluster of giant split-leaf philodendrons, she squeezed herself as far back in as she could. The broad green leaves would conceal her from view while shedding the rain that had begun to fall. This time of year it was likely to turn to a downpour, and she was glad of the makeshift shelter.

Crouching there in the dead darkness, listening to sounds she could not identify and wasn't sure that she wanted to, she felt more isolated than she had at any time in her life. Lullabied by the night sounds, not knowing what might be happening to her family, it was some time before she finally fell into a hesitant and fitful sleep.

Distant crashings in the brush disturbed her several times, but nothing came near, and the much-feared noxious body odors never assailed her nostrils. Once, a mournful cry involuntarily escaped her throat. Terrified, she was careful not to repeat it lest she attract unwanted attention.

It was nearly morning when the sound of something im-

mense and purposeful advancing through the trees nearby
finally woke her. Instantly alert, she blinked at her surroundings, illuminated now by the hazy sunrise. Her eyes scanned
the visible brush and her nostrils twitched.

When the crashing intensified, she tucked her head and
neck as far back into her shoulders as she could, not daring
to move. She'd been told what to do in such a situation, but
only casually. There was no need for intensive instruction
because such incidents were all but nonexistent. One simply
didn't go for an afternoon stroll in the Rainy Basin.

However, as often happens when academics prove inadequate, instinct took over.

Utterly motionless, eyes as wide as possible, she watched
while something the size of a small mountain strode through
the trees just off to her right. Its head was in the lower canopy and overtopped most of the ferns. A burning yellow eye
half as big as her skull blinked in the mist.

It was only an outline, a suggestion of great power and
strength, all the more terrible for not being completely visible. She was glad she couldn't see the curving, serrated teeth
that she knew filled the cavernous maw, nor the powerful
three-clawed hands that flexed methodically in anticipation
of tearing and rending.

The allosaur was a big one, perhaps thirty-five feet from
nose to tail and weighing many tons. Even though she
couldn't see it clearly, she could hear the rhythmic *chuff-
chuff* of its breath as it passed, its capacious lungs working
like an ironmonger's bellows. If it were so inclined, she
would make no more than hors d'oeuvre for its insatiable
appetite.

As she held her breath, it lowered its head to the earth and
sniffed. Was it following a trail? And if so, was it hers?

No, she decided recklessly. It had come from the south
and could not have crossed her path. But what if it picked
up her scent now? Given the amount of rain that had fallen
last night she doubted it was possible, but an allosaur's sense
of smell was especially acute. If it sniffed out her hiding
place, could she reason with it? She knew little of the carnosaurs' crude dialects, but it was sometimes possible to talk
to them. A great deal would depend on how hungry this one

was. The carnosaurs had a distressing tendency to bite first and leave conversation for later.

She had one natural advantage: she wouldn't make much of a meal for a full-grown *Allosaurus*. It might not think her worth the effort. A couple of bites of bone and tough tissue, that's all she was. Not even a morning snack.

Small comfort that would be.

Keeping absolutely still, she tried to will herself not to be. *I am a rock*, she thought intently. *A gray spot in the forest. Nothing alive, nothing here, nothing good to eat.*

Raising its massive jaws, the allosaur exhaled with a whoosh and shook its head. Perhaps it had inhaled something that didn't agree with it. The floor of the rain forest was thick with spores and mold. If it had encountered her trail the night before, prior to the heavy rain, she didn't doubt that it would have been on her in an instant. Now the path she'd taken was filled with mushrooms and other confusing odors.

Straightening like a construction crane, the huge meateater rose to its full height. It looked left, then right. Trembling in her hiding place, Keelk shut her eyes.

When she opened them, the allosaur had gone. She could hear it crashing away through the trees, heading south. Aware that the move might be a hunting ploy to trick anything in hiding, she remained exactly as she was for another hour. Only then did she feel safe in emerging from her place of concealment, knowing that the longer she lingered, the farther her family receded from help. Her muscles ached from staying in one position for so long, but she didn't mind. She was still alive, still in a position to seek help for her parents and siblings.

The only sound came from a garrulous parrot, the only movement from the last of the falling rain. With a final backward glance she resumed her journey, pacing herself and fighting down the fear that shrieked at her to run, run, before it was too late. Though she knew she was quicker and more agile than any allosaur, it could cover ten of her strides with one of its own. Toying with such a monster would be the height of folly.

Hunger forced her to slow. She couldn't run all day on an empty stomach, and she'd been taught to take care of her body. The Rainy Basin was full of food for an adventurous traveler. None of it had been properly inspected or checked for parasites, but she had no choice. She had to keep her strength up.

Locating a tree heavy with ripe rambutan, she reached up with one hand and pulled down a branch. Standing on tiptoe she was able to pluck one fruit after another. Once picked, it was a simple if delicate matter to peel the spiky red hide away from the sugary pulp within. Beak and claws did the work, and she swallowed one core after another. They were cool and delicious, and she knew that the hard seed within the pulp would pass harmlessly through her digestive system.

Invigorated and refreshed, she resumed her run. That afternoon a nest of white ants provided a protein-rich snack, which she excavated with her front claws. Fruit was to be had all along the way. She missed the elaborate and entertaining rituals of family dining, but mostly she missed her kin: mother and father's love and sage advice, Tryll's perky curiosity, even Arimat's constant teasing. Such thoughts sustained her as surely as any rations.

The sound was so subtle as to be almost inaudible, but she heard. Coming to a sudden stop, she raised her head and looked back the way she'd come. It might be nothing more than a bird, she told herself. It hadn't *sounded* like anything more than a bird.

Except that it would have to have been a ground-dwelling bird.

What an awful place the Rainy Basin was, she told herself. If she made it out successfully, she vowed, she would never return. As she recited this resolution, a second sound echoed the first. Her head jerked around to the right. A third soft thump sent her neck swinging in the opposite direction.

They were trying to box her in. Each muffled footstep marked the presence of another stalker. As yet she didn't know who *they* were, save that they intended no good. Potential friends didn't sneak up and surround you, and there was little friendly about the inhabitants of the Rainy Basin.

Strain as she might, she could see nothing. No giant carnosaur loomed against the treetops. There was only the occasional muted echo of a footstep.

But *something* was stalking her.

Had the strange humans been more determined than she'd thought and pursued her through the night? Were they that crazy? The footsteps *could* be those of humans. The young humans she played with in happier times were very adept at hide-and-seek.

Backing slowly, unsure which way to run, she felt that if she bolted she'd have only one chance to make the right choice. Her eyes detected movement in the brush, and then she saw it: a stealthy, athletic shape slightly smaller than herself. A flash of fang and a surfeit of talon and claw.

Velociraptors. A pack of them.

There would be more than three, she knew. From her studies she remembered that minimum pack size was comprised of six or more. The little brutes weren't very big, but in spite of the bounty afforded by the Rainy Basin, they hadn't forgotten how to hunt, and they were all tooth and claw.

If she jumped wrong, it would carry her right into the midst of them. She'd go down beneath their jaws and the terrible sickle-shaped claws on their hind feet. They'd make short work of what, for them, would be a substantial meal.

Well, I'm nobody's meal, she thought stubbornly. *Not today. Not ever.* Certainly not for a family of uncivilized, undersized carnivores, and not with her family in danger.

From their movements and the sound of their pacing, she knew they were working to enclose her. Probably she had little time left in which to act before they closed the circle. She looked around wildly. In a few moments it wouldn't matter which way she leaped. *Velociraptors* could run as fast as any struthie, and this time the dense rain forest wouldn't be of any help in losing her pursuers. The little carnivores were as agile as she was, could jump any obstacle or run beneath any intervening log.

For a mad moment she considered dashing to her right, directly toward the nearest cliff. But with their powerful claws and talons, raptors could climb even better than she could. Out in the open there would be no cover at all.

Could she beat them to a high place and kick rocks down on them? They were notoriously hard to discourage, and there was the danger of slipping. Even a dumb *Velociraptor* was smart enough to see such danger and avoid it.

It was no use. They had her already. They were just unwinding the string of fate to its end, playing out the game to its inevitable conclusion.

She was determined not to give up without a fight. There was a suggestion of a faint hunting trail off to her right. As yet she'd heard nothing from that direction. Clearing a mound of agitated ants in a single bound, she tore off down the narrow gap, her legs pumping like pistons, not even bothering to dodge the vines or thorns that reached out to snatch at her. Damp air whistled past her head. She felt as if she were flying.

In seconds the footsteps she'd been hearing coalesced behind her. The chase had begun. Though it could have only one outcome, she ran on, buoyed by the knowledge that she had at least escaped their initial trap. Now they would have to work for their supper. They would have to drag her down, and she'd give them a run for their efforts!

She was under no illusions as to what would happen if even one caught up with her. Though larger, no *Struthiomimus* could fight a *Velociraptor*. She was no invincible sauropod, safe within the mountain of itself; no armored ankylosaur or spear-and-shield carrying ceratopsian. The ornithomimosaurs, of which the struthies were one tribe, had only their intelligence to rely upon.

Nothing would discourage a pack of raptors on the hunt, she knew. No doubt they were relishing the chase. It would add spice to the eventual meal. Such thoughts enabled her, somehow, to increase her pace, lengthen her stride. She'd never run so fast in all her life, not even when fleeing the strange humans.

It didn't matter. The spine-chilling, high-pitched whistling was close behind, on all sides.

A lake, she thought frantically, or a swift-moving river might be her only chance. In the water they would be equals, and desperation would lend strength to her efforts. As she processed this frantic thought, a strange scent crossed her nostrils. It was thick and pungent and reeked of the familiar.

Feeling she had nothing to lose, she made a reckless turn in its direction, wondering as she did if the frenzy of the chase had already driven her mad. For surely what she had in mind was insane. But if death was assured, she told herself, lungs heaving and threatening to burst, then what mattered the source? If she was correct in her assumptions, at least this way would be quick.

Directly ahead a small, open glade appeared in the woods. A curving gray mound lay athwart the path she was taking, a high, smooth-sided boulder settled in the midst of lush greenery. On the far side, pristine rain forest flared skyward.

She slowed her pace slightly as she approached. The distinctive odor was very strong now. Behind her, the whistling of the *Velociraptors* increased in intensity. Would they detect the same aroma and retreat? Or would they embark on a final sprint, expecting to overtake her? This close to a kill, she knew it would be hard for them to turn away.

Looking back for the first time, she could see several of them, running hard in her wake, tongues hanging from the sides of their mouths. They were closing rapidly, and she could sense others following just behind. Teeth and talons caught the intermittent early sunlight like mirrors. Their eyes were terrible, and they were fixed unblinkingly on her.

Good, she thought. *Let them stay fixated.*

Too committed to tremble and having already consigned her life to the earth, she put one foot on a low portion of the mound and pushed off. As the leap carried her up and over the crest of the gray bulk, a whistle deeper than that of any *Velociraptor* split the air, followed by a querulous, infuriated growl.

The lead raptor prepared to duplicate her leap and follow her over the mound. As it placed its foot, the front part of the mound whipped around. Massive jaws snapped, there was a brief, startled squeal, and the raptor imploded in a crunch of bones.

The pack dug in their heels and alternately slid, skidded, and stumbled to a dead stop. Several of those in back didn't react in time and plowed into those in front, further adding to the confusion and alarm. Panicked whistles and screeches filled the glade.

A roar loud enough to rattle the bugs in the trees drowned out the panicky cries of the raptors as the mound, furious at having its sleep disturbed and its space invaded, rose up on two pillarlike legs and began laying waste to the frantic pack.

Keelk saw none of it. Keeping her attention on the path ahead, she ran on. Though her legs complained mightily, she did not slow down until the last echo of the chaotic confrontation had faded to silence behind her.

Her escape had carried her deeper into the Rainy Basin and away from the cliffs, but for the moment, at least, she was safe. The mound she had vaulted had been composed not of granite but of flesh. It was, in fact, the prowling allosaur that had come so close to her that very morning. She'd recognized its scent right away. The great meat-eater had been dozing. Crossing its scent trail, she had cast aside everything she'd ever been told about the huge carnivores and, instead of altering her path to avoid its lair, had turned directly toward it.

She'd run right over it, something she still couldn't quite believe she'd done. The feel of its flesh and ribs was sharp in her memory. Contact had awakened it, but only after she'd cleared its flank. The first thing it had seen when it had opened its eyes was the unlucky lead raptor. Irate as well as hungry, the allosaur had reacted instinctively. The raptors hadn't even had a chance to apologize.

She tried not to picture the consequences. A pack of *Velociraptors* would back down from nothing, not even an allosaur. Regardless of the battle's outcome, the survivors wouldn't be in any shape to resume searching for her trail.

Of one thing she was certain: when she next ran the Junior Olympics at Sauropolis, she would not be intimidated by the hurdles.

As she slowed to a more relaxed pace, the cramps in her legs went away. *Struthiomimuses*, after all, were designed to run. But they were not designed to do so on empty stomachs. She found she was hungry again, and the day had just begun.

Arimat was a stronger runner, but his bounds had not come loose. Circumstances had chosen her to flee, and she would have to make the best of it. Her entire family was depending on her. Who knew what the crazed humans intended? Such thoughts kept her going.

I wish I were older, she thought. *More knowledgeable,*

more experienced. But she'd been taught that knowledge *was* experience. She smiled. If that was the case, then she'd become very much more knowledgeable in the past day.

She was still alive.

The frenzied run had disoriented her. In the dense forest there were no landmarks and it was difficult to tell direction. Slowing, she paused for a drink and considered her position. The Backbones lay to the north of the Rainy Basin. That much was easy. But which way was north? Buried beneath clouds and mist, it was difficult to determine the true position of the sun.

If she guessed wrong she'd only plunge deeper into the basin, where she would eventually have a final encounter with one of its permanent inhabitants. There was no need to dwell on the inevitable outcome of such a meeting. She tried to recall the route she'd taken during her desperate flight, the twistings and turnings she'd made while fleeing the voracious pack.

Straight ahead? Or should she angle to her left? Tilting back her head, she studied the amorphous sky, trying to recall everything she'd been taught about off-road hiking.

To her left, then. Sucking in several short, deep breaths, she started off, hoping before long to see naked rock through the trees and bushes. Even if the cliffs proved unclimbable, it would show she was back on the right track.

Birds followed her progress, commenting boisterously in their comforting singsong. She was glad of their presence. It signified that no predators were actively stalking in her immediate vicinity. Nevertheless, she remained fully alert. Having escaped raptors, an allosaur, and soulless fireworks all in not much more than a day, she wasn't about to fail now for lack of awareness.

Though the rain forest enveloped her in its dark green embrace, she found it anything but comforting.

⇒ VIII ⇐

IN HIS LIFE PREISTER SMIGGENS HAD BEEN AWAKENED by a great variety of sounds: the thunder of cannon, the cry of a lookout, the crow of a cock. Even once, while hiding out from the police near Sydney, the soft grunting of wombats.

But never had he been roused from his slumber by anything like the sound that now sent him scrambling to his feet.

They were all a little on edge. He could see it in the faces of his fellow seamen as they rose from their makeshift berths. Some staggered clumsily erect while others seemed to come awake instantly like himself. Watching them react, it was easy to tell who had been longest at sea, longest on the shadowy side of the law. These were the men who were already up and alert, pistol or sword in hand.

The unearthly, droning wail drifted over the forest a second time. Its eerie sonority seemed to bypass the outer ear and go straight to a man's bones. Smiggens put one hand to the side of his temple and shook his head. What unimaginable creature was capable of producing a sound like that?

Blackstrap was adjusting his bandanna around his bald skull. Watching him, Smiggens could only admire. The captain was too hardened to be awed by anything. Had Lucifer himself materialized in their midst, Blackstrap would have planted himself right in the devil's face. Whether swords, curses, or a game of dice, the captain would not have backed away from a challenge.

Of course, Blackstrap would also bet first with the souls

of his crew, the first mate knew. The captain was bold to the point of foolhardiness, but he wasn't stupid.

Again the forest echoed to the reverberant drone. Searching the treetops and the nearby cliff face, the crew saw nothing.

Treggang clutched his kris tightly. "Lord Buddha gave voice to many creatures, but I no can imagine what this one must be like!"

"Aye." Copperhead put his back against the Malay's as they confronted the forest together. "I've never heard the like."

"I have."

They turned to one of their number who normally spoke very little. Having fled from angry members of his own tribe as well as from the white authorities in the Oregon Territory, Chumash had ended up in Hong Kong, where his temperament and instincts had led him to join the crew of the *Condor*. Holding his rifle loosely in both hands, he studied the treetops with practiced solemnity.

"You?" Blackstrap's gaze narrowed. "Where?"

"In the mountains of my homeland. It is like the sound of the *wapiti*, only much deeper."

The captain turned immediately to his first mate. "What's this *'wapiti,'* Mr. Smiggens?"

"I don't know, Captain."

"I do." Their attention switched to Johanssen. "He's talking about the American elk."

"Yes." Chumash nodded. "*Wapiti.*" The sound came again, further unnerving the others. The American Indian quietly contemplated the surrounding greenery. "White man calls the sounds it makes 'bugling.' "

"Bugling, is it?" Blackstrap lowered his weapons. "I ain't afraid of no elk, no matter how big it is. We ought to have a look at this, wouldn't you say, Smiggens?"

"If you say so, sir," the first mate replied dubiously.

"Nay, Captain." Andreas's eyes were wide. "Whatever is making that noise is no ordinary animal."

Blackstrap let out a snort. "Ordinary animals ain't worth anything to us, man. Though if it be a relative of this here elk, I believe I've heard that they make good eating."

"Very good," Chumash acknowledged.

The prospect of solid food eased the worries of the men somewhat, however irrational the connection.

"Watch the bird-things," Blackstrap advised his crew. A glance showed that their captives were ignoring the booming sounds. "They know the dangers of this country. If they be not panicked, then it stands to reason that whatever is making that noise is no threat."

Pondering this, the men finally relaxed, not for the first time admiring their captain's ability to see to the heart of a confusing situation.

Smiggens smiled. "Why, Brognar Blackstrap! To hear you, one would almost think you were a student of the scientific method."

"Watch your language, Mr. Smiggens. I'll have none of your lip."

"Yes, sir, but I was giving you a compli—"

"I said belay that!"

Smiggens promptly shut up. Blackstrap was a bomb always waiting to go off, and a man never knew whether or not by some innocent word or deed he'd accidentally lit the fuse. Sometimes the bomb fizzled, and sometimes it even smiled, but it was always, always on the verge of exploding in your face.

A new sound resonated in their ears, different from that which had preceded it but clearly made by the same creature. It lingered plaintively in the mind.

Blackstrap waved his cutlass. "Come on, then, and we'll see what's afoot." He turned and strode off in the direction of the sounds. The crew followed, careful to keep a close watch on their captives lest they engineer another embarrassing escape.

The bird-creatures followed docilely, continuing to manifest indifference to the cries even as they grew nearer. Thus reassured, the men were anxious to identify the source of such outlandish wails.

It was not long before they came to a place where trees did not grow. No glade this, or swift-flowing river, but a well-trodden path as wide as a Boston toll road. So firmly packed was the soil that marked the course of the winding trailway that it had the consistency of pavement. The rain forest reappeared in all its lush profusion on the far side.

What had pounded and beaten out such a distinctive thoroughfare they did not know, but as to the source of the echoing drones there was no longer any question. Espying it, the first two men who had burst out of the verdure close to Blackstrap hurriedly retreated back under cover, one crossing himself repeatedly as he did so. The others crowded close to the edge of the woods, not daring to expose themselves but quite unable to suppress their curiosity.

Striding down the road with its back to them was a creature nearly twenty feet tall. The mottled brown splotches that decorated its wrinkled hide had faded to an unhealthy-looking gray, and most of the distinctive maroon coloring that in youth had tinted the great bony crest had also disappeared, leaving only irregular patches behind.

It shuffled along on its hind legs, occasionally dropping to all fours to rest. At such moments the tail rose from the ground and was held stiffly out behind the animal. Except for the remarkable three-foot-long tube that formed the crest, the skull was very much equine in general appearance. When standing, the beast looked something like a giant kangaroo. Its leg motion was similar to that of their captives, though not nearly as energetic or lithe.

It also provided further evidence for the presence of native peoples, for it had somehow managed to entangle itself in long streamers of black cloth laced with silver thread. These hung from the arching crest as well as the neck and chest. For a moment Smiggens thought the silver weavings might represent some sort of known language, but when he managed a good long look at them he saw that they were only abstract designs, not unlike the footprints a chicken makes in the dirt.

Blackstrap beckoned to his men as he stepped boldly out onto the expansive path. The astonishing creature continued to ignore them, either unaware of or indifferent to their presence. For a second time it dropped to all fours. It seemed to be having some trouble breathing. Its dun-colored flanks shuddered as they processed air with evident difficulty.

Smiggens wondered at the function of that extraordinary

cranial lobe. Was it purely decorative, he wondered, or a male device designed to attract the opposite sex? As he looked on, the creature supplied the answer.

Inhaling with difficulty, it threw its snout in the air and slowly exhaled through its nostrils. Trapped air circulating through the bony lobe vibrated, producing the deep, reverberant sonority they'd heard before. Smiggens had once heard an Aboriginal inhabitant of Sydney generate a similar sound, albeit on a much smaller scale, on a long wooden instrument he'd called a didgeridoo, which in truth this beast's crest resembled in some small measure.

It was a poignant, mournful, and quite comely sound. As he listened to a second sonorous bellow, the first mate could not help but wonder what flights of musical fantasy a natural resonating chamber of such dimensions might produce were the owner of such a remarkable piece of natural instrumentation not merely a dumb animal.

It was instructive to note the reaction of their four captives. Instead of alarming them, the plaintive drone caused them to lower their heads and arms. Clearly there was no danger here.

"Like havin' a canary in a Welsh coal mine," O'Connor remarked with satisfaction. "See, all we have to do is watch the big chickens like this one to know whether there's any danger about."

"Aye," agreed his companion. "No gold in that, but value just the same."

A moment later the two men as well as their fellow brigands were left to wonder at the meaning of their captives' reaction when they began to whistle and squawk loudly.

Blackstrap's gaze narrowed. "Now what's got into the beasts? Smiggens?" But the equally baffled first mate could only shake his head in ignorance. Fingering their weapons, the men looked around restively. Save for the shuffling, droning giant before them, the forest was silent.

Chin-lee stepped over to Blackstrap and indicated the giant. "If that not dragon, Captain, then what is?"

"Do you see it breathing fire?" Smiggens spoke gently, as befitted an educated man declaiming to the ignorant. "Where are its wings? Does it look like any drawing of a dragon you've ever seen?"

"Different kind." Chin-lee was adamant.

What else could you expect from a heathen Oriental? Smiggens mused. But the smaller man was a crack shot, and a terror in the rigging of a captured ship.

"It looks ill," Thomas commented in his lilting Jamaican accent. "See how hard it work to breathe."

Blackstrap nodded agreement. "Har. A man doesn't have to be a physician to see that." He glanced at their four captives, whose frantic wailing had given way to more familiar mindless chattering. "By Triton's jewels if I don't think our brainless beasts were trying to communicate with it."

Johanssen responded with an amused sneer. "Chickens trying to talk to giant kangaroos!" He proceeded to give a passable verbal and physical impersonation of a foraging turkey, provoking appreciative laughter from his companions.

"The *Parasaurolophus* cannot help us," Shremaza observed sadly. "Arimat, Tryll, you know what this wizened duckbill is doing in the Rainy Basin."

Tryll responded first. "Going to one of the chosen places, Mother. She's wearing her funeral banners."

"As must we all, someday." Hisaulk saw that the humans were ignoring their conversation, as they had ever since the capture. "Well, there was no harm in trying."

As soon as they'd seen the big hadrosaur they'd done their best to get its attention. Though by nature no more aggressive than her distant *Struthiomimus* cousins, with her size and strength she might have been able to free them. But it was clear now she was too near the Final Passing. Her strength was failing rapidly and, since she had not reacted in any way to their calls, they realized she was also most probably deaf, a poignant ending for a member of a tribe that lived for music.

We do not get to choose our own endings, Hisaulk knew, *nor the manner in which we are fated to approach the Final Passing.*

"The beast is dying." In his home on the South African coast, Mkuse had seen many animals die. This one might be larger, stranger, but in its manner of life leaving-taking, it was no different from the elephant or eland.

"Too bad." Blackstrap grunted meaningfully as he gestured at their captives. "If this lot be worth a couple of thousand pounds, that one'd bring ten thousand by itself."

"The boats would never hold it, Captain," asserted Treggang. "How we get it out to the ship?"

"Look at its mouth, ya blind beggar. No more than a beak and lot of flat, grinding teeth. 'Tis big but harmless. Get enough rope on it and we could walk it out to the *Condor*. 'Tis tall enough to keep its head above the water, and there be no waves in the lagoon." Black eyes glittered. "Wouldn't that be a prize to unveil to the swells in old London Town!"

"Dammit, I *know* these creatures!" Smiggens's expression was a rictus of frustration as he muttered under his breath.

A huge hand smacked him on the back hard enough to make his spine quiver. "That be the awkward thing about book-learning, Mr. Smiggens. 'Tis useful only when you remember it. The rest of the time it just sits in your head and ferments, like old mush. Reflex, now, and strength . . ." He waved his cutlass with blatant disregard for any who might happen to be standing within reach. "Give me a sharpshooter or a good cannonmaster any day."

Smiggens reached around to rub his back as he returned his attention to the fabulous monster that was shuffling down the path in front of them.

"Deaf and dying," he declared. "Even if we could get enough lines on it, the poor creature would never make it back to the coast."

"Where do you suppose it's going?" wondered Copperhead aloud.

"Look at the way its skin shines." Watford was quite taken with the alien beauty of the beast.

Chin-lee sulked off to one side. "Dragon," he mumbled, unwilling to be dissuaded from that opinion by the first mate or anyone else.

Blackstrap sighed. "If you must have it so, Chin-lee, dragons it'll be, for want of a better name. Mr. Smiggens?"

"No, no; it's there, I know it's there, but for the life of me I can't think of it." The first mate's irritation with his faulty memory was undisguised.

"Dragons, then, even if these do not breathe fire and soar

above us on great ugly batwings. Right, Chin-lee?''

By way of reply the Cantonese adopted a self-righteous expression, folded his arms, and aimed his gaze significantly skyward.

"Which way, Captain?'' asked Andreas.

"Why, I think we might do well to follow this one for a while. It doesn't look apt to last much longer, and I've a fancy to study it close up." He winked. "I'm also more than a mite curious to see if that shiny thread in the cloth it has wrapped about itself is real silver." He toyed with his mustache. "It chooses to ignore us. Even if it were to turn, I don't see any threat. It can barely set one foot before the other." He gestured with the cutlass point.

"See how often it stops to rest. Its time is near, I think."

To the pirates' surprise, their captives unexpectedly chose to resist the familiar tugs on their tethers.

"Here, now,'' avowed Samuel, "we'll have none of that." He jabbed the point of his sword into the backside of the largest dragon-bird, just to the left of the tail. The creature gave a start and resumed walking. It also focused such a penetrating, unblinking glare on the sword-wielder that the latter turned away, irritated and confused at himself for having allowed a mere animal to stare him down.

"Father, you're bleeding!" Tryll moved to comfort her parent.

He swerved to block her from turning. "Keep moving. It's only a scratch."

She hesitated, then complied.

He would have to be more careful how he reacted, he told himself. These mad humans were liable to do anything.

Would they stoop to harming children? Hisaulk could hardly countenance such a thought. But he resolved to take no chances.

It seemed they had no choice but to join their captors in trailing the failing *Parasaurolophus*. To do so was to put them all in potential danger. As there seemed no way of communicating this to their captors, the best he could do was try to keep the family calm and together. Perhaps a chance at flight would present itself, leg hobbles and all.

"We must do something." Shremaza stumbled along next to him.

He responded with the distinctive bobbing motion of his head and long neck that corresponded to a shrug among humans.

"What can we do? We can only hope that when this honored duckbill's time arrives, those who will come to perform the final rites will choose to concentrate on her and ignore us."

"It is early yet." Shremaza glanced skyward. "Many who would come will still be sleeping."

"A delay would be welcomed," her mate admitted. Following the dying *Parasaurolophus* with his eyes, he wished he knew the proper song for the moment. The family could have improvised, and it would have been the right thing to do, but he didn't want to do anything that might startle their captors. His hip hurt where the human had poked him. In this case, the family took precedence over etiquette. He was sure that had she known what was going on, the senior duckbill would have understood.

The path wound its way through the woods, its slope gently descending. Gradually all sight of the Backbone Mountains was lost, swallowed up by the surrounding vegetation. If anything, the forest grew lusher still. Only Smiggens paid any real attention to the astonishing, exceptional flora. The rest of the crew had no time for any beauty that did not glitter.

Was every corner of the tropical world represented here? the first mate found himself wondering. Did nothing in this land ever perish or die out? Even the bird life hailed from every continent.

It was not Eden, he reminded himself. Eve did not weave black shrouds for dragons.

Except they weren't "dragons." He was sure of that. Curse his capricious memory, anyway!

It was Chumash who first spotted the gathering of great-winged birds that was circling high overhead. It was a sight familiar to any man who'd spent time in the open places of the land.

"Something's dead near here," Johanssen announced with certainty.

"Something big," the American Indian added.

Again Blackstrap utilized his cutlass as a pointer. "See there, in the middle of the sky-circle. I'll have a dead man's share for breakfast if those not be the biggest vultures any-one's ever seen!"

Many of them were familiar with American vultures, and several with the noted Lammergeier. Andreas knew well the condor of the South Americas, after which their sturdy craft took its name. But none among them had ever seen anything like the pair of *Argentavis* that dominated the aerial waltz of scavengers. Each had a wingspan of more than twenty feet.

Occasionally a previously unseen flier would rise into the sky and another would descend to take its place. It was clear that the flock was feeding on something.

"Why is our beast heading in that direction?" Watford wondered.

"Who knows?" Mkuse gripped his rifle tightly. "Many creatures have traditional ways of eating."

"And dying," Anbaya added. "The Lord Buddha—"

"Never mind your Lord Buddha," Blackstrap snapped. "We'll see for ourselves what be happening soon enough, I'll wager."

"Perhaps it's headed for a natural graveyard." Smiggens's vision of ivory lying scattered about for the taking put verve in everyone's step. A dead dragon would have many teeth, and perhaps tusks. At last: something of value with which the men could readily identify.

The trail narrowed and overarching trees, fighting for every square inch of available sunlight, closed in behind the stumbling *Parasaurolophus*, hiding it from their sight. Fearful of losing their quarry, the pirates increased their pace, chivying their captives along. After all, who knew but that an unwatched dragon might vanish into the ground, for anything might be possible in a place of such wonders.

The trail crooked sharply to the left. Moving at a near run, they were brought up short by the sight that suddenly unfolded before them. A sight that would have challenged the palette of a Bierstadt and the pen of a Poe. Or, as the scholarly Smiggens put it under his breath, "Truly this is a place where a church would come to pray."

Spread out before them was a wondrous panorama that not even the odor of death could diminish. It was a place of great peace and calm, of regeneration as much as disintegration. A site of leave-taking and new beginnings, of rebirth and recycling. Many were the man or woman who would have gazed upon that scene and seen only desolation, but Smiggens saw Nature in all its intricacy and wonder, hard at work remaking the world.

It was impossible to escape the smell. It was ripe, powerful, and dominating. Many of the pirates removed or adjusted their bandannas to cover their noses and mouths in a feeble effort to diminish the fragrance. Among the crew, only those who had served on whaling ships had ever experienced anything like it.

Fortunately there was not a weak stomach among them. These were, after all, men to whom the stink of dead and dying flesh was not unfamiliar.

It was a garden in which Bosch might have served as groundskeeper. Exotic flowers and succulents thrust up between the bones, climbing gigantic ribs and femurs as readily as any rose ever surmounted a willing trellis. Orchids burst from silent, sun-bleached jaws while vines drank at the water-filled basins of toppled vertebrae. There were hundreds of bones, thousands of bones, and though the awestruck visitors could not know it, this site was only one of several that lay scattered throughout the Rainy Basin. Suppurating in the sodden sunshine, decaying flesh still clung to the memory of the more recently arrived.

Gawking at the greatest of all boneyards they had seen, the pirates continued to trail the now badly tottering duckbill.

Samuel pointed at one especially imposing pile of ribs and vertebrae. "I didn't know mountains had bones. Look at the size of those legs!"

"Steady, men." Even Blackstrap was subdued. "They all be dead, they be. See the flies. They should be familiar enough to ye."

Vultures of every shape and size surrendered possession of corpses under dissection as the visitors passed, only to reclaim them in their wake. Beaks large and powerful enough to snap off a man's leg resumed scraping and tearing at the collapsing skeletons.

Having drawn himself up to his full height, Chin-lee strode along proudly, chin thrust forward, his expression one of complete vindication.

"Now," he declared, speaking with the voice of several thousand years of tradition behind him, "if these not the bones of dragon, tell me what clsc they is!"

"I'm near to conceding the point, Chinaman." Smiggens brushed his hair straight back. "But not quite. I still have thoughts hanging on the edge of remembrance. I'll reel them in yet."

"Good thing we don't have to rely on your memory to get us out of a tight spot, Mr. Smiggens." O'Connor smirked.

"Aye," agreed Watford. "Why, in the middle of a fight Mr. Smiggens would stop a moment to think about it, he would, while some jack-tar was cutting his guts out." Several of the men roared. It helped to lighten the unrelieved melancholy of their surroundings.

To his credit Smiggens smiled along with them. Unlike some, he was not above poking fun at himself.

"Bigger than an elephant." Mkuse used his stride to measure the length of a skeleton as they walked past. "Bigger than *ten* elephant."

"We've been hungering after something solid to eat, Captain," Davies reminded his master. "Maybe we can find a fresh one."

"Aye!" Blackstrap responded enthusiastically. "One of these would feed Her Majesty's whole bloody fleet for a week."

Following the tottering *Parasaurolophus*, they passed close by two more corpses. One had a head that was frozen nightmare, all spikes and horns and frill. The skull of the second was similar to that of the creature they were following. It looked, Copperhead remarked, like the mother of all ducks. Smiggens counted over a thousand flat teeth in its jaws before giving up and moving on.

A slightly smaller corpse of relatively recent demise

yielded an impressive hunt of haunch, which the pirates planned to place later over a cook-fire. Two stout sailors carried it suspended between them, the support pole resting on their shoulders.

"Look!" whistled Shremaza. "I can scarcely believe it!"

"What are they going to do with that, Father?" Arimat asked Hisaulk.

Hisaulk spoke carefully, so as not to unduly alarm his son. "It is said that before they came to live in Dinotopia, humans were in the habit of eating the flesh of other living creatures."

"Like they eat fish?" Tryll blinked uncertainly.

"Yes, like they eat fish. We cannot blame these men—for your mother and I are certain they are all males—for what they are doing. They are only ignorant, and in need of proper education."

"Can they be taught?" Arimat asked.

"Anyone can be taught." Hisaulk spoke forgivingly of their captors. "It should not be held against them. After all, they are only mammals."

The adult struthies made no attempt to shield their offspring from the horrid sight. It was well known among both human and dinosaurian parents that any attempt to hide something from a child only intensified the child's desire to learn its secrets. Better always to reveal through explanation than tease with obfuscation. This was a hallmark of Dinotopian education.

Hisaulk let his gaze wander past their prattling captors, past the tectonic architecture of the boneyard, past the flowers and bromeliads and trees, and out into the muggy vastness of the Rainy Basin. His eldest was out there somewhere, alone and afraid.

Keelk, he thought forcefully, *you must find help, and find it quickly. Preserve yourself for that.*

If these humans were barbaric enough to consume the flesh of the deceased, what might they do one day if they found themselves with nothing to eat in, say, the Great Desert? Might they look differently upon himself and his family? Though many parents would have found such a notion impossible to contemplate, Hisaulk did not shy from the possibility. It was reality, and however distasteful, he had no choice but to confront it.

The inhabitants of Dinotopia had been confronting reality for more than a hundred million years, and as a consequence had managed to survive where others had died out.

Blackstrap raised his cutlass. "Cease your babbling! Haven't you noticed that the thing's stopping?"

It was true. Surrounded by the bones of a dozen different creatures, the duckbill had finally halted alongside a fallen forest emergent. Perhaps its roots had been exposed by a heavy rain. The result was a temporary gap in the ferociously competing greenery.

Dropping to all fours, her powerful hips higher than her shoulders and head, the *Parasaurolophus* inhaled prodigiously. The pirates could hear the whistle of the formidable intake. Venerable lungs expanded to their utmost to contain it all.

Then it was expelled, with such exquisite modulation as to bring a tear to the eyes of several hardened seamen. It was a song, no question about that. A song, and a dirge, intricately crafted and rife with all the memories of a long and vibrant life. That single breath carried it along, high and sweet, for several moments.

When the last breath had died upon the air like a wisp of foam on a receding wave, it took with it the soul of the creature who had done the singing. With great dignity the duckbill slumped down on its belly in the manner of a hound settling itself before a warm fire and closed its eyes. The great chest trembled twice, thrice, like a foresail in the last zephyr of evening, and then was still.

It was over.

"Well, now." Smiggens wiped self-consciously at his eyes.

"Well, what?" Blackstrap was not in the least moved by the display. "The beast's up and died. About time, too. I was afraid we were going to have to follow the blasted thing halfway across this bloody island, for surely an island it must be.

"What say you to that, Smiggens? Mebbee fancy a name

for the place, do ye? Get your name in the bloody encyclo-
pedia—you'd like that.''

''I'd settle for a footnote,'' the first mate muttered tersely.

Blackstrap frowned at him. ''What was that, Mr. Smiggens?''

''Nothing, Captain.'' The first mate took a deep breath.
''Perhaps we can jerk some of the meat.''

''I will see to that,'' declared Thomas. ''We can fill the
ship's hold easy. Have enough to last all the way 'round
Africa.''

Blackstrap gazed past the sphinxlike body. ''What think
you, Mr. Smiggens? Ought we to take some of these bones
back with us?''

''Not a bad idea, but let's see what else we can find, first.
Myself, I'd think live specimens rather more valuable.'' The
silent, motionless, and as yet undisturbed corpse of the creature they had been following unsettled him. It had died with
too much composure for a mere animal.

Or perhaps we do not die with enough, he told himself.

''A skin, now,'' he recommended, more to take his mind
off the recent passing than for any other reason, ''that might
be really valuable. Think of the unique boots it could make.''

Blackstrap was ignoring him. Taking note of the mental
state of some of his crew, he waded in angrily among them.
''Here, now, what's this!'' He turned a slow circle, eyeing
each man in turn. ''When was the last time any of you cried
over a dying dog?''

''Never was the day when I heard a dog sing its own death
song, Captain.''

Blackstrap glared back at O'Connor. ''Have you not?''
Moving close, the captain removed one of several knives
from its scabbard and thrust it under the sailor's chin.
''You've a fine Irish tenor, Mr. O'Connor.''

The seaman eyed the blade nervously. ''Well, now, Captain, I don't know about that. There's some who say—''

The point of the knife pricked the Irishman's throat and
he flinched. ''Some who say? Why, I says it, Mr. O'Connor.
Give us a song, then.''

''What, now?'' The seaman looked bewildered.

''Aye. Don't you want to give us *your* 'death song'?''

O'Connor was sweating profusely, and not from the humidity. "Captain, I—"

Blackstrap withdrew the blade. "What, no interest? Well, then, let it be something livelier. Something to cheer your mates." He searched their faces again. "This bloody graveyard could use a spritely tune or two."

"Right, surely." So saying, O'Connor promptly launched into an edgy sea shanty, a favorite among the crew. As Blackstrap continued to ignore him, his voice grew stronger, the tune steadier. Several of the others joined in, and their strong voices soon rang off silent bones.

"Listen to them." Shremaza spoke from beneath the shade of the tree where the family was standing, carefully attended by half a dozen of the alert humans. "They're making a lot of noise." She looked around nervously. "Too much noise."

"I know." Tilting his head and neck, Hisaulk inspected his restraints. "We have to slip free of these ropes before—"

The smashing of saplings and the snap of breaking branches interrupted his pronouncement. All four struthies turned instantly to the source of the noise. But it was only some innocuous smaller creature, fleeing from the raucous singing. Hisaulk relaxed slightly.

"Not only is there too much noise," Shremaza went on, "but there is the recent dying." She nodded toward the silent duckbill who had just made the final passing. The body, like the spirit that had been restrained within, was now at peace.

"There's nothing we can do. We can't warn them because they don't understand us, don't even want to try to understand us."

"They'll find out," declared Arimat firmly.

"Yes, they'll find out." Hisaulk probed the brooding depths of the forest. "I would just rather be somewhere else when they do."

IX

"A FINE JOB." STEPPING BACK, BLACKSTRAP SUR-veyed the progress they'd made so far. "What say you, Mr. Smiggens?"

The first mate conceded his approval. "A strong palisade, to be sure, Captain. When it's finished, this will make an excellent base camp from which to explore the surrounding countryside."

The circular enclosure crowned a small hillock in the middle of the boneyard. Fashioned mostly of enormous ribs gathered from close by and bound together by lengths of liana, the protective wall they were constructing would form an impenetrable barrier, with the base of each rib firmly posted in the ground and the sharp points facing outward. It would be a foolhardy creature indeed that would attempt to surmount such a fortification.

They intended to fill Fort Dragon, as it was unanimously christened, with booty taken from territory yet to be explored. That they had as yet encountered no sign of such booty did not in the least discourage them.

The simple bone gate was decorated with a pair of skulls also removed from the immense graveyard. Though they noted the glee with which these were mounted, the struthie family did not shudder. Bones were not flesh, and the use of them for utilitarian purposes was not unknown to the civilized inhabitants of Dinotopia. It was, in fact, a quite acceptable means of honoring the deceased.

Hisaulk would not have thought their captors so enlightened. It was perhaps the first civilized action they had demonstrated.

And thank goodness they had stopped singing.

However, the humans had constructed their temporary habitation entirely too near the recent passing for comfort. The danger had only been postponed, not avoided. Hisaulk and his family remained alert.

Mist and night enveloped the Rainy Basin, enclosing all who dwelled within in damp darkness. Inside the pirates' encampment a bonfire blazed hot enough to withstand the wandering vapors. Those who benefited from its cheery sputter took turns feeding the crackling pyre, drying the wood they had scavenged or cut before consigning it to the flames.

O'Connor wandered over to engage the first mate in conversation, nodding in the direction of the softly chattering *Struthiomimuses* as he did so.

"Sure, and for funny animals they're plenty vocal. What do you suppose they're on about, Mr. Smiggens?"

Relaxing on the ground, the first mate didn't bother to look up as he replied. "Who knows, O'Connor? It's in the nature of birds to make noise, and these things are very like birds. All they lack are feathers and wings."

"I've seen parrots by the dozen gather on a single branch," Thomas commented from nearby. "They rattle away like old women on market day."

"A sort of beautiful, aren't they?" O'Connor studied their captives.

"Aye." They all turned to the captain, who had come up behind them. "As pretty as a chest of new-minted coin. They be our fortunes, mates. Now, if we could just manage one or two more, perhaps a little larger next time, I think I might be content."

Uncharacteristically cold, a gust of dry wind whistled through the camp, ruffling hair and nerves. Thomas scrutinized the sky uneasily.

"Don't like that breeze, Captain. That storm, she still out there mebbee."

"Forget the bleeding storm, Mr. Thomas. We be safe enough here, and those aboard the ship will cope. 'Tis that very storm which carried us to this land. Ill luck turned good, says I.'' He scanned the surrounding trees, their tops visible above the rampart of bone.

''We'll mark well the latitude and longitude of this country, har. She'll become our own private hunting ground, from which we'll supply the zoological societies and scientific institutions of the world. Not to mention the idle rich, eh? Can you not see the queen herself walking one of our smaller pretties on a jeweled leash?'' He nudged his first mate with a foot.

''What think you of that, Mr. Smiggens? After years of plundering and stealing goods and currency, we find ourselves in the blooming pet trade!'' He guffawed mightily, delighted with his own witticism. The others laughed with him, and even the first mate found himself grinning.

Laughter and smiles alike evaporated as a deeper-throated chuckle sounded just outside the pale palisade.

Thomas gazed nervously at the inner wall. ''Did you hear that?''

''Aw, there were nothin' there to hear.'' O'Connor grabbed the other man's leg and pinched.

The Jamaican jumped, his gaze narrowing. ''I warn you, Irishman, don't do that.''

''See here, you're spoiling a fine night. It were nothing, man.''

The ''nothing'' outside the wall growled again, sufficiently distinct and loud this time to convince even the cynical O'Connor. ''Mother MacRee,'' he muttered. ''I hear it now, for sure.''

A grim-faced Blackstrap shoved past them, a revolver in each hand. ''Look to your weapons, gentlemen. It seems we have a caller. Apparently there be no respect for the lateness of the hour.''

There was a scramble as guns and swords were drawn and made ready. Everyone except those guarding the captives clustered in front of the fire. As for the struthies, it did not escape the first mate's notice that they were now standing utterly motionless, gazing out into a night become suddenly sinister.

Vegetation rustled just beyond the fence. Blackstrap whispered to his first mate, "Can you make it out, Mr. Smiggens?"

"No, sir. I can't see a thing."

"Heard it, though, didn't you? A lion?"

"That was no lion, Captain." Instinctively, Mkuse held his rifle out before him, like a spear. "I have heard many lions. They moan or cough. They do not make noises like that."

For a third time that unearthly growl rolled over them. One man retreated slowly, until the fire singed his pants.

"What the devil?" Copperhead was muttering.

"Aye," murmured Smiggens softly. "The devil indeed."

Beyond the line of anxious men and outside the palisade they had raised, eyes that were curiously intent and intensely curious were examining the structure. It hadn't been there three days ago, when last this place had been visited. Had the humans violated the unspoken covenant and begun to build in the Rainy Basin? Nothing had been said about it. There had been no mention of any such thing passed among the rain forest tribes.

It was difficult to believe the humans were serious. One swift kick, a simple matter for a fully grown, thirty-foot-long *Megalosaurus*, could easily collapse the feeble wall they had built.

It blinked at the fire and the milling human shapes silhouetted by the flames. Like every dinosaurian inhabitant of Dinotopia, the megalosaur was intelligent. As did the rest of its kind, it simply rejected the trappings of civilization, preferring to live in the Rainy Basin in a state approximating that of its ancestors.

This could prove unfortunate for those unlucky enough to stumble across its path.

According to the law, anything that came into the Rainy Basin was fair game, be it a giant sauropod or tiny human. All humans knew that. *These* humans should know that. It made their presence here as much as their pitiful construction all the more inexplicable.

He considered advancing and breaking through the flimsy wall. The thought of seeing the humans panic and scatter amused him. Saliva dripped between great teeth and down the side of one powerful jaw. Having never had the opportunity to hunt live humans, having never been one of those carnosaurs who'd chosen to confront a caravan, the megalosaur was somewhat taken with the possibilities. It might be entertaining, and the taste of human was one that had escaped him.

It wouldn't be very sporting, though. They were not armored, and their only dinosaurian escort appeared to consist of a quartet of *Struthiomimuses*, who would be worse than useless in a fight. Humans were slow and fragile. Certainly not much of a challenge for a mature megalosaur.

Were they hiding something? The big meat-eater might be slow, but he was not ignorant. One thing humans were notorious for, even within the Rainy Basin, was trickery. Were they tempting him to attack, only so they might unleash some unknown mischief upon his unsuspecting person? Fang and claw could only do so much.

He sniffed hard. These humans reeked powerfully, which in itself was unusual. They also smelled of the ocean, but not of the eels or fish with which travelers through the Rainy Basin usually purchased safe passage from the carnivores who lived there. This absence of tribute was itself reason enough to attack.

Moving closer, the megalosaur peered over the top of the makeshift barrier and into the enclosure. As it did so, it entered the circle of illumination cast by the central fire.

One of the humans let out an ear-piercing shriek and turned to flee. A much larger human with distinctive facial hair intercepted him and struck him on the head with a small, curving device. The first human immediately fell down unconscious.

This struck the megalosaur as exceedingly eccentric behavior, even for humans. Were they playing some sort of game? Or were they hunting each other? The large human showed no signs of trying to eat the one he'd knocked down.

Swerving his great head to the right, he locked eyes with the largest of the *Struthiomimuses*. There, at least, he encountered the proper quotient of fear. Then the carnivore saw that they were bound arm and leg with ropes, the ends of which were gripped by several humans. Definitely some kind

of game, the megalosaur decided. The question was, did he
want to play?

If so, it would be by his rules.

He struggled to understand. Surely this was the oddest
band of humans to enter the Rainy Basin in recent times.
Had others of his kind observed such aberrant behavior before? Though conversation between carnosaurs was stilted
and infrequent, he resolved to inquire and try to find out.

When he saw the haunch of meat Blackstrap's party had
scavenged, his confusion deepened. Had some humans suddenly turned carnivore? It was rumored that they had once
eaten meat, but that was only a rumor, and one the megalosaur had no way of verifying. He knew they ate fish, but
that was all.

It made a certain sense, though. Did they not walk on two
legs like the great carnivores? Did not their eyes point forward instead of off to the side? Of course, their teeth were
altogether inadequate, but they fashioned teeth of metal to
cut for them. Wondering as much about their taste as their
motivation, the megalosaur was torn between trying to talk
to the strangers and eating them. He took another step forward.

Several large bangs resounded and the megalosaur jerked
reflexively. The noise came from a handful of long tubes the
humans were pointing in his direction. Knowing nothing of
fireworks sophisticated or otherwise, he could only blink at
the noise. Some small unseen things stung his chest and
stomach.

Was this part of the game? Were they inviting him to
participate? If so, how ought he to react? Was he supposed
to eat the tube holders or ignore them and consume their
quieter companions instead? It was at once intriguing and
confusing.

The largest human had begun by knocking down one of
its own kind. Then had come the tube pointing. The megalosaur considered jumping the fence and knocking down the
big human. Would that be considered proper procedure? The
human would not survive the attention, of course, though he
would make a nice snack.

Again the tubes boomed and flashed, and again something

tiny and superfast stung his chest. Reaching across with a three-fingered claw, he scratched at the places that burned, then lowered his head and sniffed of himself. There was an odd odor in the air, as of burned earth.

Deciding suddenly that whatever else he might be, he wasn't hungry, he favored the cluster of humans with a final contemptuous snort and veered away, plunging back into the familiar depths of the forest. The humans presented him with too many choices, too many new things all at once, and it was most perplexing. Carnosaurs do not respond well to confusion. The humans demanded too much thinking for too little reward. Rending and tearing is a megalosaur's forte, not curiosity. Like all his kind, his attention span was short.

Perhaps, the big meat-eater reflected as he strode away, he would return in a couple of days when his appetite was renewed and eat them all, game or no game. For now, though, with his belly full, all he wanted was to sleep. It was one of the three things a megalosaur did best.

Shouts rose behind him and he paused to glance back over a shoulder. The humans had advanced from the fire to their fence. Pressed up against the spaces between the bones, they were yelling and gesticulating at him. Several more of the long tubes they carried spoke loudly.

Stranger and stranger! Were they so anxious to be eaten that they were calling him to come back? He hesitated.

No, he decided. If they lingered in his territory he would eat them in his own good time and not before. His digestive system was calling for rest, not renewed activity. Resolving to return in a fortnight, he turned away from their camp and considered where he might find a soft wallow in which to rest. As he strode along, his long tongue licked out and up to clean dirt from one bright yellow eye. Thinking made him sleepy.

A towering form appeared in the darkness, threatening to cross his path. As was expected of him, he slowed and waited for the other to pass. Though they shunned organized civilization, the inhabitants of the Rainy Basin did recognize and adhere to certain protocols among themselves. The megalosaur was only one carnivore among many, and by no means the largest. He gave way readily to one more dominant than himself.

Back within the palisade, the pirates congratulated one another with whoops and hollering, convinced that by their resolve and boldness they had driven off a monster straight out of the imagination of a Dante.

"Look at it run!" Andreas could hardly contain himself as he peered between a pair of gigantic upturned ribs. "It won't be back."

"Aye!" Blackstrap scabbarded his cutlass. "See, then, how with a little courage and some good shooting a man can stand against anything, even nature's greatest horrors. Boys, I'll wager we hit it a dozen times or more."

"I didn't see any blood."

"What's that, Mr. Smiggens?" The captain whirled on his first mate.

The other man rose from where he'd been sitting. His breathing had finally dropped back to something close to normal. Instead of facing the captain, he was gazing out into the now menacing dark.

"I said that I didn't see any blood. I don't think any of our shots penetrated. Its hide was too thick."

Blackstrap was taken aback. "Maybe 'twas so. In that event, I expect that the sight and sound of our guns were enough to frighten it off."

"Were they?" Smiggens turned to face his master. "Why should they frighten it? There must come lightning aplenty in this country. Why would the crack of a few rifles scare it?"

Blackstrap considered, his expression twisting with the effort. "Well, then, ye bloody pissant smart-mouth, why did the beast turn away from us and run?"

"Maybe it got a good look at you, Captain Blackstrap." Copperhead was careful to keep his voice down.

"Aye," whispered Samuel. "That'd be enough to scare off half a dozen devils."

Blackstrap spun. "What be you two mumbling about?"

"Nothing, Captain," replied Copperhead innocently.

"All I'm saying," Smiggens went on, "is that we've no reason to believe that we're responsible for its flight. There's no proof that our shots had any effect on it."

"Then why the bloody hell did it leave?" Blackstrap demanded to know.

The first mate spread his arms. "Who can say? Maybe it just got bored. Perhaps it heard something else, or scented prey that was potentially more alluring. Possibly it thought us not worth the effort, or did not like our smell." He turned back to the palisade and the night beyond. "I thank Providence for whatever turned it. Did you see its teeth?"

"Teeth be damned." Johanssen was cleaning his rifle. "Did you see the size of the thing?"

"These from larger animal." Chumash ran a hand down the smooth curve of one rib. Next to him, Chin-lee looked glumly satisfied.

"You tell me that no dragon, Mr. Smiggens, sir."

Blackstrap glowered at his first mate. "Dragon or no, I says that we drove it away." Smiggens sensibly chose not to argue. "There, then, that be settled." As quickly as it had blossomed, the captain's anger vanished.

"A million pounds sterling, boys! That's what the London zoo would pay for a creature like that. And we'd be famous, we would!"

"Easier to drive one off than capture it," commented one of the suddenly tired sailors. "Mighty difficult, it would be."

"There's got to be a way." Blackstrap's eyes narrowed as he twirled the tip of one mustache.

Smiggens gaped at him. "You're not *serious*, Brognar."

The captain glanced over at him. "Whenever that kind of money is at stake, Mr. Smiggens, I be nothing less than dead serious."

"*Dead*'s the word, sir," the first mate mumbled by way of reply.

"Even if we could catch and subdue one, Captain, how would we get it back to the ship?" Watford eased his revolver back into its chest holster. "No matter how it were turned, we could never squeeze the beast's body through the canyon we traversed. It'd be like trying to run a forestay through a needle."

"True enough, Mr. Watford." Blackstrap had been pondering that very problem. "But maybe, just maybe, there be another way."

The men crowded close or listened intently from where they were standing. Convinced they had just driven off an ogre from their deepest nightmares, they would at that moment have denied their captain nothing. Their morale was at its highest point since they'd left the *Condor*.

Blackstrap feigned indifference, a malevolent twinkle in his eye. "Oh, 'tis probably not worth repeating, boys. 'Twas just a notion. Let me polish it and we'll see if she shines. Meanwhile, I think we could all do with a sleep."

He caught Mkuse's eye. "We'll post four men, Mr. Mkuse. One at each point of the compass. Choose your companions for the first."

"Yes, Captain." The Zulu glanced in the direction of their captives. "And two more to keep a close watch on our prizes."

"Aye, look at 'em," murmured one of the others.

At the sight of the advancing carnosaur, the two young ones had released their bladders. Restrained as they were, they could do no more than huddle behind the adults, who were clearly engaged in trying to reassure their offspring. Those among the pirates who might have found this domestic tableau pitiable rather than amusing kept their feelings private, lest they expose themselves to the ready ridicule of their shipmates and their captain.

Reliving their great victory over the attacking gargoyle, the men parted and settled down to sleep, each retiring to whichever patch of ground struck his fancy. Samuel tossed several sections of log on the fire to keep it blazing high.

Only Smiggens did not snug down beneath a fragrant bush or against a complaisant tree root. He remained standing for a long time, staring over the crest of the palisade into the cloaking darkness beyond, listening to the multitude of night sounds both familiar and alien. Occasionally a distant thrashing or rustling of branches sent a chill down his spine.

Had they driven the monster away? He was far from certain. But Blackstrap would hear nothing else. They were responsible for its flight, and that was that.

The creature had shown no indication of panic or distress.

If their bullets had done it no real harm, then why had it fled? He shrugged wearily. The mysteries of this land came too fast and frequently for any one man to comprehend. Maybe Blackstrap was right. Maybe he, Smiggens, thought too much for a good seaman. Certainly he thought too much for a good pirate.

But, he told himself firmly, *someone in this lot has to do the thinking*.

Something distant boomed at the moon. He shivered again, despite the warmth of the air. He'd listened to the cries of large, dangerous animals in the Indies and the Raj. This was different, unimaginably different.

Perhaps they had, after all, driven the creature away. But he was convinced that if such a monster fixed its determination irrevocably upon a mere man, then that individual could do no more than compose himself and prepare to meet his maker, the efficacy of whatever weaponry he might be carrying notwithstanding.

It was not a pleasant thought to carry with one to bed.

X

ALTHOUGH THEY DID NOT KNOW IT, THERE WAS NOT one of the great meat-eaters lurking in the vicinity of their camp but half a dozen, and the crew of the *Condor* encountered them not in their nightmares but on the following morning, which was bright and filled with sunshine.

The mist had risen and the clouds had not yet gathered themselves for their daily rain party when the sound of the crunching of bones induced the avaricious party of intruders to retrace their steps of the day before. After their encounter the previous night they advanced with fresh caution, taking care to keep under cover despite their renewed confidence.

Not one but two adult megalosaurs were scavenging the body of the dead *Parasaurolophus*. The larger of the pair was working on the flank, using its curved teeth to remove large gobbets of flesh with each bite, while its companion rooted about in the opened belly. And they were not alone.

"See the horned dragons!" exclaimed an excited Chinlee.

A quartet of ceratosaurs hung about the fringes of the feed. Slightly shorter and less massive than the megalosaurs, they remained fearsome carnivores in their own right. Looking out of place on so efficient a meat-eater, a short, pointed horn not unlike that of a rhinoceros thrust upward from each toothy snout.

One tried to sneak in for a bite of leg. The largest megalosaur lowered its head and growled, but that was the extent of the confrontation. Having been granted permission to approach, the first ceratosaur began to feed. It was quickly followed by the remaining trio.

To Mkuse it was akin to watching lions gorge on a dead elephant, except that two different kinds of meat-eater were involved here. *Surely they did not come from one family*, he thought. Still, it almost appeared as if they were cooperating to strip the corpse as quickly as possible.

Fascinated, the men watched as the edible parts of the duckbill disappeared down multiple throats. One megalosaur finally stepped back from the body, its belly grossly distended. With its mouth shut and eyes closed, it reminded O'Connor of a banker he'd once confronted in downtown Boston. O'Connor had coveted the man's pocket watch, and it was only the intervention of other pedestrians that had prevented him from obtaining it. The encounter had also precipitated his hasty departure from that lovely city, not to mention the whole of the eastern seaboard of the United States.

The ceratosaurs took their time gleaning the bones. With plenty for all, there was no infighting. Occasionally one would raise its head and look around sharply, as if fearful that something might arrive to drive it away. That could not be the case, though, Johanssen argued. Surely nothing walked the earth that could drive such monsters from their meal.

A light went on in Smiggens's head, illumination that he chose to share with his companions.

"No wonder the beast we saw last night decided not to take the measure of our resistance."

Blackstrap turned to him. "What do you mean, Mr. Smiggens? We chased it off fair, didn't we, boys?" Several of the crew heartily confirmed this explanation.

But with the solution spread out before him, this time Smiggens wasn't about to back down. "Don't you see? Why should a creature with an appetite which doubtless is appropriate to its size trouble itself over small bites like ourselves, when it knows that a small mountain of food lies close at hand, already deceased and ready for the digesting? For surely if we were able to encounter and track this strange crested beast's presence it would not escape the notice of any predators in the vicinity." He gestured at the all but concluded banquet. "As we see, it has not." He waved at the vast sea of bones bleaching slowly in the bright sunshine.

"Nature is ever efficient in her arrangements. Clearly many of these great beasts come here to die. Left alone to degrade by natural processes, the decomposition of so many gigantic corpses would quickly poison the soil and water. No flock of vultures and buzzards such as we saw when we first arrived at this place could possibly begin to keep up with such immense quantities of decaying flesh.

"Instead, it is the prodigious requirements of these monstrous two-legged meat-eaters which keeps this land clean and fertile. With so much food freely presented to them, it is entirely possible that many of them have never hunted in their lives. Which is not to say they cannot, but even a dumb dinosaur exerts no more energy in the pursuit of its daily sustenance than is necessary."

"A moment, Mr. Smiggens." Blackstrap frowned at his first mate. "What did you call the beasts?"

"Dinosaurs." Smiggens looked gratified. "It finally struck me where I have seen them before."

"You still say you have seen animals like these before?" Chumash eyed him suspiciously.

"Not alive." As he spoke, the first mate continued to monitor the silent orgy of consumption. "It was in London several years ago, at the Great Exhibition in Hyde Park. There was a man, a scientist by the name of Owen, I believe. He'd found bones like those now scattered around us, only they had been turned to stone. Ancient bones. He'd had them cleaned up and stuck together to form skeletons. Dinosaurs, he called them."

Blackstrap felt of the strange word with tongue and palate. "Dinosaurs, eh? What manner of creatures be they, then?" He jerked a thumb in the direction of their hobbled captives. "This lot look like birds."

"Who is to say to what line or family of nature they belong? Not I." For once, Smiggens had no answer. "I am no scientist, Brognar. It may be that since these look like birds, they are indeed related to birds. Those indulging their appetites before us resemble the kangaroo. Perhaps that is a closer relation. It was stated at the exhibition that such creatures had disappeared from the surface of the earth untold eons ago. It is now clear that this is incorrect, and that some, at least, have survived in this country to the present day.''

"Well, it makes them no less valuable,'' Blackstrap grunted.

"Indeed not, Captain. People paid good money to see reconstructions fashioned of wood and plaster. I do not doubt that they will pay whatever is asked to see them alive and in the flesh.''

"As your brain is so active this fine morning, Smiggens, I ask that you apply it to the problem we discussed briefly last night, namely, how to secure and transport a larger representative of this remarkable breed back to the ship.''

The first mate considered. ''Should it somehow prove possible, how would we keep such a beast alive all the way to England or America?''

Blackstrap's response showed that he did not rely on his first mate to do *all* the thinking. ''Most flesh-eaters are happy to take fish, Mr. Smiggens. The sea is full of fish. You work on the means of acquiring one, and leave matters of maintenance to me.''

Smiggens nodded, his attention still drawn to the frightful but fascinating panorama. A cart, perhaps, built on site from available woods. Failing that, a sledge. They had good carpenters among them, and willing muscle. Nothing inspires a man to pull more than his weight so much as the knowledge that a pile of gold awaits him at the end of his pull.

Deep in thought as he turned away, he was brought up short by the unblinking stare of the largest of their captives. The bird-dinosaur was gazing directly at him. For an instant Smiggens thought he saw something other than dumb animal indifference in that stare.

Then it looked away and the momentary spell was broken. Foolish, he told himself, to allow one's emotions to be seized by the wide eyes of an animal. Any large bird, an owl or hawk, could generate an equally captivating if brief stare.

All his life he'd sought recognition from his peers in academia. Because of his lower-class background they'd shut him out, forcing him into the desperate life he now led.

Well, with these animals in tow they'd have no choice but
to let him in. A sneer curled his lip. Let those puerile, pon-
tificating pundits refuse him membership in their learned societies now! Let Blackstrap and the others have their gold;
he would have his triumph.

"Dinosaur." Chin-lee rolled the word on his tongue. "English word for dragon. Is okay."

It brought Smiggens out of his reverie. "No, no," he explained patiently. "Dragons are creatures of the imagination.
These dinosaurs are real."

"Are they?" the Cantonese replied. "Is this place real?
Are we real anymore? What is real, Englishman?"

When Smiggens hesitated it was Blackstrap who supplied
an answer. "See this knife, Chinaman? Want to see if its
blade is real?"

Chin-lee drew himself up with as much dignity as he could
muster. "You should study Confucian thought, Captain
Blackstrap. You would be enlightened."

Blackstrap put the knife away and snorted scornfully.
"Gold's enlightening, Chin-lee. Everything else is smoke."

"Maybe . . . maybe this is the outskirts of hell," Thomas
mumbled, "and these are demons."

"Dinosaurs, dragons, demons: all that matters is what
they'll fetch on the open market. I'll sell any one of 'em or
all three, and if the devil objects, why, I'll remind him that
I made my bargain with him long ago."

As have we all, Brognar. Pressed for further explanation
of what they were seeing, Smiggens was given no time for
further dour reflection on the state of their souls.

"If this be hell," Blackstrap was telling the men, "with
its clean water, ample fruit, and wonders to see, then I'll take
it over Limehouse any day, har."

"There was fruit in the Garden of Eden," Samuel pointed
out.

"Aye," Blackstrap agreed readily, "and it were Eve who
picked it. I see no Eves among us . . . unless one of you lot
has been holding out on the rest."

There was a pause and then every man broke out laughing.
Not for the first time, Blackstrap had used humor to shatter
tension and uncertainty. Whatever you might think of him

personally, Smiggens knew, you had to admire the captain's innate cleverness.

It did not occur to the men that their jollity might be noticed. The smaller of the two megalosaurs raised its head to stare directly at them. But just as Smiggens surmised, it saw no reason to bother with a group of scrawny, bony humans.

The men lingered in the vicinity of the feed, watching and marveling at the appetites of the six carnivores. It was after several hours of profound reflection that Smiggens declared himself unable to solve the problem of how to capture and transport one.

"They're just too bloody big, Captain. We might squeeze one through that canyon we found, but any cart built to haul it would barely fit sideways."

To his surprise, Blackstrap agreed with him. "Aye, I'd reached that same sad conclusion meself, Mr. Smiggens. We'll just have to be satisfied with something smaller. Surely we can find an interesting example of these dinosaurs that's larger than our present captives but smaller than those meat-eaters we see before us. Something in between. I ain't greedy. One more will do me."

The first mate nodded. "That sounds to me like a fine plan, Captain. With persistence, surely one of suitable size can be located."

It took less time and effort than any of them imagined, for they came upon a perfect specimen later that very afternoon. It was actually shorter than their two adult bird-dinosaurs, shorter even than Blackstrap or Smiggens, but much more massively built.

Mkuse and Chumash found it sleeping within a cluster of soft plants, its head drooping forward, the scaly chin almost resting on the muscular chest. It closely resembled the much larger meat-eaters they had been observing that morning. But in addition to size, there were significant other differences.

The skull seemed oversized, as did the legs and feet. Instead of long, useful arms ending in three-fingered hands, the forelegs of this new beast were comically short and had only two fingers, though the claws on the feet were substantial enough. There was no horn on the snout, though tiny bony projections did thrust slightly outward above each closed eye.

The chest rose and fell softly with its breathing and the belly bulged, indicating that this smaller carnivore had recently eaten its fill.

When standing erect, it would still be shorter than the tallest of the bird-dinosaurs they had captured, though more muscular. The pirates congratulated themselves on locating such a perfect specimen with such ease.

They jumped when it let out a snort, but the eyes did not open and it quickly returned to its deep slumber.

"The captain will want something bigger," Mkuse commented.

Chumash let out a grunt of his own. "Captain half crazy. This enough to carry on any ship." He eased backward into the brush. "We must tell the others and come back before it awakes."

"Yes," agreed the Zulu as he noted the presence of oversized teeth and talons.

"Get the nets!" Blackstrap roared as soon as he received the report. "Mkuse, you position yourself to port of the creature and you, Mr. Smiggens, take the starboard. Beware its teeth. The rest of us will make a frontal charge at the beast and drive it toward you. Be ready lest it try to jump."

"I'm not sure that's such a good idea, Captain." Mkuse measured a length of rope with his big hands.

Blackstrap regarded the warrior. "And what's wrong with it, may I ask?"

"You haven't seen it, Captain."

Blackstrap's mustache quivered. "You said it was a small one."

"That is true." Chumash spoke up in support of his shipmate. "But you have not seen it. It is small, but there is something about it. I think maybe it will not be driven. What will you do if it runs straight at you?"

"Don't be a bloody fool, man! Consider its size in relation to our number. Of course it'll turn and run. 'Twould be the sensible thing for any wild beast to do."

"That's just it, Captain." Mkuse looked uneasy. "From its look I am not so sure this is a sensible creature."

Blackstrap's eyes flashed. "What's happened to you two? You're acting like consumptives. Did we not frighten off a brute big enough to have one like this for dessert?''

"Yes, Captain, but—''

"Look to your nets, then, and let's be about the business.''

Mkuse and Chumash offered no further argument as the men shouldered the heavy ropes and nets and started off into the forest, but both silently resolved to find themselves on the back end of the lines when the time came to ambush their quarry. Their four captives shuffled along placidly, unaware of the enterprise on which their captors were now embarked.

Led by the two warriors, the capture party took no chances. Though there was little in the way of a breeze, they were careful to approach downwind of their quarry, and to lower their voices as they approached.

"Powerful-lookin' little bugger,'' Thomas commented when they finally had it in view.

"Aye,'' agreed O'Connor in a whisper. "All legs and head, it is. But sure and it'll be no match for several dozen stout seamen, I'll wager.''

"I will take that wager, Irishman.''

O'Connor grinned at his shipmate. "Why? If I'm wrong you probably won't live to spend your winnin's, man.''

"Belay your blabbering! Luck, she smiles on us still.'' Blackstrap pointed. "The little devil sleeps on. Look at its gut. This one won't be doing any mad jumping about anytime soon.'' He strained to see to his right and left. "That malingering Smiggens and that black sourface Mkuse best be in position. I'll have their hides if this prize escapes us.''

"Mr. Smiggens is on the move, sir,'' declared Watford.

Blackstrap nodded. "Yes, I can hear their bloody clumsy stumbling about from here. Better they not wake it before time.''

"Not to worry, Captain. See—it sleeps on.''

And why should it not? Smiggens was thinking as he carefully positioned his own men. It would take a carnivore the size of the one that had menaced their camp to put fear in the heart of so stout and powerful a meat-eater. Even in slumber its aspect was ferocious.

There was no need for Blackstrap to lead his men in a noisy rush. Together with Smiggens's and Mkuse's groups they approached as silently as possible, closing the trap around the unsuspecting sleeper. Mkuse himself was within arm's length of their quarry when it finally opened one eye and blinked groggily. A querulous snuffling sounded from its snout.

That was the signal for someone to shout "Git him!" and for nets and ropes to be cast. Cautious intent gave way to mad confusion and frantic activity as men scrambled to assert themselves. Mkuse was bellowing orders in a smattering of English, Dutch, and Zulu, while sputtered imprecations in a dozen languages added spice to the general chaos.

Both of the big nets were over the creature before it could fully awaken. Working as if the devil himself were critiquing their efforts, Johanssen and Anbaya managed to fasten a hobble to the short, muscular legs.

Startled out of a deep sleep but rapidly coming awake, the beast let go with an incongruously high-pitched roar that was chilling enough to straighten hair on a bald man. A lasso was slipped over its jaws, then another, and another, and then it could no longer snap at the men or generate anything louder than an outraged grunt. More ropes were coiled around legs and neck, and attention was paid even to the ridiculously short but powerful arms.

By the time it was fully alert it was utterly helpless, secured by thick ropes and weighted down by sections of netting. The encounter had cost the pirates only bumps and bruises and the loss of one rope, bit through as cleanly as a seamstress would measure off a foot of thread. With its legs hobbled in the manner of the struthies, their captive could not even make use of its semiflexible tail. It could only glower at them and snarl menacingly under its breath.

After a few feeble attempts to kick and disembowel several of its captors, it recognized the futility of such efforts and began to settle down. It was breathing hard, and its yellow eyes flicked from one man to the next. That murderous, relentless stare would have set the legs of many an individual to shaking, but these were men who had looked death in the eye before and were no stranger to it. To Mkuse, the dinosaur (as the first mate had called its kind) was nothing more than a lion on two legs.

Perspiration glistening on his naked brow, a jubilant Blackstrap threw an arm around his first mate's shoulders. "What think you, Mr. Smiggens, of our latest acquisition? Look at those teeth! Why, I'd wager there be some nearly two inches long."

"It's a fine example of whatever it is, Captain." Smiggens was breathing hard, exhilarated by the brief tussle. "You there, Andreas! Make certain of those jaw ropes!"

"Aye, Mr. Smiggens!" came the boisterous reply. "We'll keep 'er tight, don't worry!" With the danger now past and their quarry secured, the men relaxed. They swapped jokes and eyed their new captive with curiosity, speculating freely on what it might be worth.

So hugely and single-mindedly were they enjoying themselves that they failed to notice that their other captives were literally shivering with apprehension and terror. The four struthies huddled together, their eyes bulging in fear.

"How will we feed the thing, Captain?" someone asked.

"We'll tie it down good and proper," Blackstrap replied without hesitation, "and free nothing but those jaws. It'll eat or starve. I've yet to encounter man or beast that'd refuse to eat if hungry enough. Caught the devil by the tail, we have! Give yourselves three cheers, boys!"

As usual, it was left to the first mate to put a damper on the general celebration. Blackstrap growled at him. "Why the long face, man? Must it always be the long face, no matter how much fortune favors us? Must you live always under a dark cloud?"

"I try to sail out from under, Captain, but I can't stop my mind from working."

"Aye, that pestilential encumbrance troubling you again, is it? Well, what be it this time?"

Smiggens considered their silent, bound new acquisition. "I was just wondering if this individual was a mature example of its kind, and if not, how much bigger it was going to get."

"Bigger?" Blackstrap's brows semaphored his puzzlement. "What makes you think it's going to get any bigger?"

The first mate reflected on the possibilities. "You remember the one that surprised our camp. This creature is as nothing compared to it. Look at the size of its head and feet compared to its body. Does that not suggest a youthful specimen with growing still to do?''

''Are you now an expert in the maturation of these dinosaur beasts?'' Blackstrap was not daunted. ''Be you conversant with the ratio of their foot to body size? Let it grow a little, says I! By then we'll have a proper cage made for it, or have it sold to the right authority. Let them deal with it. Worry instead about how to spend the gold its sale will bring you. If that troubles you still, there be many a seaman ready to swap you his share of the spoil for that of a mate.''

Smiggens sighed. ''It just struck me that it might not be representative of an adult of the species.''

''Belay such wasteful prattle. 'Tis plainly big enough to terrify the ladies out of their skirts. That be big enough for our needs.'' He gestured to Mkuse. ''Group this pretty with the others.''

Designating several of the burliest members of the crew to handle the key ropes, the Zulu supervised as their new captive was alternately walked and dragged over to join the rest of their small menagerie. It soon saw the futility of trying to resist and complied with their demands.

As it drew near, the four struthies did everything possible to flee. They were restrained by their hobbles and their handlers, but they continued to shy as far away from the new arrival as possible. Though not human, their body language was easy enough to read.

''Look at 'em.'' Characteristically, Blackstrap found the captives' unmitigated terror amusing. ''They've reason to be frightened, I'd wager. 'Twould be beaks versus teeth if all were set free together, and the outcome of any consequent conflict easy enough to predict.'' He indicated the new prisoner's bound jaws. ''I haven't seen cutlery like that since I was last in a duke's kitchen.'' He laughed uproariously at his own jest.

Bright, intense yellow eyes followed his every move.

''What now, Captain?'' Johanssen gripped one leg rope firmly.

''Aye, Captain,'' asked Treggang, ''haven't we got enough for one journey?''

"That we do, that we do." Hugely pleased, Blackstrap eyed their prize fondly. "Why, we may not even have to escort these pretties all the way back to England or the Americas. Perhaps some Zanzibari sultan or Lamu potentate will shower us with pearls as payment for a new plaything. We'll sell them all dear, we will." He chuckled contentedly. "No need to run up skull and bones any longer. Mr Smiggens! What be the flag of the pet trade?" Even the dour first mate had to smile at that.

Blackstrap waited for the laughter to die down. "And when these have been sold and we've spent our new fortunes, why, we'll come back and help ourselves to another half dozen beasties. That's what this land will become: our own private hunting ground, whose location will be known only to us. We'll outfit a better ship for our return, with comfortable cabins all 'round and proper cages built into her hold."

"But those currents, Captain, and the wind," muttered old Ruskin.

Blackstrap shrugged off the helmsman's pessimism. "We'll find a different route, make our approach from another quarter. You worry too much, old man. One fortune at a time."

Having finally overcome her initial shock not only at the humans' insane temerity but at their success, Shremaza used her long neck to nudge her mate.

"Speak to it, father of our children. You must speak to it."

Hisaulk brooded over the possibilities, less than enamored of any of them. "I don't know the dialect. If ever we needed a translator among us, it is now." As he concluded, the new captive growled softly in their direction. Though as thoroughly bound as they were themselves, it was much too close for Hisaulk's comfort.

He tried to reply, mimicking the gruff tongue as best he could. At the same time he kicked out as far as he was able with first one bound leg, then the other, trying to show by action as well as voice that they were also prisoners of these improbable humans.

"See," he tried to explain, his throat protesting the effort required to generate the rough, raspy sounds, "our condition is as unacceptable as yours. We are comrades in distress."

The other snarled a response. Hisaulk could not make out the meaning, but for the moment, at least, the young carnosaur did not look at them as if they represented a potential meal.

"What did it say?" Shremaza crowded near, with Arimat and Tryll close behind her.

"I'm not sure."

Arimat pushed his head against his father's flank. "It must have said *something*."

Hisaulk's face was not flexible enough to allow him to frown, but he conveyed the same feeling with his voice. "I'm not confident of the exact translation, but I do know that we must find a way to escape. As quickly as possible."

"What about Keelk?" Shremaza was hesitant. "When she returns she will expect to find us here, in the company of these humans."

"If I'm understanding this new captive correctly, we'd better not wait for her. We have to find a way to help ourselves, or else we're going to find ourselves in the middle of something uncomfortable." His head twisted anxiously from side to side, large eyes studying the surrounding forest. "We have to get away from these people *soon*."

"But why, Father?" Tryll gazed up at him uncomprehendingly.

"Isn't it obvious, daughter? This juvenile was caught out alone, asleep and lethargic from several days of eating. Solitude for one so young is not the usual state of affairs." He was looking past the new captive, past the celebrating, carousing humans, deep into the enigmatic forest.

"From its look I would say it is the near equal in maturity to your older sister Keelk. We must get away before the *parents* return and see what has happened. They will be rightly outraged and inclined to react without thinking. I don't want to be anywhere around when a pair of adult tyrannosaurs start reacting without thinking."

"Yes, that's right." Tryll's eyes widened as she, too, began to peer anxiously into the woods.

"These foolish humans have no idea what they've gotten themselves into." Shremaza allowed her two offspring to huddle close, though she could not put her arms about them. *Struthiomimuses* have an especially strong maternal instinct, which was why they often served as nursemaids for the human children of Dinotopia.

"We need a *translator*." Hisaulk added something under his breath. Not an obscenity, for such language was not in the nature of dinosaurs, but rather an expression of urgency. "When they return, this one's parents are going to be extremely agitated, and not exactly amenable to reason."

WHEN THE TWO ADULT TYRANNOSAURS FINALLY DID RE-turn from their wanderings to the sleeping site, night had progressed a fair ways down its nocturnal road. A light rain had been falling for hours, cloaking trees, flowers, and soil in a slick blanket of damp. With their captives in tow, the pirates had long since departed.

Crookeye and Shethorn carefully walked the circumference of the glade. Despite the rain, their offspring's scent remained strong on the short grass and surrounding flowers. Crookeye bent forward until his nostrils grazed the grass and methodically circled the opening, sniffing as he walked, his pillarlike legs leaving basin-sized footprints in the wet earth.

There was no mistaking it: this was the place where they had left their offspring and agreed to rendezvous. What had happened? It was unthinkable for a young tyrannosaur to willfully disobey its parents. Nor was there any reason to abandon the glade. There was food aplenty in the immediate vicinity and fresh water in a nearby stream. No Rainy Basin carnosaur would bother a juvenile *Tyrannosaurus* for fear of incurring the wrath of its parents.

The adults were frustrated and baffled. Even more puzzling was the presence near the glade of multiple human spoor. What were humans doing in this part of the Rainy Basin? It was far from the routes they usually used when crossing. And why was their scent mixed with that of many struthies?

The familiar convoy smell of armored sauropods and ceratopsians was absent. Was there a group of humans so foolish as to think they could move freely about the Rainy Basin without the protection of other dinosaurs? Unbelievable as it seemed, such appeared to be the case.

Crookeye's mate growled at him and he lumbered over to join her. The strong integrated odor she had located was unmistakable: human and young tyrannosaur, moving out of the clearing and off into the forest in intimate contact with each other. Both knew that their offspring would not accept human company voluntarily. Though neither was a philosopher or teacher in the manner of certain of the civilized dinosaurs, neither were they especially dense. What the implausible confluence of scents suggested was something too infuriating to be believed.

Their confusion was only compounded by the lingering smell of *Struthiomimus*.

The multiple scents trailed away to the east. That, too, made no sense. Nothing lay in that direction; no human trade routes, no Places of Passing, nothing but empty forest. Yet that was unquestionably the direction the unprecedented group of travelers had taken.

Snout to snout, the parents conversed in low grunts and growls. Their progeny would never voluntarily have abandoned the glade. Had the unthinkable happened and the unknown humans resorted to coercion? Would they dare? Or had something else occurred, something they had no knowledge of?

The human scent smelled strongly of the sea. Humans who traveled the Rainy Basin always brought fish with which to appease the carnosaurs they encountered. Had these travelers taken to eating their own tribute? There were too many questions. Grimly, the two adults strode off in search of some answers.

They found the humans' first camp quickly enough, and soon after that the palisade of bone. This peculiar and unprecedented structure both angered and perplexed them. Civilized constructions did not belong in the Rainy Basin. Using their heads and feet, it took the angry tyrannosaurs only a few minutes to demolish the entire edifice.

This accomplished, they resumed tracking those who had raised the structure in defiance of all previous understandings and common sense. Advancing with long, patient strides, snouts dipping occasionally to the ground to reconfirm the presence of the scent trail, they tracked the departed. No matter how fast the humans moved, they could not outpace the adult tyrannosaurs.

But as the rain continued to fall, the trail grew progressively fainter. Frustration mounted. Instead of stepping over a tree that had fallen in their path, Shethorn grabbed it in her jaws and snapped it in two, slinging one section twenty feet into the woods as easily as a dog would toss a piece of chicken bone. Their fury was palpable, and those creatures who happened to be passing nearby gave the marauding giants an even wider berth than usual.

The tyrannosaurs would find these humans who had dared to enter their territory unannounced and without proper tribute, and who had somehow induced their only offspring into traveling with them. When that meeting occurred, there would be no silken translator talk of treaties and compacts. Words would be set aside and it would be tyrannosaur tradition that would be honored.

Many Confucians had settled in Dinotopia, and it was one of their number who had propounded this sound maxim: "When encountering a tyrannosaur in a bad mood, the wise man prefers strong legs to a facile voice."

XI

KEELK COULDN'T REMEMBER HOW MANY DAYS
she'd been on the move, alternately walking and running from the sound or smell of anything larger than herself, before she found the way up.

It was an ancient walkway, much overgrown with weeds, bushes, and flowers. It scaled the otherwise sheer cliff face in a series of dramatic switchbacks that were barely discernible from below. Who had hacked the path from the solid rock, when, and for what reason, she did not know. She knew only that it offered salvation in the form of a way out of the frightful Rainy Basin.

As she started forward she thought she could see signs of human handiwork. How wonderful it must be, she mused, to have an opposable thumb. So narrow and treacherous was the crumbling pathway that not even a small carnosaur could have made use of it.

But a *Struthiomimus* could, especially one as young, agile, and resolute as Keelk.

Drinking her fill from a pool of pure rainwater that had collected at the base of the cliff, she steeled herself and started up. As she did so, she looked longingly at the scattered fruit trees she was leaving behind. There was plenty to eat in the Rainy Basin, but gathering food took time and energy. Ignorance of her siblings' and parents' current condition drove her onward. Somehow she would have to derive nourishment from desperation.

Primitive and unmaintained, the path promised death to

the unwary. She was careful to spy out the condition of the surface before placing her weight on any section. This slowed her progress, but a long fall would slow her far more. In this fashion she ascended, until she was able to turn her neck and look out across much of the Rainy Basin, a vast sea of undulating green capped this morning by a thick froth of low clouds and mist. Resignedly, she returned her attention to the route ahead.

Once, she came to a place where the path had eroded away entirely, leaving a gap equal to several strides. A misstep would result in a fatal plunge of several hundred feet. Try as she might, she could see no way around.

Retracing her steps all the way back down to the Rainy Basin and beginning her search for a way out all over again was out of the question. She was too tired and had expended too much effort in coming this far. Backing up carefully, she settled herself on her haunches and gauged the distance. In the trials she had been accounted a good leaper, but this was not the long jump at the Junior Dinosaurian Olympics. If she missed here . . .

She thought of Hisaulk and Shremaza, always close by when she needed them, and of querulous Tryll and irritating but loyal Arimat. What obstacles were they being forced to confront? What dangers besides mad humans threatened them?

Exploding forward from her preparatory stance, she strained to increase her stride on the absurdly narrow runway formed by the path, keeping her head and body low. Planting her right foot on what must surely be the last solid bit of trail, she pushed off into the air. She dared not look down until she felt herself starting to descend.

Her landing was awkward but not injurious as she slammed hard into the rocky surface on the far side of the gap, having cleared the missing section by several feet. She stumbled once, sending gravel spinning off into space, and then steadied herself. Her heart was pounding like an agitated pteranodon's and her lower legs throbbed from absorbing the impact of her landing . . . but she was across!

She resumed climbing without looking back.

That was the worst place. There were no more gaps in the

trail, and the switchbacks began to grow wider as sheer cliff finally gave way to a more gradual slope. The ascent was still steep, but the slope below her no longer was precipitous. She estimated she had climbed nearly a thousand feet from the floor of the Rainy Basin.

Now a new conundrum presented itself. Having guided her clear of the basin, the ancient trail soon petered out, losing itself among scrub and grass in a dry creek bed. Higher up she could make out deciduous trees, mostly oaks and a few sycamores. Higher still she knew she was likely to encounter pines, firs, redwoods, and ginkgoes.

Following the dry tributary led her to a rushing stream from which she drank deeply and gratefully. From here on she was unlikely to lack for water. Food was another matter. She was painfully aware of the void in her belly. The cooler temperature helped.

Though her knowledge of stellar navigation was woefully deficient, she tried to guide herself as best she could by using the stars. In this fashion she pressed on in what she hoped was the general direction of Bent Root, pausing only to eat whatever looked edible while praying it would stay down. Though dry and tasteless, most of it did.

The Backbone Mountains were not accommodating, cliffs and gullies and impassable lakes forcing her farther to the west than she would have liked. She had no choice but to go on and hope to find a way that would allow her to double back. If she missed Bent Root entirely, she might easily wander around in the mountains until she dropped from exhaustion.

Remembering the bounty of fruit available for the picking down in the Rainy Basin, her stomach growled constantly, unsatisfied by her meager diet of tubers, roots, insects, and seed cones. Above the four-thousand-foot mark food became scarcer than ever, and she had to rely on eating insects more than she would have liked. They took time and energy to catch, and she had neither to spare.

Somehow she kept on, driven by the thought of what the odious humans might be doing to her family. She *would* find her way to Bent Root! She had to.

She wasn't sure how high she'd climbed, but it didn't

really matter. She was weakening rapidly now. Insects had become difficult to find at all, and the few nuts she was able to reach were harder to digest and more difficult to reach than the fruit she was accustomed to gathering on family or group outings. Foraging was an art in which she was not especially skilled.

Ever since she'd fled her captivity she'd been walking a fine line between pressing onward and stopping to find food. As she began to stagger instead of pace smoothly, a part of her was aware that she'd stepped dangerously far over that line. She was no longer walking normally, her long smooth strides having given way to short steps marred by a distinct wobble. Instead of carrying her head high, she allowed it to sway from side to side. As strength seeped out of her, so did any semblance of grace. Though she did not know it, she was in the last stages of physical exhaustion.

Topping a saddle between two peaks, she determined to follow the stream that flowed down the other side. That was when she saw the smoke.

Her first thought was that it was a natural fire, perhaps started by lightning. There was a lot of that high up in the Backbones. Blinking, she found she could separate the smoke into a dozen distinct plumes, each regular of shape and of similar density and color. Not a forest fire, then. The cook-fires of a settlement. Bent Root!

Heedlessly plunging downward, she fairly flew between the boles of the towering trees that clung to the northern slope of the mountain. Firs and sequoias swollen to astonishing proportions became blurs on either side as she lengthened her stride recklessly.

The creek that paralleled her flight might contain freshwater crawfish, or mussels, or tasty snails. She knew she should stop to eat, but with help so near at hand she raced onward. At this point she felt it would take almost as much energy to gather food as to run, and she had nothing left in reserve. She chose to run.

The stream leveled off and widened out to form a small mountain lake. Water fell in a shaft of silver over a rock precipice. Slowing, she was astonished to see spread out below her an entire community. It was not Bent Root, but it *was* known to her through story and traveler's tale if not from personal experience. Those unique arboreal dwellings, the special sauropod barns, the aerial walkways . . . she *knew* this place.

Everyone had heard of Treetown.

Humans bustled about in the treetops like bees in a hive, while on the ground more humans picked their way between or worked alongside dozens of dinosaurs. Dinosaurs of every shape and description, from genial duckbills to waddling ankylosaurs. Petite coelurosaurs darted swiftly through the crowds, often ducking beneath the bellies of their larger cousins to save time.

So vibrant with life and energy, with good feelings and doings, was the panorama that she was nearly overcome with relief. Opening her mouth, she found that she lacked the strength to shout. She was simply too tired. Not that she was likely to be heard at such a distance anyway, she told herself.

She really *had* wandered far to the west.

As she started down the steep but easily negotiated slope, she saw that the main north road was crowded with heavily laden dinosaurs and carts. Household goods bobbed on ankylosaurian backs, while big clay jars of milled rice jostled with amphoras of wine on the flanks of frilled ceratopsians.

The Northern Plains evacuation, she reminded herself as she staggered and stumbled down the slope. *It must be well under way.* It was the same evacuation her father had alluded to and that had precipitated the family's departure from the foothills of that same region.

Thinking of the evacuation, she did not look where she was going and so never saw the rock. It slid out from beneath her left foot. Too exhausted to regain her balance, she felt herself falling.

Maybe, she thought as she hit the ground, *I should have stopped and looked for some crawfish.*

This was silly. She was almost there, almost to Treetown. She would walk in and tell her story to the first person, human or dinosaur, that she saw. They would take her to the authorities, who would send a rescue party to free her family. All she had to do was attract someone's—anyone's—attention. Then she could relax. Why, the road was just ahead.

She half rose before collapsing, too spent even to exhale a final sigh. Her legs had never betrayed her before. She argued with them, but they refused to listen. Was this, she wondered, what her teachers called irony? Lying there unable to move, she felt she could hear the distant hootings and rumblings of other dinosaurs, the entertaining babble of humans. It made her feel sleepy, so sleepy. . . .

Everything made her feel sleepy now.

It was a very peculiar bird indeed that dropped down next to her motionless, recumbent form. Cocking its head to one side, it peered curiously at her face. Fluttering its bright red wings, it landed on her back and began to pace back and forth, using its clawed feet to maintain its perch. Occasionally it would open and close its beak, the tiny teeth within making a distinctive clicking sound.

Hopping down to the ground, it plucked gently but insistently at her forearm with its toothy jaws and the claws on each wing. When she still didn't respond, the *Archaeopteryx* spread brilliant wings, flashing streaks of iridescent gold amid the crimson. Hooting mournfully in a manner somewhat like a cross between an owl and a pigeon, it launched itself skyward, swooping low before accumulating enough air beneath its flashy but primitive wings to begin flapping. Still hooting, it soared off into the trees, leaving the unconscious struthie behind.

"DOES!" SHOUTED ONE OF THE BOYS.

"Does not!" insisted the girl next to him.

She had just turned seventeen, as had her three friends. Hiking south, they had left Treetown as much to get away from the noise and dust of the many arriving evacuees as to avoid being roped into work they thought none of their business.

Presently they were arguing as to whether or not a mutual good friend was too much under the thumb of his parents or simply doing the right thing. The young woman who'd just objected continued to do so energetically, because to admit that what their absent friend was doing was right would be to confess that what they were presently doing by avoiding their work responsibilities was wrong.

"They don't need us down there," her boyfriend claimed. "Look." He waved loosely in the direction of town. "We'd just be in the way. We don't have any experience at this sort of thing."

"But that's how you get experience," argued the other boy. "By doing. Don't you think so, Mei-tin?"

The girl next to him brushed dark hair out of her eyes. "I don't know, Ahmed. I think in all the confusion you might get stepped on, but at the same time I think we probably ought to be helping."

"Come on." The other girl made a face. "Have you ever heard of a dinosaur stepping on someone?"

"Well, there are stories—"

The first girl cut her off. "There are always 'stories.' You need facts, not stories. Have you forgotten your schooling along with your responsibilities?"

The shorter teen halted and wagged a warning finger at her friend. "Don't lecture me, Tina! You're here, too, don't forget."

"That's right," added her boyfriend. "Don't forget that . . . hey, there's Redwing! I wondered where she'd gone off to."

He extended his right arm and the *Archaeopteryx* glided to a landing, touching down on the leather patch sewn onto the shoulder of the boy's jersey. Instead of settling down as usual, the bird continued to flap its wings and hoot excitedly. Before its owner could reach up to calm it, Redwing rose again into the air and soared away southward. Landing on a branch, it continued to hoot and flap energetically.

"Now, what do you suppose that's all about?" Her owner's expression reflected the puzzlement he felt at her unusual behavior.

"Mating display?" quipped the other boy.

The bird's owner sniffed. "Very funny. Look at her, jumping up and down. What's wrong with her?"

"Can't you tell?" Mei-tin had already started forward.

"She wants us to follow her. Just like in the stories."

"More stories." The owner shook his head wryly. "You read too many stories, Mei. Nothing ever happens in Dinotopia, and especially here in Treetown. It's a dull, boring country hamlet. Nothing like Sauropolis." His eyes glittered. "Now, *there*'s a town!"

Once more the *Archaeopteryx* rose, flew southward a few yards, and landed on another branch, whereupon the active sound and sight display was promptly repeated.

"You have anything better to do?" asked the other boy pointedly.

Josiah considered. "No, I suppose not. I'm willing to see what Redwing has on her mind, if anything. Especially so long as it leads *away* from town." He followed in Mei-tin's wake.

She looked back. "Aren't you coming, Tina?"

Her friend glanced townward. "I think we really should be helping with the evacuees' unpacking. It's a long, hard walk from the far reaches of the Northern Plains, and they can use all the help they can get." She hesitated. "But if you're all going . . ." She gave in and hurried to catch up to her friends.

"This is stupid." Ahmed pushed a branch aside. "Tina's right. We should go back and help. I'm feeling guilty enough as it is."

"Don't let it bother you." The bird trainer ducked the same branch. "I agree that this is dumb, but doing work that hasn't been specifically assigned to you is dumber still. I don't think that—"

"Look over there," exclaimed Mei-tin sharply. "Isn't that somebody on the ground?"

"It's a struthie." Tina was staring. "She's not moving."

"I can see that," responded her boyfriend impatiently. In a softer tone he added, "She looks like she's in a bad way."

The four teens crowded around the recumbent form. "Do you think she's dead?" Ahmed murmured. No bravado now; only genuine concern.

Ignoring his hooting, hopping pet, the bird trainer bent down and put an ear to the struthie's chest. His friends went silent. After a moment he sat up and favored them with a relieved smile.

"No, she's alive, but her breathing's very shallow. She needs real medical attention."

"I'll go." No one tried to argue with Mei-tin, knowing her to be far and away the best mountain runner among them.

"We'll all go." Ahmed started to turn, but Tina intercepted him.

"No. One's enough. Let Mei-tin go. The rest of us should stay here and try to do what we can." She nodded down at the limp form. "What if she wakes up and wanders off a cliff or into the lake, or just asks for a drink of water?"

Ahmed nodded slowly. "All right."

"I've got an idea." The bird trainer was eyeing a nearby grove of young birch trees speculatively. "You all recall your woodlands training?"

"Woodlands training?" Mei-tin stared at him. "I didn't think you'd remember any of that, Josiah. After all, that kind of dumb information's only useful to people who live in small country towns."

"I'm sorry," he apologized. "Just when you think your life's impossibly dull, something like this happens." He gestured at Keelk, who had not moved since their arrival and gave no indication that she was in any way aware of their presence. "This female needs help, and she needs it right away. Ahmed, have you got your knife?"

The other teen patted the large blade sheathed at his hip. "I don't know what you're thinking, Josiah, but I can tell you that I don't know anything about woodland surgery."

"No, but I'll bet you can cut down some of these saplings. We'll make a travois."

"A what?" Mei-tin inquired.

"You'll see. Here, let's give Ahmed a hand. We'll need some vines or bark strips to tie the saplings with."

With all four of them contributing, the work went faster than anyone dared hope. Certainly faster than Mei-tin could have run back to town and returned with help. "You think it'll hold her?" Tina gazed uncertainly at the triangular apparatus that now lay on the ground before them.

"If I didn't, I wouldn't have spent the time on it." Josiah

had his own knife out and along with Mei-tin was testing the last of the knots. "I'm more worried about being able to pull her all the way back."

"We'll do it." Rising and stepping back, Ahmed wiped perspiration from his face. "It'll work so long as she doesn't wake up, panic, and hurt herself."

The crude travois looked sturdy enough, but the only way to be sure was to put it to use. Carefully they dragged the struthie's body toward the stretcherlike contraption.

"All together, now," Josiah urged his friends. He and Ahmed each gripped one of the leathery legs while the girls took the unconscious dinosaur by her forearms. "On three. One, two, three . . . heave!"

They half lifted, half rolled Keelk's body onto the travois. The weave of saplings, bark, and vines sank in the center but held. With a boy and girl on each of the two lead poles, they easily raised the front section of the conveyance off the ground.

"All right, everybody. Let's pull!"

Straining at the poles, the four youngsters began dragging the limp *Struthiomimus* toward Treetown. They were helped by the fact that it was mostly downhill, though a single small rise nearly defeated them.

"Once we get over this hill we'll be all right." The straining Ahmed was perspiring heavily. "It's all downhill into town the rest of the way."

It was at that moment that a two-wheeled cart hove into view, rumbling down a side path. Each of the wheels was twice the height of a tall man. The *Triceratops* doing the pulling halted without being bidden and mumbled at the four teens. So did the young farmer ensconced high above in the driver's seat. Two young children peeked out curiously from behind him.

"Hoy, what have here?" The farmer pushed back on the brim of his hat.

Grateful for the momentary respite, the teens paused. "She's sick or something." Mei-tin gestured at their motionless burden. "She needs help right away. We're trying to get her into town."

"Enough said. Come on, then, Friere."

The man's wife appeared behind him. Descending from the bench atop the front of the cart, they quickly disengaged the vehicle from its harness. As the *Triceratops* backed carefully, the teens' hastily fashioned travois was hitched to the big ceratopsian.

Leaving her husband behind to attend to their worldly goods and the two children, the young wife settled herself into the saddle located behind the *Triceratops*'s frill. Josiah and his friends climbed up behind and hung on as best they could. Giving its passengers a warning rumble, the *Triceratops* took off at a fast trot, clearing in moments the hill that had nearly defeated the four youngsters. They hung on tightly. Like any ceratopsian, a *Triceratops* can make a good bit of speed over a short distance.

Humans and dinosaurs alike turned to stare as the unlikely arrivals hauled into town, dust settling in their wake. They were quickly directed to the sequoia in which resided one learned and respected Dr. Kano Toranaga.

In the next tree over, Will Denison was discussing wind shear and air flow with two friends, debating the best way to handle a skybax under such difficult conditions. Should one try to give directions or simply hang on and allow the *Quetzalcoatlus* its head, offering encouragement only where necessary?

"Wonder what's happening down there?" The young man nearest the railing had noticed the arrival of the *Triceratops* and its peculiar cargo.

Will turned to look. "Don't know. Looks like they're bringing in an injured struthie." Humans and other dinosaurs were swarming around the clumsy rig at the rear of the *Triceratops*.

As they watched, the struthie was gently placed in a hammock-basket. A young apatosaur, still in training, was given a command by its human companion (also in training). The juvenile sauropod promptly started off in the opposite direction, smoothly winching the basket upward toward the waiting branches by means of harness and straps. As it ascended, the basket rotated slowly. Will's gaze rose with it, following its progress curiously. Its single occupant had not moved.

Upon reaching the prescribed level, signals were exchanged and the basket halted its ascent. Waiting hands drew it sideways, and its immobile passenger was removed.

"She looks awfully thin," observed Moon, the third sky-bax rider.

"There's plenty of food around," declared their companion. "She's not dead or they wouldn't be taking her to the doctor."

Will glanced at her. "Doctor?"

"Kano Toranaga has his office in that tree. I've heard he's the most respected physician this side of Sauropolis. He's a vet, which means he's qualified to treat humans as well as dinosaurs."

"It's probably nothing." Moon turned away from the ground. "The struthie probably fell and hit her head or something."

"I don't know." Will tried to see what was happening. "Everyone seemed awfully anxious for it to be just a bump on the head." He came to a sudden decision. "I'm going to go see."

"Go see?" Ethera blinked at him. "But why? You can't do anything."

"Not true." Will had already started for the exit. "I can learn."

"You're supposed to be learning about the wind currents above the Backbone Mountains." She pouted accusingly. She was certainly fond of him, Will knew, and she was undeniably attractive, but his heart belonged to another.

"I know. Don't worry, I'll be back."

Exiting the dormitory, he turned left down a branch walkway, crossed a ladder to a higher offshoot, and stepped out onto a sling rope bridge. A hundred feet above the ground, he hustled across without even looking down. The drop was nothing to a skybax rider accustomed to executing barrel rolls at two thousand feet.

In the tree he'd left, his companions had resumed the conversation without him. It was just like a dolphinback, Moon declaimed, to see intrigue in everyday activities. Though the Denisons had lived six years in Dinotopia, young Will still found the commonplace fascinating. And while they were on the subject, why didn't Ethera find him, Moon, as interesting as she did Will?

Will eventually came to Dr. Toranaga's tree by a roundabout route through the branches. After identifying himself, he was passed on through to the infirmary with an admonition to keep quiet. Dr. Toranaga had no objection to eager youngsters observing his procedures. Indeed, he welcomed their attention, as long as they kept their often overactive mouths shut.

At present the infirmary contained three recuperating patients, all human. Most cases of dinosaurian illness were, out of necessity and concession to size, treated on the ground. Much easier to bring the staff to the side of an ill *Diplodocus* than vice versa. A seventy-ton sauropod would more than strain the infirmary's facilities.

But the smaller dinosaurs could be treated alongside sick humans, and at Toranaga's request the unconscious *Struthiomimus* had been raised to that level.

An attentive nurse intercepted Will, her white sari swirling about her. A small cabochon ruby flashed in the center of her forehead and plain gold earrings dangled freely.

"Can I help you?"

Will tried to see past her. "I'm an apprentice skybax rider from Waterfall City. I was told I could watch."

The nurse glanced over her shoulder. "The doctor's current patient is a young struthie."

"I know. I saw her brought in. How is she doing?"

"She's extremely weak and still unconscious." As if to deliberately contradict this diagnosis, an excited, high-pitched babbling issued from the rear of the infirmary. Will instantly recognized the fear-laden squeals of a terrified struthie. Just audible above the squealing were the impatient shouts of a man yelling for assistance.

"I have to go," explained the nurse hastily. Pivoting, she raced away from him.

"Hey, wait! Maybe I can help!"

He hesitated. The worst they could do was chase him away. Besides, if they had a delirious dinosaur on their hands, even a juvenile struthie, another set of muscles would be welcomed. If the patient was suffering from threatening hallucinations, it might react out of ancient instinct instead of modern good sense. For a struthie, that meant running. Not a good idea when one was lying abed one hundred twenty feet up in the branches of a giant sequoia.

Hurrying after the nurse, Will slowed as he approached the circular nestlike bed. The struthie was lying in the middle, kicking violently and fighting to rise. A small bespectacled man with close-cropped black hair and diminutive features was struggling to hold her down. Two nurses, one large and male, the other the woman who had confronted Will, were doing their best to help.

No one objected when Will silently lent his assistance. He did his best to follow Toranaga's orders. For a supposedly incapacitated individual, the young struthie was still plenty strong, especially in the legs. As she kicked and twisted, she babbled in the high-pitched tongue of her kind. While struggling to subdue her, Will managed to catch a word or two, but not enough to make any sense of her uncontrolled squealing.

Eventually the doctor and his aides managed to wrap the frantic youngster in a damp sheet heavily scented with herbs. This seemed to have a calming effect. The kicking ceased entirely and she slumped back into the center of the round bed. Her mumbling gradually died down but did not cease entirely.

"I'll want a number four potion, please, with extra *vivar* root." Kano Toranaga spoke without looking at his nurses. His attention was focused entirely on his patient. "And I will want to talk to those youngsters who found her and brought her in."

"Yes, Doctor." The male nurse scribbled something on a pad.

A moment later Will found himself gazing back into small, dark eyes that reminded him very much of Levka Gambo's. "And who, please, is this helpful if slightly heavy-handed young man?"

The female nurse eyed the opportune visitor uncertainly. "I don't know, Doctor. He says he's an apprentice skybax rider from Waterfall City and that he wanted to observe."

"So. What did you observe, young man?"

Will couched his reply carefully. "That even a seemingly helpless patient can be dangerous and needs careful attention."

For an instant there was no reaction. Then the doctor smiled in amusement. "Not so bad. Who are you, then?"

Will straightened. "Will Denison, sir."

Toranaga's eyes twinkled. "Ah, yes, the son of the esteemed Arthur. I have heard of him. Though not of you."

Will slumped visibly.

Chuckling softly to himself, the doctor came around the bed to greet him. "The impatience of youth to do great things. How well I remember. Well, skybax apprentice, tell me: what do you think we have here?" He gestured at the bed.

"A very sick young struthie, sir."

Toranaga nodded. "Observant, if not analytical. That will come with time. She is sick indeed but should recover rapidly with proper food and modest medicating. There seems to be nothing desperately wrong with her. No broken bones, no internal injuries. She is simply very run-down. At the moment she is quite out of her head. Her condition will have to be closely monitored for several days, at least." An afterthought caused him to regard his visitor afresh. "You may stay and learn, young man."

"Thank you, sir." A grateful Will returned his attention to the softly moaning *Struthiomimus*. "Is it known what happened to her?"

"I do not believe so. She was found by some youngsters who were out hiking."

Will didn't try to hide his surprise. "She was alone? Where is her family?"

"That is one of the things we are trying to find out. As I speak no Struthine and I doubt she talks Human, I have already sent for a translator."

"I think I understood a little of what she was saying, sir. A very little."

The doctor's eyebrows rose slightly. "You? Human-dinosaur translation is an unusual hobby for a skybax rider. I thought you only needed to know the commands for your mount. Very few humans can manage any of the dinosaurian dialects.''

Will smiled shyly. ''It's a hobby of mine, sir. And as a skybax rider, I get around and overhear more than most people. I've made it my business to try and learn a few words of each tribe's tongue.''

Toranaga nodded approvingly. ''And what have you managed to learn from our distressed young patient here?''

''Not much, really. But I do recognize some of her utterances as names. Struthie names are quite distinctive. She keeps repeating these over and over.''

''That makes sense. In her discomfort she would naturally call out first for her family. How many names?''

''Both parents. I can tell from the honorific glottal stops. One, maybe two siblings.'' He shrugged helplessly. ''That's all I could make out. She's not speaking very clearly.''

''To say the least,'' Toranaga agreed. ''While I applaud your linguistic efforts, young Denison, it is apparent we still require the assistance of a professional translator.''

''I quite agree, sir.''

''Meanwhile, we'll see if we can't get some real food into her. Room-temperature soups and broths, for a start. We will try to revive her gradually. Until then not even a translator will be able to get much out of her.''

The nurse in the sari looked across the bed at him. ''Do you think the authorities should be notified, Doctor?''

Toranaga considered. ''Not now. We do not have any idea as yet as to the cause of her condition. Though appalling, it may have a quite natural explanation. Also, all the relevant authorities are working overtime to help with the evacuation from the Northern Plains. There is much still to be organized.'' He glanced outside, scanning the cloud-splotched sky. ''If the storm is a bad one they will have much more to do than worry about one sick *Struthiomimus*. Let us see if we can deal with this matter ourselves before we go bawling for help.''

''Yes, sir.'' The woman bowed contritely.

''And as for you, young man.'' Will stiffened self-consciously. ''Since you have volunteered your assistance in this case, perhaps I can impose on you to remain with us until a translator does arrive. If you know three words of Struthine, that is three words more than myself or my assistants. Your help is valued.''

"Of course I will stay, sir.'' This was much more interesting than analyzing wind currents.

He gazed curiously down at the softly moaning struthie. What had happened to her out there in the mountains? Where was her family? How had she been reduced to such a dire condition?

And perhaps most importantly of all, what had left her so badly frightened?

≫ XII ≪

I T TOOK SOME TIME TO FIND A TRANSLATOR. THOUGH the farmers of the Northern Plains had long ago learned to communicate with their dinosaur helpmates by means of commands and gestures, there was still plenty of need for translators to help with the more complex elements of the massive evacuation. Long hours passed before Dr. Toranaga's call for linguistic assistance was answered.

Will was deep in the throes of a nap when a horn blast sounded from below. Rising from his hammock, he walked to the nearest wall and peered over the side. Down on the ground he saw Skowen, the male nurse, conversing with several other humans as well as a male *Protoceratops*. The latter made the best translators, being able to speak nearly all of the dinosaurian dialects as well as fluent Human. They had a feel for language, and many of them entered enthusiastically into the highly respected profession. Will had once listened to a biologist lecture on the unique positioning of the larynx in the protoceratopsian throat.

Will noted that the hog-sized male wasn't very big, even for one of his modestly proportioned tribe. It was difficult to tell from a distance, but to Will he appeared even smaller than Will's old friend Bix. His opinion didn't change as he watched the yellowish, rust-tinged quadruped step into the empty basket-elevator. The sauropod on lift duty promptly lurched forward, away from the trunk of the sequoia, and the newly arrived translator began a slow ascent toward the infirmary.

Will looked on as the *Protoceratops* was greeted by the nurse in the sari. It trundled along in her wake as she led it toward Dr. Toranaga's office. His early estimates of its size proved correct. Standing on hind legs, its beak would barely have come up to Will's nose.

In the company of Hapini, the nurse, it ambled into the infirmary proper, surveying its surroundings with a curious glance. To Will's considerable surprise, it fixed its eyes on him and barked sharply in his direction. Its Human was fluid and easily understood.

"I know you."

Will studied the simple, frill-backed face; the bright, intelligent eyes; and the beaked, parrotlike mouth. There was a notch missing from the upper right side of the frill—a consequence, perhaps, of some excessive juvenile frolic.

"I'm sorry, but I don't remember ever having met you," Will replied honestly.

"Didn't say we'd met." The *Protoceratops*'s manner was somewhat brusque. "Said I knew you."

Will stiffened slightly in response to the unexpected tartness of the other's tone. "Then you have the advantage of me." He was not intimidated. Judging from its size and inflection, the translator was no older than himself. A linguistic sage like Bix the new arrival was not.

It wasn't the most auspicious of first encounters.

"You're Will Denison, aren't you?" chirped the *Protoceratops*. He spoke as he ambled over to examine the sleeping struthie.

"That's right." Will trailed translator and nurse.

"I've heard of you. You're well-known to the protoceratopsian tribe."

"Really?" Will beamed.

"Yes." Putting his forefeet up on the side of the nest-bed, the young translator studied the softly breathing patient. "You're the one whose father nearly broke the leg of the famous translator Bix with a rock."

Will bristled. "That was an accident! We'd just been shipwrecked, we didn't know where we'd fetched up or what was likely to happen to us, and we knew nothing of the inhabitants of Dinotopia or how special they were. To my father, Bix looked like a potentially dangerous animal. He had only his own personal experiences to go on."

"That's no excuse," snapped the *Protoceratops*. "By the way, my name is Chaz."

"I'm gratified to make your acquaintance," Will replied dryly, employing a more formal greeting than he'd planned. "You shouldn't judge how others react in a difficult situation unless you've been in one yourself."

"I hope not to be." The *Protoceratops* still refused to look in his direction. Or perhaps, Will thought, it was simply deciding how best to open communications with the recovering *Struthiomimus*.

"Anyway, I didn't throw any rocks."

"You could have. Bet you would have if your father hadn't done so first."

"Now, look here—" Will began. His ready retort was interrupted by the arrival of Dr. Toranaga.

"I would prefer that you youngsters work out any personal problems later, please. At the moment we should concern ourselves with the status and well-being of the patient."

"How is she doing, sir?" Will was thankful for the doctor's arrival.

"A great deal better, I am happy to say. Her strength is returning rapidly. Good food and plenty of rest is often the best medicine." He eyed the round bed thoughtfully. "She has been asleep for some time. I think we would not be remiss in awakening her."

Leaning forward over the bed, he began to stroke the struthie's face, bringing his palm down from the forehead, between the eyes, and ending with a caress of the graceful snout. Following the third such stroke, the patient blinked, let out a startled whoop, and straightened her neck, her head swiveling to look in all directions.

As the doctor stepped back, the translator moved to the head of the bed.

"Let her get her bearings first," Will suggested.

The little dinosaur finally looked over at him. "Are you trying to tell me how to do my job?"

"No, of course not. I'm just concerned for her comfort." Will was by now thoroughly irritated with this patronizing

Protoceratops. He was almost as arrogant as . . . as . . .

As a certain strutting skybax rider? Nonsense, Will told himself. He wasn't arrogant. Merely confident. Who was it who had told him that the line between the two was a thin one?

No matter. He was caught up in the reaction of the struthie. As her initial panic subsided, her gaze became open and comprehending. There was none of the delirium that had characterized her previous wild ramblings.

"I am Kano Toranaga," the doctor gently informed her. "I have been seeing to your care these past several days." As Chaz translated, the young patient relaxed enough to reply. The *Protoceratops* listened briefly.

"She wants to know where she is."

"Well, tell her, tell her," Toranaga urged him.

Chaz nodded briefly and explained to the patient that she was in Treetown infirmary and under medical care. This prompted a rapid-fire and extended response. She rambled on until Toranaga and Chaz finally succeeded in calming her.

Will could barely contain his curiosity. "Well? What's she *saying*?"

Chaz favored him with a silent glare before addressing himself to the doctor. "She says she was trying to get to Bent Root but couldn't find her way and ended up here. She's happy enough to be in Treetown, though. In fact, she's glad to be anywhere. She doesn't remember arriving and does not recall how she came to be in this place."

"That can be explained to her later." Toranaga was gazing reassuringly at his anxious young patient. "I need to know what happened to her. What is a young *Struthiomimus* doing alone and debilitated out in the mountains? Did she become separated from her friends and family, or has some misfortune befallen them?"

Chaz acknowledged the series of queries and put them to the struthie. This time she responded more slowly. "Come on, come on," Will urged him impatiently.

"Do not interrupt my train of thought. Struthine is not an easy tongue." This was said, for a change, without any hint of rancor. Will forced himself to wait as silently as the nurse and doctor.

Only when the patient was finished did Chaz lower his forelegs from the edge of the bed and turn to his expectant audience.

"It's a very strange story she tells."

"Sure you got all the details right?" Will pressed him.

Few dinosaurs possess the flexibility of face required to produce varied expressions, but the translator managed to summon up a withering stare without much difficulty.

"Yes, I'm sure." In a less frosty tone he continued. "Her name is Keelk. She says that her family was captured and made prisoners by a group of strange humans."

Toranaga frowned. "Captured? Prisoners? All part of some game, surely."

"No." The frilled head swung back and forth. "It's not a game. They were bound and hobbled so they couldn't run away, and pulled along by ropes." The translator glanced back in the struthie's direction. "She thinks, or at least her parents think, that these strange humans are all new arrivals to Dinotopia, but that they're not dolphinbacks. Nor have they been shipwrecked in the manner of the Denisons." He didn't look at Will.

"She says," he continued, "that the clothing, equipment, and attitudes of these humans are intact and undamaged, which suggests that they somehow made a safe and successful landing on our shores."

The nurse couldn't keep herself from commenting. "That is impossible."

"So I've always been taught. I am only relaying what she has said. She also says that they carry explosive tubes which shoot invisible fireworks."

"Guns!" Will blurted.

Toranaga eyed him solemnly. "I have read about such devices." He turned back to the translator. "Is there more?"

"Yes. She says that these humans wear peculiar garb, that they smell strongly of the sea, and that they are all males."

"Normal enough for a ship's crew," Will murmured to no one in particular.

"She says that among them are represented many of the human subtribes, and that they talk and act as if they own everything they touch. They are, of course, completely ignorant of Dinotopia and its ways. They treated her and her family like ignorant animals and made no effort to try and understand their speech.''

''They couldn't anyway,'' Toranaga observed. ''What about gestures? All humans understand simple gestures.''

Chaz conveyed this to the struthie, who replied without hesitation. ''She says that she and her family were tied up as soon as they were captured. You can't make gestures with all your limbs bound. Her father, Hisaulk, can recognize a few words of Human. One word these intruders kept repeating over and over was 'gold.' '' The *Protoceratops* let out a derisive snort. ''Why would they be obsessed with gold? Can they be preparing for some sort of festival?''

Will had been compiling a list in his head and didn't much care for the picture it added up to. All males, guns, acted as if they owned the place, spoke frequently of gold, the taking of prisoners . . .

''Excuse me, but I think I may know the source of these strangers' intentions and the reason behind their unfriendly actions.''

''Please,'' murmured Toranaga expectantly, ''enlighten us.''

''I'm just guessing, of course.'' Will hastened to qualify his thesis before delivering it. ''But it sounds to me like Keelk's family has been captured by a group of roving adventurers or brigands or pirates.''

''Pirates? What are 'pirates'?'' Toranaga turned to his nurse. ''Hapini, have you ever heard of such?''

''No, Doctor.''

Both of them had been born and raised on Dinotopia, Will knew. Unlike him, they had little knowledge of the outside world. Nor were they historians. He tried to explain.

''These people are bandits, thieves.'' Even thievery was a concept he was forced to elaborate on. He mentioned the recent antisocial exploits of Lee Crabb, but they had not even heard of the recent activities of Dinotopia's resident rapscallion. Dinotopia was a big place. Still, he eventually managed to get his point across.

''Extraordinary.'' Toranaga was clearly taken with his young guest's explanation. ''Almost as extraordinary as the notion that a vessel may have landed here intact.''

"Without talking to these people we have no way of knowing anything for certain.'' Will continued. ''If they have managed to anchor here successfully, then they may believe they can also leave with whatever they can acquire. If they think *that*, there's no telling what they might do.''

Toranaga was shaking his head in disbelief. ''I still don't understand why they would imprison a family of harmless struthies.''

"Neither do I, sir.'' Will forbore mentioning that ships' crews embarked on long voyages often kept live animals aboard as a source of fresh food. ''But it's not important. What matters is that they're being held against their will.''

"Yes. The situation is quite unprecedented.'' The doctor considered. ''Sauropolis must be notified immediately.''

"Sauropolis!'' Will exclaimed. ''That's a long way from here, sir.''

"Not so far for a qualified skybax rider,'' Chaz commented coolly.

"There are plenty of skybax riders in Treetown,'' Will shot back, ''because of the evacuation. I don't have to be the one to go.'' He looked at Toranaga. ''I agree that the council needs to be made aware of the situation, sir, but that will take time. Just as it will take time for them to formulate a reply and respond. In the meantime, if my supposition is correct, this struthie's family is in grave danger. We have to do something *now*.''

"We?'' Chaz had no eyebrows to raise but managed to convey the expression nonetheless.

"We will call a meeting of the local elders and those town officials who can be spared from the evacuation work,'' Toranaga decided. ''This is obviously a matter of some importance, but at the same time the welfare of many families cannot be imperiled so that one can be aided.''

"I'm sure she will understand.'' Chaz nodded at the struthie, who was watching them uncomprehendingly.

But Will, staring into that anxious, hopeful, drawn face, wasn't so sure.

➤➤ XIII ◄◄

THE ASSEMBLY WAS HELD IN ONE OF THE GREAT barns that was used to shelter the local sauropods and ceratopsians from the depredations of the carnosaurs that on rare occasions succeeded in finding their way up and out of the Rainy Basin. Dr. Toranaga was in attendance, along with a number of local officials and academicians. Only a small percentage of those present were human.

It was something to watch them discuss and debate, as for example when a maiasaurian face was thrust inches from a human one. There was no anger involved; only enthusiasm and interest. But recommendations did differ, and it took time for individual expressions of opinion to be translated into multiple tongues.

This last task was handled by translators senior to Chaz, leaving the youngster to stand off to one side with nothing to do but observe, learn, and fidget. Will was present as well. Being the subject of much of the discussion, Keelk figured prominently in numerous gestures and contemplative glances. Now almost fully recovered, she listened to the discussion, watched the debate, and chatted exuberantly with Chaz.

"What is she saying?" Will asked the *Protoceratops*.

"That there's too much talk and too little action." The young translator tilted his frilled head sideways, the better to observe the much taller *Struthiomimus*. "I can't say as that I've ever encountered a more forceful representative of her particular kind.

"She's grateful for the help that's being proposed but is afraid it may arrive too late. Until it materializes, she wants to return to the Rainy Basin to do what she can to help her family. To the Rainy Basin! By herself! Can you imagine it?"

Will tried to picture his father as an ill-treated captive of marauding pirates. Or worse yet, Sylvia. Yes, he could understand the struthie's motivation.

Looking at Keelk, he whistled softly, modulating the sound with care and concluding with a descending series of clicks. She glanced over sharply and responded with a sequence of sounds he could barely make sense of, smiling with her eyes as she vocalized. He did manage to infer the impression that she was grateful for his concern.

"Her family's in imminent danger, and here we've got the usual old bunch of apatosaurs and styracosaurs and duckbills and humans bickering over what to do. Time is of the essence."

"Did you determine that for yourself," inquired Chaz sarcastically, "or are you parroting the opinions of your father?"

"I'm probably mimicking my father." Will was proud to be Arthur Denison's son and was not in the least upset by the comparison.

One of the senior duckbills, a wrinkled corythosaur, was speaking. "If these intruders do indeed have weapons, and contemporary weapons from the outside world at that, we don't know what havoc they might be capable of wreaking."

"Yes," agreed a solemn pachycephalosaur. "Though I sympathize with the plight of this young *Struthiomimus*'s family, we must proceed with caution lest many others be injured."

"I have been checking with our local historians, and we have no choice but to move carefully." The respected Norah, matriarch of Treetown, looked tiny, flanked as she was by the maiasaur on one side and the apatosaur on the other. "These intruders might even have with them something called a 'cannon.' "

"A 'cannon'?" queried another of the humans present. "I

confess I am not much of a historian. What sort of device might that be?''

And so the conversation went, digressing into interesting but time-consuming sidelights that were certainly relevant to the matter at hand but which did nothing to accelerate the dialogue or resolve Keelk's concern.

''They'll come to a decision and move,'' Will remarked from the shadows, ''eventually.'' The young struthie chirped at him. He caught only a word or two, but Chaz translated automatically.

''She says that something must be done right away. She can't wait and she's going to go back and do what she can.''

''She can't do anything by herself.'' Will found himself staring into the struthie's wide, limpid eyes, wishing he possessed even a small portion of Chaz's skill at translation.

''She doesn't care.'' The *Protoceratops* shuffled his forefeet. ''She says that no matter what happens, at least she'll be with her family. She feels that she's discharged her obligation to her parents by coming here and reporting the situation, and that now she's free to act as she pleases. Even if it seems foolish to us.''

''She's very brave,'' Will observed.

''You mean very stupid.''

Will found himself nodding at nothing in particular. ''She won't be alone.''

''That's exactly what I was . . .'' The translator hesitated, uncertain he'd heard correctly. ''What do you mean?''

Will whistled and clicked softly at the struthie. Showing that she understood, she extended a forearm and rested clawed fingers on his shoulder, stroking it three times. There was no misunderstanding the gesture, and he responded with a smile.

''I'm going with her.''

''You?'' The *Protoceratops*'s gaze swung nervously from the human and dinosaurian faces of his young acquaintances to the actively debating circle of elders. ''Shouldn't you wait for a formal rescue expedition to be proposed?''

''Like she said, she can't wait,'' Will replied.

''But what can the two of you do against a whole party of armed adult human males?''

"Keep an eye on them, for one thing. Track them. Lead others to them." Will grinned. "Who knows what else we might accomplish? My father says that the man who doesn't make his own opportunities usually doesn't find any."

"You humans and your goofy affinity for aphorisms," the translator muttered. "I don't see how they will do you any good against these gun-weapons."

"We're wasting time." Putting an arm around Keelk's shoulders, Will led her toward the exit.

Chaz watched them go. Then, with a last backward glance in the direction of the noisy assembly, he clip-clopped hurriedly after them.

"Wait, wait a moment! Wait for me, you inconsiderate long-legs!"

Will and Keelk stopped to allow the translator to catch up. It was a good thing the tribe of protoceratopsians was so eloquent, Will mused, because they weren't very big or very strong or unusually smart.

"Listen to them talk. They'll go on like that all night," Will commented as they exited the barn.

"Out of consensus comes wisdom," Chaz retorted.

Will smiled down at him. "Now who's resorting to aphorisms?"

"I was simply making an observation." By way of changing the subject, the *Protoceratops* examined the night sky. "What will we do if we're caught in the Rainy Basin when the big storm hits?"

"I don't know." Will likewise inclined his gaze toward the still-visible stars. "Float, I hope."

Chaz looked up at him. "That's not funny. I don't know how to swim, and my kind can't climb trees."

"You take care of the translating and I'll handle the swimming," Will assured him breezily. This was going to be a real adventure! It was going to be fun.

Provided no one got shot, he reminded himself somberly.

"You can stay here, Chaz. I won't think the less of you for it. In fact, it's the sensible thing to do. You can tell the elders where we've gone and what we're doing."

"What do you mean, stay here?" The *Protoceratops*

puffed himself up. "And who cares what you think, any-way?"

"You're still coming with us?"

"Don't think it's because I really want to. It's just that I'm tired of hearing about the accomplishments and insight of the wondrous Will Denison, and I want to be there when you fall flat on your face."

"Why, Chaz, I thought jealousy was generally considered to be a human failing, one from which dinosaurs were im mune."

"Jealousy? I'm not jealous of you. Besides, you need me. Not to talk to these peculiar humans, should we have the opportunity to do so. I'm sure you can manage to converse with representatives of your own kind, no matter how per-verse their habits."

Will considered. "If many nations—or tribes, as Keelk refers to them—are represented, then I should be able to converse with at least a few of them."

"Precisely. But you need me to translate for her." He nodded in Keelk's direction. "Also for her family. So long as everyone understands everyone else, we may, I hope, be able to minimize the foolishness that already marks this ex-pedition. Struthies are notoriously impulsive."

"We'll be glad of your company." Will spoke warmly. "With only three of us, we should be able to move fast."

"Yes," agreed Chaz as they turned toward the nighttime bustle of Treetown. He lifted first one stubby foreleg and then the other. "But not *too* fast."

They had no difficulty acquiring packs and supplies. In the confusion of the evacuation there was little time for ques-tions. Plenty of food was available: dried fruit and nuts for Keelk; yams, potatoes, and other vegetables for Chaz; dried fish and fruits for Will. If necessary, they were confident, they could survive off the land. After all, Keelk had man-aged, and their trek would be easier since the worst of it was nearly all downhill. But everyone felt better departing with full backpacks.

She spoke confidently of being able to find the old switch-back path that had led her out of the rain forest and up into the mountains. They would have to find it, Will knew, for neither he nor Chaz was familiar with the trails that led in and out of the Rainy Basin, much less one that was so clearly off the usual trade routes. To this day there were many parts of the Rainy Basin that had never been visited except by the uncivilized carnosaurs who lived there.

Located in the crown of a neatly trimmed giant sequoia, the skybax roost was largely deserted when Will arrived. The sun was not yet up and it was too early for most riders to be stirring. While Keelk and Chaz waited restively below, Will climbed up to bid good-bye to Cirrus. They could not understand each other's language, but familiarity and intimacy allowed rider and skybax to comprehend the other's mouth noises and gestures.

"I'll be back soon," Will assured the giant *Quetzalcoatlus*. "You'll be all right without me. Rest your wings, and when I return we'll fly high again." He knew that the roost's human attendants would automatically see to it that any skybax in their care received proper food and attention. Still, it was like leaving a member of the family when he at last started down. Not entirely understanding, Cirrus whistled mournfully after him, then folded himself back in his fifteen-foot wings and went back to sleep.

No one challenged them as they hurried out of town, losing themselves in the confusion of preoccupied refugee workers and newly arrived evacuees. Only Kano Toranaga might have wondered at their intentions, and he was busy at his infirmary, tending to patients.

Hiking out of Treetown, they passed a convoy of apatosaurs and ceratopsians, heavily laden with supplies intended to assist the evacuees from the Northern Plains. No one paid them the least mind. A pair of farm families greeted them cheerily; others called out, their dinosaurs hooting or whistling. The hikers waved back. Turning south, they ascended the hill nicked by the waterfall that had marked where Keelk was found and started up the first slope. In the distance lay alpine ridges, and beyond, the Rainy Basin.

"This is absurd." Chaz was grumbling under his breath as he trundled along, twin saddlebags slung across his back. "We should have waited to join the formal rescue expedition."

"You could have." Will's pack felt light on his shoulders, and he strode along briskly. The air above Treetown was crisp and bracing where the cool atmosphere of the mountains mixed with oxygen-rich fog rising from the basin.

Just as Keelk had warned them, there were few conspicuous landmarks. It was fortunate, Will mused, that struthies had an excellent sense of direction. Dazed though she'd been, Keelk led the way with assurance. It helped that she'd kept to valleys and streams during her desperate dash through the mountains.

"I am a good tracker." Chaz translated for Will as she spoke. "My parents always encouraged me in the hobby."

Will nodded approvingly in reply, noting that she seemed to be gaining strength with every passing day. Her resolve, of course, had been strong from the start.

Will and Chaz had to extend themselves to keep up. Whenever she was forced to hesitate, uncertain of the way, crisscrossing whichever valley they happened to be traversing at the time soon produced a shelter half remembered, a drinking place keenly recalled.

Eventually they came to a place where a spindly cascade spilled over a sheer cliff, only to lose itself in swirling spray below. Spread out before them was a sea of mist, as substantial as a dream, as solid as memory. *Vanilla cotton candy*, Will thought, *cupped in the hands of the mountains*. Below the impenetrable cloud layer the swarming, fecund, noisy, colorful Rainy Basin awaited.

The perilous Rainy Basin, he reminded himself.

A leery Chaz peered over the edge. "I don't see any way down."

Neck extended to its full length, Keelk hooted softly as she glanced right and left. Then she vocalized a rapid stream of booming clucks and pointed excitedly to her left. Following closely, Will and Chaz soon found themselves standing at the trail head. It was partially concealed by trumpet flowers and night-blooming *ochela*. Anyone not aware of its existence could have walked by within a few feet and missed it completely.

Without a word, they started down.

Will had no trouble negotiating the narrow, crumbling

path, striding along confidently behind Keelk. Once again, his skybax training proved its worth. The intimidating drop-off did not trouble him.

It was a different matter for poor Chaz. He kept falling behind, forcing man and *Struthiomimus* to wait for him to catch up.

"What's wrong?" Will finally asked the translator. "You're built low to the ground and you've four legs to our two. You should be more stable on this sort of terrain than either of us."

"Precisely the point." The *Protoceratops* hugged the cliff face, keeping as far from the edge of the trail as possible. "Because we don't climb or favor high places, all quadrupeds have a fear of falling." His fear was tangible. "I'll be glad when we're down."

It was fortunate that Keelk hadn't thought to mention the missing section of trail, Will decided when they eventually reached it. Had she described it accurately, Chaz might never have agreed to join the expedition. Nourished by mist rising from the rain forest below, numerous small trees grew from cracks and crevices in the mountainside. After arriving at a delicate consensus on how best to proceed, Will and Keelk reluctantly broke several of these small saplings off at the roots. With these they were able to bridge the gap.

Will admired Keelk's athletic ability as the struthie cleared the opening in a single leap. Working together, they succeeded in lining up four trees side by side. Each held one end of the logs steady while Chaz, with eyes more than half closed, tiptoed over. Will followed more easily.

Safely across, Chaz struggled to control his breathing. "Are . . . are there many more places like this one?" When Keelk replied that this was the only such break in what was otherwise a solid path, he relaxed visibly.

"What was that about?" Will inquired as they resumed their downward march.

Chaz sniffed. "I was just saying that if that's the worst place on this trail, the rest of our descent will be a snap."

"Oh." Will kept his expression carefully neutral. The look in the *Protoceratops*'s eyes belied his carefully chosen words.

I can go anywhere you can, Will Denison, Chaz found himself thinking. At the same time he wondered why he was comparing himself to a human. It was an undinosaurian sort of thing to do. Must be the stress they were under, he told himself.

The trail grew steeper still, but there were no more breathtaking chasms. Even Keelk had to slow down lest the perfidious footing catch her unawares and send her stumbling to her doom.

They heard the Rainy Basin before they could see it: insect and bird calls in profusion rising up through the mist, the notes so sharp and clear as to be almost solid. Then trees became visible, and beneath their sheltering crowns small bushes, vines, lianas, flowers, and bromeliads. Orchids and other blossoms filled the air with a sudden rush of fragrance, as if competing for some ethereal olfactory prize.

"It's beautiful," Will murmured. "Just like I remember it."

Chaz cocked an eye up at his human companion. "You've been here before?"

"Not in this place." He waved at the rain forest. "Much farther south, on the main convoy route. And elsewhere. But not here." He glanced at the sky. "The cloud cover is much heavier here than where I was, the mist a lot thicker."

"Lately there is more humidity in the air everywhere across Dinotopia." The *Protoceratops* hunched forward, shifting the position of the twin saddlebags slightly. "It's the six-year storm. The air is becoming saturated."

The increased oxygen count compensated for the higher heat and humidity, so that their energy level was little affected when they stepped off the trail onto the damp soil of the basin itself.

Winded from the effects of the hurried descent, Chaz suffered more than his companions from the change of climate. "It's not exactly comfortable down here. I prefer a drier environment myself."

"Not a place to linger, no." Keelk's apprehensiveness, however, had nothing to do with the weather. Her wide eyes scanned the forest depths as efficiently as any pair of binoculars.

She noticed that her human companion was busy examining a large pink flower, seemingly oblivious to his threatening surroundings.

"You do not seem frightened," she told him via Chaz.

"I've been in the Rainy Basin before. Had my share of close calls." He indicated the surrounding forest. "It seems reasonably quiet here."

"But you know what there is to be afraid of."

"Of course. I may seem relaxed, but rest assured I'm listening and looking as intently as you."

"Well, I have never been here." Chaz sniffed of a small succulent, took a thoughtful bite of one large, spatulate leaf, and chewed reflectively as he spoke. "Keep in mind that if we run into any danger, I'm the one who's going to be caught first. I can't run like a struthie or climb like a human."

"You can dig a hole," Will suggested.

"I will certainly keep that in mind," the squat translator replied sardonically.

"Oolu, my skybax instructor, always says that it's foolish to borrow trouble. Keelk made it through safely."

"Not without several close calls," she countered, in response to Chaz's translation.

"That's right," the *Protoceratops* grumbled. "Be encouraging." He cast a sour eye on the forest. Every direction looked the same as every other. "Which way?"

She didn't hesitate, pointing eastward. They headed off into the trees, trying to keep the cliffs and slopes of the Backbones always on their left.

"The humans who captured us tried to hug the cliffs as well. If they are still doing so, we should be able to find them."

"Then what?" Chaz demanded to know.

She looked down at him. Ceratopsians were not known for their patience. "Find my family first."

From time to time she would pause to sniff the moist earth. The soil was rich with scent, none of it familiar. The incessant rain had washed away not only any hint of her family and their captors but also of her own recent, reckless passage.

"I'm looking forward to seeing this slot canyon the visi-

tors found.'' Will stepped easily over a gnarled root con-
testing his progress. ''I didn't know there was a way through
this part of the Backbones.''

''I am not sure anyone does,'' she replied in response to
the *Protoceratops*'s translation. ''I think these humans found
it by accident. It was almost completely hidden by plants.''

''It must be very narrow,'' Chaz commented thoughtfully,
''or the farmers of the Northern Plains would find themselves
plagued by meat-eaters from the basin, who would use such
a route to travel northward.''

''It is. Very. Narrow, that is.'' She bent her neck to take
another sniff of the ground.

Will watched her work. ''Do you think you'll be able to
pick up a scent? Everything's so wet here.'' Chaz conveyed
the question.

She raised her head and resumed walking. ''I do not know,
but I can try. Any member of my family I would, of course,
detect instantly. As for the humans, there were many of them,
they stank powerfully, and they were very dirty in their personal habits. So there is a chance, I think.''

''Odd,'' remarked the *Protoceratops*. ''It's been my experience that the majority of humans enjoy bathing. But then,
it's obvious that these humans are thoroughly uncivilized.''

''If these visitors are the kind of men I think they are,''
Will replied, ''you don't know how right you are.''

In the lush depths of the forest something vanished
abruptly in a terse rustling of green. Chaz eyed the spot nervously. ''Perhaps we should reconsider our intentions. Having found the way down, we could mark it clearly and return
with more help.''

''What kind of help?'' Will kicked a rock aside. ''Are we
going to get an armored ankylosaur or *Tarbosaurus* down
that little spit of a trail?''

''More humans, then.''

''The Treetown Council will decide. By then it might be
too late for Keelk's family. What we're doing may not be
the most sensible thing, but it's the thing that needs to
be done.'' He glanced in the struthie's direction. Not understanding Human, she hadn't reacted to his words.

''I know, I know,'' Chaz groused. He used his sharp beak

to snip off a tempting twig and chewed reflexively. It had a sharp, pleasantly minty flavor. "This is quite good. A last tasty meal for the noble condemned."

"Don't be so pessimistic." Will waited for the *Protoceratops* to get ahead of him. "If trouble comes, we can always scatter."

"Oh, really? All well and good for the two of you. What about me? Am I a pterodacytl, to cling to sheer rock?" He sighed dramatically. "How did I get talked into this, anyway?"

Will rested a friendly hand on the crest of the *Protoceratops*'s frill, which came just up to his stomach. "As I recall, you refused to be left behind. Your natural bravery and compassion wouldn't let us go on without you. You care about others and, as a consequence, you're not afraid to put your own life in danger on their behalf."

"Well, yes." The translator put some spring in his step. "That's all true, of course."

Something snapped a heavy branch. They all froze, staring intently in the direction of the sound, hardly daring to breathe. Standing utterly motionless, Keelk resembled one of the smaller trees while Will, slim and straight, could slip easily behind one. Only the rose-yellow bulk of Chaz stood out distinctively amid the sea of green.

"Nothing," whispered Keelk, resuming her stride. Chaz shuffled along close to Will.

"Tell me again," the translator murmured quietly, "about my bravery. Just so I won't forget."

➤➤ XIV ◄◄

BY THE FOLLOWING MORNING THEY HAD TRAVELED a respectable distance. It was early midday when they paused to make a lunch. Intending to ask Keelk's opinion on a matter of direction, Will was startled to see the struthie standing motionless, a cluster of small green fruit dangling absently from one hand. Pupils dilated, her stance indicative of the utmost alertness, she was staring fixedly into the forest.

"What is it?" Looking around sharply, he saw nothing out of the ordinary, heard nothing save the usual bird and insect calls. Perspiration dotted his forehead. It was close to noon, the hottest part of the day in the Rainy Basin, and very little ought to be stirring.

He looked at her again. Certainly she heard or saw *something*.

"Is it the intruders?"

Without turning, she drew the back of her right hand across her beak, unmistakably signaling him to silence.

Then he heard it.

A heavy, deep breathing, like a bass-pedal counterpoint to the twittering of the rain forest birds. It was accompanied by what could only be described as a muffled crashing in the woods. Chaz retreated on all four legs until his backside was pressed up against the nearest large tree. A vine dropped across his spine, and Will thought the little *Protoceratops* was going to jump out of his frill, but to his credit he made not a sound.

Keeping his voice to a whisper, Will leaned in the translator's direction. "Ask her what's going on. Ask her what's—" Before he could finish, Keelk responded with a series of sharp, rigidly modulated chirps.

"She says we have to move." Chaz listened intently. "No, not move: run. She says we have to run." Even as Chaz translated, the *Struthiomimus* was edging sideways, stepping carefully over a fallen log.

"Run? Run where?" Strain as he might, Will still couldn't see anything.

"Deeper into the forest." Chaz reluctantly abandoned the bulwark of the tree while Will scrambled to pack up the remnants of his lunch. The two of them did their best to follow their agitated guide.

Chaz had a hard time keeping up, especially after Will broke into a trot. Furthermore, unlike his two companions, the *Protoceratops* could not look back over his shoulder to see if anything except nervous suspicion was gaining on them.

"Ask her if anything's chasing us." The struthie was continually urging them to greater speed.

"She's not sure." Chaz was puffing like a little steam engine. The forest kept deliberately placing obstacles in his path: roots, tree stumps, fallen logs, termite mounds. "She says that—"

Skidding to a halt, Keelk let out a squeal unlike anything Will had heard before, not even when she'd lain delirious on the infirmary bed. This time it wasn't necessary for Chaz to translate.

By then his eyes had grown almost as wide as hers.

It stepped out from behind a huge cecropia, having concealed itself with a stealthiness wholly unexpected in so formidable a creature. Nearly fifteen feet tall, the *Albertosaurus* weighed several tons. Not all of that was teeth, though at the moment those seemed to hold all of Will's attention. He focused on them as completely as he did the buckles on his safety harness when he was doing acrobatics with Cirrus.

A thickly articulated growl emerged from deep within the muscular throat. Will took a step backward, only to find his retreat blocked by Chaz. The *Protoceratops* didn't need to explain his intent. Flight would only be likely to precipitate an attack, and at such close range they had no chance of escaping or avoiding the huge, agile carnivore.

It wouldn't have mattered anyway. Will sucked in his breath as two more of the giants emerged from the forest behind them. They were slightly smaller than their predecessor, each being no larger than your average couple of elephants. Any kind of retreat was now impossible.

There was nowhere to run, nowhere to hide. Which left only one small and very unencouraging possibility.

Will whispered urgently to his protoceratopsian companion. "Talk to them!"

"I'll try."

"You'll have to do more than try, or we're canapés."

Nodding nervously, the translator took a shaky step forward, shifted his weight to his back legs, and put one foreleg in the air, waving it in the universally accepted manner. He then ventured a reasonable facsimile of the meat-eater's tongue. As a respectable growl it bordered on the comical, but it was enough to make the big theropod hesitate. Querulous rumbles rose from the equally intimidating pair behind them. Will was quietly impressed.

Not that he felt their chances much improved. There were three of the carnivores and three of them. The albertosaurs might be trying to communicate . . . or they might be arguing over the sharing out of prey.

Whose snack will I be? he wondered. Just their bad luck to encounter a trio of theropods wandering about in the heat of midday. The fact that they had lost out to long odds was small comfort.

The largest of the meat-eaters rumbled something low in its throat. Will moved to stand alongside the translator.

"What is it saying?"

"Be quiet," Chaz snapped. "I want to be sure I understand perfectly. Inflection is very important to carnosaurs." Will obediently subsided.

"It asks . . . what the three of us are doing out in the heat of sunhigh." The *Protoceratops* gaped at him. "What are you smiling at, Will Denison? Do you find our situation amusing?"

"No. It's only that I was wondering exactly the same thing about them."

"I do not think the commonality of curiosity will help us, since this one professes itself delighted by our choice. And not because it and its friends are in dire need of refined conversation."

A quick lunch, Will found himself thinking. *So that's how I'm going to end up.* After all he and his father had survived—the storm at sea, the shipwreck on the shores of Dinotopia, the mastering of the ways of this strange land—he was fated to end his days as food. It seemed a terrible waste of accumulated knowledge.

"Tell them what we're doing here. Tell them our purpose in coming this way."

"Do you really think that will have any effect on them?"

"You have a better idea?"

"No," replied Chaz morosely, "I don't." Returning his attention to the albertosaur, he resumed his elegant growling.

Will fought not to look back over his shoulder. He fancied he could feel warm, fetid breath on his neck. One bite, he knew. It would all be over in one bite.

Chaz was speaking to him again. "It's as I feared. They're not interested in our reasons. Their only interest is in sating their hunger, which at present appears substantial."

"Surely you can do something!" Will declared. "Reason with them, tell them that if they let us go we'll return with fish. A whole convoy full of fish!"

The terrified Keelk chirped in with comments of her own, forcing the stressed *Protoceratops* to listen to two simultaneous sets of suggestions in two very different languages.

"You can't reason with a carnosaur."

"Yes, you can! You can reason with any creature that thinks. I know, I've seen it done. Translator Bix—"

"Oh, *Bix*. Who do you think I am, Will? I'm only an apprentice, like yourself. I don't have the redoubtable Bix's experience or linguistic skills. I do well enough to make sense of Struthine. Not that it matters. I don't think even the famous Bix could talk three carnosaurs out of an easy meal. Why should they hesitate? We have no armor, no sauropodian support, and it's obvious we're out here by ourselves."

"Then you've nothing to lose by trying, do you?" Will replied firmly.

The lead albertosaur snorted impatiently and took a step forward. It was a considerable step, but the three travelers could not back away. There was nowhere for them to go but into waiting maws.

Will saw the bright, hungry eyes flicking between himself and Keelk, as if trying to decide which would make the more respectable mouthful. A single lunge and it would all be over. At the last instant he would close his eyes, he decided. His only regret was that he wouldn't have the chance to say goodbye to Sylvia or his father.

Give Chaz credit: the little translator was doing his best, grunting and growling strenuously in the albertosaur's tongue. The theropod didn't hesitate to reply.

"I told this one that we're on a mission of mercy and that there are many strange humans prowling their territory. They find this news pleasing. It offers the promise of easy hunting. As for our mission, it means nothing to them. Any last clever ideas?"

Now Will was certain he could feel a decaying breath hot on his back. He tried desperately to think of something, anything else for Chaz to say. It's hard to stall when you're given no time to think, much less when your prospective audience consists of such poor listeners.

A thunderous roar echoed through the forest, sending birds streaking from their perches and obliterating the normal buzz of background sound. The head of the lead albertosaur, now less than an arm's length from Chaz's snout, immediately rose to its full height and spun southward, as did those of its two companions. A startled Will turned in the same direction. So did Keelk and Chaz.

A second, even more awesome bellow reverberated through the rain forest before the echoes of the first had faded away, followed by a thrashing of the trees and bushes off to their left. The ground trembled as if a highly localized earthquake had been summoned forth and sent crashing toward them.

Abruptly disregarding their imminent prey, the three albertosaurs whirled as one and ran off in the opposite direction, their thick, powerful legs carrying them rapidly into the dense verdure. They fled in single file, the two smaller specimens trailing the larger.

Keelk mustered a querulous hoot. It sounded incredibly lonely in the ensuing, unnatural silence. There was no need for Chaz to translate. The struthie was saying "Now what?" in no uncertain terms.

Whatever it was, Will told himself, it couldn't be any worse than what they'd just faced. He was wrong, of course.

The pair of full-grown adult tyrannosaurs came straight toward them, massive jaws half agape, yellow eyes burning with anger. Their tiny, muscular forearms were turned toward one another, the tips of the heavy claws nearly touching. Between the two of them they massed more than fourteen tons. Compared to them, the absent albertosaurs were as jackals fleeing the unexpected arrival of lions.

No time now even to argue, Will thought wildly. He tried to prepare himself for the inevitable first bite. He couldn't close his eyes, though. There is little in nature more majestically terrifying than a tyrannosaur on the attack. Will felt very much like a man caught in the middle of a high train trestle with a locomotive bearing down on him at full speed.

The male tyrannosaur was advancing straight as an arrow, the great skull dropping down, its weight counterbalanced by the heavy tail, which stretched out in back of the animal like the rudder of a ship. Fully five feet in length and lined with six-inch-long serrated teeth, the head did not so much dip as plunge toward him. Frozen to the spot, Will had a glimpse of flashing yellow eye and a dark, black pupil. The gaping maw blotted out everything else. He closed his eyes and tensed.

Nothing happened.

What was it waiting for? He was barely a mouthful, hardly even worth chewing. Certainly nothing worth pausing to think about.

A rippling snarl, deeper and more impressive even than that of the albertosaurs, formed words of a kind. It reminded Will of an idling steam engine. His ears twitched. Slowly he opened his eyes.

He almost wished he hadn't. The nightmare head was still

there, less than a yard from his face. A part of him became aware that Chaz was speaking, albeit in an uncharacteristically unsteady voice. Thoroughly terrified, the little *Protoceratops* was somehow still doing his job.

"It says . . . it says that you're human."

Will saw no need to respond to this. He would have had difficulty forming words in any case. The tyrannosaur snarled at him anew. Its breath was unimaginably vile, pure essence of carrion.

I will not faint, Will told himself shakily. *I will go out like a man and not like a meal.*

Ongoing existence lent strength to the *Protoceratops*'s voice. "I can hardly believe it. The male tyrannosaur, whose name is Crookeye, demands to know what you've done with their offspring. Their daughter, to be precise."

Will blinked. As curiosity overcame fear, his lower limbs stopped quivering. He was face-to-face with the fiercest, most imposing carnivore nature had ever put on the face of the land, and instead of swallowing him down in a single gulp, it was asking him a question.

Clearly, it behooved him to come up with a reply.

"Their daughter? I haven't done anything with their daughter."

As Chaz translated, the second tyrannosaur came near. If the presence of one was terrifying, proximity to a pair, both equally attentive, left no room for emotion of any kind. It growled steadily at him for several minutes.

"That's Shethorn, the mother." Chaz went on to clarify this for Keelk. It had to be a strain on him, Will knew, shifting between so many languages, and under such difficult circumstances.

"I don't understand," he said. "Ask them for an explanation, for more details."

Clearing his throat, Chaz resumed his comical mimicry of the tyrannosaurs' dialect. The rumbling response his inquiry engendered was immediate and undercut with an almost painful urgency.

"They had left their daughter Prettykill to sleep after feeding on a carcass. It seems she overate and did not want to go with them. When they returned for her, she'd disappeared.

She would not do this voluntarily. Tyrannosaur offspring do not disobey their parents."

Who would? Will thought uneasily as he stared back at the seven-ton meat-eater.

Chaz continued. "To their astonishment, they found signs of a brief struggle. There was also evidence of the presence of many humans, in the form of strong smells, localized spoor, and footprints. These were integrated with those of their daughter as well as those of several struthies. All vanished together into the forest.

"Since then they have been desperately trying to track their daughter and these humans. The added presence of struthies only confuses them further."

Will deliberated. "Ask them if the human scents they detected were tainted with the smell of the sea."

Chaz complied. The two tyrannosaurs actually exchanged a look before the male responded.

"He says that they were, though the connection was very faint. They recognize the sea smell because of the fish they have been given by the convoys passing through the basin. They have never before had reason to connect it with humans traveling on foot." A barely controlled growl punctuated his last words.

"He would like very much to know," the *Protoceratops* went on, "how you happen to be aware of this connection." Chaz added more softly, "Couch your reply carefully, Will. These two are very edgy."

"I can see that." With a five-foot-long skull eyeing him intently on either side, he knew there was no room for linguistic error. How much longer would the tyrannosaurs' curiosity continue to override their fury and frustration?

Putting hands on hips, he boldly returned their attention, wondering as he did so if his confident stance looked as futile as it felt. He tried to see them as individuals, as concerned parents, instead of as gigantic, two-legged eating machines.

Fortunately, he was possessed of an excellent imagination.

"Tell them that our friend here is also someone's daughter." He gestured in Keelk's direction, and the young *Struthiomimus* gazed back at him hopefully. "The struthie prints they found belong to her family, which has been taken prisoner by these humans, who are not residents of Dinotopia but who come from far across the sea. She managed to escape and go for help.'' He shrugged modestly. ''Right now, we're all the help she's been able to muster. But others will follow.'' As soon as Chaz had finished translating this, Will continued.

''These humans are not civilized. They know nothing of Dinotopian ways. They seem to be lacking in morals of any kind. I know that those who live in the Rainy Basin think and act differently from those of us who live in the developed regions, but at least we understand each other. These new arrivals know nothing of our conventions, compacts, or agreements. They act solely out of unenlightened self-interest.

''I think that since they've shown themselves eager and able to capture and hold an entire family of struthies, they are also capable of capturing and holding a young tyrannosaur. I think that may be what's happened to their daughter. How old was she, anyway? How big?''

Chaz translated first for Keelk, then for their audience. When the *Protoceratops* had finished, the female tyrannosaur leaned toward Will. He forced himself to stand still as the enormous skull passed over him. A stubby but powerful two-clawed hand reached toward his head and stopped, the claws level with his hairline. Then Shethorn withdrew.

''Not very big, then,'' he observed sympathetically. It was hard to imagine any group of humans restraining a tyrannosaur of any size, but somehow these intruders had managed the feat. This Prettykill was no taller than Keelk, though certainly more muscular.

With the two tyrannosaurs hovering so close, the stench that emanated from their mouths was doubled. He tried to breathe only through his mouth.

''Tell them we want the same thing they do: to find these humans and free their prisoners. They want their daughter returned; Keelk wants her family back. Tell them . . . tell them that we'll help them rescue their daughter.''

He waited while Chaz translated. All that growling and grunting must put a terrific strain on the throat, Will reflected as he listened admiringly to the *Protoceratops*'s eloquent efforts. He tried to remain poised as the tyrannosaurs exchanged seismic rumblings of their own.

At last the male lowered his head and nudged Will's chest with his snout—gently, so as not to knock the human down. Will stumbled backward a few steps but didn't fall and quickly gathered himself.

"What's the problem?" he whispered anxiously to Chaz. Keelk held her ground nervously, watching the tyrannosaurs' every move and saying nothing.

Chaz hastened to inquire. "Crookeye says that he doesn't see why they need our help. He doesn't see what we can do for them. He says . . . he says he doesn't understand why they shouldn't make a quick snack of us and be on their way."

"A fair question." *My, but it is hot here*, Will thought. *And not giving any indication of cooling off anytime soon.* "Go on; translate that."

Looking as though he'd already resigned himself to spending the evening in the stomach of a distant relation but not knowing what else to do, Chaz complied with his friend's request. Will continued.

"Tell them that without us they wouldn't have any idea of what's happened to their daughter. Tell them that no matter how big and strong they are, there are some things we can do that they can't. Humans understand tools better than any dinosaur, and if it becomes necessary to parley with these intruders, they'll need the services of a translator. As for Keelk, if it wasn't for her, none of us would be here." As an afterthought he added, "Tell them also that there's hardly enough meat on the three of us put together to put a dent in their appetites. I'm bony enough myself to stick in their throats."

"Anyone who thinks tyrannosaurs have a sense of humor is more than a little crazy." Despite his uncertainties, Chaz translated Will's response exactly as given.

"Tell them also," Will added when the *Protoceratops* had finished, "that no matter what they think, we'll be of much more help to them alive than digested."

It was just as well that the tyrannosaurs could not smile. Such a display of teeth would not have been reassuring. But in response to Chaz's speech they both straightened slightly.

To maintain eye contact, Will was forced to tilt his head back until his neck throbbed. It was like watching a pair of tall buildings converse.

Shethorn growled down at him. Will wanted to cover his nose but didn't dare, afraid that the tyrannosaurs might recognize the gesture.

"She says that they've had dealings with humans before but that they've never encountered one like you. Our boldness in entering the Rainy Basin without any kind of armored escort has impressed them." The *Protoceratops* lowered his voice slightly. "I've always heard that the big carnosaurs respect courage. That doesn't mean that they're averse to consuming the courageous."

"What else did they say?" Will prompted his friend.

Chaz sucked in a deep breath. "They said that if we can really help them find their daughter, then they will be forever in our debt and that even if you never pass this way again you will be able to number at least three of their kind among your friends."

"Excellent." Will gazed evenly back into feral yellow eyes as the male tyrannosaur continued to growl softly.

"They also say," Chaz continued, "that if we're wrong about all this and we lead them down a false trail and as a consequence anything bad happens to their daughter, they'll hold us personally responsible."

"Tell them that I understand, and I accept the condition."

"It doesn't matter anyway," the *Protoceratops* mumbled to himself. "It's not like we have anything to lose."

"No, it isn't. Their daughter's name is Prettykill?"

Chaz translated and listened closely to the rumbling response. "Yes. They're very fond of her and they miss her very much."

"Tell them that Keelk misses her family as much as they miss their daughter. So they have something else in common besides both being bipeds. Tell them that we have to move quietly. We don't want to do anything to startle or alarm these humans. If they're the kind of people I think they are, they won't hesitate to maim or kill their captives if they think it'll be to their benefit."

The *Protoceratops*'s translation sparked a savage snarl

from the mother tyrannosaur that chilled Will's blood. It was completely terrifying even though it wasn't directed at him. Keelk's head drew back almost to her shoulders and Chaz was visibly shaken. He could almost feel sorry for Pretty-kill's captors. To envision oneself the target of such unimaginable fury was almost inconceivable.

"They're also impressed with Keelk's boldness," Chaz added.

"So am I." Will's gaze shifted from one tyrannosaur to the other. "What do you think, Chaz? Can they be trusted?"

"Do we have a choice?"

"I mean, what happens if they wake up in the middle of the night and feel the urge for a quick meal? I've heard that carnosaurs have short memories."

The frilled head turned toward him and its owner managed to sound slightly superior. "That won't happen. There's a lot you don't know, Will, because you haven't lived here long enough. The meat-eaters have their own rough code of ethics. They won't eat someone they've made a compact with. They might grow irritable or angry or impatient, but they won't forget. They've given their word. You needn't worry about waking up in someone's belly."

"Then we're safe." Will finally summoned a smile.

"Not entirely." The ever-cautious *Protoceratops* corrected him even as he translated for Keelk. "These *are Tyrannosaurus rexes* we're dealing with here. We'd best hope that nothing untoward has happened to their daughter."

"If anything has, it's not our fault."

"That won't matter to them," Chaz replied knowingly. "However, you have managed to convince them that we need each other. So everything is indeed all right . . . for now." The *Protoceratops* turned to the male, who was grumbling impatiently at him.

"Crookeye says that they'll do the tracking. Their sense of smell is better even than a struthie's."

"Perfectly agreeable." Will took a step forward. "We should formalize it."

"Formalize it?" Chaz succeeded in frowning with his voice.

"You know. The usual gesture of agreement?"

"Ah, you mean this?" The *Protoceratops* raised a forefoot and Will placed his palm firmly against the flat pad.

Following the demonstration and Chaz's growling explanation, Will approached Shethorn. With not a little trepidation he extended his hand, palm outward. Grunting, the female bent low and turned slightly to her right in order to keep an eye on the human. Reaching out with a powerful forearm, she touched the base of the twin claws to his soft human hand.

At the contact a shiver of excitement ran through Will. For all he knew, this might be the first time in Dinotopian history such an exchange had taken place. He sensed the enormous lower jaw hovering just above his head. The touch concluded, he stepped back.

Crookeye was snarling insistently at an uneasy Keelk and Chaz hurried to reassure her. "Breathe deep. He just wants all the information you have on these humans who have so outraged common convention."

Keelk nodded reluctantly, her respiration slowing. Through Chaz she began to relay everything she could remember about her captivity. The two tyrannosaurs listened closely. Aside from the unnerving intensity of their stares they betrayed no reaction.

When Keelk had finished, each of them touched a snout to the ground in front of her. Separating, they began to sweep the soil with their sensitive nostrils, their great heads swinging from side to side as they searched for any hint of their daughter's presence . . . or that of unidentified humans. Will watched in fascination.

Nearly ten minutes later Shethorn straightened, growled gently, and gestured with both head and right forearm to the southeast.

"That's the way," the *Protoceratops* declared.

"You didn't have to translate that," Will admonished him. Chaz simply gave his human companion a look.

As they carefully traced the faint scent trail through the rain forest, the tyrannosaurs stopped frequently to sniff the ground, bushes, and anything that might retain a lingering odor. Occasionally they would engage in brief, grunting conversations Chaz would not bother to translate. Then they would resume tracking.

These brief pauses were welcomed by Will and his friends, who could not begin to match the effortless, earth-spanning strides of their new companions. It was a struggle even for Keelk to keep up, and Chaz was having a seriously difficult time of it.

At least they didn't have to worry about trying to follow a marked path. The tyrannosaurs made their own road. As the old Dinotopian saying went, "Where does a tyrannosaur go? Anywhere it wants to."

Despite their best efforts they eventually fell behind, Will doing his best to help Chaz, and Keelk having to slow down to remain with them. Shethorn looked back and growled impatiently.

"Look, I'm sorry!" Will was panting hard, and poor Chaz was nearly done. "We can't go any faster." It occurred to him that he'd just spoken sharply to an always irritable tyrannosaur, but he was so tired he didn't care.

Crookeye rumbled at his mate, then spoke to Chaz. The *Protoceratops* was grateful for the opportunity to translate. It meant he didn't have to run.

"They're saying—let me catch my breath, Will—they're saying that they recognize that we are having trouble keeping up with them, but that you said yourself time was of the essence."

"I know, but what do they expect us to do? Fly? A skybax rider needs his skybax."

"They are willing to sacrifice dignity in order to expedite matters."

Will frowned. "I don't think I understand."

Chaz nodded at Shethorn, who was kneeling and lowering her head. "They want us to ride."

"Ride? Ride them?" He'd thought riding Cirrus, his skybax, was the greatest thrill anyone could have. And any of the larger dinosaurian citizens of civilized Dinotopia were quite happy, under most circumstances, to provide helpful humans with individual transportation. Many carried saddles and harnesses specifically designed for the purpose.

But to ride a *Tyrannosaurus rex* . . .

Crookeye had crouched down alongside his mate. Now he growled his impatience.

"They want us to get on with it," Chaz elaborated.

"I can see that. Tell them . . . tell them that we'll give it a try." He started toward Crookeye while Keelk advanced tentatively on the waiting Shethorn.

Even crouched low, the two tyrannosaurs presented a difficult proposition. How was he supposed to mount? Keelk had sharp claws on her hands and feet with which to climb and grip. Will was good in trees, but there were no convenient branches here. No place to put his foot. . . .

Crookeye's jaws parted slightly and he gave Will a slight, encouraging nod. Trying to avoid looking down at those six-inch teeth, Will put one foot on the edge of the lower jaw and gripped the horny projection above the tyrannosaur's right eye with his left hand. Kicking off and pulling, he found that he could swing his other leg up and over. It wasn't very different from mounting a horse, which he'd done as a child in America. The only difference was that he was seating himself across a head instead of a back.

That, and the fact that his current mount could have any horse for breakfast.

He saw that Keelk had chosen a position on Shethorn's neck, just behind her head. With her claws and talons the struthie could just hang on, maintaining a strong grip without penetrating the thick therapodian skin. Having no such built-in hooks, Will would have to find a way to sit.

Crossing his legs beneath him, he balanced himself near the center of the skull, which was more than broad enough to provide an adequate seat. The horny projections above each eye made serviceable handles. Thus positioned, he rapped the top of the skull with the palm of one hand.

Instantly he found himself rocketing skyward as Crookeye stood up. From his new perch fifteen feet above the ground, the forest looked very different. A brachiosaur rider would have an even more expansive view, but not the same feeling of absolutely invulnerability. It was a heady sensation even though he knew nothing in Dinotopia (or anywhere else on earth, for that matter) would dare confront his mount.

Easy, he reminded himself. He'd been granted a unique

privilege. It could just as quickly be withdrawn.

Looking to his right, he saw that Keelk was comfortably attached to Shethorn's neck. But Chaz presented a problem. The stumpy *Protoceratops* possessed neither Will's simian agility nor the struthie's natural gripping apparatus.

The impatient tyrannosaurs solved the dilemma themselves. Bending down, Shethorn gripped the reluctant translator behind his forelegs and lifted him easily. A tyrannosaur's arms are stubby but very powerful, and she had no trouble holding him. Though reasonably comfortable, Chaz found the actual position, hanging as he was with backside dangling toward the ground like that of a human infant, highly unbecoming.

"Relax." Will fought to suppress a grin. "No one's going to see you. And if they did, they wouldn't laugh. Shethorn might think they were laughing at *her*, and I don't know anybody who'd take that chance."

"This is most undignified." Chaz was not mollified.

Will worked to keep his balance as Crookeye started forward. So smooth was the tyrannosaurs' stride that there was very little up-and-down motion. The slight side-to-side jostling was not uncomfortable, and he soon got the hang of rolling with each step. Before long they were racing instead of walking through the forest. Buttressing roots, thick vines, depressions and rises, small creeks and ponds flew past beneath him.

Let's see a brachiosaur rider do this! Will thought ebulliently. The combined feeling of speed and security was positively intoxicating.

As they raced through the rain forest, the two tyrannosaurs paused from time to time to perform their scent checks, but the pace of the pursuit picked up exponentially. Not only that, but since he no longer had to exert himself, Will could relax, let his leg muscles recuperate, and enjoy the sights that were flashing past. It was a unique and probably unprecedented way to explore the Rainy Basin.

He'd expected more bouncing, but the only time he was nearly jolted from his perch was when the tyrannosaurs unexpectedly cleared a deep creek in a single jump. The landing on the far side of the stream, cushioned as it was, still nearly

sent him flying, and only a last-minute grasp of the eye horn
on his right kept him from taking a serious tumble.
Thereafter, he paid more attention to his riding and less to
passing scenery.

He'd seen pictures of Arabians riding their camels. His
situation was more analogous to that of a Hindu mahout,
perched grandly upon his pachyderm's supercilious brow.
Gaining confidence with each successive giant stride, he
crossed his arms in front of his chest and pushed out his
lower lip, disappointed no skillful daguerreotypist was present to permanently immortalize his pose.

Nor did he lack for entertainment, as Chaz maintained a
running commentary on the ignominy of his position.

Birds and the smaller inhabitants of the forest understory
fled from his approach, screeching and screaming as they
rushed to get out of the way. Though under complete control,
to anything in their path the two sprinting tyrannosaurs must
have given the appearance of a pair of runaway locomotives.

Rain forest sped past on either side, a kaleidoscope of
brilliant flowers and colorful bromeliads and darting insects.
While he noted each of them in passing, he was more concerned with the occasional low branch that loomed suddenly
out of the oncoming verdure. More than once he was forced
to duck low, feeling the leaves and branches stroke his hair
in passing.

Beneath him the great organic engine that was Crookeye
thundered along effortlessly, covering huge chunks of forest
with each stride. Occasionally Shethorn paced her mate,
other times she fell in behind.

A pack of half a dozen ceratosaurs was working on the
half-consumed carcass of a recently deceased protosauropod
when the searchers burst upon them. Instinctively the ceratosaurs turned to defend their food, only to flee at the sight
of the onrushing tyrannosaurs. Disdaining the carcass,
Crookeye and Shethorn rumbled past, leaving the baffled ceratosaurs to emerge from hiding only after their much larger
cousins had passed.

If there was any drawback to the extraordinary experience,
other than the unfortunate insects that occasionally splattered
against his face and chest, it was that Will could not escape

the fetor of the tyrannosaur's breath. Not that he was about to venture any criticism. Only a most unwise person would criticize a tyrannosaur to its face. A late, unwise person, Will decided.

From time to time he would lean to his right and peer down at a saucer-sized yellow eye, which would roll up to look back at him. He always smiled and offered words of encouragement, wondering as he did so if they had any effect.

As to one discovery there was no doubt, however. Like most dinosaurs, the tyrannosaurs loved music, and Will's early musical education had not been neglected. It developed that Crookeye and Shethorn were particularly fond of Liszt, Berlioz, and traditional marches.

Most unexpectedly, Will had found another use for his skill at whistling.

»» XV ««

"THESE HUMANS ARE CRAZY!" TRYLL WHISPERED.
"I know." Shremaza did her best to calm her daughter. "We can only hope that Keelk will bring help, or that the opportunity to escape will come also to the rest of us."

The four struthies were tied to two trees. As always, their captors had fed and watered them conscientiously. Damaged goods, as Blackstrap so calmly put it, never fetched as high a price as those that had been well cared for.

Having seen to their more docile prisoners, the pirates proceeded to the far more delicate task of feeding their most difficult captive. With great caution the thick hawser line that secured the young tyrannosaur's jaws was unwound. It was the first time since its capture that they had ventured to feed it, and everyone was being more than usually cautious.

There being none of the enormous quantities of carrion they had encountered in the immediate vicinity of their first camp currently available, the men had trapped a strange crocodilian in a nearby stream. After saving the best part, the tail, for themselves and proceeding to grill it over a hot fire, they had quartered the rest of the carcass and were preparing to offer the sections one by one to their most prized prisoner. Dead, it would still bring them money, Smiggens avowed. Alive, it might well make all their fortunes.

Blackstrap's call for volunteers to feed the captive devil was met with thunderous silence. "What be you all afeared of? Look at the poor blighter! Why, it can hardly move, with its arms and legs and, yes, even its tail so tightly strapped down. On top of that 'tis tied fair and square to a tree big enough around to do for a clipper's mainmast. What more protection could a man want?''

"Why not feed it yourself, Cap'n?'' suggested an anonymous voice.

"What's that, what say you?'' Seeking the speaker, Blackstrap encountered nothing but hard-bitten visions of angelic innocence. "Who dares to suggest that I don't do my share? No one? Come on, then, speak up! Be there not a man among the lot of you?''

"I will feed the dragon.'' Chin-lee, the smallest among them, stepped forward. Picking up a haunch of croc in both hands, he dragged it forward. Halting at what he perceived to be a respectful distance, he swung the heavy piece of meat back and then heaved it directly at their captive.

With a single snap of powerful jaws that sounded like a sack of wet mud striking pavement after falling from a height of several stories, the young tyrannosaur plucked the gobbet from the air. Swallowing jerkily in much the same fashion as a large bird, she gulped the chunk down. Eyes of feral topaz glittered as she gazed hungrily at the rest of the carcass.

Chin-lee stuck out his chest as he confronted his shipmates. "See! Smart man can even teach dragon tricks.''

"Not dragon,'' corrected Smiggens softly. "Dinosaur.''

Chin-lee ignored him. He knew a dragon when he saw one, and no white devil was going to disabuse him of that notion. He tossed a second hunk of reptilian roast at the beast, noted with satisfaction how easily it caught the heavy piece.

"Nothing to it, then.'' Stepping out of the semicircle of onlookers, Mkuse duplicated the Chinaman's effort. Their captive took meat as readily from him as from his predecessor.

"Best sell it to someone who can afford a zoo's feed bill, Captain.'' It was with no little awe that Andreas admired their prisoner's capacity.

"Me, I'd like to see it jump for its dinner,'' avowed Copperhead.

"Now, there's a stroke of brilliance.'' Smiggens gazed

across at the seaman. ''You, of course, will do the honor of
untying its legs, Mr. Copperhead.''

The sailor chuckled. ''Not I, Mr. Smiggens. This is near
enough to those claws for me, thank you.''

''Bragh! There's nothing to be afraid of here. You're all
a lot of mewling babes.'' These words from Guimaraes, the
big Portuguese, as he stepped forward. Shouldering Mkuse
aside, he hefted the last section of crocodilian in one big,
callused fist.

Striding boldly up to their captive, he stopped to stare
directly into its ugly, blood-smeared face. The two adult struthies squealed a warning that, of course, none of the humans
present either understood or appreciated. Tilting his head to
one side, the Portuguese considered unbound jaws and teeth.
With the captive sitting back on its haunches, the seaman
actually towered over it by a full foot.

Satisfied he'd stared the creature down, he raised his right
arm and waved the chunk of meat close to its snout. Accepting the offering meekly and with delicacy from the
sailor's fingers, the tyrannosaur tilted her head back and
swallowed with what almost amounted to a certain decorum.

Guimaraes glanced back at his comrades. ''There, you
see? There is nothing to it. Hobbling an animal like that will
tame it quick.'' He sniffed scornfully and then committed
the unfortunate error of turning his back on the subject of
his contempt.

He managed half a step before that vulpine skull darted
forward like a snake's and serrated teeth clashed. A number
of the pirates had grown bored with the show and had turned
to other tasks. Guimaraes's scream drew their attention back
to the feeding session right quick.

Mkuse and Treggang hurried to help their wounded col-
league. But when they descried the nature of his injury, their
initial concern and fear turned quickly to amusement, which
soon melted into uncontrollable laughter. Blackstrap could
hardly contain himself, and even the usually dour Smiggens
was momentarily overcome with merriment.

''Hold still, man!'' Still chuckling, Mkuse had removed
his shirt and rolled it into a bandage. With the injured Guimaraes twitching about, it was difficult to secure the fabric

over the wound, which bled copiously but was in no way life-threatening.

The vicious bite had removed a piece of flesh some six inches in length and five across but fortunately not very deep from the Portuguese's left buttock, leaving a gaping hole not only in his backside but his trousers. Being the nearest thing on the *Condor* to a physician, it was left to Smiggens to further treat and bandage the injury.

Through it all, the young tyrannosaur simply stared and watched, her hunger appeased but by no means sated. Crocodilian or human, it was all the same to her. Her appetite was as democratic as it was ravenous. It was difficult for some of the onlookers to believe she wasn't laughing along with them, though they knew by now that the strangely sinister smile on her face was a function of her physiognomy rather than her temperament.

Stepping forward, the stocky Thomas tossed the remnant of his share of crocodilian tail to their captive. "There you go, old chap. That's a sight worth an extra feed! Have another piece of tail." This jest brought forth renewed guffaws from the men.

Only one among them was neither smiling nor laughing. Guimaraes glared at the West Indian. "When I get up from here I am going to stick you head in its mouth. Then we see who laughs, yes?"

Thomas was not impressed. "You got to catch me first, man." White teeth flashed in a broad grin. "And somehow I think you not going to be doing much running anytime soon, you know?"

"True enough," declared tall Samuel. "Be grateful for small favors, Guimaraes. You're lucky it waited till you turned your back!" Gales of laughter followed.

All of which affected the unhappy Guimaraes far more deeply than the pain behind him. Far rather would he have suffered the kiss of a saber's blade than his shipmates' laughter, though it was at heart good-natured. The Portuguese was no stranger to pain. He was missing half his right ear, carried away by a bullet fired from an obstreperous merchantman they'd cornered against a reef in the South China Sea. An imposing scar ran crosswise down the upper half of his chest, a gift from a now deceased sailor on a Dutch spice ship.

Those were wounds he could display and boast of. What was there to boast of in this? Fortunately, most would never see it. But he knew it was there, as did his comrades-in-arms. The louder their laughter, the more it seared his soul and the hotter his anger blazed.

That night he was unable to sleep until it was his turn on watch. Though the moon was three-quarters full, its lambency was significantly diluted by the incessant clouds that masked the heavens.

There was just enough light to enable him to find his way to the far side of the camp, where their captives were secured to a trio of stout rain forest trees. The four svelte dinosaurs slept squatting on their haunches, their heads resting on their backs like so many chickens on their nests. They neither awakened nor looked up at his approach. He thought this odd, but who was he to speculate on the sleeping habits of such creatures?

He glared unblinkingly at the beast that was the source of his dishonor. Dragon, the Chinaman had called it. Dinosaur, the first mate had instructed them. Guimaraes had since invented a number of other names for the creature, many prefaced by or embellished with coarse profanities.

His tone was soft and deceptively cordial. "Hello, little devil-beast. Are you awake?" One yellow eye flickered open, followed quickly by its counterpart. "Ah, good."

Though the creature was once more thoroughly and completely bound, Guimaraes kept his distance. Once bitten, he thought bitterly . . . The hawser rope once again circled several times around the strong jaws, preventing them from opening. The beast was harmless and helpless. He could do anything he wanted to it, anything at all, and it would not be able to resist.

He dare not act now, however, in the midst of his shipmates. Blackstrap would have him drawn, quartered, and fed to the next monster that came along if he so much as damaged a single scale of that precious, vicious hide. No, Guimaraes knew that despite the desire for revenge that simmered deep inside his heart he would have to bide his time.

Until then he would have to content himself with planning it in his mind, and periodically visiting the source of his discontent.

"Sleeping well?" The beast did not reply. It could not, with its jaws securely bound. But it could stare at him, which it did. "Hate me, do you? That's good. That's very good. We understand one another, then. When I come for you in the night the final time, I will have no regrets, no sorrows." His bandaged backside burned, but not as badly as his shipmates' laughter.

Walking was painful, and for a while he would limp. He didn't mind. Every step reminded him of the incident, every stride fueled the flame of his hatred. Every new joke made at his expense helped to solidify his determination.

Not much longer, he told himself. *The right place will come and the right time present itself. Then . . .*

"You think you are smart, don't you? Taking that meat so carefully and then waiting for me to turn my back. Do you feel smart now, with your legs hobbled and your mouth tied shut? Do you?" His voice rose slightly as he jabbed at the tyrannosaur's snout with the muzzle of his rifle.

A sharp hiss issued from the captive's throat. Guimaraes held his ground and grinned. "Yes, go on and sputter at me. I'll bet you'd like to take another bite out of me, wouldn't you? Wouldn't you?" He wiggled his fingers tauntingly beneath the prisoner's lower jaw. Aware of its bound condition, it wasted no strength trying to bite.

Again the Portuguese jabbed teasingly with the rifle. "See this, little devil-beast? This is *my* tooth, and it bites hard. Next time I won't have my back turned to you. Next time it is I who will do the biting." He was very close now, all but eye to eye.

The captive twitched forward, trying to head-butt her tormentor. Guimaraes was ready this time and jumped back. His smile widened. "You are very quick. Very damn quick. Your mother was a cobra who mated with a tiger. You know, I have seen both, in India. They are deadly, but the Hindoos kill them anyway. They die just as quickly from a knife or bullet as any duck or pheasant." His grin twisted into something highly unpleasant.

"I wonder what you'd taste like. How will you like it when I take a bite out of you, eh?"

A shuffling noise made him whirl sharply. He knew it wasn't the captain. When he wanted to, Blackstrap could sleep like a dead man. But that damned inquisitive Smiggens was always about and underfoot, snooping and sticking his long nose in where it didn't belong. Trouble was, the first mate was as smart as he seemed. Seeing Guimaraes so close to their prize prisoner might set the mate to thinking, a dangerous proposition.

For long moments the Portuguese waited without moving, relaxing only when it became apparent no one was sneaking up on him. Then he turned a last time toward the captive.

"You had your fun. Soon enough now, I will have mine. You will see. There will come a certain moment when no one else is looking, when no one else is around. It will be just you and me. Then you'll catch an accidental bullet in one of those bright eyes, and maybe a few more elsewhere." For a second time he stepped close.

"Look at me close, little demon. Look at me well. Because someday soon, I am going to be the death of you." He prodded the young tyrannosaur in the neck with the muzzle of his rifle, and she drew back as far as she could, hissing. Grinning nastily and thoroughly satisfied with his visit, he turned and walked back toward his guard station.

Prettykill was elated. A formal challenge! And from a *human*. Though she couldn't understand a word he'd said, his actions and attitude had left no doubt as to his intent. A challenge from something as puny as a human would be meaningless to an adult tyrannosaur, nothing more than an amusing diversion. But this one was her size. He would do. She had accepted his challenge and would have replied appropriately had her jaws not been bound.

The prodding she'd received from the long tool had clinched it. Normally she was only challenged by others of her own kind, or the juveniles of some of the other carnosaurs. Such scuffles were entered into solemnly and in full accord with ancient conventions. In keeping with the natural temperament of the participants, such contests were sometimes bloody affairs, though only rarely fatal. It would be interesting to see how a human would do. She'd been told by her parents that humans, while not very strong, were very tricky and often made use of artificial devices to compensate for their small stature.

So be it. She was ready, even eager, for the confrontation this particular human seemed to promise. It would be a character-building experience. Much more interesting than the endless talking and reasoning humans usually preferred. If only she could free a foreleg or her jaws, she could slice through the ropes that restrained her and fulfill this accommodating human's desire.

She spotted one of the young struthies peering in her direction and glared back. The juvenile quickly turned away and made a pretext of returning to sleep. If only she could free her jaws, she could shred the rest of her restraints in minutes. Alas, the tricky humans knew how to handle such implements. She could not slip free.

Well, the human was obviously willing to wait for the right time to consummate his challenge. Could she do less? Settling herself back on her haunches, she shut her eyes and concentrated on going back to sleep. Around her, the rain forest hummed its familiar discordant lullaby. . . .

THE PARTY WAS ADVANCING THROUGH THE TREES THE following morning when Mkuse stopped and pointed. "That's odd. Look at the sails."

"Sails!" Anbaya let out a whoop and rushed forward. "Boats, commerce, people!"

"Wait up there, man!" Smiggens tried to restrain the Moluccan, but the smaller sailor was too quick for him.

Through a gap in the tree line they could see the sails plying the surface of a broad lake, the slim, arching shapes weaving slowly back and forth in the wind like the triangles of rough brown linen that propelled Arab feluccas. The silhouettes of these were distinctive and unusual.

Peculiarity of design was not sufficient to explain the shout that next reached them, followed by a short scream. It suggested that not everything was as it seemed, a condition they were becoming accustomed to the longer they remained in this outlandish country.

Anbaya burst back through the short brush. His shipmates gathered around the swart Moluccan, whose eyes were wide and whose breathing was agitated.

"Not boats," he gasped. "Not boats, not people!"

A deep-throated growl caused everyone to turn toward the opening in the forest. The massive perpetrator of that intimidating noise shoved its upper body forward through a cluster of branches. Jaws parted to reveal sharp teeth dripping with saliva. Two nearly identical monsters crowded behind.

The trio closely resembled the dinosaurs the pirates had previously observed feeding on carrion, as well as the singular monster they had chased from the boundaries of their bone-fenced campsite. What differentiated these from their predecessors were the large, leathery sails that protruded from their backs. Supported by bony spines, these astonishing structures did indeed resemble the sails of small ships. They quivered slightly with each step. When their owners were crouched down in the vegetation only the "sails" would be visible. Hence Mkuse and then Anbaya's understandable error of perception.

Given the nautically embellished creatures' ferocious appearance, it quickly became apparent that more was at stake than a little visual confusion. Nearly twelve feet tall, a second monster snarled at them. Sails and all, the three lurched in the direction of the travelers.

Spinosaurs, thought Prettykill. Three of them would make short work of the humans and their captives as well. Would they dare to attack her? She was bound, helpless, and without adult protection. Not that she could defend herself for long against a fully grown spinosaur in any case. But fighting back would be a better way to depart life than wrapped up like one of the human's bundles.

"This way, for your lives!" Mkuse whirled and sprinted for the nearby foothills.

Blackstrap had drawn his cutlass and was backing away from the newly arrived nightmares. "Hell and damnation!

Will the devil never let us rest? Do not his minions have other tasks to attend besides troubling us?'' Though he was the last man to turn and run, he did not fall behind. Blackstrap could move with surprising speed for so large a man. Also, he had no intention of abandoning a single one of their hard-won prizes to the slavering, sail-backed predators and was as determined to shepherd them to safety as he was any of his men.

He gripped both pistols tightly. Not to threaten the pursuing carnivores, which were still struggling to ascend the slight slope that led down to the lake where they'd been dozing, but to cajole his crew.

''First man who abandons his pet post is dragon—no, dinosaur food!'' With blows and words he coerced the men handling the tethers that led their captives. As they were far more afraid of their captain than any beast of the forest, the men hewed to their assignments, alternately dragging, leading, and bullying the creatures forward. Very little effort was actually required, since neither the struthies nor the young tyrannosaur had any desire to linger in the vicinity.

Initially they succeeded in putting some distance between themselves and the three carnivores, but this temporary margin of safety began to contract as the spinosaurs levered themselves up onto level ground. The men could hear the meat-eaters crashing through the thick growth behind them.

''We'll have to find a place to make a stand, Captain!'' insisted a sailor as he fought to shove his way through the dense verdure.

''A fruitless notion, Mr. Johanssen.'' Though breathing hard, Blackstrap kept up with the younger, more limber members of his crew. ''One such monster we might bring down, but not three. Not with rifles and pistols. They be too fast, and they'll be on us the instant we stop.''

''We have to try something, sir!'' No athlete, Smiggens was having a hard time. Several of the others were likewise beginning to slow. It was obvious from the start they would not be able to outrun their pursuers, designed as the carnivores were by a ruthless nature to run down and dispatch far fleeter prey than the humans.

Once more in the lead, Anbaya let out another cry. This

time, however, it smacked of excitement rather than fear.
Smiggens could see gray granite looming above the thinning
canopy and forced his complaining legs to move faster. What
had the nimble Moluccan found?

"There's a canyon, Captain! Another canyon!"

"For your lives, then, you lazy lot of limp lizard-dung!"
Looking back over his shoulder, Blackstrap saw a narrow,
fanged snout pushing through the greenery. It was close
enough to snap at him. Bits of dead, dried flesh clung to the
sharp teeth that just missed his waist sash. A crosswise tree
slowed his pursuer, but only for an instant.

Whirling, the captain fired his pistols repeatedly, emptying
both fine American revolvers and sending off each shot accompanied by an appropriate curse. The bullets only irritated
the lead spinosaur, but the unexpected flash and noise of the
guns caused it to pull up short, momentarily uncertain and
confused. This sudden stop caused the second monster to
crash into the first. Sails flailing, growling and snapping at
one another, they tumbled to the ground. Though uninvolved
in this brief dispute, the third and last of the carnosaurs was
held up by the confrontation that had ignited in front of him.

This unexpected respite proved the pirates' deliverance.
Suddenly they found themselves running past *Livistona*
palms and isolated bushes instead of dense rain forest. Anbaya was frantically beckoning them on from atop a smooth,
dinoursized boulder.

The slot canyon was wide enough to admit their pursuers,
but at least it would force a frontal attack. They couldn't be
surrounded now, Smiggens saw. Like the first canyon they
had traversed, this one also boasted sheer, towering walls and
a fine level floor of sand and gravel. Running was much
easier without projecting roots and hidden holes to worry
about.

One of the struthies tripped and fell. It lay kicking its
hobbled legs as it fought to regain its footing, hooting and
squealing piteously. The other members of its family gathered around the fallen one, refusing to move no matter how
hard the frustrated pirates pulled and kicked at them.

"What's the matter with you idiots? Make them move!"

Blackstrap roared, scanning the still empty canyon behind them for signs of pursuit.

"Maybe it sprained a leg!" Smiggens suggested loudly. There was no time to find out. Under his direction four of the men picked up the fallen creature bodily and resumed their precipitous flight, supporting the squealing animal between them. The ropes with which it was bound provided excellent purchase for its reluctant bearers.

Encouragingly, the canyon continued to narrow. A dead end would not be so encouraging, Smiggens knew as he pounded along. Glancing in Blackstrap's direction, he saw that the same thought had occurred to the captain. Both men kept their thoughts to themselves lest they alarm their unimaginative and already frantic companions.

A better running surface underfoot notwithstanding, they knew there was no way they could outpace the three monsters if the dinosaurs chose to continue the pursuit. Sure enough, a pair of fanged skulls soon appeared behind them, peering around a bend in the canyon. An angry, frustrated bellow echoed off the smooth canyon walls as the spinosaurs redoubled their efforts.

"Hurry, hurry!" Anbaya was shouting from somewhere up ahead. "Canyon narrows, Captain, it narrows!"

Heart pounding, lungs burning, Smiggens offered up a silent prayer to whatever god of geology might be attending their flight. A narrow canyon was just what was wanted now. "Just let it not be a cul-de-sac," he whispered fervently.

Already the walls had closed in enough to force the spinosaurs to pursue in single file. They were very near now.

Lunging forward through the rapidly narrowing gap, one caught the terrified Treggang by his right ankle with the tip of its mouth and dragged the unfortunate man down. Clawing madly at the sand, the diminutive Malay howled frantically at his fleeing companions. In a fine display of determination and bravery, Mkuse raced back to grasp his shipmate's wrists, locking them in a steel grip. The Zulu warrior dug his heels into the sand.

It was no use. Treggang might as well have been hooked to a steam winch and not a living creature. Bellowing and roaring, the other two spinosaurs crowded close behind the first, anxious for their chance at prey but unable to pass to either side of their relative, whose robust form now filled the whole of the rocky passage. Tough, knobby skin rubbed dust and small shards of rock from the unyielding walls as the three meat-eaters pushed and shoved.

Suddenly Mkuse fell backward, nearly tumbling head over heels. The spinosaur had lost its fragile grip and Treggang had popped free. Eyes wide, the liberated sailor saw that his boot had been sheared off clean just below the heel, as neatly as if by a cobbler's saw. A small scrape bled slightly into the sand, but the wound was not serious.

Scrabbling frantically on his backside, he scuttled away from the stymied, enraged meat-eater. The pirates could not understand a word that was being bellowed in the carnivore's language, but the meaning of those roars was clear enough. "Catch you and eat you!" they were snarling, over and over. "Catch you and eat you, puny humans!"

Only they no longer could. Like the first canyon the pirates had traversed, this one had narrowed to a point where only one or two men could advance abreast. Dig and push as they might against the solid walls, the spinosaurs could not advance another step.

Ignoring Smiggens's warnings, Blackstrap turned and walked back down the cleft until he was within a few yards of the exasperated, irate carnosaurs. Swirling his contempt within his cheeks, he spat scornfully in their direction.

"That be for thee, you dumb beasts! I've watched senile lions with more sense bring down stronger prey than we." None of the incensed spinosaurs spoke Blackstrap's language, of course, but his manner and tone were eloquent enough. They redoubled their efforts—grinding their shoulders against the indifferent rock, flailing with clawed hands, raising an impressive cloud of dust—but, despite their rage, penetrating no farther into the canyon.

Spitting a second time into the sand, Blackstrap pivoted on his heel and with great deliberation walked slowly away, indifferent to the frantic teeth and claws that shadowed his retreat.

"Well, Mr. Smiggens," he declared upon rejoining his men, "it seems that since we cannot go back, we may as well go forward. But first I would rest awhile. My legs insist upon it.'' With sighs and whistles of relief the exhausted men sunk down upon the sand. The struthies were no less grateful for the respite.

Tilting back his head, Blackstrap squinted up at the thin line of blue sky that separated the rims of the canyon. Thick clouds interrupted the azure streak, many of them dark and heavy with rain. Was the terrible storm that had driven them upon these shores dissipating at last or still gathering strength? He had no way of knowing.

''Different canyon, Captain,'' offered Suarez conversationally.

''I can see that, idiot.''

The sailor tried a different tack, nodding in the direction of the spinosaur-clogged gap behind them. ''What d'you think they do?''

''I expect they'll grow bored and leave.''

''Surely you don't mean to go back that way, Captain?'' Mkuse was eyeing Blackstrap intently.

''Did you not just hear me say that we should go forward, man? We'll not return to that blasted jungle unless there be no other way out. Meanwhile, we'll explore the farthest reaches of this timely refuge and see if we cannot convince it to deliver us to the coast.'' He twirled one tip of his great mustache.

''Aye,'' muttered a spent seaman. ''Gold's no good to the man who doesn't get the chance to spend it. We've teased Lady Luck enough, I think.''

''Yes, back to the ship,'' agreed Samuel fervently.

''You know what they say about luck.'' Several of them turned to Guimaraes. ''It is like a jug with a hole in it. You can still drink from its mouth, but it is a smart man who drinks fast.''

''What think you, Mr. Smiggens?'' Blackstrap crouched next to his first mate, who lay prone and exhausted on the sand. ''Does this crack in the mountains also go all the way through?''

Smiggens raised himself up on one elbow and considered the enigmatic, winding boulevard of sand and stone. ''Only one way to find out, Captain. Only one way.''

"Aye." Blackstrap clapped him on the shoulder and Smiggens winced. " 'Twill be good to see our shipmates and the old tub again." A few weary cheers rose from the resting seamen.

"We needn't hurry, Brognar."

Blackstrap's expression narrowed as he peered down at his first mate. "What mean you by that, Mr. Smiggens?"

The other man looked away. "It's just that there's so much to learn here, Captain. When we depart, who knows if and when we'll be able to come back this way?"

"Here, now, Mr. Smiggens, what's all this about not hurryin'?" Copperhead dwarfed the spindly first mate. "Have you no care for your life?"

"Of course I do." Smiggens rose and brushed sand from his trousers. "I want to live as much as the next man. It's just that I want to learn as much as possible about this place in the event we're not able to return."

"What's so important about 'learning'?" growled O'Connor. "We're pirates, we are. It so states in the covenant of the *Condor*, which each of us has signed." He glared accusingly at the first mate. "Including you, Mr. Smiggens."

"Or is it, then," wondered Watford, coming dangerously close, "that you value learning above the life of an honest seaman?"

Seeing which way the wind was blowing and not liking the smell of it, Smiggens hastened to clarify his position. "No, no, it's nothing like that." He gestured up the canyon. "Best we not linger here, but move on while the light's still good. The quicker we're away from this place, the quicker there's money to be made."

The ominous expressions on the faces of the two sailors gave way to contented smiles. "That's more like it, Mr. Smiggens." O'Connor turned to the others. "A cheer for the first mate, boys!" A few ragged huzzahs rose from the exhausted crew.

Watford clapped him on the back hard enough to rattle his ribs before stalking off through the sand to help with the animals. Moments later the procession had resumed, captives in tow, leaving in their wake three incredibly frustrated but helpless spinosaurs. Their fear now behind them and protected by ramparts of impenetrable rock, the jovial pirates tossed a few well-chosen epithets in the direction of their former pursuers.

Though he maintained his place in line, Smiggens could not keep from glancing repeatedly back over his shoulder. What exotic lands still lay hidden and unseen on the other side of the rain forest? What marvels and wonders, what astonishing creatures were there to be found on the far side of the lake they had seen, or within its crystalline depths? Greater spectacles, perhaps, than any they had yet encountered?

The simple seamen who were his companions lacked the imagination to wonder or to care. Even Blackstrap, with his demonstrably greater intellect, cared nothing for discovery if it could not somehow be turned into gold.

He should be content, he told himself. They had done well, having encountered and survived marvels beyond imagining. Their amazing captives, living dinosaurs, would make all of them wealthy men.

Somewhere in the distance thunder rolled, causing him to glance skyward. If this canyon did not go all the way through the mountains, it would be an especially bad place to be caught in a downpour, he knew. As long as the floor remained level and flat his confidence stayed high. The sand was soft and warm beneath his boots, a great comfort to his feet after the difficult terrain of the rain forest.

Don't think so much, Preister Smiggens, and you'll be a happier man for it. But try as he would, he never had been able to escape his own thoughts.

⇒ XVI ⇐

THE PIRATES SPENT A RESTFUL NIGHT IN THE depths of the canyon. Swept into mounds like giants' jackstraws by periodic flash floods, piles of driftwood gathered jagged and broken in hollows and low places. The delighted seamen had only to collect what wood they needed for their fires.

For the first time since they'd entered the rain forest, they felt reasonably safe. It was clear that no carnivore of dangerous size could squeeze into the canyon and reach their campsite. They would be able to sleep in relative comfort. The sandy floor of the cleft was clean and sterile save for the occasional wandering insect. No one objected to the idea of being bitten, as long as the biter was smaller than themselves.

So fatigued were they from their narrow escape that it took an effort of will to prepare and eat supper. Nevertheless, and much to the struthies' dismay, the ever-cautious Blackstrap posted guards to keep a watch over both ends of the canyon.

With the fall of night the central campfire cast its stained-glass light on the canyon walls, throwing men and dinosaurs alike into eerie silhouette. The reassuring crackle of the fire was broken only by the murmur of conversation and the occasional chuckle of a seaman laughing at a comrade's joke.

"What do you think, Mr. Smiggens?" O'Connor nodded up canyon, past where the stolid Mkuse stood silent watch. "Does she cut all the way through, then?"

"Blackstrap asked the same question of me earlier." The

first mate studied the few stars visible between the gathering clouds. "There's no way to tell from our present location, Mr. O'Connor. I believe the floor of this chasm to be at least as low as the one that originally brought us this way, but I'm no surveyor. Still, I think it possible that this entire range of mountains, or at least the portion we are visiting, may be cut by such canyons. We can but hope this is one such."

Prettykill listened absently to the human babble. Of all the species who inhabited Dinotopia, they alone were famed for talk more than action. Even a garrulous *Gallimimus* appeared mute beside the least long-winded of them.

Their words meant nothing to her. Despite their verbosity she knew they were not entirely useless. She had heard from others of her tribe that on the rare occasions when they could be safely caught, they were quite good to eat, though one had to watch out for all the small bones.

Turning, she scrutinized the struthies. One of the young-sters noted her stare and began to shiver slightly. She smiled. That was as it should be. Though civilization had come to Dinotopia long ago, it had not succeeded in wiping out every ancestral memory.

In these modern times kills were rarely made. The car-nosaurs of the Rainy Basin did not need to hunt. Not when the aged and dying of the civilized regions betook themselves down into the basin to expire. It was a mutually beneficial arrangement, allowing the carnosaurs to survive without kill-ing while at the same time permitting the inhabitants of the civilized regions to get on with their lives without having to dig hundreds of graves the size of ships.

But the hunting instinct remained strong within Prettykill and her kind. While its fulfillment took the form of games instead of reality, her skills and those of her fellow juveniles remained sharp.

Crouching quietly in her shackles and ropes, conserving her strength, she shut her eyes until only a thin line of yellow was visible. *Better this way*, she thought. *Better a life of freedom and unfettered individuality than the constrictions of a town or farm.* What need had her kind for the trappings of civilization? What need for morals and books? They re-mained true to their wild ancestry, the occasional covenant with the meandering convoys that passed through the Rainy Basin notwithstanding.

She would continue to bide her time. Her jaws twitched, eager to be free of the restrictive ropes. When the moment was right—and she had no doubt there would come such a moment—she would strike. She would show them what even such a young one of her kind was capable of when aroused.

I am the apex predator, she reminded herself. *There are none above; all lie at my feet. I have nothing to fear.*

"Look at that critter, squattin' there like a sleeping shark." Old Ruskin gestured in the direction of their prize captive. "You'd think it were dead, so still it sits."

"Not that one." Chumash had lit his last cigar and sat puffing contentedly. "Not sleeping, either."

Ruskin squinted, his eyes sharp, for an oldster. "You're wrong, Indian. It's sound asleep, it is."

"You think so?" Chumash grunted. "You go give Big Tooth a kiss. Then you see how hard it sleeping." He took another drag on the battered stogie.

"Wouldn't matter none. It's tied fast. The Portuguese made the mistake o' gettin' too close when its jaws were loose."

Chumash nodded once. "You bother it too much and captain will take a bite out of you. Healthy it worth ten thousand American dollars. I hear first mate say so."

Ruskin whistled softly. " 'Tis a strange place we've come to and a strange business we're about, even for so much money. I don't like it here."

"Eh-tah," the Indian murmured in his own tongue. "You belong to sea. I belong to tall woods. Yet we work these things together in this place. For gold."

"Aye," Ruskin agreed, feeling a little better. At the thought of gold the canyon walls felt a little less like the halves of a gigantic vise. Unlike many of the others, he would relax only when his beloved ocean was once more in sight. "For gold."

It was Watford who, in the course of their trek northward the next morning, first remarked on the distinctive nature of a certain side canyon. They had passed many such offshoots since rising, fanning out like capillaries from a vein. Blackstrap had sent men to explore several, only to have them return within no more than an hour to report that in every instance the offshoots rapidly narrowed to dead ends or impassable fissures. Such reports further convinced Smiggens that they were indeed hiking a major canyon, one likely to cut all the way through the mountains.

It was the singular color of the canyon floor, a distinctive darkening, that caught Watford's attention. After a moment's hesitation, he decided to bring it to Blackstrap's notice.

"Sir, there's something about that side crevice over there, the one coming up on our right."

"What about it, man?" His eyes focused single-mindedly on the route ahead, Blackstrap didn't turn to look. Despite the perpetual shade provided by the narrow canyon, it was still hot and humid, what with the Rainy Basin on one side and the Northern Plains on the other. The occasional breeze was a most welcome visitor. At present it was notable for its absence, and Blackstrap was perspiring profusely.

"Well, look at the sands there, Captain." Watford was from Cornwall, which at least partly explained his interest in rocks.

Blackstrap squinted to his right. "A little darker they be, Mr. Watford. What be that to us?"

"I'm not sure, sir. There's something about the color that reminds me of that which I've seen before. I just can't quite place it."

"Place it quickly, then, Mr. Watford, or hold your tongue. 'Tis too hot for mindless prattle."

Undeterred, the sailor broke from the main party and trotted over to the entrance to the tributary gorge. Halting where the sands shone sooty, he dug experimentally at the ground with the heel of his boot. Sand and gravel flew backward. The deeper he dug, the darker the surface became, until it was almost black.

Thomas waved at him. "Come on, then, man! What are you wasting time there for?"

"Aye," yelled another. "We'll not wait for you, Cornishman!"

Only Smiggens showed any interest, wandering back to watch the sailor at his work. He searched the ground carefully, looking for anything out of the ordinary.

"What is it, Watford? What do you think you see?"

"I ain't sure, Mr. Smiggens, sir. A suggestion, maybe. A hint, an inkling."

"Of what, Mr. Watford?"

"Tin, mostly, sir. And other things."

"Well, we've plenty of cups and flagons on the *Condor.*" The first mate's sarcasm was leavened with gentleness. "Perhaps you should conserve your curiosity for another time."

"I suppose you're right, sir." Raising his right leg, Watford brushed accumulated sand from his boot. "But back home I'd swear this were familiar."

It would have ended there, finished and forgotten, had Smiggens not slipped in the process of turning to depart and fallen hard. Laughter rose from those men who'd witnessed his clumsiness.

"Best watch your step there, Mr. Smiggens!" shouted one. "We're not back aboard yet."

"Yes," added another from behind his beard, "the ground here doesn't roll."

Smiggens's backside had taken most of the impact, his legs the rest, and his scabbard just a little. It was the metal scabbard, however, that had kicked up the bright flashes. The glint of cloud-masked sunlight caught his eye as Watford helped him to his feet.

Most likely mica, in rock like this, he reasoned. Or perhaps quartz. His gaze narrowed as he stared hard at the place where his scabbard had struck. The gleam was different, somehow. Brighter and more intense.

"Captain," he called out even as he started to crouch down for a better look, "you'd best come and have a look at this."

"At what?" Blackstrap growled. "More dirty dirt, Mr. Smiggens? You know better than to waste my time with your poking and classifying."

The first mate was kneeling now, scratching with his knife at the surface where his scabbard had given birth to buried light. The more blackness he shaved away, the larger became the patch of reflected sunshine. He was sure now it wasn't mica or quartz. Beneath his knife it was almost soft.

An alloy of some kind. His pulse quickened.

Then Watford was on the ground next to him, digging furiously at the surface with his own blade. His face was alight. "Not tin, sir. No, by God, not tin."

Smiggens held a pinch of the black stuff up to the light. "Tarnish, Mr. Watford. Incredibly thick and old it is, but no more than that."

Holding the tether that was secured to the neck of the largest *Struthiomimus*, Mkuse paused curiously to hail his suddenly frenetic shipmates. "Hoy, you two! Have you found something, then?"

"Worms," ventured Samuel. "They going fishing."

"That we are, Mr. Samuel, that we are," Watford called back. "And you'd best be nice to me or I'm liable to not share my catch with you!"

One at a time, and then in small groups, the men turned from the path and wandered toward the furiously digging first mate and his companion. Blackstrap built himself into a fine fury over the delay until he, too, saw what the labors of the two men had revealed.

"By the sea-god's beard, that be silver or the Chief Justice on his high perch doesn't piss into a long john!" His anger was quickly put aside as he fell to digging and scratching frenziedly alongside his equally ecstatic men. Whoops of astonishment and delight soon rang from the canyon walls.

As for the captive struthies and the young tyrannosaur, they watched the frantic activity and found themselves wondering in equal measure what all the fuss was about. The gleaming metal bricks the men were slowly uncovering certainly constituted an unusual choice for road paving material, but hardly one capable of driving otherwise sane humans into a maddened frenzy. It only reinforced Hisaulk's feeling that their captors were mentally unbalanced.

"Look at them," Tryll exclaimed. "Have they all gone mad, Mother?"

"It may be that this lot of humans was mad from the beginning, daughter." Shremaza wished she could cuddle her offspring close, but she was prevented by the tightness of her bindings. Nearby, restrained only by her hobbles and the wavering attention of several guards, Prettykill ignored the childish goings-on.

Swords and knives joined bare hands as the men scraped excitedly at the accumulated tarnish. Shirts flew off backs and were pressed into service as polishing rags. Before long they had a substantial area cleared. The sunlight gleamed so brightly on the result of their efforts that several of those with light-colored eyes were forced to look away while tears ran down their unshaven cheeks.

"See." Smiggens traced the lines in the pavement with the tip of his sword. "Here's where the bricks were poured. Not mortared into place, mind, but *poured*."

"How thick do you reckon it be, Mr. Smiggens?" Blackstrap's eyes glittered greedily.

"No way to tell without digging some of it up, Captain." Rather than concentrate on their impressive if shallow excavation, the first mate had turned his attention up the side canyon. "At the moment, I find myself more interested in how far it runs rather than how deep it goes."

With swords and axes they sliced away at the thin blanket of sand and the tarnish beneath, following the silver road up the tributary cleft, their baffled captives in tow. The little canyon wound its way steadily eastward, the silver pavement beneath their feet showing no sign of giving out.

After a respectable distance the sheer-sided cleft, instead of narrowing further as had been their experience with similar crevices, began to broaden out. The silver paving widened to reach from side to side. They proceeded now with caution, as the chasm was more than wide enough to accommodate those species of large meat-eaters whose unwelcome attentions they had so recently escaped. Their concerns were muted by the ever-present shimmer of silver underfoot. *Livistona* palms thrust their trunks skyward, but there was no suggestion of intruding rain forest or woods.

"Nickel, I should think," Smiggens was muttering.

"What's that, Mr. Smiggens?" Blackstrap spoke with unusual calm, their discovery sufficient to awe even him.

"In the alloy. Pure silver would be too soft for a road, even one that carried only light traffic. Nickel would, I think, make it sturdy enough to serve its intended function." As they advanced, the narrow canyon became a trail, then a thoroughfare, and lastly a boulevard broad enough to make each man rich beyond his maddest dreams.

"This much silver..." Blackstrap was murmuring, "why, even the conquistadors never took so much out of the New World."

A shout made them both look up. As the discoverer of the astonishing avenue, Watford had earned the right to walk point. In the rain forest such a position would have been considered suicidal, but here it was a mark of honor.

"Har, what has our sharp-eyed Cornishman found this time?" The captain's gold tooth glistened as he smiled. "Rouse yourselves, boys! Mr. Watford is hailing us, and when Mr. Watford hails now, why, 'tis the wise man who snaps to his call!"

Increasing their pace to a jog, which their captives had no difficulty matching despite their hobbles, they turned a sharp corner in the enlarged canyon and found themselves confronting a wall. Simple of design and solid of construction, it ran from one side of the chasm to the other. Perhaps two feet deep and twenty high, it was fashioned entirely of bricks a foot long and several inches thick. A large opening was visible in the exact center of the barrier, with loose brass hinges showing where an ancient wooden gate had long since rotted away.

Dusty and dirty, every brick in the wall had been coated with brass to protect it from decay at the hands of the elements.

"Why brass, I wonder?" murmured Blackstrap as they advanced on this relic of an unknown civilization. "Mayhap they had access to a lot of it."

"Brass." Smiggens wore a strange expression, peculiar even for him. "If it's brass, then it should be as tarnished as the silver. Unless someone hereabouts has dedicated a lifetime to polishing."

The reality was so overwhelming that for several moments more it continued to evade those hardened and experienced buccaneers. It struck them as forcefully as a hammer blow to the back of the head only when Blackstrap tried to pry a loose brick from its setting on the edge of the ancient gateway.

For a long moment the captain was actually speechless, the first time in their long acquaintance that Smiggens had ever seen him so. Cradling the brick in both hands, the big man sat down on the hard ground. He tilted his head back and stared silently up at the wall. Two feet thick, twenty high, how far from canyonside to canyonside they had yet to measure or estimate. Except for the long-vanished gate, a solid barrier across the chasm.

"What is it, Captain?" asked Thomas.

"Aye, Captain, what's the matter?" Samuel pressed close, curiosity if not actual concern written in his expression.

"The matter? Why, nothing be the matter, Mr. Samuel." Blackstrap let his eyes rove the faces of his men. "Nothing be the matter at all. Be so good as to take this for me, Mr. Samuel."

So saying, he tossed the brick to the seaman, who caught it easily . . . and then yelped as it slipped through his fingers to land heavily on his right foot. Despite the protection of his boot he collapsed to the ground, howling in pain that passed almost immediately.

The brick was solid gold.

The wall was composed entirely of identical bricks.

Therefore, the wall . . .

Untrained as they were in Aristotelian logic, the men were soon digging and hammering at the barrier with anything and everything that would do duty as a tool. Knives, swords, axes, gun butts, even whalebone combs were pressed into hysterical service. A second brick was extracted and proved to be as heavy as the first. Digging patiently into the surface of the captain's block, Smiggens ascertained that the brick was indeed gold all the way through and not, for example, lead coated with poured gold.

"I'm no goldsmith, but I would guess it at eighteen karat," he finally announced. "Of course, one would expect the purity to vary from brick to brick."

"Oh, to be sure, Mr. Smiggens, to be sure," replied Blackstrap through pursed lips. "That be no problem, that." He gazed anew at his crew. "Anything under fourteen karat, why, we'll simply use for ballast!'' The men roared.

"Ha-weh." Chumash was looking past his fellow pluto-crats. "Has anyone see Cornishman?''

"Yes''—with a grunt, Smiggens set the small fortune aside—"where has Watford got to, anyway? One would think he'd be here celebrating alongside us. After all, he is the legitimate discoverer of our fortune.'' At a thought he returned his attention to the wall. "What is this place, any-way? Who built this wall here, and why?''

Blackstrap was not entirely without learning. "Atlantis, perhaps. Lemuria. Ancient Mu. Cimmeria. All the half-forgotten, half-remembered civilizations of the world. The Cathay that Columbus looked for but never found. This be them, all rolled into one grand golden artifact.'' He rested one palm possessively on the impossible fortification. "Now 'tis ours. Where are you going to live with your share, Mr. Smiggens? Meself, I thinks I may buy Warwick Palace. Or half of Devonshire.''

"I don't know.'' The first mate could manage no more than a dazed mumble. "I haven't thought that far ahead yet.''

"You know what this means, Captain.''

Blackstrap turned to face the sailor. "What say you, Mr. Guimaraes?''

The other sidled close and nodded in the direction of their stolid, indifferent captives. "It means we do not need those animals anymore. Why should we trouble ourselves to trade living creatures for gold when we already have more gold and silver than the ship can carry?''

"The Portuguese speaks smartly,'' agreed Samuel.

Smiggens woke from his daze. "We have to bring them back with us, Captain. They're worth more than just gold. Their value to science is incalculable.''

"Science!'' Contempt dripped from Guimaraes's lips. He ran one hand along the golden wall. "Will your 'science' make us richer than this?''

No, the first mate thought anxiously, *but if you'd give it half a chance it would make you smarter, you sneering ba-boon*. Aloud he said, "We haven't anything to carry the gold back with. The animals carry themselves. Why not take them back to the ship with us? Then we can return with sacks and sledges.''

''Nothin' to carry it with?'' Ruskin's graying whiskers quivered. ''Why, I'll carry it in me teeth!'' Several of the men guffawed.

''Also,'' Smiggens added desperately, ''I'll pay for them out of my share.''

This time approving murmurs instead of laughter greeted the first mate's words. The splitting of shares was a profound matter to any crew engaged in piracy, and the men took the offer seriously.

''That be fair enough.'' Blackstrap bestowed his blessing on the proposal. ''Though I think you've spent too much time in this heat, Mr. Smiggens. Be that as it is, you may have your animals. May they bring you as much satisfaction as your gold will bring us.'' Fresh laughter arose from the men.

Curious and hopeful as ever, Hisaulk studied the antics of the crew. They seemed overjoyed by the discovery of the wall, though for the life of him he could not understand why. Surely this was the most peculiar clutch of humans ever to set foot on Dinotopia. When their guards glanced away, he worked at his bindings, with the usual lack of success. A human thumb would have been a great help.

''At least my cargo will weigh less,'' Smiggens pointed out.

Guimaraes didn't give up easily. ''The first mate makes a generous offer, but is there enough gold even in his share to compensate us for the pain and trouble we'll have to put up with if we are to carry these noisome beasts clear across the Southern Ocean?'' A malign gleam came into his eyes. ''And besides, is there a man among you not hungry for the taste of fresh meat? I myself have eaten tortoise, iguana, and snake, and if these here possess flavor similar in any wise to those, they will make a fine repast indeed.''

Mkuse eyed the struthies appraisingly. ''More like ostrich, I would think, but that is good eating as well.''

''We have our gold,'' remarked another man. ''A feast would seem to be in order.''

Before the cry could be taken up by the rest of the crew,

before a worried Smiggens could protest further, a shout came from beyond. The absent Watford had announced himself.

"Har, now what else has that wandering Cornishman found?" Blackstrap rose from where he'd been sitting to peer through the gap formerly occupied by the long-vanished gate. "Another wall, perhaps?"

"Sure, and 'tis not possible, Cap'n," declared O'Connor. "There could be no more gold than this in any one place."

"We'll go and have a look anyways. I find I've grown rather fond of Mr. Watford's discoveries."

"Your pardon, Captain," interjected Guimaraes, "but what about our feast?"

Blackstrap looked from Smiggens to the Portuguese. His thoughts and heart, however, were presently with the insistent, unseen Watford. "There'll be no killing of anything for now. Time enough later to settle this."

"But, Captain—"

"That's me word on the matter, Mr. Guimaraes." Blackstrap's tone darkened ominously. "Have you any difficulty with that?"

Muttering under his breath, a disappointed Guimaraes turned away. "No, Captain. No difficulty at all."

Bunching close and keeping their captives in the middle, they strode through the opening, marveling as they did so at the straight lines of the primeval wall and the precision of its construction. Following Watford's echoing calls they advanced up the canyon, which had now expanded to the point where it ought more properly to have been called a hidden valley.

Watford's shouts were growing louder, indicating that they had all but caught up to the Cornishman. There was another sharp bend in the now expansive gorge. This they ambled around . . . and stopped where they stood, overwhelmed by the sight that greeted them.

It was fortunate indeed, Smiggens decided as he gaped wordlessly alongside the others, that the sky was filled with clouds, else every man-jack among them would likely have been blinded.

The most wondrous vista lay spread before them, no less

overpowering for its compactness. Flanked by brooding walls of sheer gray and red rock, the complex of temples and ancillary edifices thrust into the clear air. Neat avenues separated the step pyramids, the columned public buildings, and the more modest, single-story structures that had once served as living quarters for the masters of the community. Smiggens recognized a host of architectural influences, from Egyptian to Greek, Chinese, and Incan. It was an olla podrida of styles. The results were confusing, but they worked.

Of more interest to the rest of the crew was not the engineering but the choice of building materials.

Many of the structures were fashioned of the same solid gold brick as the wall they had left behind. Others used gold and silver brick in alternating line. Those must be the cheap houses, a dumbfounded Smiggens decided. Though every building had suffered in some way from the ravages of time, many of the ornate embellishments and decorations were still intact. In their own way, these were even more fascinating than the amazing structures themselves.

Silently, the stunned intruders made their way along the silver boulevard that ran between the principal edifices. In a whorl of engravings and gold inlay it halted before the largest and most complex structure in the sunken valley.

Pillars inscribed with detailed bas-reliefs and finely wrought sculpture decorated the front of the temple. People were the subject of much of this art, along with creatures large and small that for the most part the men did not recognize. It was Smiggens who pointed out that several of the nonhuman sculptures resembled creatures they had already encountered in this land, as well as their own captives.

Each of the pillars had been cut from a single piece of malachite. The bas-reliefs that wound around their circumferences were set with amethysts and citrines, chrysoprase and turquoise. Lintels of lapis lazuli supported the roof of the porch, so dark blue they were almost black. The ramshackle crew of the *Condor* were simple men whose tastes had been only partly elevated by their choice of career. Here was wealth beyond their comprehension.

"And to think," O'Connor was mumbling, "all I ever wanted out o' life was a decent house in Dublin."

"Why think so small?" Suarez stood next to him, gaping up at the inlaid columns. "Buy Dublin."

The golden walls behind the columned porch were inlaid with large squares of jasper and agate, carnelian and opal. These had been carved as deeply and intricately as the pillars.

A grinning Watford stepped out from behind the nearest. "Well, boys, what do you think? Myself, I think Buckingham Palace would be but an outhouse compared to this country cottage."

Blackstrap peered past the energetic sailor. Panels of translucent jade passed light through the ceiling onto the wide porch, while circular ports of flawless rock crystal served as windows into the structure.

"You will have an extra share from all this, Mr. Watford. As for meself, me ambitions have changed. I think now I will not buy myself a county, but rather a country. If you hear of one for sale, Mr. Smiggens, you will let me know. Perhaps you will buy the country alongside and we can be neighbors."

They mounted the last of the golden steps, which were trimmed in polished onyx, and found themselves confronting a pair of ten-foot-high doors. These had been cut from purest rose quartz and inlaid with rubies, sapphires, padparasha, and pearls. Staggered by the riches they had found, they leaned on the heavy barrier until it parted, admitting them to the temple.

Though fashioned of the same precious materials, the interior was surprisingly sparse. Rooms were devoid of furniture and, save for a few scattered sculptures, the main hall was deserted. The floor was a detailed mosaic of animal life that all but Smiggens found incomprehensible and nightmarish. The mosaic chips themselves engendered far more comment, each being fashioned from an appropriately colored semiprecious stone.

As he studied the floor, Smiggens ignored the sound of boots clicking softly on the smooth stonework. "I think this may represent the history not only of this land but of life on earth."

"Belay that kind of talk, Mr. Smiggens." Johanssen, too, had been examining the beautifully inlaid surface. "There's no depiction of the flood, so this can be no more than a scene from someone's imagination.''

Smiggens chose not to reply, certain he was the only one among them who was in any way familiar with the recent writings of those intrepid Englishmen Darwin and Wallace.

"See how they empty their minds through their eyes," Shremaza whispered to her mate. "They are completely obsessed, though with what I cannot imagine."

"Perhaps they will forget us." Hisaulk ignored their splendiferous surroundings. "I don't like it in here. It's cold.''

Perhaps the pirates were beginning to feel likewise. Sunset threatened, and no one was anxious to spend the night in that venerable, mysterious temple. Returning the way they had come, they exited through the rose-hued entrance and busied themselves with knives and swords, prying precious gems from the bas-reliefs and sculptures.

By the time darkness enveloped them, Smiggens had a cheery fire ablaze on the golden porch. Copperhead had managed to accumulate a hatful of fine emeralds. As Thomas played a Caribbean jig on his hornpipe, the other man, inebriated by wealth, danced for his comrades, tossing flashes of green fire at them like an Arab potentate dispensing alms to the poor. Laughing all the while, the men snatched lazily at these offerings. In the context of the fortune surrounding them, such baubles were pretty but of no especial worth.

Masticating their dry evening meal, which now did not seem so tasteless, they swapped grandiose dreams, each man trying to top his mate with a description of what he planned to do with his newly acquired, incalculable wealth. To amuse themselves, Thomas and Andreas pried bricks from the wall of the temple and used them to construct a solid gold fire pit around the first mate's blaze. They had no difficulty finding fuel with which to feed the fire. Ample plant matter, dry and ready for the gathering, lay scattered everywhere, having fallen or been blown down from the enclosing canyon rim.

Seeing no reason to conserve it further, Blackstrap magnanimously ordered Smiggens to break out their small flagon of medicinal grog and measure out a ration to each man. While this was insufficient in quantity to enable the men to get roaring drunk, it did lighten their already elevated spirits considerably. Ruskin brought out his Jew's harp and joined its metallic twang to Thomas's hornpipe, whereupon the porch of the temple soon echoed to the merry tunes of sailor and landsman alike. Not even Blackstrap objected when several of the men chose to fire off their weapons in celebration.

"Their dancing is execrable." Shremaza watched the humans stumble and totter about. "It would not pass entry at the simplest festival."

"I hear the fireworks but see only flashes of light." Tryll hovered close to her mother. "Where are the pretty colors?"

Hisaulk watched one man aim his rifle skyward and let loose a succession of shots. "They're noisy enough, but these are not fireworks as we know them. They emerge from long tubes, which is right, but without color. Just as the lives of these humans must be devoid of color."

As usual, Prettykill paid no attention to the family discussion. Even were she conversant with the struthie tongue she would not have been inclined to participate. The pops and bangs of the humans' toys she ignored.

Guimaraes might not have joined so wholeheartedly in the celebration had he known that his every move was being followed closely by a pair of burning yellow eyes.

⇒ XVII ⇐

FOR THE PAST HOUR CROOKEYE HAD BEEN RUMBLING like a threatening storm. Will knew that the tyrannosaur was baffled and frustrated.

They'd spent most of the morning wandering aimlessly through the rain forest. The intruders' trail had finally faded beyond the ability even of the great carnivores to detect. It had rained hard several times and the trail repeatedly crossed small streams. Will was surprised that the dedicated tyrannosaurs had managed to follow it for as long as they had.

From his lofty perch atop the great head, he looked to his right and down. "What is he saying?"

Held securely if not comfortably in Shethorn's grasp, Chaz kicked his legs and tried to turn his head. "You think, Will Denison, I have nothing better to do than dangle here and translate at your whim?"

"Well, do you?" Will waited for a reply.

The *Protoceratops* had none. "Oh, well, I suppose you're right. Crookeye says that they've lost the trail. Time and dilution have weakened the scent beyond their ability to follow it. They don't know which way to go."

Will considered the impasse. "I guess the best thing to do is continue eastward while keeping the mountains on our left. That's what I'd do if I were a stranger here needing a way out."

"Yes, that's what you'd do, but you're familiar with the dangers of the Rainy Basin. These intruders must be ignorant of such things. Who's to say they aren't heading due south across the basin?'' The *Protoceratops* looked like a giant tadpole in the female tyrannosaur's grasp.

"Their trail's followed the foothills for the past two days, and from the time our friends picked it up, it's never strayed far from the mountains. Isn't it more reasonable to assume they'll hew to the same pattern than suddenly change direction?''

Clinging comfortably to the back of Shethorn's neck, Keelk chittered at them. Though she addressed herself to Chaz, who alone among her companions could understand her speech, her gaze remained focused on Will. She had beautiful eyes, he thought. All struthies did.

"She wants to know what's happening, why we're hesitating here.'' Chaz looked to his human companion for assistance. "I don't know what to tell her.''

"Tell her the truth,'' Will replied.

As soon as Chaz had finished explaining, Shethorn chipped in with a series of sonorous rumblings. Again the *Protoceratops* translated.

"She says that we'd better find her daughter in good health.'' Chaz shuddered slightly. "I agree. I've no desire to learn what a *Tyrannosaurus rex* looks like in the throes of a mad rage.''

"Nor do I.'' Shifting his backside against the smoothly pebbled skin of his mount's skull, Will peered over the side. "Somehow we have to pick up the trail again. I've been watching for footprints and broken branches.''

"Footprints would help,'' agreed Chaz. "Other creatures besides humans also break branches.''

"Oh, that's right.'' Will was slightly crestfallen. "Remember, I'm new to this. I'm used to looking for signs from a lot higher up.'' He leaned over the other side. "You'd think with there being so many of them we'd see *some* trace of their passing.''

Chaz translated for Keelk and then translated her reply. "She says the ground's too wet and too soft. I don't know how we're going to—''

He was interrupted by a long, loud ringing noise. It echoed through the trees and reverberated off the precipitous cliffs of the nearby foothills. It was followed by another, and another.

"Odd sort of thunder," Chaz remarked. Shethorn growled querulously.

"Tell her that's not thunder." Will was excited and concerned all at the same time. Excited because he now knew which way to go, and concerned for what they might find when they got there.

Not many people could have stood confidently atop a tyrannosaur's head, shielding their eyes as they searched the surrounding country, but Will managed it. In addition to a disdain for heights, he had an excellent sense of balance. As he scanned the enveloping rain forest, trying to see through the trees, the sharp pealing came again. The five-foot-long skull beneath his feet twitched slightly, forcing him to spread his arms to maintain his stability.

"Crookeye wants to know what that is," Chaz explained, "and frankly, so do I."

"Gunfire! Those were gunshots."

"What is gunfire, and what are gunshots?" The history and use of such weapons were unknown in Dinotopia except to historians.

Will considered carefully before replying. The two tyrannosaurs were already edgy enough. "They're kind of like fireworks."

"Fireworks." From his undignified position the translator tried to meet Will's eyes but could not. "Why would the people we seek—or anyone else, for that matter—be setting off fireworks this deep into the Rainy Basin?"

"Why ask me to speculate on their motives?" Will responded quickly. "Maybe they're celebrating something." *Please let them be celebrating something*, he thought anxiously, *and not shooting at any of their captives*. He tried not to think of what might happen if they encountered the intruders only to find that they had injured young Prettykill, or worse. If such turned out to be the case he knew that sympathetic words were not likely to calm enraged tyrannosaurs. Remembering their bargain, he was acutely conscious of the immensely powerful skull on which he stood.

They could avoid such a possibility by sneaking off at the

first opportunity, he knew. They could find a way up the cliffs or hide in crevices in the rock until the deceived predators gave up and went away. They could do that . . . except that he'd given his word. In Dinotopia it didn't matter if you gave that to a dinosaur or another human. In a society based on barter, a person's word was their bond.

Of course, the tyrannosaurs were uncivilized and not formally a party to such covenants. But he was.

Resuming his cross-legged seat atop Crookeye's head, he pointed northeast with his left hand. No trail lay in that direction, but that wouldn't be a problem. The tyrannosaurs made their own trail.

"Tell them to go in the direction of the sounds. The sounds mark the location of the intruders."

"Then we must be fairly close." Chaz hastened to translate for the tyrannosaurs.

As he was doing so, Will reached down to rap his mount on the upper lip. A yellow orb rolled up to look at him, and he saw his face reflected in the tyrannosaur's eye.

"That way." He pointed again. "The ones we seek are that way."

The big male didn't wait for Chaz to finish the brief translation. With a lurch he started forward, snarling in anticipation. Breaking into a run, the two colossi smashed their way effortlessly through the forest, scattering a host of smaller creatures from their path. Will hung on to the pair of knobby projections that rose above each eye and focused on the rocking scenery ahead. They were speeding now, the tyrannosaurs moving as fast as they could, and the sensation was breathtaking.

If Will lost his seat and fell off, he knew, it would be more than that.

Off to his right he could hear Keelk chirping away encouragingly. She appeared to have no difficulty maintaining her grip on Shethorn's neck. Below, Chaz kept up a constant litany of complaint that the female tyrannosaur ignored as usual.

A flock of birds-of-paradise exploded from a small, densely vegetated tree directly ahead. The tree went down beneath Crookeye's belly, only to spring erect again in his wake. Off to their left, the Backbone Mountains beckoned. Soon, Will hoped, he would be at home in their cool heights once more.

But first he had a rescue to perform.

Where gravel and rock replaced soil, the rain forest began to thin. The tyrannosaurs were finally forced to slow as they approached sheer walls of gray granite. Both bent low to the ground and sniffed energetically, their great heads once more sweeping methodically from side to side.

Shethorn came near. Shoving her snout close to Will, she snorted several curt phrases. Her breath made him reel, but he managed to muster an attentive smile. Keelk peered anxiously around the tyrannosaur's neck.

"What . . . what does she say?"

From below, Chaz looked up at him. "They've picked up the trail again."

Moments later they found themselves pausing outside the entrance to the slot canyon. Confirmation of the correctness of their course came in the form of hundreds of overlapping footprints that marred the rock and sand underfoot. Many were those of resident dinosaurs, but enough showed the unmistakable outline of well-worn boots. Hardly able to restrain their impatience, Crookeye and Shethorn strode into the well-shaded gap.

They soon encountered not human intruders, nor Keelk's family, nor even the adult tyrannosaurs' missing daughter. Three very startled spinosaurs whirled around at their approach. Their initial snarls of challenge quickly gave way to panic and desperation as they saw what was coming up the canyon behind them. With nowhere to go, they scrabbled and clawed at the rocks and one another, each trying to force itself into a smaller and smaller opening behind its companion.

Parting massive jaws, Crookeye bellowed his own challenge. It was echoed by his mate. This only increased the spinosaurs' panic, and Will found himself sympathizing.

One of the smaller sail-backed carnosaurs dropped to its belly and put its head on the ground. This gesture of abject submission was quickly duplicated by the other two, until all three lay prone on the sand, their colorful sails swaying slightly from side to side. In such fashion were bloody conflicts between the dominant inhabitants of the Rainy Basin avoided.

Half crawling, half groveling, the spinosaurs slithered sideways, pressing as close as possible to the southern wall of the chasm. Properly appeased, Crookeye and Shethorn backed themselves close to the opposite wall to allow their smaller, deferential cousins to pass.

"Tell them to stop, and find out if they know anything," Will abruptly told Chaz.

The *Protoceratops* looked up at him. "What, me?" he squeaked.

Will couldn't help but grin. "What are you afraid of? You think they're going to take offense?"

"I prefer not to dwell on the possibilities." Turning to the subservient spinosaurs, he addressed them in their own tongue. He did not have to translate for the tyrannosaurs, whose own dialect was near enough to that of the other meat-eaters to be readily understood.

"They say that they chased a whole covey of humans down this canyon until it became too narrow for them to go any farther. The humans had four struthies with them as well as a young tyrannosaur, and these were all bound with ropes. It puzzled them, but not enough to halt their pursuit. To a carnosaur, an easy meal is not to be questioned."

Will was satisfied. "Tell them they can go." To emphasize his words, or perhaps to make a statement of his own, Crookeye took a ponderous step in the other carnivores' direction and dropped his lower jaw, emitting the loudest hiss Will had ever heard. It sounded like an angry hundred-foot-long snake.

In their haste to flee, two of the spinosaurs ran into the wall behind them. Flailing frantically at each other, they scrambled to hightail it out of the canyon. Shethorn punctuated their departure with a derisive snort before she and her mate turned to study the terrain ahead.

The unseen sun was well down and night fell faster within the confines of the canyon than outside. Despite the failing light, Will could clearly see the imprints of many booted feet in the sand below, as well as those of the intruders' captives and the agitated spinosaurs.

"Tell them to go carefully," Will directed the *Protoceratops*. "We only know that these people have guns. We don't know how many or of what caliber."

Chaz relayed this information to their mounts. Crookeye growled a curt reply.

"They're not impressed."

Will considered. "I suppose that's not surprising, since they don't know what guns are." Even as he discussed the situation with Chaz, they were advancing steadily up the chasm. It was already so narrow that the two tyrannosaurs had to travel in single file.

"I don't think it would matter if they did," the stocky translator told him. "They know that their offspring is a prisoner somewhere up ahead. No human contrivance is going to prevent them from reaching her."

Very soon, however, they encountered an obstacle that not even an adult tyrannosaur could surmount: the same attenuated passage that had thwarted the spinosaurs. As they examined the barrier, a volley of shots rang out in the distance, threatening to drive the already frustrated adults into a frenzy.

"Easy, easy." Wondering if he could even feel the gesture, Will leaned forward to stroke Crookeye's snout. Whether it had any effect or not Will would never know, but the big tyrannosaur settled down. The echoes of the multiple shots faded into the distance.

Chaz translated Keelk's comment. "She says that we must be very close now."

"I think we are, too, though echoes in a canyon can be deceptive. Skybax riders learn that right away."

"Is that a glow in the sky off to our right?" Chaz would have pointed, but his awkward position prevented him from doing so.

It didn't matter. As the darkness deepened, Will saw it, too. "Somebody has a fire going. A big fire." *I hope not a cooking fire*, he thought grimly. "They're up ahead somewhere, all right."

Growling her frustration, Shethorn bit at the obstructing cliffside, her saberlike teeth leaving inch-wide gouges in the raw stone. But not even she could chew her way through to her daughter.

"They can't go any farther," Chaz declared.

"I can see that," Will replied, deep in thought. "The question is, what do we do now?"

Having come to the same conclusion as her friends, Keelk wasn't waiting to debate their next step. Already she was climbing carefully down the back of Shethorn's neck, making her way to the ground. The narrowness of the chasm might have halted the tyrannosaurs' advance, but it would not stop her, not even if she had to continue on by herself.

Bounding forward across the soft sand, she halted ten yards on and turned to hoot at her companions. One clawed foreleg beckoned repeatedly.

"Surely we can't go on by ourselves?" Chaz was fidgeting in Shethorn's grasp. "The closer we get, the more irrational you make these intruders sound."

"We don't have any choice. We gave our word." Leaning to his left, he met Crookeye's stare while stabbing a finger downward. "Don't worry. We'll get your daughter back. Somehow."

The great carnivore grunted a response. He understood nothing of the human's words, but the young man's tone and gesture were readily fathomed. Settling slowly into a crouch, he lowered his head and neck to allow his passenger an easy dismount.

Hopping off, Will found himself standing next to Chaz, who had been gently set down by Shethorn. Even resting flat on the sand, the tyrannosaur's skull came up to Will's chest. As soon as his passenger was clear, the big male straightened. Will turned to regard them both.

"Tell them that I promise we'll do everything we can to return their daughter to them, safe and unharmed. But in order to do that we have to go on by ourselves. We all know that they can't go any farther. If the spinosaurs couldn't get through this pinch-point, they surely can't."

"I think they know that," the *Protoceratops* replied.

"Well, tell them anyway."

Chaz bristled. "Don't tell me what to do. Nobody elected you leader of this expedition." Ahead of them, Keelk was gesturing anxiously. "I think I'll go ahead and tell them anyway."

Will repressed a smile. "Good idea." He waited while the *Protoceratops* translated.

As soon as the stocky quadruped had finished, a massive skull gave Will a gentle but firm nudge. "All right, all right, I'm going! Don't be so impatient."

"What do you expect?" Chaz told him. "He's a tyrannosaur. And if I were you, I wouldn't talk back to him."

Will considered Crookeye, who could snap him up in a single bite and have room left over for most of Chaz. "Aw, they're all right. They just have their own code of conduct. And they're anxious because of their daughter."

"That's fine with me." The little *Protoceratops* edged away from Shethorn. "So long as they're worrying about her, they won't be thinking about food."

Keelk raised her voice sharply and turned to trot another few yards up the canyon. Her intent was clear. If they weren't coming, she was going to go on ahead without them.

Will raised his right palm to the tyrannosaurs in the traditional sign of greeting and farewell. "Try not to worry. We'll be back with your daughter as soon as we can." In the onrushing tide of night, the yellow eyes of the tyrannosaurs seemed to glow like lanterns. He turned and broke into a jog to catch up to Keelk.

Behind him, a reverberant keening filled the air. It was an eerie, haunting sound. As a youngster he'd once heard an opera chorus make a sound similar to that as it mourned the death of the story's heroine. But no human voice could reach so low a register.

The two tyrannosaurs persisted in their melancholy wailing until they dropped from view. "What was that all about?" Will inquired as they turned a bend in the narrow cleft. No gunshots had sounded for some time now, but he felt confident of finding their source. What he and his friends would do then was beginning to be a matter of some concern.

Chaz kept up easily. His tough, splayed footpads were much better suited to running on sand than they had been to the dips and sumps of the rain forest.

"They are lamenting the fact that they can't accompany

us. They have also made the three of us honorary members of their tribe. Each of us has been given a tyrannosaurian name.'' He nodded at Keelk, who continued to lead the way.

"Hers is Walkthrustone. Because of her determination.'' He translated for the struthie, who responded with a surprised but pleased chirp. Lengthening his stride, Will gave her a friendly slap on her left flank.

Chaz was starting to puff slightly but showed no signs of slowing down. His tone turned slightly self-important.

"I am Slayswithwords.''

Will grinned. "Very appropriate.'' Beneath his feet, the footprints that had preceded them showed the way clearly even in the failing light. "What about me?''

"You?'' A hint of amusement crept into the *Protoceratops*'s voice. "You are Hat.''

"Hat? That's all? Just Hat?''

"What did you expect, riding about on that male's head all this time?''

"Just Hat?'' Will's expression fell. "Keelk is Walksthrustone, you're Slayswithwords, and I'm just Hat?'' His gaze narrowed as he regarded his companion. "Wait a minute. Are you telling me everything?''

Chittering sounds emerged from the translator's mouth: protoceratopsian laughter. "Let me think. Hmmm . . . possibly hat isn't the correct interpretation.''

"I thought so!'' Suddenly he found himself grinning down at the chunky dinosaur. "You little . . . All right, what's my real tyrannosaurian name?''

Will could tell from his companion's tone that this time he was being serious. "Thinksthrufear.''

"Thinksthrufear.'' Will repeated it to himself. "Maybe the carnosaurs aren't as dumb as we think.''

"They're not dumb.'' Chaz easily surmounted a small dune face. "They just prefer a rigid form of anarchy to the rest of Dinotopian civilization. That makes them antisocial, not stupid.'' He was silent for a while, during which time more of the canyon slid past beneath their feet.

"You know, Will, it is a great and rare honor we have been given. I do not know of anyone else, not even respected convoy masters, who have been granted tyrannosaurian names. I know that such a thing is possible because I have heard of it in stories, but I've never met anyone who was actually so honored.''

"Can you teach me, Chaz, to say my tribal name in their tongue?''

"It's not easy. You have to use your deepest voice, and it hurts the back of the throat.''

"Tell me anyway.''

Chaz proceeded to do so, and Will repeated the consonental growl until the translator assured him he had it right . . . or nearly so.

"You might say,'' the *Protoceratops* said with a chuckle, "that you have the Will, but not the throat.''

Will swallowed. "You were right. Pronouncing it does hurt. I guess I'll never be able to say it precisely, but then, I'll never be a tyrannosaur, either.''

"Only in your dreams,'' Chaz assured him.

Will glanced skyward. Considering the heavy cloud cover, they were fortunate to have as much moonlight as they did. "We can't wait, you know. We'll have to think of something to try right away, before the body of the storm hits. This would be a bad place to have to wait it out.''

"Most assuredly. This canyon could easily become a river running higher than our heads. Yours as well as mine.'' He translated for Keelk, who hooted a vigorous reply.

"What did she say?'' Will asked.

"She's not worried about the weather,'' Chaz informed him. "She's not worried about anything except rescuing her family.''

"We will.'' He was surprised at his self-confidence. Given what they knew about the intruders, it was quite unwarranted, but that was how he felt nonetheless.

"We'd better.'' Chaz kicked sand aside with his feet. "Because I, for one, am not going to go back the way we came and tell those two tyrannosaurs that we failed.''

"Cheer up,'' Will told him. "This is a worthy thing we're doing. Ethical.''

"Maybe so, but I'd still rather be lying on a clean bed of straw in a warm barn back in Treetown.''

"What about me? Where do you think I'd rather be?''

The *Protoceratops* cocked an appraising eye up at his slim human friend. "You're a strange one, Will Denison, even for a dolphinback. I'm not sure you'd rather be anywhere else than right here."

"That's kind of a hasty judgment, isn't it? Don't you think I'd rather be . . ." his voice trailed off.

There was a very good chance that the *Protoceratops*'s assessment was correct.

They'd traveled for what seemed like quite a ways up the canyon when Keelk, who was determined to inspect the entrance to each and every side chasm, called to them sharply. Human, *Protoceratops*, and struthie gathered to examine what she'd found.

Chaz nodded appreciatively, absently clacking his horny beak. There was no mistaking the profusion of footprints. "She says they've turned off this way. I find myself in agreement."

Will frowned as he straightened and peered up the sandy tributary. "I wonder why." He glanced to his left. "This is obviously the main canyon and the most likely way through the mountains. Why would they turn off here?"

"I expect we'll find out." Chaz chirped fluently at the *Struthiomimus*. She nodded sharply before turning and once more taking the lead.

"What did you say to her?"

"I told her that her nose was more sensitive than yours or mine and that if it grew too dark to see, we'd do better to follow her."

Will agreed. Since the gunshots had long since ceased, they could no longer track the intruders by sound.

It was not long before they came upon the ancient wall and its missing gate. The glow of the intruders' fire was once more clearly visible against the night sky, and they advanced with extreme caution.

"Soon now," Will whispered to his companions. Keelk responded with a very subtle whistle.

Closing on the firelight they entered the temple complex and marveled at its beauty, which even the darkness could not mitigate. It was Keelk who spotted the guard, contracting her neck to lower her head and putting out a foreleg to restrain Will.

Fortunately for them, the guard's enthusiasm was matched only by his exhaustion. He was lying back against a pile of zealously accumulated gold bricks, hands folded across his chest, rifle at his side, and snoring prodigiously. They gave him a wide berth, Will marveling at Keelk's ability to advance in complete silence on her wide, three-toed feet.

The glow from the campfire was very bright now. Wordlessly they crept close, using a low, intricately inscribed wall for cover. Slowly raising their heads to peer over the barrier, they finally saw the men they had been following for so long.

Some sprawled indifferently on the silver boulevard, their heads resting on packs or gold bricks. Others lay where they had collapsed on the steps leading up to the portico of the main temple. Some clutched close to their bosoms piles or sacks of jewels pried from walls and pillars, their slumberous embrace as ardent as that of any lover's.

"I don't understand." Chaz rested his forelegs against the sturdy wall. "Look how soundly they sleep. What's the matter with them?" At the same time Keelk had her head back and was sniffing intently of the air.

You didn't need a struthie's nose to identify that odor, Will knew. "They're drunk. Maybe not deeply—the smell's not that strong—but they've had enough to hurry them to sleep. A stroke of luck for us."

"Drunk." Chaz considered the situation. At a festival he'd once seen a *Stegosaurus* who'd imbibed too much in the way of enlivening spirits. It had unintentionally but rapidly cleared an entire game field, until a pair of disapproving apatosaurs had succeeded in flanking it on either side and escorting it to a suitable resting place. Upon awakening, the stegosaur in question had been mortally abashed. The authorities were not entirely displeased, as they were able to utilize the episode as a lesson with which to instruct the youngsters in attendance, human as well as dinosaurian.

Nevertheless, the *Protoceratops* reflected, it was fortunate that the great majority of sauropods were teetotalers. The thought of a drunken brachiosaur lumbering uncontrollably about was more than daunting. Obviously these intruders felt differently and were more than a little fond of intoxicating spirits.

Keelk had difficulty keeping herself under control as she gestured excitedly to their left. Four familiar shapes and one stranger squatted there, secured to malachite posts. They, too, slept soundly, though no aroma of alcohol rose from their vicinity.

Taking careful note of the intruders' garb, the condition and variety of their weapons, and their diverse ethnic backgrounds, Will felt that his initial guess had been correct, though it awaited final confirmation.

"Pirates for sure."

"Pirates?" Chaz glanced over at him.

"Thieves of the sea. Men, and sometimes women, who sail for plunder. They'll attack other ships, or towns, and steal anything they can make off with."

The *Protoceratops* nodded somberly, finally asking innocently, "Why?"

"Because it's easier to take something than work for it."

"But that's wrong."

"Exactly. These are people who live for wrongness. They're common criminals." Again he surveyed the scattered sleepers. "They don't look beat up. Their weapons and clothes are intact. I don't think they've been shipwrecked. They look like they've managed a successful landing. Is it possible for a ship to get through the fringing reefs?"

"I was always told it wasn't. But strange things have been known to happen at the end of every six-year storm cycle. In any case, the actions of the sea are not a specialty of mine." The *Protoceratops* shuddered visibly. He was neither a good swimmer nor particularly fond of the water, though Will knew many dinosaurs who delighted in the activity.

Keelk was hooting at them soft and urgently. "Yes, I know," Will whispered in response. Some thoughts did not require translation. "I see them. We'll get them out of here somehow."

The sleeping pirates filled the air in front of the temple with their snoring and breaking of wind. There were a lot of them, more than he'd imagined. Every man looked healthy and in good condition. In a fight he and his friends wouldn't

have a chance. Keelk might outrun the fleetest of the brigands, for struthies were very fast. But she couldn't outrun a
bullet, he reminded himself.

"We must try to get closer," he heard himself murmuring.

"Are you sure?" Chaz had dropped back on all fours. "I
don't like the look of these humans. I don't like it at all."

"That doesn't matter. So long as we don't wake them,
everything will be all right." He gestured to his left. "We'll
circle around behind the prisoners, keeping well clear of the
guard. Then we should be able to get close enough to untie
them."

"Optimist," Chaz muttered as he trailed along behind the
two bipeds.

Will's plan proved as efficient as he'd hoped. The single
guard snuffled noisily but did not awaken. Soon they were
near enough to discern the individual knots and shackles that
secured the captives.

"See how many ropes." Chaz ground his lower jaw
against the upper. "I think I could bite through the lower
ones."

"That'll take too much time." Will strained for a better
look. "Those look like ship ropes. They'll be tough and well
seasoned." He glanced at Keelk, whose smaller beak and
digging claws were equally ill-suited to the task. "I guess
it's up to me. This is what humans are best at, anyway. Intricate manipulation."

"Of things or words?" Chaz offered the rejoinder gently
to show that he meant no anger.

"You two keep back here, out of the way." Bending low,
Will started forward.

"What are you going to do?" Chaz asked anxiously.

His friend smiled encouragingly back at him, his teeth
white against the darkness. "Free everyone, of course. That's
what heroes do in books."

After their human companion had moved off, Chaz whispered to Keelk in the struthie tongue, "Of course, this is no
book."

Keeping to cover and shadows, Will succeeded in reaching
the three posts unnoticed. With their acute hearing, the struthies heard him coming. Senses fully alerted, they spoke not

a word as they watched the young human approach. His clothing was reassurance enough, a familiar Dinotopian style.

Putting a finger to his lips in the universal sign for silence, Will ducked down behind Hisaulk and began to work on his bindings. The two youngsters did not have to be instructed by their parents on how to behave. Feigning continued sleep, they kept silent despite their rising excitement.

Tied slightly apart from the others, Prettykill sensed voices and motion. One eye opened slightly, the only movement in the squatting mass of muscle. She watched silently and without comment as the new arrival busied himself undoing the adult male *Struthiomimus*'s ropes.

"Easy, now." Will's face contorted with his efforts. The tough sea ropes were proving as difficult to undo as he'd feared. "I'm getting it." Fortunately, he'd had plenty of time to study similar knots on the long voyage out from America that had eventually shipwrecked him and his father here. As an apprentice skybax rider, his knowledge of knots had only improved.

It took more time than he'd hoped but less than he'd feared for him to free the adult male. Hisaulk stretched surreptitiously, keeping his movements slow and subtle. From her place of concealment Keelk waved anxiously. Relieved to see her safe, Hisaulk acknowledged her presence with a nod. But while he was free to join her, he did not, refusing to leave until the rest of his family had been liberated. While the big male loosened cramped muscles, Will started in on the female's bonds.

The instant she was free, he turned his attention to the two youngsters. His fingers were raw and sore, but he refused to rest. When all had at last been freed, he had the pleasure of watching them depart silently to join their long-separated sibling. Graceful necks entwined in heartfelt, silent embrace.

His own participation in the celebration would have to wait. One more set of ropes needed to be undone. Rising from behind the malachite post, he advanced on the young tyrannosaur. She was fully awake now, tracking his approach with intense yellow eyes.

He was halfway to her when he felt something catch his ankle. Looking down, he saw to his horror that between a pair of fallen poles he'd been carefully stepping over lay a dark, wiry man with a thick mustache. Bright brown eyes glared inquisitively up at him. Fingers like steel bands held his right ankle in an unyielding grip.

"Hoy, now, mate. Where did you drop from?"

⇒ XVIII ⇐

DESPERATELY WILL WRENCHED FORWARD, TRYING to free his leg. The man held on with the tenacity of a starving cat. Twisting and reaching up with his free arm, the pirate got his right hand around Will's other leg and began shouting at the top of his lungs.

"Avast, there! To arms—we are betrayed!"

The call of the abruptly awakened pirate sparked an explosion of activity on the part of the young tyrannosaur. Until that moment seemingly sound asleep, she was now fighting furiously with her restraints, twisting and writhing and throwing a veritable fit as she did everything possible to try to free herself. But her captors had tied her well. Unable to bring even her comparatively tiny forearms to bear on the ropes, she couldn't move more than a foot in any direction.

Will turned and tried to kick at the man's face. Having survived dozens of battles and street fights, the wiry seaman was not about to be so easily dislodged by a comparative boy. While continuing to yell, he ducked his head down between his arms so that Will's frantic kicks only glanced off his shoulders.

By now, anxious shouts and queries were rising throughout the camp. Seeing that all was lost, Will yelled toward the others.

"Run for it, Chaz! Run for the gate!"

The last he saw of his friends and the liberated family were the eyes of the mother *Struthiomimus*, eloquent with compassion and helplessness as she shepherded her reunited brood toward the main canyon and freedom. He hoped the translator could keep up with them. Even a *Protoceratops* could manage a fair pace over a short distance.

As he shouted toward them, he kept trying to free himself. He might as well have been caught in an old-fashioned trap, so unyielding was the smaller man's grasp on his legs. Twisting and bending, he tried to remember his early boxing lessons as he gave his tormentor a glancing blow on the side of the head. The pirate grunted and cursed but did not let go.

Left to his own devices Will might have worn down his captor and freed himself, but just as he felt the man's grip beginning to weaken slightly, he was surrounded by powerfully muscled, unyielding arms.

Highlighted by torchlight, the circle of faces that stared back at him were as hardened and disreputable as any he'd ever encountered in a newspaper, book, or bad dream. Filthy beards and mustaches framed scars and vacant eye sockets. Many of the men had assorted fragments of ears missing, and one showed clearly where the front part of his nose had been bitten off in a fight. The frailest among them looked tougher than driftwood.

I'm sorry, Father, he said to himself. *I did what I thought was right*. Maybe back in Boston they'd think it a strange choice, but he was no longer a citizen of Boston and his ethics were no longer Bostonian. He was as much a part of Dinotopia now as the half dozen dinosaurs racing to safety somewhere in the darkness behind him.

It didn't take long for the pirates to discover that the majority of their captives had been freed and were nowhere to be seen. By whose hand was obvious enough. Muttering threateningly, several of the men edged forward. Will saw dirty, gnarled hands reaching for him.

Andreas stepped forward. "Let the captain handle this business. As for the chicken-dragons, I says good riddance to them!" Turning, he waved expansively. "We've the fortune of the world about us, and the prize turkey to boot." He nodded toward the still-restrained young tyrannosaur. "Let Mr. Smiggens be satisfied with the one. The others gave us nothing but trouble." The men debated softly among themselves, and the tenor of their discussion showed that

Andreas's opinion was shared by more than a few.

Among the growing body of hastily awakened seamen only Anbaya sounded disappointed. "Would have made good eating," he mumbled, gazing off into the darkness that had swallowed their former prisoners.

"Trouble, is it?" growled a new voice. "There be trouble aplenty this night, it seems." Will saw an individual of massive size and girth approaching, shadowed by a tall but much thinner companion. Still buckling his belt about his impressive waist, Blackstrap strode into the light, the others parting before him like mackerel giving way to a prowling tiger shark.

His mustache, Will decided, was as ferocious as the rest of him. As he gazed at the prisoner, the look in his eyes reminded Will of the adult tyrannosaurs. He immediately determined that in temperament, if not in size, they and this man were not so very dissimilar.

"By my mistress's betrothed." The big man's expression turned nasty as he moved closer to Will. "What have we here? A boy, and not a particularly impressive specimen, at that."

Will bristled at the "boy" but decided it would be exceedingly tactless to venture a complaint. The longer he could stay alive, the better. He wasn't entirely displeased with the situation, as the brigands showed no inclination to pursue his friends. Whatever happened to him, it appeared that Keelk and her family, together with Chaz, were going to be all right.

"Why waste time on 'im?" growled a sleepy voice in irritation. "He's nothing to us save another mouth to feed."

"Aye, slit his throat and be done with it, Cap'n," came a cry from the back of the group.

Blackstrap turned a menacing glare on the nearest sailors, who suddenly wished themselves in the rear of the congregation. "Have you learned nothing from Mr. Smiggens? Care you nothing save for gold and your next meal?"

"What's wrong with that, Captain?" wondered a seaman innocently.

"Nothing, Mr. Samuel. My point be that a judicious question here and there can often lead to the greater satisfaction of both desires." He turned back to Will and smiled, a forced collaboration of mustache, teeth, cheeks, and accumulated grime that if anything was even more frightening than his previous expression.

"Now, then, boy, it seems you've gone and freed our dainty little dinosaurs, which we captured fair and square after a great deal of danger and hard labor. What inexplicable and foolish urge would inspire you to do such a thing?"

More than a little surprised to hear the uncouth buccaneer before him identify Keelk and the others correctly, Will hastened to explain.

"The dinosaurs of this lost land are not animals. They're intelligent, civilized, and some of them are smarter than you or I."

Blackstrap's right eyebrow jumped. "Now, what's this you say, boy?" He turned to his men. "D'you hear that, me boyos? The lad says our chickens were as intelligent as us!" The sailors roared with laughter.

No, Will thought silently, *not as intelligent as you. Rather smarter, I suspect.* Aloud he insisted, "It's true! They've lived here for millennia in the company of other humans. They've built great cities and dams and have accumulated all sorts of knowledge unknown to the outside world. They didn't die out here in Dinotopia the way they did everywhere else."

"Dinotopia, is it?" Blackstrap grinned callously down at him. "Aye, and Father Christmas will be here any minute to shower us with gifts if we will but let you go." He leaned close and lowered his voice dangerously. His breath was, if anything, nearly as bad as that of the tyrannosaurs. "Now, then, I'll have some straight answers from you, boy, or you'll be wishing I let Samuel or another cut your throat. I be Brognar Blackstrap, captain of the good ship *Condor*, at this very moment lying at anchor in the lagoon to the north of here. What be your name?"

Will drew himself up to his full height. No matter how hopeless a situation seemed or how others around him were reacting, his father had always told him to show courage.

"Will Denison, son of Arthur. Five mothers American, first time Dinotopian."

"You're a cool lad, I'll give you that." Blackstrap rubbed at his stubble. "So these dinosaur-dragon-chicken-things are intelligent, you say? Didn't see much sign of that during the time we had them in our company."

"I understand." Will struggled to explain. "The first time my father and I encountered them we thought exactly as you, that they were nothing more than fantastic animals. It took time and the help of others before we understood just how smart they are. But don't worry." He did his best to exhibit an assurance he didn't feel. "You'll find out. Because the ones you held prisoner will be back with friends, coming to rescue me."

The implied threat slid off Blackstrap as easily as hog lard off hot cast iron. "So there be other people here, then. Interesting. How long you been marooned here, boy?"

"Six years, my father and I. But we're not marooned. We're full citizens."

"Might be," commented Ruskin, "but you still sound like a Yankee to me." Several of the men snickered.

Will wondered how these intruders would have reacted had they come ashore elsewhere on Dinotopia. Near Chandara, perhaps, or even Sauropolis. Instead, they had landed somewhere on the Northern Plains just when that area was in the process of being evacuated until the six-year storm had passed. No wonder they'd encountered no evidence of Dinotopian civilization. Evidently they'd managed to miss even the widely scattered farms.

Could he somehow turn their ignorance to his advantage?

Meanwhile, he was not the only one considering his fate.

"Kill him and be done with it!" muttered someone loudly.

"Why waste him?" wondered another. "He has a strong back and good hands."

"And spirit," added Thomas with grudging admiration. "Let him carry gold for us."

"Aye," agreed Copperhead. "Put a pack on him."

Will made himself stare back at the man. "I wouldn't carry a pee-pot for you, mister!"

Copperhead only laughed, as did those close to him.

"You say there's others here," Blackstrap declared.

"Hundreds of others. No, thousands, plus the dinosaurs."

He thought rapidly. "There's a rifle for each man and woman, and . . . and they've got cannon. *Big* cannon, huge cannon."

"Do they, now?" Blackstrap's smile shrank but did not disappear. "Well, then, we ought to be proper terrified, shouldn't we, boys? Because ain't none of us would know what to do if somebody pointed a cannon at us." The concerted laughter that greeted this observation was considerably lower and more dangerous in tone than any that had preceded it.

"We should keep him alive, Captain." The skinny individual Will had noticed earlier pushed himself forward into the light. He had a lantern jaw and more intelligence in his voice than any Will had heard thus far. His eyes showed something akin to compassion.

"Not to use as a beast of burden, though I see no harm in that. But if he truly lives here and doesn't belong to some shipwrecked crew elsewhere, his knowledge of this land should prove valuable."

Blackstrap deliberated. "You think he speak fair about guns and cannon?"

"We can find out if he's telling the truth." That calm, cool comment was the most frightening thing Will had yet heard. "There might be fifteen-inch Dahlgrens hereabouts, or nothing larger than a catapult. Or not even that. The point is that the boy is full of information. It's like panning for gold. First you extract everything, then you separate the nuggets from the dross."

Talk of gold set Blackstrap's thoughts on a familiar path. "Tell me, boy, is the family you come from a wealthy one? Do they also live in houses like these?" He indicated the shadowy temple complex in which they stood.

"Until just now I didn't even know this place existed," Will replied honestly. "I've never heard of it. I don't know that anyone else knows of its existence, either. According to what I've learned, there's a lot of Dinotopia that's still pretty unexplored, especially in the vicinity of the Rainy Basin. It's a big place. You may be the first people to have set foot in this canyon since the civilization that built these buildings."

"You hear that, boys?" Blackstrap's bellow was rich with

irony. "We be the rightful discoverers of this place." Mocking cheers rose from the assembled.

"Why would you be thinking of ransoming me?" Will wondered. "Isn't this gold enough for you?"

"We need help moving it, boy. Horses, mules, wagons, and men to drive them."

"Wagons you'll find," Will told him, "but no horses or mules. No cattle, either, or pigs or common fowl. This is the land where the dinosaurs never lost their dominance. Modern mammals never took hold here, except for the smaller vermin that came floating in on logs. We have birds, though, blown in on storm fronts. And insects, arrived in similar fashion. And ancient mammals."

"So say you. We'll learn soon enough which of your words can be believed." The pirate captain peered past his new captive into the night. "As for the chicken-dinosaurs, well, what's done is done. Our standards have risen somewhat, and we still have the little devil." He gestured diffidently toward the juvenile tyrannosaur, who had been watching and listening to everything. "Besides, we can always trap more if we wish."

Will responded insistently. "I *told* you, you can't treat dinosaurs like common animals. They're as intelligent as you or I."

"You're adamant about that, ain't you, boy?"

"It's the truth, sir."

"Well, then, you should have no objection to putting it to the test." Blackstrap's previous unpleasant grin returned.

Will was instantly wary. "I'm not sure I follow your meaning."

At a sign from Blackstrap, two of the pirates grabbed Will and bound his wrists behind his back. "If these beasts be intelligent, then they should be capable of reason, should they not?"

"Of course." Will was uncertain what to make of the captain's sudden conversion from obstinacy to logic.

"Excellent. Why don't we ask the adorable one you left us what he thinks of your opinion?" Blackstrap turned and pointed toward the young tyrannosaur. As the captain's intent dawned on them, the crew began to joke with and nudge one another.

Will found himself being pushed and shoved urgently toward the bound carnosaur. "It's a her," he explained, not knowing what else to say.

"Is it, now?" Smiggens eyed the prisoner closely. "How do you know that, boy?"

Before Will could reply, two of the pirates grabbed him under the arms and hustled him forward. Meanwhile, others were carefully loosening the ropes that secured the tyrannosaur's jaws. Their shipmates gripped the other restraints tightly, restricting but not eliminating the captive's range of movement.

Mock cheers rose from the assembled crew. "There you go, lad! Have a long chat!"

"Aye," quipped another, "ask him . . . no, ask her how she's feelin' tonight."

"See if she'll give you the next dance!" guffawed his companion.

"I know." O'Connor gave Will a nudge with his forearm, sending the younger man stumbling forward. "Why don't you ask her if she's . . . hungry?" More laughter rose from the now festive crew.

In her crouch she was slightly shorter than him, Will noted. As he was alternately shoved and kicked forward she tracked his involuntary approach with eager eyes. They held none of the natural compassion and understanding one would find in, say, the face of a sensitive *Struthiomimus*.

"Go on, boy." Blackstrap moved close. It was obvious he was enjoying himself hugely. "What are you waiting for? Show us how 'intelligent' she be. Talk to her." Broken teeth showed in a wide, malevolent smile. "See if she's ready for afternoon tea."

A jittery Will tried to divide his attention between Blackstrap and the juvenile tyrannosaur. "I . . . I can't talk to her."

"What's this?" Blackstrap threw his men an exaggerated look. "You can't talk to her? Why, bless my soul, I thought she be as intelligent as we."

"It's just that the big meat-eaters of Dinotopia all live together near here in a place called the Rainy Basin. They *are* intelligent, but their languages are very rough and difficult to understand. They don't share in Dinotopian civilization. It's a matter of tribal choice.''

"I'll wager a gold brick on that!" shouted one man gleefully. His shipmates roared.

"I'm telling you," Will went on desperately, "they're intelligent, too! They just choose to live as their ancestors did, primitively and away from civilization."

"Sounds like they'd do right well as members of this crew," Smiggens quipped.

"Har, get on with ye." Blackstrap gave him another shove forward. The young tyrannosaur's jaws gaped expectantly, revealing a full complement of smaller but equally sharp versions of her parents' teeth. "Don't you know 'tis impolite not to ask a lady to dance?"

"My father could explain it better," Will insisted. "He's a respected scientist. He was a teacher in America."

"A scientist, you say." The first mate turned reflective. He badly wanted to question this young man further. If he was telling the truth and his father was truly a man of science, it suggested there were wonders indeed to be experienced in this strange new land.

But Smiggens knew he dare not go against the wishes of the crew. Their spirits, so to speak, were running high and Blackstrap had their full support. If he tried to interfere in their fun, he knew that in their current mood they were as likely to toss him to the captive meat-eater as they were their new prisoner. Presented with such a prospect, he chose to keep silent. His curiosity was powerful, but not sufficient to induce him to embark on any uncharacteristic acts of personal bravery.

"WHAT IS IT, WHAT'S HAPPENING?" CURSE THESE SHORT legs! Chaz thought anxiously.

Knowing they could now safely outrun any pursuit, for no human could keep pace with even a young *Struthiomimus* over a short sprint, the escapees had ceased their flight. Driven by a desire to see what was going to happen to their human friend, they had hidden themselves behind a low, collapsing wall of gold bricks. With their superb night vision they were able to see everything that was going on, knowing at the same time that no human's sight was sharp enough to detect them. Even at a distance, their former captors' torches lit the tense scene more than adequately.

"It's hard to say. They're all crowded together." Hisaulk strained to isolate individual figures. "They've tied your friend Will's hands behind his back and seem to be pushing him toward the young tyrannosaur."

"Prettykill," muttered Chaz. "There's no telling how she'll react under the strain of her captivity. It must be even more stressful for a carnosaur than it was for you."

"What did you say?" Shremaza blinked at the *Protoceratops* while the three children exchanged a glance.

"Prettykill. That's her name."

Hisaulk continued to watch. "Whatever her name is, I think they are trying to feed him to her."

"No!" Chaz repeatedly stomped the ground with his left foreleg. "That's barbaric!"

"I'm not surprised." Shremaza did her best to comfort him. "Nothing these humans do would surprise me."

"He has a chance." Chaz was walking in tight circles. "A small one, but only if he thinks fast. Very fast." He returned his attention to the male struthie, who had by far the best vantage point. "What's happening now?"

"Nothing yet. Oh! They have just taken the ropes off the young tyrannosaur's head, freeing her jaws. The humans are taking care to keep well clear of them."

"As well they should. What's she doing?"

"Nothing so far. She is watching Will very carefully."

Chaz tilted his head back until his frill bumped up against his shoulders. "If only I had stayed with him. I should be there! I could talk to the humans."

"You assume they would listen to you." Shremaza spoke gently. "I have spent time among these humans. They are utterly convinced we are dumb and stupid. If you spoke, they would think it was a trick and that Will was somehow speaking for you. They would feed you to the young tyrannosaur before you had a chance to convince them. Or eat you themselves, which I could tell from their looks they thought on occasion to do with us.''

"Cannibals!'' Chaz shook his head from side to side. "What dreadful creatures!''

"No.'' Like all her kind, Keelk was too empathic to hold a grudge. "They are just uneducated.''

The *Protoceratops* was consumed with frustration. He'd never felt so helpless in his life. Sure, he and Will Denison had experienced some disagreements, but the travels and travails they had shared and endured had brought them together. He felt closer to Will than he ever had to any human, even his teachers. He'd developed considerable respect and not a little affection for the young skybax rider.

There was nothing he could do. Only pray that Will could somehow do for himself.

THE PIRATES CONTINUED TO LAUGH MANIACALLY AND offer mocking suggestions as to how Will ought to proceed. Someone suggested he turn away and offer his backside. Guimaraes laughed along with his companions, but his smile was tight.

Those yellow eyes never left Will as he was shoved forward. Saliva dripped from the lower teeth. *How long since she'd last been fed?* he found himself wondering. Too long, to judge from the way she was looking at him. Those traplike jaws were now only a few feet away.

What could he do? These half-drunk brigands wouldn't listen to reason. Neither would a tyrannosaur, even if one could speak their language. Chaz might have tried, but he had fled to safety, and quite properly, too.

Unable to look away, he found himself returning the feral gaze. It was almost hypnotic, the way it seemed to pierce straight through him. *That's what happens*, he thought, *when you find yourself looked upon not as an independent, thinking individual, but as a piece of meat.*

There was no telling what thoughts were churning in her mind. Her situation must have her feeling terribly angry and confused. Not afraid, though. He doubted there was a word for fear in the tyrannosaurian tongue. She was probably looking forward to the opportunity to take out her anger on a human—any human.

He was almost within biting distance. Had her legs not been bound and hobbled, she undoubtedly would have pounced on him already. Even if his hands were free he doubted he could fend off those powerful jaws. Her breath, like that of her parents, smelled of carrion.

Her parents. A sudden rush of excitement raced through him. He *could* speak tyrannosaur. Four words of it, to be exact.

Four proper names.

He tried to frame the sounds precisely. His throat was so tight that his first attempt made him sound like a coughing kitten. The pirates found his desperate wheezing greatly amusing and urged him to try again. Ignoring their taunts, he did better the second time, uttering a passably modulated low growl. It sounded comical to his ears, a feeble imitation of Crookeye's prodigious rumble.

But the effect was unmistakable.

A startled Prettykill blinked and shut her imposing mouth, eyeing him uncertainly. *Have to lower my voice somehow*, he told himself as sweat poured down his face. His lungs being too small by several orders of magnitude to muster the correct tone, he nevertheless readied himself to do the best he could.

His second growl only deepened the young tyrannosaur's confusion. Head cocked to one side, her whole aspect suggesting intense curiosity, she waited to hear whatever he would say next.

"*Ah-veh!*" exclaimed Chumash. "The boy does talk to it."

"Not a bit of it," Copperhead objected. "He just knows how to imitate its call, that's all. Like whistling at a dog."

"That's right, Mr. Copperhead be right." Though far from

willing to concede any of their captive's points, Blackstrap was impressed with the young man's skill and courage. " 'Tis not bloody talking."

Will was within biting range now, but the tyrannosaur no longer seemed inclined to make an appetizer of his head. Instead, she was wondering how this strange young person, who had crept into the humans' camp to free the family of struthies, had come to know the names of her parents. The fury that had accumulated within her and that she had fully intended to vent on his hapless sacrificial form had largely subsided, to be replaced by curiosity. His pronunciation was terrible, of course, but no less remarkable for that. She watched him intently, waiting to see what he would do next.

Touching his chin to his chest, he intoned a name that could only be his own. It was emphatically tribal. Putting as much force and care into his voice as he could muster, he then looked her straight in the eye and called her own name. The last time she'd heard that, it had been voiced by her mother.

Sitting back on her haunches, she snarled querulously at the human, repeating first her parents' names and then his. To this he nodded vigorously and smiled. She recognized both human gestures.

"Damn me for a drunken manatee if they're not talkin'," marveled Ruskin.

"Mind your thoughts, Mr. Ruskin." Blackstrap's brows beetled as he observed the snarling verbal byplay. "Growls and grunts be all it 'tis, can't you see? A boy and his dog. 'Tis not true speech. Be that not so, Mr. Smiggens?"

"That is my opinion also, Captain."

Blackstrap snorted with satisfaction.

"But there is clearly some sort of contact," Smiggens continued. "I wouldn't call it language. Certainly not intelligent converse. But there's surely something there. Something outside our experience, anyway."

Blackstrap waved off the implications. "I had a horse once that recognized more words than that dainty devil. But I never claimed to be able to talk to the nag."

"See there." Thomas pointed at the carnosaur. "What she going to do now?"

Throwing back her head, the young tyrannosaur initiated such a plaintive howl as to put any pack of energetic coyotes or wolves to shame. Will sympathized with her lament. Though their chanting was unsophisticated, the great carnosaurs were no less inherently euphonious than any of the other tribes save perhaps the duckbills, who were noteworthy for their mastery of the musical arts.

It was a potent mix of outrage and loneliness. Not knowing quite how to respond, Will put his own head close to that of the howling tyrannosaur, half closed his eyes, and did his best to provide counterpoint. He'd attended many duckbill concerts, but the music of trained corythosaurs and lambeosaurs was like Mozart compared to the guttural baying of the youngster next to him. Yet in its own primitive fashion it was quite affecting, even moving.

In any case he sang his level best, certain he would never again have the chance to participate in such a singular duet.

Blackstrap was utterly unmoved by the raw emotion on display. "Here, now, boy, belay that racket! You there, Johanssen, shut him up."

"Aye, sir." Turning to Will, the sailor yanked sharply on the rope that had been looped around the younger man's waist. "You heard the captain!"

Unable to keep his balance, Will went sprawling. What happened next was as unexpected as anything that had gone before.

Ceasing her mournful dirge, the young tyrannosaur lunged with astonishing speed in the tall pirate's direction. Two of the men charged with restraining her were pulled off their feet, and it was only through dint of much straining and shouting that their companions succeeded in arresting Prettykill's charge. Her jaws slammed shut barely inches from the seaman's face.

For several moments all was confusion as everyone fought to secure the hawser rope around the tyrannosaur's jaws. Only when they had once more been strapped shut did any among the assembled relax. As for Johanssen, he was entirely convinced that his heart had well and truly stopped for several seconds.

Unable once again to offer anything in the way of resistance, Prettykill was forced to content herself with glaring furiously at her captors.

Struggling to his feet, Will staggered over to her, no longer afraid. "It's all right," he assured her gently. "I'm not hurt." Several times in succession he repeated his name and then hers, taking care to vary the inflection so that neither was more prominent than the other.

She met his gaze once more. Gradually her breathing slowed.

Will felt a sudden weight on his shoulders: Blackstrap's arm. The captain might look fat, but Will decided he wouldn't want to meet him across a wrestling mat.

"Interesting demonstration, lad. Most enlightening. Not that I countenance your claims for the brute's intelligence, not for a minute. Why, it just tried to eat poor Mr. Johanssen's face. Didn't it, Johanssen?" Still badly shaken, the seaman in question could only nod a reply. "Now, I ask you, boy, is that a sign of intelligence?"

"How would you expect her to react after you've gone and made her a prisoner?" Will badly wanted to rub the itchy dirt off his face.

Blackstrap ignored the question. "I will admit to this: you know the proper commands for controlling the beast."

"I can't command her. Nobody commands a *Tyrannosaurus rex*."

"Is that what it's called, then?" Smiggens was looking not at Will but at their other captive.

"D'you take me for a prize fool, lad? Bark at it if you will, but no more singing. Hurts me sensitive ears, it does." Blackstrap turned to his first mate. " 'Tis bleeding right you were, Mr. Smiggens. This lad will be far more valuable to us alive than dead, though I confess some regret as to the loss of entertainment."

"Stop calling me 'boy.' " Somewhat emboldened by the bound Prettykill's new willingness to leap to his defense, Will held his ground.

"Fair enough." Blackstrap grinned. "What shall we call you, then?"

"I told you. Will Denison's my name."

"So be it. You're a brave and clever lad, young Will. So

harken to me when I say that 'tis *my* will you accompany us back to our ship. It may be that should we meet up with any more of these dinosaur beasties along the way, your barking will prove useful.'' He leaned close, his blackened and broken teeth split in a humorless smile. ''But be aware at all times that no matter who does the barking here, I be the master and you the dog.''

''I still don't understand how you managed to anchor safely. I've been told that any vessel that approaches Dinotopia close enough to see it is invariably caught in strong currents and wrecked on her shores.''

''Har, 'tis a noble word, *invariable*. I've been proving such fine words wrong all me life, young Will. All I can say is that they've been poor captains who've surveyed these shores, weak no doubt in spirit as well as in seamanship.''

''It was a big wave,'' Smiggens explained. ''Carried us right over the reefs, it did. We were lucky.''

Blackstrap scowled at his first mate but said nothing.

''*Over* the reef.'' Will considered. ''I guess that's possible. No, obviously it's possible. How will you get out again? There are no channels through any of the reefs.''

''We'll find a way,'' Blackstrap assured him. ''Blast one open, if need be. We've plenty of powder aboard.''

Could they do it? Will wondered. *This Blackstrap was just obstinate and foolhardy enough to try such a crazy venture.* A distant echo of thunder drew his attention skyward. The storm was still out there somewhere, still intensifying. Could these brigands' vessel ride it out behind the protection of the reef? Just how violent could a six-year storm be? Would it miss Dinotopia, or were the ultimate predictions of the weathercasters going to be proved right?

''There's a big storm coming,'' Will began.

It was Smiggens's turn to grunt sardonically. ''Don't tell us about big storms, lad. It was a monstrous great one which brought us to this land.''

''That was nothing compared to what might be coming. It's due to hit land any day now, and the area most in danger is the Northern Plains. You can't go back there. Everyone's already left.''

"Now, why would they do that?" Ruskin wondered. "The land seemed fertile enough."

"I . . . I don't know, exactly," Will went on. "I only know that when a big six-year storm is predicted, everyone who lives on the Northern Plains is told to leave until the storm has passed."

Smiggens considered. "The ground we first crossed was fairly flat. I've seen such country along the southeast coast of India. A monsoon-season cyclone could bring some local flooding." He smiled at Blackstrap. "Nothing the *Condor* can't ride out."

"My thinking exactly, Mr. Smiggens." The captain stared out into the darkness. "We'll carry what gold and jewels we can back to the ship, secure our playful little demon and this lad in the hold, and return with proper gear for hauling off half a temple or so." He raised his voice lustily. "Won't we, boys?" A number of tired but willing cheers greeted his cry.

"You can't!" Will began. "The storm—"

Blackstrap grabbed him by his shirt collar. "Now, lad, that be a word that's not in old Brognar's vocabulary." Letting go of his captive, he looked to his men. " 'Tis back to sleep, then, and whoever's on guard keep a weather eye on these two. Already they're too fond of one another's company." He stalked off into the night, heading for his golden bed.

They couldn't get away with it, a distraught Will worried. It could not be allowed to happen. If they managed to escape with such treasure, others would learn the location of Dinotopia. Ship after ship would come searching, and some would find it. The elegiac, peaceful civilization humans and dinosaurs had so carefully constructed after millennia of cooperation would come under intolerable pressure. It would be invaded by people, politics, and philosophies from the outside world. Was Dinotopia strong enough to resist such an invasion? Was any wholly independent country?

There was little in the way of weaponry in Dinotopia besides the purely defensive armaments convoys used to hold off stubborn carnosaurs when crossing the Rainy Basin. How could Sauropolis defend itself against modern warships? Would its citizens even try? If a successful anchorage could be found, a foreign power could land troops and . . .

He couldn't think about it anymore. His schooling had been thorough and he knew far too much of human history. Dinotopia's unique society would never survive the pressure of regular contact with the outside world. The pirates' departure had to be prevented at all costs, for their own benefit as well as that of all Dinotopia. It was all up to him.

Well, perhaps not entirely.

XIX

FROM THEIR HIDING PLACE THE STRUTHIE FAMILY had watched the unfolding of developments within the pirate encampment.

"What *is* that sound?" Tragic and fueled by sorrow, it made Chaz wince.

"Some sort of tyrannosaurian lament." Hisaulk peered over the wall. "There, it's stopped. The humans are not moving around so much and their laughter has faded. Things seem to be quieting down."

"What's the young tyrannosaur doing?" the *Protoceratops* asked.

"She looks to have reached an accommodation with your friend. I don't think she's going to eat him. At least, not right away."

The translator continued to pace in a small tight circle. "Somehow we've got to get him out of there."

"I agree."

"There has to be a way to . . ." The *Protoceratops* paused in his pacing. "You do?"

"Certainly. He's given us back our freedom. We can do no less for him." Hisaulk continued to peer through the darkness. "We must wait. Until the proper time presents itself, we will play the game of statue. These humans think we're running away. Let them continue to think we're running away."

Chaz was uncertain. "I don't mind being a statue for a

while. The questions is, what will they do to Will in the meantime?''

MANY OF THE PIRATES HAD THEIR HANDS TO THEIR EARS.
''Make it stop!'' Treggang winced as Prettykill hit a particularly discordant note.

''*I'll* make it stop.'' Guimaraes raised his rifle.

''No!'' Will rushcd to interpose himself between the Portuguese and the wailing tyrannosaur. ''That's not the way.''

''Aye, belay that!'' Blackstrap stepped forward to slap the muzzle of the rifle aside. ''You forget what the little devil is worth.''

''It's worth a lot of trouble, Captain.'' A sullen Guimaraes nodded sharply in the direction of the main temple. ''Do we really have need of such trouble when we already have more wealth than we can carry?''

''Mayhap,'' Blackstrap agreed. ''However, I find meself fancying a bit of fame to go along with the gold, and Mr. Smiggens assures me that bringing back a creature such as this will surely buy me that. So there'll be no killing as yet.'' Turning to Will, he fingered the cutlass at his side.

''That said, lad, if you don't find a way to quiet the little horror, we'll find a means of silencing her while still keeping her alive.''

Will vigorously nodded his understanding. ''All right, I'll do it. But you have to untie my hands.''

Blackstrap stared hard. ''As you will, then. But first you must give me your word of honor, lad, as a representative of whatever 'civilization' you say you belong to, that you'll not try to escape.''

''I . . .'' Will hesitated only an instant, ''give you my word, Captain Blackstrap, that I'll do nothing to flee by my own hand.''

The big man grinned through broken teeth. ''Still expecting a rescue, are we? Looking to walk into the nearest telegraph office?''

"There's no telegraph on Dinotopia. Not the kind you're thinking of, anyway."

"So be it. I'll take your word, boy. Thomas, untie the lad."

As soon as the big Jamaican had undone the knots, Will stood, rubbing circulation back into his wrists. Then he turned to the young tyrannosaur. Repeating her parents' names and keeping his tone gentle, he made silencing motions with both hands. As Prettykill observed his approach she went silent.

Carefully he advanced until he was standing next to her. Then he reached out gingerly and began to scratch the underside of her lower jaw. A few murmurs of admiration arose from the hardened seamen. Guimaraes's fingers whitened as he gripped his rifle.

"What's happening now?" Chaz asked.

Hisaulk glanced down. "The humans have untied his hands, but he is not trying to run. He's going toward the tyrannosaur. Now he . . . I don't believe this . . . he's petting her!"

"He's *what*?" Chaz found himself wishing for the neck of a *Mamenchisaurus* to stand upon, ridiculous as that would make him look.

"IT'S ALL RIGHT." WILL STROKED PRETTYKILL'S JAW and whispered soothingly. She couldn't understand a word he was saying, of course, but he felt that his feelings, if not his exact meaning, would be clear enough. "We'll get out of this somehow. Together. I know you think these people are crazy. If it helps, I think they're crazy, too." The young carnivore did not reply. Will felt her breathing steadily, like a bellows.

"See him soothe small dragon." Chin-lee made an arcane sign in the air. "We must watch him carefully. He is a sorcerer."

"Nay, not a sorcerer." Smiggens was not quite as flabbergasted as his more superstitious colleagues. "Remember, he told us that his father was a scientist."

"Scientist or sorcerer, he got the beast to shut up. That be what matters." The ever prosaic Blackstrap grunted his satisfaction.

When Will let his hand drop, he was startled to find the young tyrannosaur nudging his shoulder with the blunt end of her snout. He resumed scratching under her chin and was rewarded with a distinct sigh of pleasure. Though his arm was growing tired, he continued as best he could. *What a tyrannosaur wants, a tyrannosaur gets*, he reflected. *Even a young one*.

"That's not what matters here," he heard himself telling Blackstrap. "What matters is science and morals and ethics and education."

"Bah! You can't spend any of those."

"You don't understand. You don't see the larger picture, the greater meaning. Dinotopia is not only a place where humans have learned to live side by side with dinosaurs, who are older and wiser than we, but it's also a country where people of all backgrounds and nationalities have learned to live peaceably with one another. All of history and humankind is represented here. It's a model for what the rest of the world could be like.

"There's plenty of trade but no money. Everyone tries to help everyone else. There's free learning available for any who wish it. Academics for those who want books, apprenticeship for those who prefer to learn a skill. Even the simplest professions are respected."

"What are you getting at, boy?" Mkuse demanded to know.

"Why don't you stay?" Will put as much urgency into his voice as he could muster. "Give up the idea of trying to sail back to America or Europe or wherever. Stay here. Breathe deep and seek peace. That's worth so much more than a pile of pretty rocks and metal. You'll see." He eyed the captain hopefully.

"Well, now, lad, each to his own." Blackstrap stroked his mustache. "Me, I'll keep me pretty rocks and me gold. But I'm a fair man. Let's ask me shipmates." He turned to the watching seamen. "Did y'hear the lad? He asks us to give up all this"—and with a sweep of his arm he encompassed the temple complex—"to sit and converse peaceably with a bunch of big lizards. And learn a trade, of course. So I leave it to you, me boyos. Which'll it be? A carpenter's trade or lives of wealth and luxury? By my dome, 'tis a hard choice to make."

The pirates' response was predictable.

"No," Will began, "you mustn't look at it like that! You don't understand."

"I understand." Anbaya let out a derisive snort. "You people are stupid to ignore all this." He gestured at the golden buildings.

The opinion was unanimous. Give them plunder and loot over work and learning any day. Several stated what they thought of Will's proposition in more colorful terms.

"You hear them, young Will?" Blackstrap waited until the catcalls and hoots had died down. "If the folks hereabouts aren't interested in this wealth, why, me and the lads will be happy to relieve them of the burden of looking after it."

"But I told you," Will replied, "I don't think anyone else knows this outpost, or whatever it is, is here. It's a part of the history of Dinotopia. You can't just carry it off. It needs to be properly researched and documented."

"Har, you may write a full report if you wish. You may note each brick, each gem, as we remove it for safekeeping aboard the *Condor*. But remove them we will, have no doubt of that." His expression softened. "Won't that be the day, lads, when we sail up the Thames or into Boston Harbor in a ship ballasted with solid gold." Another murmur of approval rose from the assembled sailors.

"You'll never get away with it," Will told him. "Even if you manage to ride out the storm, you'll never get back across the reef."

"Why, boy, I've dealt with more difficult bits of seamanship in the past six months than you will in your whole life. Don't think to frighten me with tales of giant storms and uncrossable reefs. You'll have the opportunity to see for yourself, because you'll be accompanying us."

"What?" Will gaped at him.

Blackstrap grinned. "Did you think once we had our treasure aboard we were going to let you go? Who'd mollify our new pet? You ought to be on your knees thanking me, lad. We'll be carrying you safe away from this godforsaken place, back to civilization."

"But I want to stay here." Visions of Sylvia and his father filled his thoughts.

Blackstrap leaned close. "Now, boy, don't be going and making the mistake of thinking this a democracy. You've no choice in the matter. The sooner you accept that, the easier it'll go on you."

"You'll be stopped." Will was unable to control his anger. "Stopped and . . . and reeducated."

Raising his hands in mock fear, Blackstrap chuckled at the threat. " 'Reeducated.' Did you hear that, Mr. Smiggens? Mercy me!"

Will nodded in Prettykill's direction. "Also, her parents are looking for her."

Smiggens blinked. "You mean, this one's not an adult?"

"That's right." Having caught the first mate's interest, Will wasn't about to let go of it. "Surely you didn't think she was full-grown?"

"How young?" Smiggens involuntarily found himself glancing in the direction of the main canyon.

"*Very* young. I don't know enough to give you an equivalent in human terms, but she's really just a child."

"A cub. Interesting. If this is a cub, what must the adults be like?" A few nervous mutters rose from the gathering. The first mate's glance canyonward was quickly duplicated by others. None of them was sharp-eyed enough to detect Chaz or the well-concealed struthies.

"You can't imagine," Will informed him. "You just can't imagine. The adults are to Prettykill here as a lion or tiger would be to a housecat."

Blackstrap stepped between Will and Smiggens. "What's all this, now? Haven't we dealt with bigger versions of our dainty little one? The lad's doing his best to scare you. Did we not turn one away from our camp in the jungle?"

"Your guns wouldn't stop a big carnosaur." Will spoke

with complete confidence. "Or turn it, either. Probably it just wasn't interested enough."

Suddenly Blackstrap was right up in Will's face, his voice low and menacing. Prettykill fought against her ropes but could do nothing.

"What's that, boy? You wouldn't be calling old Brognar a liar, now, would you?"

Will swallowed hard and thought fast. "It's not me. I'm just saying what I think happened. Of course, I wasn't there."

"No." Blackstrap took a deep breath and drew back slowly. "No, you weren't. Don't think to frighten us, boy. I'm not afraid of anything that walks or flies or swims on this earth."

"That's admirable, sir." In a hushed voice Will added, "But if you ever were going to be afraid of anything, Prettykill's parents would be it."

A few of the men laughed nervously, and Will saw that they were far more afraid of Brognar Blackstrap than of anything their prisoner might describe.

"Get a good night's rest, boys," Blackstrap urged them. "We're safe here. You saw what happened to those sail-backed devils that chased us. Nothing bigger than ourselves can make it through the lower canyon, and there weren't no toothy beasts where we landed."

"Does that mean no watch tonight, Captain?" Thomas inquired.

"Nay, Mr. Thomas. Just because we're in a place where these dinosaurs can't get in doesn't mean we're in a place where people can't get in. On the odd chance this lad's tale has some truth to it and others be out searching for him, we'll post a lookout. I ain't half afraid of no lot of scientists and philosophers, but I don't want them sneaking up on me while I'm asleep in me bed, either." He grinned. "Not that they're likely to find him, since the lad himself said no one knows of this place.

"So it's to sleep, lads. Tomorrow we'll take what we can carry, and then it's straightaway back to the ship."

"Three cheers for Captain Blackstrap!" someone shouted.

The spontaneous tripartite hosanna that followed was more muted than usual. The men were tired.

Will waited patiently while two of the pirates tied him to the post that had formerly held Hisaulk and Shremaza. He might have given his word, but Blackstrap wasn't fool enough to allow his new captive the run of the camp.

When they were through, Will tested his bonds and found them as intransigent as he'd feared. Shifting his backside against the hard ground, he struggled to find a comfortable position in which to try to sleep. Nearby, the young tyrannosaur watched him silently. Her face was inflexible and unreadable, but he sensed a certain amount of trust, if not actual friendship. The latter would be too much to expect. Tyrannosaurs weren't even especially fond of each other's company.

Two of the pirates settled themselves on either side of the prisoners. Clearly Blackstrap was going to have Will watched at all times. There would be no opportunity for anyone else to repeat the silent nocturnal visit he'd employed to free the struthies. Blackstrap wasn't a man to be fooled twice.

Will closed his eyes. Best to get some sleep. Perhaps along with daylight the morning would bring some new ideas.

"WHAT ARE THEY DOING NOW?" UNABLE TO RESTRAIN himself any longer, Chaz was peering around the wall they had adopted for concealment. Since his night vision was nowhere near as acute as that of the *Struthiomimuses*, he couldn't see much, but it made him feel better to try. Keelk, Arimat, and Tryll crowded close behind him.

"It looks like they're going to sleep." Shremaza spoke softly from her position near the top of the wall.

"Yes," agreed Hisaulk. "See how they are crowding close to their fire." He and his mate turned and hopped lithely down to the ground, where all of them gathered in a circle.

"How can we help Will?" Keelk spoke freely in her own

language, knowing that the linguistically versatile *Protoceratops* would be able to understand.

"We must try to free him," Chaz muttered, "and the young tyrannosaur as well."

Hisaulk blinked down at him. "We have no obligation to the wild meat-eater."

"No, but Will and I do. We . . . we promised her parents."

"What strange compacts this whole peculiar business has forced us into," Hisaulk remarked.

"We can't just rush in," Chaz went on. "Will explained to me about these 'guns.' They might not hurt a big carnosaur, but they can kill someone our size."

"Then what are we to do?" Shremaza wondered.

Hisaulk regarded his family, so recently reunited. Now, it seemed, they would have to be separated once more.

"Among us I am the fastest and have the greatest endurance. Keelk and the *Protoceratops* can describe to me the path they took to get this far. Without having to search for a route out of the Rainy Basin, it should not take me half so long to reach Treetown and return with help."

"It will be very dangerous." Shremaza was understandably uncomfortable with the idea.

"Keelk did it." Hisaulk eyed his daughter, who swelled with pride. "While I am gone, the rest of you can shadow these humans. Perhaps a chance to free Will Denison . . . and the young tyrannosaur . . . will present itself. Chaz can try to overhear what the humans say and interpret it for you. This is the ethical thing to do." He entwined necks with each of his offspring in turn. "It will be a learning experience, albeit a dangerous one. Make a game of it."

"A most serious one." Shremaza considered the high walls that enclosed the complex of strange golden buildings. "Do you think, husband, that either this canyon or the one to which it leads runs all the way through to the Northern Plains?"

"I don't know, but we know of another which does so. Where one cuts through, it's certainly possible for another to do the same. If I can reach Treetown in time, it should be possible for a rescue team to intercept these humans before they can reach their vessel." Tenderly he wrapped his long neck twice around that of his mate, first from the right side, then from the left. Beaks rubbed gently against one another.

"I will be looking for you between the land and the sea, in that place where love waits. Children, abide by your mother's words. Translator, do your work well. Farewell." Turning, he broke into a run and had soon disappeared into the depths of the side canyon.

Shremaza called softly after him. "Go like the wind, husband. Breathe deep, and may only your shadow touch the ground."

Chaz knew the male *Struthiomimus* was risking his life for Will. But Will had done the same for them. "Much as I'd like to, we shouldn't stay here all night. One of their guards might wander over this way. I think we should go back and sleep in the main canyon. There's no reason for them to explore that far. Not at night."

"I concur." Shremaza gathered her brood around her. "We could all use a good night's rest."

"How can such strange humans be?" Keelk strained for a glimpse of the human encampment as her mother led her away from the wall.

"I don't know." Chaz was planning for the morning. "Will says that in the outside world humans fight over pieces of rock and metal. It's all very bizarre and incomprehensible."

"Don't they have enough to eat, or a place to sleep?" wondered Arimat.

"Not all of them do, but according to Will that has little to do with it. I don't pretend to understand. I'm only a translator."

XX

THE FOLLOWING MORNING THE UNDERSIDE OF THE cloud cover was ominously darker, as if it had been tanned by rain. Will doubted it would do any good to point this out to his captors. Blackstrap had already told him that neither he nor his crew was about to be intimidated by inclement weather, and after what Will had seen and heard the previous night he had no reason to doubt the captain's word.

Having never experienced the full force of a major six-year storm, he didn't know if a ship lying at anchor in the northern lagoon could survive one. If it did, he had no doubt that Blackstrap would make good on his promise to find or fashion a route back to the open sea. If that happened, Will knew he'd jump overboard rather than abandon Dinotopia. He shrugged his shoulders, in his mind's eye already seeing himself swimming hard for shore. Could a young tyrannosaur swim? They might have the chance to find out.

One of the pirates brought him breakfast, a noxious medley of water, corn, bully beef, and salt pork all cooked together, with hardtack on the side. It was a long way from the fresh fruits, vegetables, and fish of Treetown. Knowing it was important for him to keep his strength up, he forced himself to chew and swallow the gruel. Prettykill looked on without comment. Tyrannosaurs could go a long time without eating.

She was not his only company. The two guards on duty squatted together nearby, slurping their rations as if they were gourmet delicacies. A glance showed none of the other members of the crew, including Blackstrap, was within hearing range.

"I don't know what kind of life you've been living," Will began conversationally, "but Dinotopia offers a chance to start over."

Copperhead elbowed his companion. "Hear the boy. Next he'll be telling us this is the earthly paradise."

"Aye, paradise," snorted Thomas. "Only with dragons. No, what did Mr. Smiggens call them? Dinosaurs. Yes, paradise with dinosaurs that try to eat you."

"That's only back in the Rainy Basin," Will told him. "All the big carnosaurs are confined there. The rest of Dinotopia is pretty safe. You can't imagine how beautiful it is. The constant lullaby of Waterfall City, the classical glories of Sauropolis, the rural loveliness of Treetown and Cornucopia, the quiet coves and beaches, the rolling farmland and the lush orchards."

"Hoy, that's paradise, all right," Copperhead snickered. "Sounds like a bloody lot o' work to me." Thomas shared his friend's amusement.

Will hesitated, wooden spoon halfway to his mouth. "Isn't piracy work, and dangerous work at that? At least on a farm or fishing on a river or working in a shop, nobody's trying to kill you."

Copperhead's smile frayed. "Put me in jail for stealing a loaf of bread, they did. To help feed my sister's family. After that things just got worse somehow, till I ended up on the *Condor*."

"I worked in the cane fields all my life. Be there still if not for Captain Blackstrap." Thomas pushed out his lower lip belligerently.

"He can stay, too," Will assured them. "It doesn't matter what you've done in the outside world. Everyone who's cast up here starts life anew. It doesn't matter who or what you were in your previous existence. It's a chance to really begin over."

"Doesn't matter." Copperhead waved his spoon. "If the authorities find us here, we'll still hang."

"I don't know how you managed to survive landfall with your vessel intact. Yours may be the first ship to do so in

the entire history of Dinotopia. I do know that it had to have
been a freak occurrence and isn't likely to be repeated, even
if a warship somehow managed to find us. I also know that
no matter what Captain Blackstrap says, clearing the lagoon
with your hull in one piece is going to be a lot harder than
it was coming in. The winds and currents that surround Dinotopia tear ships to pieces.''

"That's true enough," muttered a thoughtful Thomas.
"We saw many wrecks coming in."

"Everyone who's shipwrecked automatically becomes a
citizen of Dinotopia. Sure there are problems, but it's nothing
like in America or Europe. Even the big meat-eaters aren't
really a concern since they're confined to the Rainy Basin.
All the other dinosaurs work side by side with humans."

"Like the ones you set free," Thomas reminded him
darkly.

Will didn't back down. "Yes. Like them. You'll see,
they're a lot like us. Bigger or smaller, they're just people.
We're all just people working together here, citizens of Dinotopia. You can be, too."

"I ain't sure I'd like working alongside folks from everywhere else," declared Copperhead. "Chin-lee, now, he's
okay, but a whole town full of Chinee, well, I don't know
about that."

Will smiled reassuringly. "Believe me, the first time you
find yourself taking mail from a *Gallimimus* or plowing behind a *Triceratops* or participating in field games with a couple of ankylosaurs, you'll wonder why you ever looked
sideways at different-colored skin or eyes shaped otherwise
than yours."

Will shook his head ruefully. "What happens when you're
too old to run anymore? Assuming you live long enough to
get old."

"Why, then," Copperhead replied, "at least we'll know
that we lived!"

"You can do that here. There are more exciting things to
do in Dinotopia than I can begin to mention. Think of it!
Your pasts will be as if they'd never been." He concentrated
on Copperhead, trying to hold his interest. "You say you
were arrested for stealing a loaf of bread. No one here will

know about that or care. Or care about anything you've done since." He shifted his gaze to Thomas. "The same holds true for you. Both of you can start new families here."

For the first time Thomas showed a flicker of real interest. "There are women here?"

"Women from every part of the world, from every civilization." He couldn't keep from thinking of Sylvia. "Relationships here are open to all." He hoped he was handling the subject properly. It was one he still knew very little about.

"Each of you could start a family, become responsible members of a unique community. Can you say that opportunity is open to you anywhere else in the world?" He lowered his tone pleadingly. "Is your present life, then, such a satisfying one that it won't even let you contemplate another?"

Copperhead looked troubled. "Well . . . I have to confess there are times when I'm not sleeping belowdecks, just lying in my hammock watching the overhead, when the ship's tossing in a heavy swell and everything's all wet and damp, when I think it'd be nice to be lying in a warm, dry, real bed somewhere, not wondering if a shell from a warship's going to come flying through to take off my legs."

"That's very so," agreed Thomas. "I come from the islands, where everyone still talks about Mr. Henry Morgan and his ilk. It's not like it was in his day. Pirating is a difficult business now. This *is* the nineteenth century, after all."

Copperhead abruptly snapped back from the idyll he'd been visiting. "What are we blathering on about? There's nothing we can do about our situation. What are we supposed to do, walk up to Captain Blackstrap and tell him we want to desert? Stand on the beach and wave good-bye with lace hankies?"

Thomas nodded knowingly. "He would have us strung up as mutineers and violators of the *Condor*'s compact. A new life's no good to a man whose neck has been stretched." The Jamaican stared evenly back at Will. "Forget it, boy. The life of a settled landsman's not for us. We've cast our lot with Blackstrap, and that is the way things are."

"But the authorities here would offer you protection," Will explained.

Copperhead's inner torment was written clearly on his face. "No more of this, boy. Let us have no more of this!" He dropped his hand to his rifle.

The gesture didn't alarm Will. He knew they didn't dare touch him without word from the captain. But he subsided. He'd planted the seed and seen it take root. Both men were pondering a life outside piracy. He hoped they would mention what he'd said to some of their companions. If he could get a significant portion of the crew to contemplate jumping ship, they might gather enough courage between them to defy Blackstrap.

After their morning meal, the men began gathering their gear to move out. Pockets bulging with gems pried from walls and sculptures, packs heavy with gold bricks, they headed not for the main canyon but the doors of the central temple.

"The captain's not a man to depart without looking into everything," Smiggens remarked in response to Will's query.

Once again the magnificent rose quartz doors yielded to the pirates' touch and they found themselves striding down the exquisitely decorated hallway. Will marveled at the sculptures and wall carvings, the bas-reliefs and mosaics. *What Nallab wouldn't give to see this place!* he thought wonderingly.

The hall split. Led by Smiggens, the pirates chose the left-hand passage, which led toward the center of the structure. Clear quartz portals admitted light, which bounced back in a thousand colors from the semiprecious gems that had been used to decorate the walls. The craftsmanship was as fine as anything Will had seen anywhere on Dinotopia. Who had built this place, and why? So intriguing did he find it that he was almost able to forget that he was a prisoner. Behind him, Prettykill's occasional grunts reminded him.

The pirates advanced in uncharacteristic silence, awed by the magnificence surrounding them. By the time they encountered a pair of solid, intricately carved amethyst doors,

they had long since exhausted their limited store of super-
latives.

Johanssen pushed experimentally on one, and it surprised
him to see it swing silently aside. The immensely heavy
doors were perfectly balanced on stone pivots.

Stepping through, they found themselves in a circular
room with a ceiling over a hundred feet high. It was more
of an atrium, really. Lush plants hauled from the Rainy Basin
thrust their leaves toward the distant skylight. Six feet across,
it had been cut from a single piece of yellow diamond.

The curving golden walls were teeming with mosaics.
Most depicted ancient Cambrian sea life. Will admired a *Hal-
lucinogenia* rendered in agates even though he had no idea
what it was. Judging from the design of the creature, nature
hadn't been too sure, either.

Scattered about the chamber were several pieces of handmade wooden furniture, the wood stark and yet somehow
inviting amid all the gold and jewels. Against the far wall
stood a short, round nest-bed woven from cane and packed
with palm leaves. On the bed was an occupant.

"Is it dead?" Samuel whispered as the men crowded into
the room.

"A mummy," swore O'Connor. "Sure, and it is, I've seen
them in the British museum."

The motionless figure was draped in the robes of an ascetic, one who had chosen a life of solitude and contemplation. Legs crossed before him, tail stretched out behind, head
drooping on his breast, the room's sole inhabitant did not
appear to be breathing. Will noted the huge claws on the
forearms, intricately entwined with one another. The whole
posture was suggestive of contentment and a deep inner
peace. Though large for one of its kind, when erect it would
stand no taller than Chin-lee.

Even Blackstrap was taken with the solemnity of the
scene. "Here, now, lad, what manner of dragon be that?"

"A *Deinonychus*. They're very dexterous and are often
employed as scribes. I can't imagine what one's doing here."

"Look at those claws on its hands and feet," Watford
commented. "See the big middle toe. Like a bloody scythe,
it is."

"Teeth, too," murmured Andreas. "That's no plant-eater."

"The *Deinonychuses* are very fond of shellfish," Will informed them.

"So well preserved." Smiggens advanced on the figure. "Perhaps it died only recently. Denison?"

Grateful to have someone call him by name, Will professed his opinion. "He's wearing the robes of an ascetic. He came here seeking peace."

"Bloody well found it, I'd say." O'Connor was examining the exquisitely decorated walls.

"Avast there!" someone screeched suddenly.

The diminutive figure was moving.

It sounded like an invasion of crickets as rifles and pistols were hastily unlimbered and made ready. Slowly the *Deinonychus*'s head came up. Eyes opened to regard them with indisputable awareness. The crossed legs and entwined hands did not move.

"Well," it remarked in perfect, if heavily accented English, "it has been a long time since I had visitors."

"Beggorah," exclaimed O'Connor, "the little dragon speaks!"

"I told you," Will insisted to any who would listen, "I told you." What he didn't add was that this was the first dinosaur besides a *Protoceratops* that he'd ever heard speak a human language. And not just the Latin-derived Human of Dinotopia, but English! Here was a very learned dinosaur indeed.

"Mark that burr in its voice," Watford was muttering. "Sounds like a blooming Glaswegean, it does."

Blackstrap's thoughts were racing down other paths. "Har, now, this could be useful, it could." He advanced on the nest-bed, towering over the squatting *Deinonychus*. "You live here?"

"It is my choice, yes." The ascetic shifted his position ever so slightly. "I am Tarqua."

Smiggens contemplated the incredible shaft overhead. "Must get pretty lonely."

The *Deinonychus* turned its toothy snout toward the first mate. "There is no loneliness where there is cogitation."

"Oho!" Blackstrap grinned. "Now, what have we here? A philosopher?"

Will stepped forward. "Tell me, meditative one, what do you do here?" He was pretty sure he knew, but he wanted the *Deinonychus* to get a good look at his ropes.

Tarqua took note of them immediately. "You are bound." His alert gaze traveled past Will to fasten on Prettykill. "And there is a young *rex* among you who is similarly restrained. What curious manner of journey is this?"

Blackstrap idly fingered the hilt of his cutlass. "Go on, lad. Might as well tell him."

Will explained the situation. The *Deinonychus* listened in silence, then sighed. "It is a sad thing to import such habits from the outside world."

"We ain't interested in your opinion." Blackstrap leaned forward menacingly. "The boy asked you what you did here."

A slitted pupil focused on the captain. "I contemplate the great mysteries. For this I find silence and solitude conducive."

"Silence and solitude, is it?" Blackstrap backed off to indicate the surrounding gem-encrusted walls. "Looks more to me like you're contemplating treasure."

"Treasure?" Tarqua blinked. "There is no treasure here save in the colors and the silence. But I understand whereof you speak. I have read much history, and I know that in the outside world humans have an inexplicable hunger for the tears of the earth. They are blinded by them, and so only rarely see and understand their true beauty."

"We finally find one of the boy's intelligent dinosaurs," Smiggens mused aloud, "and it talks in riddles."

"No matter." Blackstrap was once more relaxed and at ease. "He can sit on his rump and contemplate the silence all he wants. We'll leave him to it." An unpleasant grin crossed his face as he pointed to a mosaic depicting a swarm of *Orthoceras* swimming through a sapphire sea. The most prominently depicted had one very large red eye.

"Except for that there big ruby. Before we leave I'll have that for my purse, I will." Removing a wicked-looking knife from his belt, he took a step toward the wall.

The *Deinonychus* was instantly out of his crouch to confront the captain. "Do not touch that."

Blackstrap paused. "Oh? And why not? I thought you didn't care anything for treasure."

"I spoke the truth. But as my name is Tarqua, I will not allow the integrity of the inner temple to be violated. You cannot disturb anything in this room."

"Be that so, now?" Blackstrap's fingers tightened on the haft of the knife.

Smiggens was eyeing the *Deinonychus*'s impressive assortment of talons and claws. "Captain, we have ample booty. Maybe it would be better if—"

"Hold your tongue, Smiggens. Mr. Philosopher here and I are discussing matters of some importance."

The first mate bit down on his reply.

Though originally as carnivorous by nature as any inhabitant of the Rainy Basin, the family of dromaeosaurs, to which Tarqua's kind belonged, had long ago renounced ignorance to become respected members of Dinotopian civilization. Will personally knew several, including Enit, the head librarian of Waterfall City. Until now, he'd never thought of their teeth and claws as offensive weapons. All the dromaeosaurs and deinonychuses he knew tended to be bookworms.

"Here be a fine opportunity," Blackstrap was saying, "to add to our private zoological reserve." He addressed his crew. "What say you, lads? If our little devil will bring ten thousand pounds, what d'you think a talking one would be worth?"

Enlightenment having visited the first mate, he was suddenly at the captain's side, whispering urgently. "Brognar, don't you see the import of this? It means that the boy's been telling the truth all along! These creatures *are* intelligent. They *have* created some kind of unique civilization here."

"Get hold of yourself, Mr. Smiggens." Blackstrap was not so easily convinced. "One talking dinosaur does not a civilization make." His grin returned. "Besides, when did it ever bother you to have intelligent captives aboard? Have you forgotten the blackbirding we did in New Guinea and the Fijis?''

Dismissing the first mate by looking past him, the captain raised his voice. ''This here parrot's worth twenty thousand pounds at the minimum, men! More than its weight in gold, and it conveys itself. We've rope enough still to add it to our collection.''

''I dunno, Captain.'' Samuel eyed the silent *Deinonychus* uneasily. ''It's got a lot of claw.''

''What are you afraid of?'' Blackstrap glared at his crew. ''Why, 'tis no bigger than the smallest among you, an eagle without wings. Spread out on all sides now, and we'll take it easy.''

Unlimbering their nets and remaining ropes, a dozen or so of the pirates encircled the nest-bed and its contemplative occupant. Making no effort to flee, Tarqua quietly watched the humans' approach. Will held his breath, and even Prettykill looked on intently.

Taking the first step, Suarez flung a loop of net toward the *Deinonychus*'s head. At the last possible instant Tarqua leaped straight up into the air and turned a perfect somersault. The huge sicklelike claw on his second toe flicked out, there was a small snicking sound, and he landed exactly where he'd been standing. Only a slight ruffling of his robe indicated that he'd moved at all.

Neatly severed in three places, the half-inch-thick section of hemp netting dropped harmlessly to the smooth golden floor.

Several of the other pirates made similar attempts. In each instance the result was the same: Tarqua remained unrestrained while a number of neatly sliced ropes and nets piled up on the ground. The men looked to their captain for instructions.

Blackstrap's tone hinted at admiration rather than displeasure. ''Very impressive, aye. For one who says he just sits around contemplating, you're damnably fast, little dinosaur. I'd say in a tight situation you could meditate right well with your fists as well as your feet.''

Tarqua returned the captain's stare unblinkingly. ''An ancient art learned, interestingly enough, from humans whose

ancestors came to Dinotopia from places like Ch'na and
Kr'eah. I have modified it somewhat the better to suit my
abilities. I find performing the kata both physically and mentally relaxing.''

"Relaxing, aye. I expect you could relax a man clean
through from belly to backbone with those claws. Of course,
being a philosopher and all, you'd never consider such a
thing."

Tarqua gazed evenly back at Blackstrap, and for just an
instant Will thought he saw the pirate captain flinch. Civilized the *Deinonychus* might be, even highly civilized, but
somewhere deep inside, the ancient memories of a time when
he and his kind had hunted much larger dinosaurs in ferocious, unrelenting packs still lay dormant. Tarqua had flashed
just a glimmer of that, and the impact on the captain had
been profound.

Mkuse dangled the neatly sheared end of his rope. "That
could just as easy have been my wrist, Captain."

"I can see that." Blackstrap was not happy. Teeth and
talons notwithstanding, he'd just been stared down by an
oversized chicken with the manner of a bishop. "I wonder
if he's fast enough to cut down a bullet." Taking a step
backward, he drew one of the two pistols slung at his belt.
Noting the captain's reaction, the rest of the men followed
suit. Rifles were made ready. Tarqua looked on, silent and
unmoving.

Will stiffened, not knowing how to react, what to do, or
if indeed he should try to do anything. The tension in the
chamber was palpable. Looking at the calm, composed, and
supremely confident *Deinonychus*, he found himself wondering if maybe the dinosaur *could* deflect bullets.

The opportunity to find out did not arise. It was Smiggens
who filled with reason a momentary void that could have
turned tragic.

"Here, now, Captain," he whispered to Blackstrap, "we
have all the treasure we can carry and can come back for
more at our leisure. With more men from the ship, and if
needs be, more arms. Why risk an unnecessary confrontation
with this creature now? So long as we leave its sanctum
alone, it doesn't seem to mind if we carry off everything else

in sight. Is it really worth risking even one man just to bring it down?''

Blackstrap considered himself challenged, and his gut reaction was to meet a challenge head on. But that was one reason why Smiggens had been made first mate. Sometimes—not always, but sometimes—his calm reason could override the captain's congenital fury. The fact that Blackstrap was willing to listen to the advice of others was a major reason he was still plying the high seas while so many of his peers were languishing in foreign jails . . . or foreign graves.

Eyes never leaving the *Deinonychus*, he slowly holstered his pistol. ''Right you are, Mr. Smiggens. Right you are. Put your rifles up, boys.'' He forced a smile. ''After all, this be a place of contemplation and tranquillity, don't it? No reason to disturb things.'' Will could hear the sighs of relief as the men relaxed. None of them had been looking forward to a fight with the chamber's occupant.

Doing his best to turn the confrontation into a joke, Blackstrap bowed mockingly in the nest-bed's direction. ''Sorry we are to have disturbed you. We'll be on our way now, we will, and no harm done.''

''But Captain—'' Suarez began, mindful of Blackstrap's comments on the *Deinonychus*'s potential worth.

The big man glared at him. ''I said we're leaving, Mr. Suarez. If that sack on your back be not full enough for you, I'm sure we can find more gold for you to carry.'' The bewildered sailor subsided.

It was impossible to tell the *Deinonychus*'s exact age, but Will estimated that it was quite an elderly representative of its kind. Notwithstanding its advanced years, it hopped lithely from the center of the nest-bed onto the floor. The pirates tensed.

''There is one more thing.''

Blackstrap's gaze narrowed dangerously. He was used to dictating conditions, not accepting them. ''And what might that be, Mr. Philosopher?'' Smiggens put a hand on the captain's arm, but Blackstrap irritably shook him off.

''That once you have left this place you promise not to return. I have been listening to you for more than a day, and that has proven to be a day too long. Unsullied contemplation requires absolute peace.''

The broad grin that creased the captain's face this time was genuine. ''Why, I see no difficulty with that whatsoever, Mr. Tarqua, sir. None whatsoever. The problem is, you see, that we be strangers hereabouts and are having some difficulty finding our way. To make sure we're out of your hair—pardon me, your scales—as swiftly as possible, perhaps you can show us the quickest way from here to the Northern Plains?'' He winked at Smiggens, and the first mate was left to admire the speed with which Blackstrap had turned the awkward encounter to their advantage.

Blackstrap's promise, of course, was worth less than the palm leaves with which the dinosaurian ascetic had padded his bed.

''The Northern Plains?'' Tarqua looked puzzled, but raised a taloned hand and pointed northwestward. ''Continue out the back of the temple. You will see three clefts in the valley wall. Take the left-hand one. In places it is so narrow a *Deinonychus* or a man must turn sideways to squeeze through.'' He eyed the massive human speculatively. ''*You* will have to inhale deeply. But it does go all the way through the Backbone Mountains, and if you follow this course you will eventually emerge onto the Northern Plains, as you desire.

''Be quick about it, now, so that I may have back my peace and quiet.'' With a hop he returned to his bed and settled himself into a comfortable position for meditating, crossing his hands in front of his chest, lowering his head, and closing his eyes.

''Absolutely, your dinosaurship, oh, most rapidly we will depart!'' Blackstrap gestured at his crew. ''Come on, then, now, men. You heard the Solemn One. Let's hurry to be away from here.''

The seamen were careful to give the deceptively quiescent *Deinonychus* a wide berth as they filed out the back way. Hemmed in by pirates, Will prepared to call out in the hope that so wise a dinosaur might question his captivity. Given the *Deinonychus*'s arrantly antisocial nature it seemed unlikely Tarqua would protest Will's condition, but Will felt calling attention to himself was worth a try.

He never had the chance. Divining his intent, Johanssen slapped a heavy, callused hand over the younger man's mouth and grinned down at him.

"Belay that, boy. We wouldn't want to disturb the old dragon's meditatin' any further, now, would we?" Will struggled in the pirate's grasp but was unable to free himself. Assisted by shipmates, Johanssen hustled him out of the chamber. With her jaws tightly bound, Prettykill was afforded even less of an opportunity to comment on their involuntary condition.

Approximately an hour after the room had been vacated, Tarqua briefly raised his head, surveyed the empty chamber, and muttered something in his own tongue about "bad karma" before returning once more to a state of profound inner contemplation.

⇒ XXI ⇐

Having seen or heard nothing of the pirates or their captives by the following morning, Will's friends decided to take a chance and carefully made their way into the temple complex. While keeping a wary eye out for Will's captors, they took time to marvel at the unfamiliar and wondrous structures that towered around them.

They had no difficulty tracking the thick, pungent smell of the pirates into the main temple, located at the rear of the complex. By herself Shremaza and her brood would have been unable to open the outer doors, but using his horn-covered snout and frill like a miniature earthmover, the compact Chaz easily forced the portal wide.

"What's this?" At their cautious approach a testy Tarqua looked up from the nest-bed. "More interruptions?" He sighed deeply. "If this keeps up I will never achieve Nirvana."

Chaz gaped at the *Deinonychus*. "Who are you? What do you do here? Are you all alone in this place?"

"I am Tarqua, and I rejoice in solitude. More importantly, what do you do here? Heretofore, visitors to this valley were nonexistent. Suddenly I find myself compelled to deal with two groups in as many days."

"Did you hear, Mother? Then they *did* pass this way!" Arimat commented excitedly.

"Pity." Chaz's attention focused on the open corridor that led off to their right. "I was so hoping there was no other way out. This will save them time and make it even more difficult for Hisaulk and a rescue team to intercept them.''

"You must leave.'' The *Deinonychus* sounded tired. "So that I may resume my contemplations.''

Gathering himself, Chaz trundled forward to confront the ascetic. "Now, you listen here, whoever you are. We're trying to rescue a friend and we need your help. Was there a young human traveling with those who preceded us? One who was bound with ropes?''

"A young human and a young tyrannosaur,'' Shremaza elaborated helpfully.

"I believe so.''

Chaz cocked his head sideways as he considered the *Deinonychus*. "Didn't you wonder about their condition?''

"To tell you the truth, I did not pay much attention. I had all the others to watch closely, lest they cause me injury.''

"The boy and the tyrannosaur are prisoners, taken by these intruding humans.''

"Truly? Why did the boy not say anything?''

Chaz and Shremaza exchanged a look.

"I don't know,'' Chaz explained. "One way or another, his captors probably made it difficult or dangerous for him to do so.''

"I see.'' The *Deinonychus* pondered something unseen in the air before him. "What are these two to you?''

It was Keelk who stepped forward now, bowing to show her respect for the *Deinonychus*'s age and learning. "These strange humans took my whole family prisoner. It was the young human Will Denison who returned to help me free them. These humans do not think we are civilized and intend us no good. They intend Will no good. What they want with a juvenile tyrannosaur I cannot imagine.''

"The young tyrannosaur's parents helped us,'' Chaz elaborated, "and in return we promised to help free their daughter. We gave our word.''

The venerable *Deinonychus* nodded slowly. "The situation is more complex than I believed. I wish your young friend had said something to me. Now they are well away. To alter your friend's unfortunate status will be difficult.'' He sighed. "It does not matter. They are all doomed anyway.''

Shremaza blinked. "What are you talking about, wise one? What do you mean?"

Tarqua gestured skyward with his snout. "The storm-that-is-a-circle, which has been building for so long, will not miss Dinotopia but will pass directly over it. I have been reading the clouds and the stars. If you know your history you know where the worst of it will be felt."

"The Northern Plains," blurted Chaz. "Of course we know that. Everyone does."

Sadly, the *Deinonychus* lowered his head. "Then you must know that if this storm is a bad one—and I believe it will be so—that out on the plains he has no chance, nor do those who restrain him against his will, nor would even a tyrannosaur." With uncanny timing, thunder boomed somewhere high up in the unseen crags of the Backbone Mountains.

Its significance did not pass unnoticed. "It is starting already."

"But we have to save Will!" Chaz had dispensed with any attempt at formality or etiquette. "We have to! Not only did he save all these struthie lives, but it's the right thing to do. The *necessary* thing to do."

"For you, perhaps." The *Deinonychus* was unmoved. "I have removed myself from the world and its concerns. I think you will be safe from the storm if you remain here. We are far from the lowlands of the Northern Plains, and these temples have stood thus for many centuries."

Chaz backed away. "I'm sorry, sir, but I can't do that. I can't stay here knowing that we're safe while Will's life is in danger."

The struthie family crowded close around the indomitable *Protoceratops*. "Neither can we," declared Shremaza. "The young human put his own life at risk to save us. We must do what we can to try and help him."

"As you wish." Tarqua shrugged. "I cannot stop you. I would not if I could. The cosmos offers each of us choices."

"That's right," agreed Chaz readily. "We're stuck in it, and no matter how much *some* of us might try, we can't pretend we're not a part of it."

The look that flashed in the ascetic's eye momentarily reminded Chaz of the *Deinonychus*'s highly aggressive and carnivorous ancestors.

"Thus far I have done reasonably well at that, thank you. Each day I try to isolate myself a little further."

Tryll stepped forward. "Please, sir, if you can help us at all, you must."

The *Deinonychus* peered down at the smallest *Struthiomimus* and his tone seemed to soften slightly. "There is nothing I can do, little runner. They have too much of a head start, and there are many of them, armed with what I believe to be exotic and dangerous weapons from the outside world. If they can subdue and capture a young tyrannosaur, what makes you think you can unsettle them?"

"We don't know that we can," the stalwart Chaz replied, "but we're honor-bound to try."

"When my wanderings brought me to this place I vowed that I would remain here and do nothing save strive to achieve spiritual and mental perfection. Everything else I renounced. Now it seems that I am to be dragged, kicking and screaming as it were, back into a reality I believed I was finished with." The *Deinonychus* took a deep, weary breath.

"Yet there is merit to be gained in goodness, and your cause and motivation are noble. I will try to help you." At this the three young struthies hooted with joy, and Shremaza bowed low as a sign of thanks.

"There is one possible way we might overtake them," Tarqua confided, "but it means breaking the only law I have made for myself."

"There are laws higher than those we set for ourselves," Chaz told him.

The *Deinonychus* looked surprised. "Truly. For one so young, you have insight."

"I just want to help my friend," the *Protoceratops* replied.

As Tarqua hopped off the platform, the young struthies retreated behind their mother, wary of teeth and claws they would not have given a second thought had they been in Sauropolis or Treetown. Despite his encouraging words, they did not entirely trust this solitary *Deinonychus*, for he was surely the most eccentric dinosaur any of them had ever encountered.

Observing their reaction, the ascetic hastened to reassure them. "There's no need to be afraid of me, little ones." Robes trailing behind him, he set off at a relaxed lope for the rear corridor. "Come."

Keelk followed uncertainly. "Where are we going?"

"Going?" The *Deinonychus* was as serious as ever. "Why, we are going toward the place I have devoted my life to reaching. We are going toward heaven." He turned a corner and they had to lengthen their strides in order to keep up with him.

NO QUADRUPED IS VERY FOND OF STAIRS. CHAZ WAS NO exception. The swerving stone stairway they had been climbing for what seemed like hours wound its way interminably up into the mountains.

"How much farther is it to heaven?" Tryll asked innocently.

Tarqua glanced back at her. "I do not know, little one. That is one of the things I am trying to find out. Do not worry. We are not aiming to climb nearly so high. Only in that direction."

"We're just climbing to the top of the tallest temple, silly," chirped her brother. Tryll stuck out her tongue at him. It was surprisingly long and quite flexible.

"Not exactly." In the wake of the more agile bipeds Chaz huffed and puffed along as best he could. They had to pause often for him to catch up. "For one thing, we're not climbing in a spiral but in a long, continuously ascending, more or less straight line. For another, we have already, by my estimates, climbed far higher than the top of the tallest temple spire."

"Then where *are* we going?" Shremaza whispered edgily.

"I don't know." Chaz kept his eyes fixed on the metronomic sway of the *Deinonychus*'s tail, a shifting shadow in the light of the ascetic's torch. Fused vertebrae kept it from dragging along the floor. "This is the most peculiar dinosaur

I have ever encountered. Dromaeosaurs normally are brusque and irritable. This one is calm and serene. Usually they love to fuss and argue. This one speaks only of living in peace and quiet. They tend to shun the Rainy Basin. This one lives alone on its fringe. I don't understand him at all. I know only that his kind are but one step removed, albeit a very big step, from the rain forest carnosaurs.''

"You don't think . . .'' a wide-eyed Shremaza began.

"No,'' replied Chaz quickly. "He's much too educated to have fallen back to the old ways. He just puzzles me, that's all. But I don't care if he's from another planet so long as he helps us to rescue Will.''

"It feels like we're climbing to another planet,'' Arimat grumbled.

The beautifully hollowed-out corridor through which they were ascending gradually gave way to a natural tunnel decorated with stalactites, stalagmites, helectites, and other speleothems. At regular intervals the *Deinonychus* would pause to light one of the many torches set in holders attached to the walls.

"I'm getting tired,'' announced Tryll.

"*You're* getting tired?'' Chaz's short, stumpy legs ached from the strain of the steady climb.

"Be of good cheer.'' Tarqua's hearing was as acute as his eyesight. "We are almost there.''

"To heaven?'' Shremaza inquired uncertainly.

The *Deinonychus* chittered under his breath, a form of laughter. "Not quite so high. We are almost to the place I call the Balcony.''

The struthies exchanged glances. Having no one to look at, Chaz kept his reaction to himself.

The stairway opened into a huge, vaulted chamber hung with exquisite cave formations. Disturbed by their arrival, a turmoil of bats flashed past their heads, black confetti propelled by squeaks.

Chaz's beak sampled the air. "Stinks in here.''

"Ammonia.'' The *Deinonychus* led them deeper into the expansive cavern. "From the guano. Pay no attention to it and, like most disagreeable things, it will soon pass.''

"I wish those humans would soon pass.'' Keelk's claws

clicked rhythmically against the stone floor. "I wish they would let Will Denison go and leave in their boat."

It wasn't necessary to ask for a description of the Balcony. A short climb and turn to the left brought them to it, whereupon the source of the name became clear.

It was completely hidden from below. Anyone looking in its direction from within the temple complex would have seen only the protruding ridge of rock that completely blocked from view the gaping cavity in the mountainside.

As they arrived they also saw the workshop: stone benches set with orderly clusters of tools, many of which were unfamiliar to Chaz. The walls were decorated with more of the fine bas-reliefs that adorned the buildings in the hidden valley. These depicted humans working with strange machines and devices.

"There are no dinosaurs," Chaz commented as he examined the reliefs.

"No." The *Deinonychus* doused his torch in a rock cistern. Ample light poured in through the high opening in the cliff face, passably illuminating this portion of the cavern. "All that you have seen here was fashioned by an ancient human cult. They had access to great knowledge, much of which has been lost."

"What happened to them?" Chaz inquired.

"The picture writing they left behind is not conclusive," Tarqua explained, "but from what I have been able to gather and infer, it seems that they came to this place bent on restoring a culture built upon the accumulation of artificial wealth. They found and mined many gems and metals. So busy were they finding and mining and raising impressive monuments to their false riches that they forgot to grow food or catch fish. So they began to starve. When they found they couldn't eat the gold or jewels they'd slaved so long and hard to stockpile, they began to leave. Most rejoined the rest of Dinotopian civilization. Those who remained gradually died off. With their passing went all memory of this place."

Keelk marveled at their surroundings. "I bet Will Denison would find this interesting. His father is a scientist. Will wants to become a master skybax rider, but while his heart may fly, I think he has a scholar's eyes."

"Truly? It sounds like his father and I would have much in common."

"I didn't think you wanted to talk to anybody," Chaz remarked.

The *Deinonychus*'s gaze flicked in his direction. "I will always break silence when knowledge is to be had." Turning from the *Protoceratops*, he strode out onto the natural stone porch. "I come here often, not only to study and learn from these ancient artifacts and pictures but to enjoy the view." He beckoned with a clawed hand. "Come out. Are you afraid? It is perfectly safe."

Slowly they filed out into the light.

"Ho-shah!" exclaimed Shremaza. "It's beautiful!"

Golden buildings and silver walkways agleam in the sunshine, the entire temple complex lay spread out below them. Brilliantly faceted gems and semiprecious inlays set in walls and rooftops glittered like stars in an upside-down sky. Ahead and to the right the crests of the Backbone Mountains marched north and east in majestic, snowcapped succession.

"See, Mother!" An exhilarated Tryll pointed excitedly. "Isn't that Mount Spiketail?"

"I don't know, child. Perhaps Keelk . . . ?" When her eldest daughter did not respond, Shremaza turned querulous. "Keelk?"

They found her farther back in the cavern, examining a large irregular device of unfamiliar appearance that seemed to crouch in the deep shadows. "What's this? It looks more like a sky galley than anything else."

Tarqua's tone was complimentary. "You are observant. This is indeed an aerial vehicle of my own manufacture, similar to yet very different from the sky galleys which ply the mountain vastnesses of Dinotopia. It is based upon an ancient human design and employs novel methods of propulsion and fabrication."

Chaz studied the outlandish mechanism dubiously. The function of the gondola, fashioned of reeds and ropes, was obvious enough, as was that of the rigging that draped much of the craft. The prow took the form of a wooden sculpture in the shape of an ennobled *Deinonychus*. Clearly not their host, but perhaps some honored ancestor.

Instead of balloons filled with helium, half a dozen metallic globes hovered above the body of the device. They were held in place and secured to the gondola below by finely woven mesh nets and elaborate rigging. It seemed they should fall and crush the rest of the craft. Instead, they strained visibly at their moorings, obviously capable of providing considerable lift.

A single large wooden propeller protruded from the back of the craft. It was attached by means of a complex sequence of gears and shafts to a treadmill inside the gondola. Steering vanes, or rudders, flanked it on either side.

Chaz rested his forefeet on the craft's railing, the better to see inside. "That looks like a scroll reader," he commented, nodding in the direction of the treadmill.

"One that has been regeared and strengthened," Tarqua admitted, "so that instead of cycling a printed scroll, it operates this geared mechanism here. Observe."

Exhibiting an agility Chaz could not have matched even in his dreams, the elderly ascetic easily hopped over the railing and into the gondola, whereupon he proceeded to explain the mechanics to the attentive *Protoceratops*.

"The treadmill engages this gearing, which turns this screw, which drives the propeller, which pushes the vehicle through the air."

"Sky galleys have two such devices," Shremaza pointed out.

"Truly they do." Tarqua looked over at her. "But since there is only one of me, I built this craft so that I could operate it alone."

"But you have no balloons to provide lift." Chaz indicated the metal spheres. "Only those odd silver globes."

Tarqua was patient. "How do you know these are not balloons also?"

"Because balloons are made from silk, not metal. Metal is too heavy to be woven."

"That is so. But these are not woven, you see. They grow naturally, in the depths of this cavern, and with proper care can be increased in size like cabbages."

Chaz snorted in disbelief. "How can you 'grow' metal?"

Tilting back his head, the *Deinonychus* gazed proudly at

his spherical creations. "These are hydromagnesite balloons. They form slowly, as do the other more common cave formations you see about you. Employing the arts of the ancients, it is possible to greatly increase their size. When they have inflated to the degree necessary for my purposes, I carefully detach them and bring them here.

"I replace the gaseous mixture they contain with hydrogen, which is freely available from natural vents that permeate this mountain. Helium is safer, but requires artificial production facilities which are denied to me. Once the balloons have been refilled, their fragile surfaces are coated with a special transparent varnish, which strengthens them greatly."

"What in the name of the Great Egg can you want with such a device?" Shremaza regarded the outré contraption uncomprehendingly. "Of what possible use can it be to you here?"

Tarqua blinked at her. "Why, when I am ready to die I hope to use it to ascend to the proverbial heaven. Its lifting power is considerable."

"Metal balloons." Keelk studied the gas-filled globes. "What remarkable conceits has nature."

"It does seem to contradict natural law." Arimat had walked over to peer into the gondola. "Yet here it sits."

"There is room for all," Tarqua told them. "High winds may make navigating difficult. But my real fear is that if we use it to rescue your friend, I may not have enough hydrogen left to return to the Balcony. The balloons are not perfect, you see, and tend to leak. If we reach the Northern Plains but are unable to return, how then will I ascend to heaven?"

Stepping boldly forward, Keelk put a clawed forehand on the *Deinonychus*'s arm. There was a time in the archaic past when Tarqua's ancestor would have killed and eaten her on the spot. Much had changed in the past sixty million years, however, and the *Deinonychus* listened while the young struthie spoke.

"You are a fine person, Tarqua. Virtuous and moral. When the time comes for you to pass on to the next life, no matter which direction it lies I don't think you'll need a conveyance like this to carry you there.'' Her mother looked on with quiet approval.

''I confess there are occasions when similar thoughts occur to me.'' The ascetic gazed fondly at the contrivance that had cost him so much time and effort. ''Perhaps this is a better use for it.'' Turning, he scrutinized the lowering sky beyond the Balcony. ''The weather is not promising.''

''Neither is Will Denison's future,'' remarked Keelk solemnly, ''and his prospects are worsening by the minute.''

Tarqua nodded solemnly. ''The winds will be difficult, especially as we shall be sailing into them.''

''Excuse me,'' barked Chaz. ''We? Am I a pteranodon, to take to the air? You can't be serious.''

''We're going to fly, we're going to fly!'' Without waiting for instructions, Tryll and Arimat hurdled the woven railing into the gondola.

''Ah, the unquestioning enthusiasm of youth.'' Murmuring to himself, Tarqua leaped lithely into the rear of the craft and opened a door in the side. ''If you are ready?''

''Wait a minute!'' insisted Chaz. ''Ready for what?'' He cocked a disbelieving eye at Shremaza. ''Surely you're not going up in that thing?''

Ignoring the prattling *Protoceratops*, she fixed her attention on the sky boat. ''I have often watched the skybax and their riders and wondered what it would be like to be able to look down upon the ground from a great height. I had hopes Will Denison could somehow convey the feeling to me. But why not find out for myself?'' She stepped through the open gate and into the craft. More out of courtesy than necessity, Tarqua graciously extended a hand to help her aboard.

''Listen here, now.'' Chaz approached the vehicle but did not board. ''What happens if we do manage to overtake Will and his captors? Has anyone thought about that? What do we do then?''

''We could drop rocks on them.'' Arimat always had been an aggressive youth.

''Or pieces of log,'' his sister added, not to be outdone.

Tarqua looked on disapprovingly. ''I abhor violence. Perhaps we can frighten them away somehow. It may be that in the outside world flying machines are not yet a common sight. In any event, I will devote all of my considerable intellect to the problem.''

''Oh, now, that's reassuring,'' groused Chaz sarcastically.

''We'll drop down on them out of the sky, snatch Will up, and flee with him into the clouds where none can follow.'' Keelk eagerly examined the rigging. ''We'll substitute this craft for his skybax.''

''Then it's settled.'' Shremaza turned glistening, limpid eyes on Chaz. ''We may need your help, translator. Are you coming?''

''Oh, my,'' Chaz mumbled. ''Are these, my legs carrying me forward? Are these, my feet stepping up into this preposterous contraption? I am betrayed by my own body!''

Keelk bent over to place a forehand on the *Protoceratops*'s frill. ''Thank you, translator. I'm glad you're with us.''

''I'm not,'' he muttered. ''Actually, I'm back on solid ground, acting sensibly, watching you bounce and lurch through the air like a bug trying to negotiate a thunderstorm. But my body, it seems, has other ideas, and my brain has no choice but to go along for the ride.'' Ignoring his complaints, Tarqua closed and latched the door behind him.

''I'm not much on heights, you know.'' Chaz studied the comfortable, tightly plaited interior of the craft. At least the rails and walls were higher than his head. Unless he stood up on his hind legs he wouldn't be able to see the ground. And he had no intention of standing up.

Using the middle claw on his forefinger like a knife, Tarqua began cutting the ropes that secured the straining craft to the ground.

''Calm yourself, translator. The vehicle is perfectly safe.''

''I suppose.'' Chaz flinched as the gondola lurched forward. ''I guess you've tested it many times.''

With the last anchor rope cut, the silvery hydrogen-filled hydromagnesite balloons began to drag the heavily laden craft toward the Balcony and the open air beyond.

''Actually,'' Tarqua replied with serene nonchalance, ''this is the first time it will have been airborne.''

''*What*?''

''Oh, yes.'' Hopping onto the treadmill, the *Deinonychus*

began to run, loosely, easily, with fluid, measured strides. The treadmill scrolled, the gears meshed, the propeller began to hum, and the craft accelerated forward as it rose from the stony surface.

"Then how do you know it will fly?" an increasingly agitated Chaz sputtered.

"Because we *are* flying," the *Deinonychus* replied, quite unperturbed.

Chaz turned away, closed his eyes, and pressed his face against the nearest wall. He could feel as well as hear the wind whistling outside.

"I am not here," he recited under his breath. "I am not doing this. I am at home in my bed, preparing the next day's lessons. I am not here, I am not . . ."

Indifferent to his insistence, the sky boat soared out through the breach in the cliff face, over the edge of the Balcony, and up into the open sky.

They pitched sharply and the *Protoceratops* moaned.

"Interesting." Tarqua sprinted furiously, without evident effort. The treadmill's footpad cycled beneath him. "There are bumps in the air. I have heard of such." The lighter-than-air craft continued to pick up speed.

Beneath them, slot canyons rent the high plateau like dark veins. Most were less than a foot wide. Locating one of the gondola's corners, Chaz pressed his face into it as far as it would go and stood silently, isolated and shivering. Part, but not all of his reaction, could be attributed to the fact that as they rose higher, the air cooled noticeably. He did his best to ignore the elated singsong of the struthies, all of whom were glorying in the experience.

Wind began to catch and buffet them. Rain fell fitfully from dark clouds while thunder echoed all around. There was lightning, but only in the distance, off to the north.

If our situations were reversed, Chaz told himself angrily, *Will Denison wouldn't be cowering in a corner like this*. Of course, Will was a skybax rider and as at home in the clouds as on land. Flying held no fear for him.

What was that fear? A mental condition. Couldn't Chaz control a simple mental condition? His trembling eased, then ceased altogether. Tarqua had done his work well. The sky

boat rocked and bounced, but not so much as a single plait
came loose. Chaz began to approach a state somewhere between utter panic and stoic resignation. It was a great improvement.

The resin-coated hydromagnesite balloons drew them ever
higher. Thin as paper, they gleamed like steel in the fitful
light.

On an off day, this might be considered fun, Chaz told
himself. Instead of simpering in terror he should try to enjoy
himself. Give himself over to the experience. The struthies
were leaning against the railing, pointing out sights below
and squealing delightedly at the adventure. When Tarqua began to tire, they each took a turn on the treadmill, with the
result that no speed was lost. The *Deinonychus* adjusted the
gearing to suit the strength of each individual runner.

From time to time he would realign the rudders and the
remarkable craft would sluggishly change direction. Once,
they soared close by a thousand-foot-high spire of ocher
chert, and even Chaz had to marvel at the stately beauty of
the encounter. His spirits rose, if not quite as high as the sky
boat itself, at least to a level approaching that of the excited
struthies. He didn't even panic when the gondola, heeling
over to starboard, scraped its port side against the sheer stony
needle.

Who knows, he told himself jauntily as he tried to put the
best possible face on the situation, *we may even be lucky
enough to find a soft place to crash.*

XXII

SHEETING RAIN FOLLOWED BY BRIEF, FITFUL PERIODS of calm slashed at the line of pirates as they emerged from the mouth of the canyon onto the Northern Plain. There was much relieved cheering and shaking of rifles in the air. Not everyone participated. After the long, tense march many of the men were too tired to contribute to the celebration.

Starting down the easy slope that fronted the canyon, they soon found themselves on perfectly flat lowland, unable to see over the trees and palms. Somewhere ahead, their vessel rode safely at anchor, holding shipmates long unseen and the promise of fresh victuals from the galley's stores.

Between tree and sky lay an unbroken line of cloud black as night, thick with foreboding, and riven by lightning. None chose to comment on this ominous sight. They were just happy to be clear of jungle and canyon.

It was only a short, easy hike to the beach that fringed the lagoon, Blackstrap assured them, and none among the crew desired to believe otherwise. Not with hundreds of pounds of gold and jewels chafing the skin on their backs. Each man carried a fortune beyond his wildest dreams, along with the promise of returning for more.

"Straighten up, there, lads!" Blackstrap moved among them, cajoling this one here, encouraging that one there, booting those he thought weren't pulling their weight in their sweaty, bent-over backsides. " 'Tis only another day or so and we'll be back at the boat."

Fate, however, cared nothing for Brognar Blackstrap's

urgings. As it happened (and it happened very quickly indeed), they never even made it back to the mangrove forest.

Will didn't have the sharpest eyes among the party, but unlike the others he was the only one looking for what he finally found.

"There, look there!" With his wrists bound behind his back he was unable to point, and so could only nod westward.

"What ails the boy?" Mkuse looked to Johanssen.

"Don't know." The tall American strained to see. "There's a big dust cloud off to the west. Not surprising, what with this crazy wind blowing every which way." His gaze lifted. "Don't like the look of this sky, Zulu man. I don't like it at all."

Suarez overheard. "The ship, she'll be fine inside the lagoon. She can ride out any storm there." He gestured at Blackstrap's broad back, rising and falling like a swimming whale among the leaders. "I see the captain ride out meaner storms than this. Can't be worse than the weather that blew us all the way here from the Indies."

"I dunno." Johanssen blinked away sudden rain. "See how dark the horizon is. Blacker than night it be, only without stars. There's something unnatural about it."

"Then it fits with what we've seen these past several days," Mkuse observed. His companions nodded their agreement.

Only Will knew what the cloud of mist portended. It arose not as a consequence of wind but of feet. *Big* feet. They'd have to be, to stir up so much soil and water amid the all-pervasive dampness and driving rain. Though still a long way off, it was clearly headed in the pirates' direction. Only when the party surmounted a low, sandy hill overgrown with coastal vegetation did the source of the mist cloud reveal itself.

Could anyone else make out individual shapes? Will wondered. Surely they had to. The rescue team was coming straight toward the travelers.

"Lord almighty," Thomas murmured as he pointed to the west. The cloud had subsided, revealing its cause for all to see. His gaping shipmates packed in next to him, forming a line atop the provident hillock. Uneasy mutterings filled the air.

Advancing in their direction was the most beautiful sight Will had seen in a long time. A dozen giant sauropods carrying riders and extensive equipment packs shuffled effortlessly through the swampy vegetation. There was no question that the intruders had been spotted. Even at the still considerable distance that separated them, Will thought he could see light flashing from the lens of a telescope. Seated just behind the brachiosaur's head, the rider would have a commanding view of the surrounding countryside.

They were a grand sight: pennants streaming from their long necks, tassels hanging from backpacks and harnesses, the light reflecting off the gold filigree that decorated their equipage. The occasional flush of rain could not dim their magnificence.

Rising on tiptoes, he started to yell. Immediately there was a pirate in his face and a dirk at his throat.

"Let's have none of that, now, boy." Guimaraes glared at him, his hate-filled face inches from Will's.

"It doesn't matter." Smiggens looked glum. "They've obviously seen us and are coming this way."

"Mountains on feet." Like his companions, Samuel was thoroughly awestruck. "No way can we outrun them."

Old Ruskin's words were tinged with grudging admiration. "I know a Raj in Lahore who'd trade twenty of his best elephants for one of those, just for the chance to ride it in the yearly procession honoring Ganesha. What a howdah it could carry!"

Blackstrap raged among them with slaps and rebukes. "Why are you all standing about like gawping children? These be not Arabian thoroughbreds threatening us." He raised a burly arm. "The beach be that way. Surely the beasts cannot swim."

Actually, brachiosaurs and apatosaurs and diplodocids were quite at home in deep water, Will knew, but he sensed that to dispute Blackstrap at that moment would be to invite disaster. The captain might shoot him simply out of frustration. So when the group hurried down the far side of the little hill, Will increased his hobbled stride and did his best to keep pace.

They hadn't traveled more than a couple of hundred yards before Treggang, gasping under his heavy load of treasure, stopped and pointed. "It is no use, Captain. See how they come faster now!"

Probably someone in the rescue party had identified Will through a scope. Whatever the reason, the sauropods had broken into a run. It was a sight Will had only seen once before, when he'd encountered a group of children playing with a pair of *Diplodocuses* on the beach. Formidable as the stupendous sauropods appeared when striding along at a normal pace, they were infinitely more impressive when bearing down at a gallop. Even at a distance, the earth shook beneath them.

The muffled rumble set pirate hearts to pounding, as well it should.

Despite his present unpleasant circumstances, Will couldn't help but recall his history lessons. What might such a cavalry have done against Caesar at the Rubicon, or the British at Waterloo? Such notions were pure fantasy, of course. Even if the opportunity to do so somehow presented itself, no sauropod would think of engaging in such an enterprise. Inherently aware of their capacity to wreak havoc, they were among the most pacific of all dinosaurs.

Not knowing that, more than one seaman was shaking in his boots. "Look how fast," stammered Chumash. "Cut us off from beach for sure."

"Not so fast," O'Connor corrected him. "But look at the length of those strides!"

"Right!" Blackstrap drew himself up behind a cluster of ivory palms. "Form a line, then. Hold your fire till I give the signal. We'll turn these same as we did the first monster that dared challenge us." He smiled ferociously. "Aim for their riders!"

Will started toward the captain and stumbled. "No, you can't!"

His plea proved unnecessary. Though valiant and experienced brawlers, none of the pirates had the gumption for a fight with an animal the size of a railway station, much less twelve of them.

"What's wrong with you?" Blackstrap roared. "Fire at will, then, if you won't form a line."

One of the pirates threw his gun into the bushes and turned to flee.

Chumash showed no inclination to participate in the futile fusillade. "Might as well try to bring down a grizzly with spit," he commented phlegmatically.

An assortment of frightened cries and wails rose from the assembled.

"They be trying to cut us off from the beach. We'll fool 'em, we will." Waving his cutlass over his head, Blackstrap beckoned for them to follow. "This way, men! Discard your treasure."

Samuel gaped at him. "Discard it, Captain?"

"Aye! There's plenty more to be had. We'll retreat back into the canyon, where the great beasts cannot follow, and either wait them out or find a way to circle 'round whatever position they take up. If their riders dare pursue, we'll cut them down like dogs."

Reluctantly, the seamen let sacks of gold and silver slide from their backs. A few furtively shoved handfuls of choice jewels into their pockets, so that their hips and chests bulged as if afflicted by some intractable disease. Which was, in fact, not far from the truth.

"They're coming!" howled Samuel. "We'll all be crushed!"

"No," Will insisted as he was swept up in the panic, "don't worry! It'll be all right. Just stand your ground and nobody will be hurt, I promise!" No one was paying him any attention.

"Run!" screamed Andreas as fresh rain struck the party.

"*Wait!*"

Will whirled on the speaker. He'd been wrong: at least one member of the crew *had* been listening.

All the uncertainties, all the confusion and troubled thoughts that had been boiling in the first mate's mind, had finally come to fruition. Slowly removing his pistol from his belt, he let it slip indifferently from his fingers. It landed in a shallow, rain-spattered puddle. He looked hard at Andreas, then turned to regard the rest of his shipmates.

"Why should we run? We'll only keep running for the rest of our lives. Do any of you really think we can get off this island, for an island it surely must be, without the permission of the people and dinosaurs who live here? They're the masters of this land, not we. Why should we not take the only chance that's been offered to us? Listen to the lad!"

The men hesitated. Exhausted and fearful, they were ripe for reason.

Something of an ambulatory mountain himself, Blackstrap strode back and forth among them. "What's the matter with you lot? Move your cowardly arses! Back to the canyon!"

"No." Astonishing himself, Smiggens gazed unafraid at his companion of many difficult years. "I'm tired of running, Brognar. I'm tired of being awakened in the middle of the night to stand to arms just in case the next vessel we encounter might turn out to be a patrolling warship. I'm tired of sneaking ashore for a few nights of drunken revelry only so I can sneak back to the ship and out of port. I'm not a young man anymore. Piracy's a dying profession whose boldest practitioners can only look forward to a short and furious life at best."

"Have a care, Preister," rumbled Blackstrap warningly.

Smiggens was not to be denied. Addressing the attentive seamen, he pleaded his case. All the while the sound of the approaching sauropods grew louder.

"Mind what the lad has been telling us. Ponder well its meaning if he speaks the truth. We've none of us a record here in this . . ." he glanced at their captive, "what did you call it, Will Denison?"

"Dinotopia," Will replied softly.

"Yes, Dinotopia. We're all free men here with the promise of a fresh start. A new life for each and every one. Who among you wouldn't gamble to lose the weight of his past? You, there, Mkuse. What were you before you became a brigand?"

"When I was not fighting in an impi, I was a river fisherman," the Zulu replied pensively. "But we've seen only small streams here."

"There are rivers!" Will leaped to the first mate's aid. "Big, fast-flowing, game-filled rivers. Wait until you see the fish to be had in the Polongo!"

"You see?" Smiggens moved from man to man, peering deep into their eyes, taking those who seemed uncertain or benumbed by their surroundings by their collars and shaking them gently. "Why compound our guilt by running? As yet we've injured no one here. Let us cast ourselves at the feet of the local inhabitants and perhaps in their mercy they will welcome us among them." He spun to face Will.

"That's what you said would happen, wasn't it, lad? That we could become citizens of this country?"

Will nodded vigorously, trying to keep one eye on the seething Blackstrap. "All who are cast up here leave their previous lives behind them. Dinosaurs and humans alike will make you welcome."

Ruskin took a step forward. "I've been three times 'round the Horn, and each time it was because I was running from something. I say now, I'll run no more." He smiled at Will, displaying a distinctive dearth of teeth. "I believe the boy."

"Used to train horses before I went to sea." Andreas was gazing westward to where the rescue party had been slowed by a rain-swollen, soft-bottomed stream. "Liked to feel the wind in my hair." He examined the gigantic sauropod in the lead, noting its massive legs, the long muscular neck, and the rider swaying in his saddle forty, fifty feet up behind the large intelligent head.

"What must it be like to ride such a beast at a gallop?"

"You could find out," Will assured him. "Every sauropod has a favorite human groom. They gladly trade rides for personal care."

"What's all this?" Stepping into the circle, Blackstrap swung his cutlass freely, forcing several of the men to duck out of the way. Rain trickling down his face and spilling from his great mustache, he turned angrily on the mate.

"We've been through a lot together, Mr. Smiggens. All the way from the hell of Hobart, we have. Be you, now, after all this, counseling mutiny?"

The first mate stood fast. "This is no mutiny, Brognar," he replied tightly. "We indeed have seen much, you and I.

More in the last year than most men will in a lifetime. But . . .'' he hesitated, *"I'm tired of running."* Looking past the captain, he gestured at Will. "The lad offers us a better end than any I thought I'd meet. It's a chance, Brognar, a chance for all of us.''

"And if he's lying, Mr. Smiggens? What of that, eh?''

The first mate shrugged. "As well a dinosaur's foot as a hangman's noose, I reckon.''

Blackstrap's face contorted into a grotesque scowl. "Why, you lying, traitorous, backstabbing, mutinous spawn of a jellyfish.''

"I'm with Mr. Smiggens." A determined-looking Watford crossed to the first mate's side.

"And I." Mkuse joined them.

Quickly the cry was taken up by all the rest of the crew save two. Davies and Copperhead, two of the most murderous of the lot, moved to flank their captain.

Blackstrap glared menacingly at the men who'd joined Smiggens. "You slimy, scurvy, useless lot of sun-baked trepang. You be not men but babes, bawling to be wet-nursed. So be it!'' Glancing to his left he saw that the sauropods and their riders were starting to emerge from the streambed. Reaching into a pocket, he scornfully flung a king's ransom in gems into the sullen, defiant faces of his former crew. Suarez started to make a dive for the jewels, only to have Smiggens grab him by his shoulder and his dignity, paining the former while preserving the latter.

"Come on, then,'' Blackstrap told his remaining companions. "We'll outrun 'em to the canyon and find a place to hide out. Paradise, is it? Har, we'll see about that! Every land has its lice and crabs. I'll raise a new crew from among them, a true crew, and we'll pillage and plunder this stinking country from one end to the other!''

He spat contemptuously in the direction of the oncoming rescue party. "I be Brognar Blackstrap, and I ain't afraid of nothing on the face of this earth. Neither man nor beast, no matter how bold the man or large the beast.'' He favored them with a last, venomous snarl. "I'll be seeing every manjack among you again, and when I do, you'll find yourselves sorry you chose to cast your lot with this coward and this boy." Replacing his cutlass in its scabbard, he drew both pistols. "There be but one thing left to do."

So saying, he turned to face Will. Those in his immediate vicinity hurried to take themselves elsewhere. Will was left standing alone, hands bound behind his back, legs hobbled. Prettykill thrashed wildly at her restraints, unable to intervene.

Blackstrap stood silently for a long moment, watching his young prisoner's eyes, which had grown very wide. Methodically he checked first one revolver, then the other.

"You've cost me me crew, boy. I can't let that pass."

"Not me, it's not me." Will looked frantically from left to right. It was clear that, willingly as they had sided with him in the matter of no longer running, none of the men was about to interfere.

"Circumstances cost you your crew, Captain Blackstrap," Will continued desperately. "Events, happenings. Not me. Listen, there's a new life here for you, too, if you'll have it. There's always work for an experienced seaman."

"Doing what?" Blackstrap let out a terse, humorless snigger. "Running a ferry back and forth across a river? Navigating grain barges? Guiding tourists? No, boy, that not be for Brognar Blackstrap." He raised one of the revolvers. Smiggens's mouth tightened, and several of the other sailors inhaled sharply. A couple of the men looked as if they were thinking of jumping in, but the presence of that second, always accurate revolver gave them pause.

Will closed his eyes. *Good-bye, Father,* he thought. *Goodbye, Nallab and Cirrus and Bix and all my friends. I never thought it would end like this. But I did what I had to do to help others. If making me a better person is what Dinotopia has done to me, then I guess it's for Dinotopia I'll die.*

Sylvia, he thought. He envisioned her soaring alongside him, her hair flying in the wind as her skybax, Nimbus, banked toward him. Saw the four of them dipping and rising together, as they might have done in life.

No, he told himself. He wasn't going to go out like this. Not with all these hardened seamen watching. Straightening, he opened his eyes and stared straight back at Blackstrap.

The captain nodded ever so slightly in approval as his finger tightened on the trigger.

A gray streak wrapped in flowing linen fell from the sky to land square on Blackstrap's shoulders, knocking him forward and down just as he pulled the trigger. Will convulsed as the bullet dug a streak in the earth just to the left of his leg.

"What the bloody blazes?" Pistol still gripped tightly in his fist, Blackstrap rolled onto his back to see what had knocked him down.

The unexpected arrival dipped its head in a slight bow. "Your pardon. I hope I did not hurt you." So saying, Tarqua sprang forward and in a single lithe, fluid motion, kicked the revolver out of the captain's hand. Had the ascetic chosen to use the great curving sickle of a talon that curved downward from his second toe, instead of the heel of his foot, it would have been Blackstrap's hand instead of the gun that would have been sent flying.

The captain was nothing if not persistent. As he tried to aim the other pistol, Tarqua simply sprang in reverse and sent the other weapon spinning into a clump of bushes. Face flushed and panting hard, Blackstrap slowly rose to his feet, not taking his eyes from his bright-eyed tormentor as he prepared to draw his cutlass.

He was distracted by the approaching rumble of the rescue team. "Blathering demons who drop from the sky. Mountains that walk." His expression twisted into an ugly sneer. " 'Tis gratifying it will be to put this land to the torch!" Gesturing to his remaining loyalists, he whirled and rushed back up the path they had taken, in the direction of the slot canyon.

The remaining pirates gazed in astonishment at the enrobed Tarqua as the *Deinonychus* turned to bow low before Will. It was Chumash who first noticed movement overhead and let out a startled cry.

"It's all right!" Will hastened to reassure them. "It's only some sort of sky galley. A boat like your own." But no sky galley like he'd ever seen, he reflected. The balloons that held it aloft looked to be made of metal, which was self-evidently impossible. Wasn't it?

As it descended rapidly toward them, a familiar, sensitive face appeared in the prow, leaning out and waving energetically at him.

"Keelk! It's you!"

The pirates strove to divide their attention between this new marvel and their young prisoner, who had begun struggling like a madman. It was left to the most recent arrival to calm him.

"Will Denison, I presume? I saw you in the temple, but we did not speak. In retrospect, that is a pity, for had we communicated at that time this precipitant journey might have been avoided."

Will nodded slowly. "I tried to call out to you, but I wasn't allowed."

"So your friends surmised. Your very persuasive friends, I might add. Please excuse me while I go to the aid of my disabled craft. I saw from above that it would not land in time and so jumped out at what I thought to be a propitious moment. I am glad you are unharmed."

Bounding past a pair of startled pirates, he leaped impossibly high into the air. Aware that his kind were among the strongest jumpers in all Dinotopia, Will was the only one on the ground not struck dumb with amazement at this feat. Snagging the side of the craft with both clawed hands, the *Deinonychus* pulled himself up and into the gondola.

"If you could give us a hand," he yelled from within, "it would be much appreciated!"

For a moment no one moved. Then Mkuse turned to his shipmates. "Well, are we to be good citizens of this country or not? Come on, then!"

Putting aside their weapons, some of the men doing so for the first time in their adult lives, they rushed to the reeling, wavering craft's aid. They crowded beneath its sturdy keel, jumping and grabbing, but it pitched back and forth in the inconstant wind and hovered just out of reach. Following Tarqua's directions, the struthies tossed mooring lines over the side, which the pirates gathered up. Digging their heels into the rain-sodden ground, they fought to bring the craft to earth. Several found themselves dragged forward so that they sprawled facedown in the mud, to the gruff amusement of their fellows.

The grounding of the gondola was a group endeavor. As soon as its keel scraped earth, Tarqua hopped out and began issuing directions in heavily accented but perfectly understandable King's English. The sailors, who had until very recently thought dinosaurs nothing more than peculiar, exotic animals, suddenly found themselves taking orders from one.

"Secure that foreline to that palm trunk . . . no, not like that . . . there, that's better . . . bring the stern down gently, gently . . ." Tarqua's instructions were as clear as those of any experienced ship's officer. "You tie a good knot," he complimented the man nearest him.

Samuel grinned at the *Deinonychus*. "That's a skill the least among us possesses."

Shremaza had popped the latch on the sky boat's door and urged her offspring out. Groaning, an unsteady Chaz stumbled out last, found a soft patch of ground, and immediately slumped down on his belly.

"Chaz!" Will shouted to his friend.

The *Protoceratops* looked up weakly. "Am I really back on solid ground? It doesn't feel like it. It feels like I'm still moving. Still rocking, still bouncing, still sliding from side to side, still . . . oooohhh!" He closed his eyes as Will looked on sympathetically. Whether through sea or sky, sailing was not for everyone.

Touchdown had taken place not a moment too soon. One of the hydromagnesite balloons had already collapsed, and two of the remaining three were in bad shape.

With a sigh of resignation Tarqua bounded into the gondola and released the air from the two damaged sacks by puncturing each with the tip of one claw. Hydrogen hissed softly as both metallic globes deflated. They could be repaired and refilled, but the sky boat would not fly again for some time.

"We did not rise very near to heaven, did we?" he murmured.

"Heaven?" Will joined the *Deinonychus* in inspecting the grounded craft. "I don't know about that, honored elder, but when you came down on top of Blackstrap the way you did, you surely looked like an angel to me.''

A familiar chirping and hooting made Will turn. Keelk was standing close by, her right forearm upraised. Smiling, he touched his own palm to hers. Then, in true struthie fashion, she wrapped her neck around his much shorter one, first on the left side, then on the right. This exchange was repeated with her brother, sister, and mother, until Will's head rang slightly from the surplus of affection.

''They are saying that you saved them and now they are glad to repay the favor,'' Tarqua translated for him. ''Allow me to release you from your restraints.''

''Thanks.'' Will turned his back on the *Deinonychus*.

''Stand very still, please.'' Taking a step back, the *Deinonychus* extended the second talon on his right foot and measured the distance carefully. A few quick, whistling kicks and Will's bonds lay in coils about his feet. He'd felt nothing except the wind of Tarqua's passing foot.

''Much better.'' Will rubbed at his wrists and legs where the ropes had chafed the skin. A glance to his left showed the rescue party bearing down on them. ''Now we need to do likewise for my friend.''

Throughout it all, Prettykill had looked on in silence, conserving her strength for a last, explosive effort should the large human point his weapons at her. Then the young human who had befriended her had been miraculously saved, and the dominant male of this disgusting pack driven off. Now she crouched silently, waiting to see what would happen next.

Johanssen intercepted Will and the *Deinonychus*. ''Wait, now, lad. It's true that we've cast our lot with you, but surely you can't mean to free that devil-beast?'' Wind whipped his long hair and rain pelted his face. ''It'll kill all of us.''

''I don't think so,'' Will responded confidently. ''Have you forgotten that I calmed it once before?''

''Aye,'' admitted another of the uneasy seamen, ''but that was when it were strapped and bound.''

''If she's been acting aggressively it's only because she's young. What would you do in her position, kidnapped and carried off by strangers? I gave my word to her parents that

I would see her free.'' He noted their troubled expressions.
''If you want to be citizens of Dinotopia you have to understand everything that means.''

''We realize that, lad, but still . . .'' Johanssen's imploring
gaze finally came to rest on the damp, lanky figure of the
first mate. ''Mr. Smiggens, what say you to this?''

''We have to do as the lad says. Although,'' he added as
he retreated several steps, ''I confess to being less than keen
on his intentions myself.''

Accompanied by Tarqua, a still wobbly Chaz, and the entire struthie family, Will approached the young tyrannosaur.
Placing a hand on the upper end of her snout, he once again
repeated both their names in her own tongue. He wasn't surprised when the masterful *Deinonychus* addressed her fluently and at length. When the ascetic had concluded, she
snorted to indicate her understanding.

''Give me some room, please.'' The *Deinonychus* studied
the tyrannosaur's bindings. ''This will take a few moments.
There is a lot of rope.'' Robes swirling, talons flashing, he
went to work. Watching the wonderfully athletic display,
Will was reminded of folk dancers in flight.

One after another the heavy tethers fell to the ground,
sliced cleanly through. When the last parted, Tarqua stepped
back to survey his footwork. Not a nick showed on the young
tyrannosaur's skin.

Prettykill stretched and yawned, the latter a most impressive display. Though only a youngster, her serrated teeth
were already larger than those of the mature *Deinonychus*.
She flexed one leg, then the other. Then she turned her head
slightly and, growling dangerously low in her throat, started
straight for Guimaraes.

Perceiving her intent, the Portuguese's friends instantly
abandoned his company. Guimaraes, who not so very long
ago had been the picture of bloodthirsty recklessness, back-
pedaled frantically and tripped over a rock. Skittering backward on his buttocks, kicking madly with his legs, he
beseeched any who would listen.

''No, stop, call her off! She'll kill me, she'll tear my throat
out! Don't let her near me!'' The terror in his face was pit-
eous to behold.

Reflexively, Will interposed himself between the whimpering seaman and the stalking tyrannosaur. "Tarqua, Chaz! Somebody translate for me, and quickly." His expression determined, he raised both hands. Breathing hard, Prettykill halted, her teeth inches from his fingers.

"Prettykill, listen to me. I know you don't adhere to the standards of civilized Dinotopia." He could hear both the *Deinonychus* and the *Protoceratops* translating in the background, an amazing series of growls and rumblings. "But just as I gave my word to free you, I've sort of given my word to these humans that they'll be safe in my company. Let the authorities in Sauropolis judge them, not you.

"You're free now, and I'll see to it that you have any help you need to return safely to the Rainy Basin. But I want you to give me your word that you'll leave these men alone. *All* of them. The one who's truly responsible for what was done to you, for what was done to all of us, has gone. Don't blame those here for the things he made them do."

Will knew that wasn't entirely true. Not all of these men had been coerced into the actions they'd taken. But it was near enough to the reality, and all now seemed ready, even eager, to begin anew.

It made sense to him, but would it make sense to a tyrannosaur?

Prettykill blinked. Using her right forefoot, she scratched at a place where a rope had burned. Then she looked back, not at the petrified Guimaraes, but at Will. The powerful jaws parted, and he found himself staring at a dark maw lined with razor-sharp teeth. He didn't flinch, not even when the long pink tongue emerged to give him a rough lick on the cheek. Like the tongue of many carnivores, Prettykill's was as rough as sandpaper. Nevertheless, he managed a smile as tyrannosaur saliva ran down his cheek and off his chin.

"Right, then: that's settled." He heard several of the pirates exhale sharply. "You can get up now, mister. It'll be all right. Mister?" He turned to reassure Guimaraes, but the Portuguese was destined to remain unaware of his salvation for several moments yet.

He'd fainted dead away.

➡ XXIII ⬅

"Y OU KNOW," REMARKED SMIGGENS CONVERSA-
tionally as they waited for the rescue party to collect
and for Samuel and Andreas to revive the unconscious Guimaraes, "I was a teacher. I've always missed teaching, but
I don't imagine those skills will be wanting here. This is a
whole new world, and I know nothing of it."

Will brushed rain from his forehead and tried to comfort
the former first mate. "There's always a need for teachers.
You can teach contemporary outside world history, or sailing, or timeless subjects like mathematics. I'll introduce you
to my father. He had some of the same fears when he first
learned we couldn't leave here. Now you couldn't drag him
away."

Smiggens regarded the confident young man. "You really
think so? That would be grand."

Will nodded vigorously. "Wait until the librarians find out
you were a teacher. You won't have a spare moment. Why,
once you learn the ancient script, you might even find yourself teaching young dinosaurs as well as human children."

"Teaching dinosaurs." A faraway look came into Smiggens's eyes. Then he blinked and found himself eyeing Prettykill uneasily. "Well, some dinosaurs, anyway." Will
grinned at this remark. "It seems a most understanding society which has been established here."

"You'll see," Will told him. "There's room here for
everyone."

Mkuse stepped forward, an unaccustomed hesitancy in his

voice. "Tell me, lad. Does anyone . . . do they make slaves of Africans here?"

"Slaves?" Will frowned. "There's no slavery in Dinotopia. I don't know about the humans of ancient times, but the dinosaurs would never hear of it. It's an alien concept to them."

The warrior muttered something in Zulu, adding in English, "There are many who I wish could see this place."

"Me, too," Will replied sadly. "But no one leaves Dinotopia."

Old Ruskin squinted at the threatening sky. "If anyone could do it, Captain Blackstrap's the one."

"Don't worry about him. A watch will be put on your ship, and he'll be found."

"You said something about contacting authorities." Smiggens looked uncomfortable. "We haven't exactly treated you and your friends well."

Will considered. "None of us has been harmed. In fact, the whole experience will make a good story. You haven't been acting as citizens of Dinotopia and aren't citizens yet, so I suppose you're not subject to its laws. I don't know exactly what will happen, but I'm sure everything will turn out okay." He smiled apologetically. "It's not for me to say. I'm only an apprentice skybax rider."

"Skybax rider?" exclaimed Andreas. "What's that?"

"You'll see." *It would be wonderful to see Cirrus again*, he thought. *The* Quetzalcoatlus *must be lonely.* "Here are our rescuers."

The seamen crowded together and gazed in awe at the gathering of sauropods that halted nearby. Wind tugged at hats and scarves. It was raining heavily and continuously now, and everyone was soaked to the skin.

Separating from the group, the lead brachiosaur advanced to within a few yards of the onlookers. Several of the pirates lost their hats, and Treggang fell on his backside as they tilted their heads back, back, to gaze up the length of that phenomenal neck. As they looked on, it slowly descended, like the scoop on the end of a crane. Red and gold tassels decorated the tack, and the saddle behind the head had been tooled by a master leathermaker.

Identical tassels hung from the shoulders and boots of the human rider, who slipped off the saddle with an effortlessness born of long practice. The head withdrew, rising skyward. As it did so, a slim, familiar shape slid and hopped free of the formidable mass of supplies that was strapped to the sauropod's back.

Hisaulk's reunion with his family was as touching as it was restrained.

"What manner of creature is this?" A reverent Ruskin tried to take the measure of the immense quadruped.

"Aye," added O'Connor. "She's as big as a house. No, two houses!"

"That's a brachiosaur," Will informed them. "They're very gentle."

"See how high the saddle sits," Samuel commented. "It must be like riding a foremast."

While Chaz chatted with the big sauropod, Will did his best to explain the situation to its rider, a stout, earthy woman from Treetown who identified herself as Karinna. The repentant seamen seemed to find her, in her boots, trousers, and overblouse, as astonishing a sight as any of the great dinosaurs.

She listened closely to all of Will's abbreviated but relatively complete tale before nodding understandingly. When she replied, a rapidly recovering Chaz thoughtfully translated her Dinotopian jargon for the benefit of the pirates. In the background thunder boomed incessantly, as if a mighty sea battle were taking place just over the horizon and drifting steadily nearer.

"So it was the leader of this collection of wayward misanthropes that we saw running for the foothills." She looked toward the Backbone Mountains, their summits now hidden beneath thickening clouds. "I saw him myself, through the glass." She patted the spotting scope that hung from a loop of her belt. "A big man."

"Only physically," Tarqua asserted.

Surprised, the brachiosaur rider blinked at him. "You're very articulate, for a dromaeosaur."

"I have spent my life in study." Tarqua rewarded her with another of his gentle, elegant bows.

"If we don't try to cut him off, he's going to get away."
Will, too, was gazing in the direction of the mountains.
"He's dangerous."

"Not now. Let him go." Karinna whistled to her mount
and the brachiosaur's head dipped earthward again. Swinging
one leg over the broad saddle and slipping both feet into the
dangling stirrups, she rapidly rose forty feet into the air. At
her request the gigantic quadruped raised up on its hind feet,
using its tail like the third leg of a tripod and boosting her
another twenty feet skyward. The pirates cringed, but the
brachiosaur maintained its balance for the several moments
her rider required to scan the horizon. When it dropped back
down to all fours, the ground shook.

Several diplodocids and another brachiosaur congressed
together, riders and mounts conversing animatedly. Eventually Karinna directed her mount to lower her groundward
once more, but this time she didn't dismount. Everyone gathered around, even the pirates, who could not bring themselves to be frightened of the brachiosaur's inherently
bucolic, affable expression.

"We must get away from here at once." Karinna spoke
in no-nonsense tones as she divided her attention between
the travelers and the distant sea. Wind bent her tall, pointed
cap almost in half. If not for the strap that ran under her
chin, it would surely have been blown away.

The wind was now howling about them. When a broken
twig struck Will on the cheek, it felt like a flying piece of
glass. Nearby, Tarqua's sky boat strained at its moorings.
Bits of trees and bushes went skimming by, some bouncing
along the ground, others already airborne. Will needed no
explanation for what was happening. He'd been expecting
and fearing it for days.

The six-year storm was coming ashore.

"The *Condor*!" Chumash had to raise his voice now in
order to make himself heard above the wind.

"There are men aboard," a fretful Smiggens informed the
brachiosaur rider. "They took no part in this and have no
idea what's happening." He started toward the coast. "They
must be told."

A neck the size of a man-o'-war's mainmast blocked his

path. "There is no time," Karinna informed him. "Your shipmates will have to cope as best they can."

Smiggens turned to Will. "I don't understand. It's just a storm. Why all the concern?"

"It's not just a storm." Leaning into the wind, Will came close. "This is the culmination of a six-year cycle. All this land"—and he waved to encompass the low ground on which they stood—"is in danger."

"In danger?" The first mate made a face. "In danger from what, lad, flooding?"

"I'm not sure. I don't know all the details, but I do know that everyone who lives around here moves out every six years, and that we'd better do the same—and fast!"

"Will Denison is right." Karinna gripped the sides of her brachiosaur's neck tightly with her thighs. "We have little time."

Smiggens was torn. On the one hand, everything the young Will Denison had described had come to pass. But the *Condor* was not only home to him and his shipmates; it was refuge, mother, and the only security most of them had known for years. It had ridden out every blow they had faced. To abandon it now meant placing themselves in the hands not only of strangers but of strange beasts. It was a decision demanding a true leap of faith, a complete break with the past.

He saw that the others were watching him, waiting for him to make the decision, waiting for him to tell them what to do. He found himself smiling in what he hoped was a reassuring manner. He was used to giving orders, but not to leading.

"From now on we have to do what these people tell us to do. It'll be all right." He looked at Will Denison. "It will be all right, won't it?"

Will nodded as Chaz waddled up next to him. "Only if we get out of here quickly," the *Protoceratops* declaimed.

Karinna was thirty feet up and staring seaward, as were all the other sauropods and their riders. "There is no more time to discuss your concerns. Nor need you think any longer about returning to your ship."

A perplexed Smiggens peered up at her. "Why not?"

"Because in a few moments it won't be there anymore." Her tone was solemn. "The sea is coming to kiss the land."

A chill ran through Will as Chaz translated this for Smiggens and his mates.

"To the high ground!" At a word from her rider, the brachiosaur began to turn.

When Will translated this for the pirates, they started a mad scramble for the all-too-distant foothills. He rushed to cut them off.

"No, no! Not that high ground. *This* high ground!"

Slowing, the seamen looked back to see a dozen massive necks all but touching the ground behind them, like so many fallen Greek columns. Karinna and the other riders were beckoning urgently.

Their actions required no translation. Shouting encouragement to one another, the pirates scrambled up those curving inclines onto backs as broad as boulevards. Will, Chaz, and Tarqua translated the riders' instructions, shouting into the wind and rain.

"Secure yourselves to the backpacks!" Will had his hands cupped to his mouth. "Grab any strap or rope you can find and hang on!"

Another band of travelers might have had difficulty complying, but not these hardened seamen. Used to walking yardarms and spars on a rolling ship in a high wind, they had no trouble obeying. Several wrapped the leather straps that dangled from the sauropod riders' saddles around their wrists. Others used their legs to climb up the muscular necks and hang on, thereby gaining height if not comfort.

Meanwhile, Karinna, the other riders, and their stupendous mounts were bunching into an arrowhead-shaped phalanx consisting of nearly a thousand tons of meat and muscle. Diplodocids shouldered as close as possible to apatosaurs, while the five brachiosaurs assumed positions at the head of the formation. Legs interlocked as much as possible, forming a solid wall of bone and muscle facing the coast. Karinna's brachiosaur, Maratyya, ninety feet long and eighty tons massive, headed up the formation.

Will sat behind Karinna on the leather saddle. It was a long way to the ground, and he kept his arms locked around her waist. Blinking away the driving rain and barely able to hear her now above the howling wind, he leaned to his right and tried to follow the line of her pointing arm.

Past the last tier of mangroves, beyond the narrow beach of perfect, uncontaminated coral sand, the *Condor* swung at anchor, her bow pointing into the screaming wind. Beyond the ship, gigantic breakers higher than any Will had ever seen were smashing against the reef.

Outside the reef and unbeknownst to any save the dolphins, the floor of the seabed angled down and out to form a great funnel-shaped slope. Every six years, when the moon was full, the tides were at their highest, and the southern Indian monsoon spun off a mutant cyclone or two southward, great storms would slam into Dinotopia's northern coast. Unchecked by any islands, seamounts, or other land-masses, the waves that accompanied the eyes of such storms swept steadily southward, their prodigious energy multiplying until it at last encountered the gradually sloping sea floor.

As these waves squeezed in upon themselves, impelled forward by the terrific winds of the cyclone, the result on rare occasions was a flawless fusion of typhoon-force waves with a stupendous oceanic tidal bore. It was this, a solid wave line stretching from horizon to horizon, that now held the full attention of the riders, their mounts, and their awestruck passengers.

Twenty feet high and still building as it gathered height and speed, the oceanic bore rushed shoreward. It swept over the broad reef as though it didn't exist, millions of tons of water pouring into the lagoon. Will couldn't hear the men left aboard the *Condor*, but he could imagine their panic and confusion. Behind him, he heard several shipmates of those unlucky enough to have been left aboard cry out, knowing even as they did so that their warning cries would not, could not, be heard.

All looked on as the sturdy ship rose like a toy in the wave's embrace and was ripped from its moorings. Chin-lee jabbered excitedly, having observed a similar phenomenon on the Yangtze River. Johanssen knew of the tremendous tides that periodically swept up the Bay of Fundy, but neither he nor anyone else had ever witnessed a spectacle like that which now unfolded before their stupefied gaze.

Furthermore, it was headed straight for them.

Crest foaming, the great wave swept over the beach, covering the mangroves, bending the palms, and swallowing the land. The sauropods steadied themselves while their riders exchanged last-minute instructions. Will gripped Karinna with his arms and the saddle with his legs, while the pirates and struthies dug their fingers deep into leather and hemp fastenings. With the best grip of all, Tarqua helped to support Chaz, who unlike everyone else once again had nothing to hold on with save his strong but inadequate beak. Prettykill's jaws were locked in a careful but unbreakable grip around one thick rope.

The last thing Will remembered before the water struck was the astonishing sight of the *Condor*, masts and sails gone but hull still intact, spinning and rolling as it surfed the breaking wave inland past palmetto and cypress.

Then the deluge was upon them.

If I ever get out of this, Chaz swore before the water rolled over him, *I'm going to keep as close to the ground as possible.*

"We're going to die, we're all gonna die!" Treggang bawled.

"Belay that!" Smiggens had no idea if the man heard him. About him now all was roaring wind and salt water, and it was all he could do to keep from being swept away. "Hang on!"

Will felt the stout neck beneath him tremble. He was glad Cirrus wasn't with him. She could never handle such winds. No flier, dinosaur or artificial, could.

Accompanied by a great sucking sound, the wave withdrew, only to be followed by a second, and then a third. The mammoth body under Will shuddered but did not stumble. Above the wild wind he heard riders and sauropods shouting and bellowing encouragement to each other.

The phalanx held. A thousand tons of determined dinosaur is not easily moved, not even by a twenty-foot-high storm surge.

By the time the third wave had slumped back out to sea, the eye of the cyclone had moved on, and Will knew that

the last of the great surges were shattering themselves harmlessly against the solid rock of Windy Point. Though still
lusty, the storm winds were falling. In their wake rain fell in
torrents, flooding the lowlands but at the same time diluting
the sea salt and washing much of it out to sea before it could
sink into and poison the soil.

Had Blackstrap and the men who'd fled with him made it
to high ground before the surge struck? There was no way
of knowing. Will was too concerned for his friends to let the
thought linger.

Twelve sauropodian bodies had challenged the waves
chest-on. Twelve necks had thrust high and unbowed above
the foam. Mud clung to pillarlike legs while fish and other,
weirder sea dwellers flopped aimlessly about in the slowly
dissipating waters.

Riders and mounts checked in with one another to make
certain all had survived the aqueous onslaught unharmed.
Water ran in streams off pale skin, backpacks, harnesses,
waterlogged sailors, sputtering *Struthiomimuses*, one stoic
Deinonychus, a single exhilarated juvenile tyrannosaur, and
one very unhappy young *Protoceratops*.

"Will there be any more?" Will spat rain from his mouth
as Maratyya lowered him to the ground.

"I don't think so." Karinna tried to shield her eyes with
one hand as she studied the horizon. "I think the storm's
moving off to the west. The old records say that such surges
can occur only when the storm is in just the right position.
It was something to see, wasn't it?"

"It certainly was." *Better, though, to have observed it
from a dry tent atop a high mountain*, Will reflected. He slid
off the back of the saddle and moved off a ways. Rain cascaded from the brachiosaur's back in small waterfalls.

Espying something flopping about in a small pool, he knelt
to examine a pair of large *phacops* trilobites that had been
cast ashore from the lagoon, only to become trapped when
the waves withdrew. Carefully he picked them up, first one
and then the other, and placed them in a rapidly receding but
still running stream. Immediately they began to ambulate
seaward, their multiple legs fanning the water in their haste
to retreat.

Stranded *Orthoceras* and ammonites lay everywhere, eyes glazed and tentacles limp. They would make excellent eating, Will knew, although he personally found their flesh too rubbery for his taste. Already Prettykill was picking through the leavings, searching for the choicest specimens. It was the first time since her capture that she'd had enough to eat. Not far away, Anbaya and Chin-lee were discussing how best to cook a six-foot-long *Orthocera*. To them it savored of a squid banquet, already prepacked.

Hearing someone moaning nearby, Will turned to see Chaz staggering slowly toward him. Water splashed beneath the *Protoceratops*'s feet.

"How are you feeling?" he inquired solicitously.

"Tired. Tired of running from Rainy Basin carnivores, tired of dangling from tyrannosaurian hands, tired of flying through the sky supported only by reeds and vines, tired of drowning atop an apatosaur's back." The little translator's head jerked as he sneezed. "Once we're back in Treetown, I'm going to make a vow never to get within a hundred body-lengths of the sea ever again."

"Don't be like that. An occasional romp on the beach is good for everyone." Will considered the fast-moving clouds. "What's needed is a bright, warm, sunny day."

"What's needed are high, dry plains and streets," the *Protoceratops* groused.

Chaz was an urban dinosaur, Will reflected. Well, not everyone was partial to the glories of the countryside.

"When we arrived it appeared you needed rescuing only from the storm and not from these men." Karinna gestured in Hisaulk's direction. "That's not what the struthie led us to believe."

"Things have changed," Will explained. "Except for the three who fled, all these have agreed to give up their antisocial ways and become good citizens of Dinotopia. I can vouch for that, as can Tarqua and the struthies who were with us.

"As for the men still on the ship, I think that once they've had a chance to talk to their shipmates here, they'll find themselves of similar mind." Will gazed westward but could not see where the displaced *Condor* had come to rest. No matter what their intentions, its crew must surely be too battered and debilitated to offer any resistance. There was no doubt in his mind that Smiggens and the others would quickly make them see reason.

The brachiosaur rider nodded somberly. "The ultimate disposition of their case will be up to the grand council in Sauropolis." Behind Will, hardened seamen shuffled about uncomfortably, looking for all the world like a party of guilty schoolboys. Karinna smiled through the diminishing rain. "For now, though, we'll take your word for it." She raised her voice.

"If you have truly put your transgressions behind you, you will be treated the same as any other shipwrecked or dolphin-backs. From this moment on you are our guests."

She raised an arm and swept it forward. Behind her, all twelve massive necks dipped low in a great, unified arc. It was a most impressive sight.

Descending from their saddles, the riders waited while their mounts settled with ponderous ease onto their bellies. Using rope ladders integrated into the tack, they then climbed up onto sauropodian backs and began to untie the supply packs. Working like cranes, the sauropods reached back over their own shoulders to help with the unloading.

Overwhelmed by gifts of food and unfamiliar but finely made clothing, several of the pirates sank to the ground with joy and relief. There were even bouquets of flowers that expanded in the last of the rain. Battled-scarred faces broke out into wide, boyish grins at the sight of several of the riders: young women clad in sturdy leather and linen. Smiling a welcome, they placed garlands of exotic blossoms around the sailors' necks.

"I hardly know what to say." Overcome by the show of unpretentious hospitality, Smiggens fingered the flowers draped about his throat. "What's the meaning of these?"

"I'm told that Polynesians were among the first humans to land in Dinotopia," Will explained. "It's an old way of greeting here."

"But flowers," the first mate murmured. "Victuals I can understand, and water, but why would a rescue team travel with flowers?"

Will beamed. "In Dinotopia people travel everywhere with flowers. They're considered as essential to a long and happy life as food or drink. Dinosaurs consider them a spice, both visual and otherwise."

The grin on his face spreading irresistibly wider, Smiggens found himself nodding at nothing in particular. And at everything in general.

"I think . . . I think my shipmates and I are going to like it here. Neither I nor any of these men have ever been treated like this before in our lives."

"I guessed as much." Will glanced skyward. The sun was starting to peek out from behind the rapidly dissipating clouds. "Sometimes the hardest thing to know how to deal with is an unexpected kindness. Or so I've been told."

Smiggens made a sound in his throat and wiped at the rainwater trickling from one eye. Or was that a tear? Will wondered.

"What will you do now, Will Denison?"

"Me? I'll go back to studying how to become a master skybax rider."

The first mate's smile turned to a knowing grin. "Is that all?"

Will glanced away, embarrassed without quite knowing why. "There *is* a young lady. A special young lady."

"I thought as much. I've known many ladies, but none of them well enough to ever think of one as special. I'd like someone like that to think of me as special, someday. Maybe . . . maybe if things work out as you say they can here I'll be lucky enough to find someone like that, someday."

Turning, he let his eyes rove southward over the sodden plains, let them climb the slopes of the Backbone Mountains. Beyond those peaks and crags lay wonders unimaginable, which the young man standing next to him had only hinted at. Wonders that even someone like himself, who'd long thought his dreams lost and his life wasted, might now have a chance to explore.

A last cloud seemed to pass over the sun and he looked away. "Don't let your friends underestimate Brognar Blackstrap," he told Will. "He's the toughest, meanest, cleverest, most vicious individual I've ever met in my life, and believe me, I've known some the mere sight of whom would curl the hair on your young head. He'll stop at nothing to have his revenge.''

Will followed the first mate's gaze. ''The authorities will deal with him,'' he assured the older man, mindful of his recent encounters with the irascible Lee Crabb. ''He's no longer your concern, or mine. Try to put him out of your mind.''

Claws gentling on his shoulder made him turn, and he found himself staring into the handsome face of Tarqua the ascetic.

''I must return now, Will Denison.''

Will blinked at the *Deinonychus*. ''What? Back to the canyon, and the temple complex?''

''Back to my life of contemplation. Back to my search for the answers to the great mysteries.''

''But what if Blackstrap's waiting for you there? There are three of them and only one of you.''

The *Deinonychus* sighed. ''I know, but if it comes to another scuffle I will try somehow to even the odds for them so it is not so one-sided. Perhaps I will fight them only on one leg.''

Will's dubiety gave way to a grin. ''Maybe you're right. Maybe that will make it more fair.'' His grin faded as he looked to his right. The place where the *Deinonychus*'s craft had been moored was empty, scoured as bare as much of the surrounding landscape. ''I'm sorry about your sky boat. I can imagine how much time and effort it cost you.''

''A useful occupation for one's time and hands. I will build another when it suits me.'' Again a clawed hand came up to lightly grip Will's shoulder. ''I would enjoy talking with you again someday, Will Denison. From what I have seen of you and from what your friend Chaz tells me, you are a singular young human, especially for one arrived so recently in Dinotopia.''

''I'd like that, too.'' Will's insides tightened. ''Why don't you come back with us? I know you'd be made welcome in Waterfall City. Nallab would love to talk to you, and the head librarian is one of your own kind.''

''No.'' Tarqua was unyielding. ''I have chosen a life of

solitude and contemplation, and to that I will hew. But perhaps . . ." he seemed to hesitate for just a moment, "I may
pay you a visit someday. It has been a long time since I was
in a place like Waterfall City. A long time since I had the
opportunity to read the great scrolls."

"I'm going to hold you to that." Will put a hand on the
sloping shoulder, feeling the muscle beneath the embroidered
robe. "Maybe when you come you can teach me how to
kick like that."

"A lowly skill useful for maintaining one's physical con-
ditioning." The curving claws slid down to touch Will's
other hand, palm to palm. "Good-bye, Will Denison. I am
glad I was able to help you and your friends. Karma shall
accrue to us both."

There was nothing more Will could do but watch as the
exceptional *Deinonychus* bade farewell to everyone from
Chaz to Prettykill. Then he was off, loping along with long
strides toward the distant mountains, pausing only once atop
a waterlogged rise to wave a last time in their direction.

Will turned his thoughts toward home. His father must
have been notified by now and would be anxiously awaiting
word of his son's fate. The same was true for Sylvia, and to
a lesser extent Cirrus, who at least knew what Will had intended. They would be greatly relieved to learn that he was
safe and unharmed.

"Look," a voice called out. "The philosopher's coming
back!"

Whirling, Will saw that Tarqua was indeed bounding back
toward them, his taloned feet kicking up water with every
stride. Once more the *Deinonychus* confronted him.

"You know, as I was running along—by myself, as
usual—it struck me that perhaps I *could* take a break from
endless solitude. For one thing, I had forgotten how addictive
good conversation and the company of friends could be. Do
you think the librarians of Waterfall City would truly be
desirous of speaking with me?"

Will's delight knew no bounds. "I'm sure of it! My father
might even help you improve on the design of your sky
boat."

"Truly? That would be a fine thing."

Smiggens had been standing nearby, listening. "Believe it or not, I once had an interest in such matters. I remember seeing the drawings of da Vinci, and reading about the work of two brothers in France. There were also some interesting experiments with balloons during the Civil War in America . . ."

Ignoring the lingering drizzle as well as their surroundings, the eager first mate and the meticulous *Deinonychus* wandered off together, deep in learned conversation. A gratified Will watched them go, until a nudge made him turn.

Encountering Prettykill's face so close to his own still gave him a start. A delicate snarl induced Will to gesture for Chaz to come and interpret.

"She's anxious to start on her way home," the *Protoceratops* explained.

"I understand." Will made himself stare back into those relentlessly feral eyes. "Tell her I'll personally see to it that she's returned to her parents, just as I promised."

As was the nature of tyrannosaurian conversations, the exchange was brief and to the point. After she had turned away, Chaz peered up at his friend.

"Be aware, Will, that this is a unique, perhaps even unprecedented friendship. For, astonishing as it may seem, she does regard you as a friend. I've never heard of such a thing. Any other human she most likely would treat as food. Should you someday, for some inexplicable reason, wish to spend time in the Rainy Basin, you know you now have a friend there." With his horny snout the *Protoceratops* nudged his companion's leg. "In fact, I'd go so far as to say that she's downright fond of you."

"Now, just a minute," Will began. "She's not my type. I like my female friends a little less, well, carnivorous." As he finished, he felt a blow to his shoulder.

"Hey, ow!" Turning, he saw that Prettykill had whacked him with the side of her snout. Bright yellow eyes regarded him intently. "Take it easy!"

"What did I tell you?" Chaz chortled softly. "Most definitely a gesture of affection. A tyrannosaurian love-pat. Be glad she's no bigger. She'd have broken your arm."

"You're exaggerating. But tell her to take it easy. After

all, I'm only human.'' At this Chaz began to hoot uncontrollably.

Ignoring both the uncomfortably attentive tyrannosaur and the greatly amused *Protoceratops*, Will let his gaze roam out across the inundated Northern Plains. Soon the farmers and gatherers would return to rebuild their informal but comfortable homes. Rice and taro fields would be replanted, ceratopsians and ankylosaurs would once more shoulder their plow harnesses, and life here would return to normal.

As would his own. He was amazed at how eagerly he was looking forward to a return to ordinary, everyday routine. He'd had more than enough excitement and adventure.

For a little while, anyhow.

COPPERHEAD CURSED AS HE TRIPPED OVER THE ROOT. His face streaked with grime and sweat, Blackstrap scowled at him.

''Belay that! 'Tis hard enough avoiding the beasts without letting them know we're here.'' He paused to catch his breath. With the passing of the storm, the heat and humidity in the Rainy Basin were higher than ever.

Davies plucked at the bigger man's sleeve. ''You sure we're going the right way, Captain?''

Blackstrap glared back. ''D'you doubt my sense of direction, man? Me, who's found his way through most of the seven seas with naught but a compass and the stars to guide him?'' He snorted contemptuously. ''Did I not find the first canyon, and are we not on course to return to the second?''

''Your pardon, Captain Blackstrap, sir,'' complained Copperhead, ''but I still don't see why we didn't just return to the temple complex direct.''

''Must I explain it again? I could not take the chance of being followed, and this way we'll be able to sneak up on that high-kicking devil when he least expects it. If anyone's looking for us at all, which I doubt, they'll be watching the route by which we returned to the lowlands.'' He grunted his satisfaction. "No one'll be expecting us to circle all the way 'round again.

"We'll catch that damnable great-clawed lizard in his sleep and slit his throat. Then we'll gather as much treasure as we can carry. If the *Condor*'s been disabled or taken, we'll steal a boat from the locals. It shouldn't be hard. The boy as much as told us the peace-loving simpletons hereabouts bear no arms."

"Aye, that's so," Copperhead admitted. "It would feel good to open a few bellics."

"That's the spirit. There's not a sound coastal craft that, properly rigged, can't cross a cooperative sea. All we'll need is a little weather luck. We'll load it with treasure and make our way to Durban. That and the promise of much more will be enough for us to raise a fleet." His eyes burned with an unholy light.

"We'll sail back here and put this unnatural society of dinosaur beasts and people to the torch. I'll have my revenge, I will!" He shook his fist at the trees, which did not respond.

"What if they decide to fight, Captain?" Davies wanted to know.

"With what? You heard the boy. As for these dinosaur creatures, though they be monstrous big I'll wager an emerald the size of me nose that modern cannon will bring them down right quick enough. Rifled artillery, har, that be the trick! We'll put an end to this 'Dinotopia,' or whatever 'tis called. We'll—"

His tirade was interrupted by a sudden parting of the vegetation before them. The brute had approached undetected. Now it confronted them in silence, the only sound that of its heavy but unlabored breathing.

"Back!" Blackstrap yelled unnecessarily to his companions as he drew both revolvers. "Look to your rifles! We frightened one such demon away with their sound and flash. Who's to say we'll not have similar good fortune with this one."

Davies shrieked and fell to the ground. "Captain, there's another one . . . *behind us!*"

Blackstrap whirled just as a second monster nearly as big as the first emerged from the trees. Fearful as he was, he still found himself marveling at the silence with which they moved, at their physical grace and the beauty of their natural camouflaged coloring. He gripped both pistols tightly.

"Steady, steady. Keep your nerve. Mayhap they'll choose to ignore us and engage one another. Move to the side. That's it, that's it. See, they have other concerns."

Hope surged through Copperhead. "Look at their stomachs, Captain. See how they bulge. These two have just eaten. If they're at all like lions or tigers, they should have no interest in killing for several days."

Indeed, the two great carnosaurs were distended with food. Though they watched the three men closely, they made no move to attack. Their entire attitude was suggestive of ennui and indifference.

"They're going to let us go," Davies whispered tautly. "They're not interested in us."

"Bloody hell," Copperhead muttered. "Would you believe there's a third devil!" His tone softened. "It's all right, though. It's only a little one."

Blackstrap's brows drew together. "Little one? What do you mean, 'little one'?" He spun around.

Copperhead was right. Standing before them and blocking their retreat was a much-reduced version of the two tumescent giants behind them.

"Go to its left." Blackstrap's fingers were numb from gripping the pistols so tightly. "It looks like it has eaten as well. There be no reason for them to trouble us with so much ready carrion about."

For several moments that seemed to be the case, and it appeared that they were destined to slip away clean. Then Davies whispered, a slight tremble in his voice.

"That small one, Captain. Doesn't it look familiar to you?"

"Familiar? What are you gibbering about, man?"

Abruptly the subject of the seaman's concern parted its jaws and emitted a series of sharp growls and snarls. In response the two heretofore disinterested monsters came instantly awake, their lethargy gone. Striding forward, they shook the ground with their tread. Mouths several feet long parted to reveal dark pink tongues and jet black gullets framed by saberlike teeth.

Only then did Blackstrap recognize the third and smallest member of the suddenly attentive trio. It was the very same young dinosaur they had taken captive. And if it was the young, then the two toothy leviathans bearing down on them must be . . .

For the second time since making landfall in Dinotopia, Brognar Blackstrap found himself speechless.

It was also the last time.

ABOUT THE AUTHOR

Alan Dean Foster's career in fiction began in 1968 with the publication of a short story in *The Arkham Collector*. His first novel appeared in 1972, and since then he has published numerous books and short fiction in a variety of genres; he has also written novelizations of many motion pictures, among them *Star Wars* and all three *Alien* films. An avid traveler, he has explored some of the most exotic places on earth, from the "Green Hell" of the Peruvian jungle to the shark-infested waters off Australia. He and his family live in Prescott, Arizona, where he is working on several book and film projects as well as teaching at Northern Arizona University.